HEAT

Vol. 0

HEAT

Vol. 0

edited by
Russell Davis

FOGGY WINDOWS BOOKS

Anthology

SCARBOROUGH, MAINE

HEAT, Vol. 0

A Foggy Windows Books Original

Foggy Windows Books
P.O. Box 2358
Scarborough, ME 04070-2358
www.foggywindows.com

ISBN: 1-930947-00-3

Cover art by Pelaez
Cover design by SQP, Inc.

First printing, October 2000

Production by Windhaven Press: Consulting & Editorial Services
www.windhaven.com

Printed in the United States of America

10   9   8   7   6   5   4   3   2   1

CONTENTS

HEAT

Vol. 0

Introduction
HEAT, Vol. 0

The word "heat" is a word of magic. A word that can conjure images of a desert sun, drops of sweat beading on tanned skin, or even a vision of the intense passion between two lovers. When we selected *HEAT* as the title for our first anthology series, it was with this provocative power in mind. We wanted to excite the erotic imaginations of our readers from the very beginnings of their journey with us.

Beginning on Valentines Day 2001, Foggy Windows Books will be releasing thirty-six original novels and twelve anthology volumes per year. These unique, plot-driven stories will possess a high level of erotic tension and passion, but with one key difference we believe makes our stories more intense than those of any other publisher in the field.

The characters in our stories are *married*.

Recently, someone asked me if what we were doing was creating some new type of "moral erotica." And, I'll admit, that the question got my wheels turning. Was that, in fact, what we were doing? I've come to the conclusion that the answer is "not ex-actly." Does the fact that the characters are married make our novels and anthologies "moral"? It might; morality is a fairly subjective thing.

But, there's no doubt at all that married people have incred-ibly active sex lives. Statistically speaking, married people have sex *five times* as often as everyone else! That's a lot of practice.

And it's our firm belief that the most erotic moments of our lives come not in the arms of a stranger, but in the arms of someone we love and trust; a person who represents a safe harbor, where we have the freedom to explore our sexuality without risk, and with the opportunity to find joy and laughter.

HEAT, Vol. 0 represents our first steps down this path. Vol. 0 is a sneak preview, if you will, of the type of short fiction we plan to offer our readers. It's also a look at what Foggy Win-dows Books is all about. Of the 12 stories in this collection, nine feature characters and settings from forthcoming novels.

There is, quite literally, something for everyone.

Foggy Windows Books is a six-imprint line, and in this and every forthcoming anthology volume, you'll find two stories from each of our imprints. Our suggestion is to skip around; whether you're in the mood for something spicy from the Old West or something totally unheard of from the deepest reaches of Outer Space, we've got stories that satisfy.

In this volume, our *Frontlines* imprint is represented by Wendi Lee's Civil War mystery, in which an amorous couple must find time to help General Grant, while fulfilling their desires for one another. There's also a "who-done-it" written by Stephen Mertz. Set during the height of the conflict in Vietnam, the enemy here is guilty of far more than just "coitus interruptus."

Our *Overdrive* imprint, which features stories of action and adventure, is represented by the tale of a husband and wife who seek out hidden treasure (and each other) deep beneath Mexico City. Written by Sean McIver, the characters from this adventure grace our cover. The second story, written by Colin Vincent, offers a unique look at what can happen when a well-known British Secret Service agent decides to marry and retire.

If you enjoy the Wild West, then the stories from our *Flintlock* imprint will leave you wanting more. The first story in the set, written by Daniel Ransom, reveals just how far one frontiersman will go to keep his wife happy. Already well known for his horror fiction, we're happy to present Ransom's first foray into the Western genre. We also have the story of newlyweds who want to catch the bad guys and still find time to consummate their union. Written by Lindsay Hart, these characters are more than just married, they're partners in the first crop of Secret Service agents.

If mystery and suspense are more along the lines of your craving, our *Undercover* imprint should quench your desire. In the first story, offered by Tim Waggoner, we're introduced to a husband and wife team of private investigators who, in order to catch a killer, must attend their first orgy. Then, well-known author Billie Sue Mosiman contributes a sensual story of reconciliation between a husband and wife.

From our *Afterburner* imprint, we have a hilarious foray into an unknown universe. Written by David Bischoff, this story is bound to make you laugh (and give some thought to what all that future technology might really be good for) as a husband and wife find out just how strange a new world can get. Our second story, by Allison Lawless, details one couple's in-depth exploration of the resources available to them in a water world.

And finally, from our *Chimeras* imprint, newcomer Jonathan Morgan's high fantasy tale is sure to please those who enjoy a bit of "swordplay" between husband and wife. The last story in the collection, contributed by Gary A. Braunbeck, is a dark story of the love and lust that one newly married couple feels for each other in this life and beyond. It's certain to send shivers down your spine, and some jolts to a few other places on your body as well.

Twelve stories in all explore the passion and excitement that can only be found in the HEAT generated by marriage. Turn on your air conditioner—tonight is going to be a scorcher.

—Russell Davis

About the Editor

Russell Davis is the Managing Editor and Book Division Director for Foggy Windows Books. He is a published author, and his short fiction has appeared in such DAW anthologies as Merlin, CatFantastic V, *and* Warrior Princesses. *Forthcoming in 2000/2001 are short stories in* Civil War Fantastic *and* Single White Vampire Seeks Same. *Davis also co-edited the anthology* Mardi Gras Madness *with Martin Greenberg. In addition to running around like a madman at Foggy Windows Books, he is currently at work on a novel called* The Crown of Sands, *as well as a number of other writing projects. Davis lives with his wife, children, and one psychotic cat in southern Maine.*

FOGGY WINDOWS BOOKS

Frontlines

Set against the backdrop of war, the Frontlines *imprint represents perhaps our most traditional romance stories. The settings for these stories could be any war or historic battle, from the earliest in recorded history to the most recent conflicts in Bosnia and Kosovo. Across the dangerous grounds of minefields and gunfire, from the hidden efforts of spy networks, to the doctors and nurses who have tended to the wounded, and been wounded themselves, men and women, husbands and wives, have loved, lusted, and fought beside each other to preserve those things that they hold most dear.*

With Malice Toward None

Wendi Lee

Wendi Lee has written mysteries, westerns, and American historicals. Booklist has said of her private eye, Angela Matelli: "This too-little-known series and its first-rank female sleuth deserve more recognition." Lee's traditional westerns, written as W. W. Lee in the early 1990s, were critically acclaimed, and her highly praised American historical, The Overland Trail, *was released in 1996. She lives in Iowa with her cartoonist husband, Terry Beatty, and her daughter, Beth.*

Louise pulled the corncakes out of the oven and placed them on the cooling rack by the window. Despite the fact that corncakes were John's favorite—so sweet and moist that they melted in the mouth—making them made Louise feel slightly nauseous. But it was a treat—John had been gone two days with General Grant, and a messenger had come to Louise earlier this morning with the news that her husband would be returning home tonight.

Rations had just been handed out yesterday, including a bag of cornmeal, and Louise was able to pick a few ears of corn from her small garden to make the cakes for John. Ever since President Lincoln had been killed three weeks ago, the nation was grieving. But it was especially hard on those who knew Mr. Lincoln well. John had met with the president a number of times in Grant's presence and had come to like and admire the man. Louise had even met Mr. Lincoln and his wife once when they were invited to the White House for an official dinner.

General Lee had surrendered to Grant almost a month ago at the Court House in Appomattox, and with the exception of a few holdout troops in Mississippi and out West, President Lincoln had proclaimed the War Between the States as ended just before he died. The War Between the States was all but over. Andrew Johnson was trying to fill the presidential void left by Lincoln's death, but there was still unrest among the Confederates.

Louise and her husband John had played their parts in the Union effort to win the war. They were only just betrothed when the war began, but John wanted to help the Union efforts. Their marriage had to be put off until he returned.

Since the war began, rations had been hard to find, even for army officials and their families. Louise had heard that it was even harder on the Confederate families.

The sound of John's horse and carriage clopping up the drive brought Louise back to the present, and she untied her apron, quickly hanging it on the hook by the kitchen door. As he entered, Louise threw herself into John's arms. He caught her up and swung her around. It had become a ritual of theirs—married over a year and they still acted like a newlywed couple.

Before John could say anything, she pressed her willing mouth against his, her softly contoured body against his hard chest, and felt his sinewy arms wrap around to hold her securely to him. Louise's heart still fluttered at the nearness of her beloved husband. She buried her nose in his jacket. The scent of outdoors clung to his jacket from his two days on the field with General Grant, and she remembered that she had almost lost him during the war.

It had been a dark day when she received word that her betrothed was missing and presumed dead. A week later, she heard from a soldier who was returning from Georgia that he couldn't be certain, but he thought he saw Major John Ames in Andersonville, a prison camp in Georgia. Louise wouldn't listen to others when they begged her to wait with the other wives and sweethearts for word of his return. She couldn't shake the bad feeling that John might not return if she didn't try to do something about it. So she donned a soldier's uniform and, posing as a man, marched down to Georgia. She even fought in a few skirmishes, but was fortunate to have come out unhurt.

As her regiment neared Andersonville, Louise once again changed identities to get into Andersonville to find out what happened to John. Her attempts resulted in his escape and return home with Confederate maneuvers for several battles that helped the Union win some major confrontations

Here at home with John out of the hands of the Confederates, Louise felt safe and loved by her husband. They pulled through their darkest hours during the early days of the War Between the States, and she was grateful for every day they had together. John now accompanied General Grant on meetings with Confederate generals who were laying down their arms and ordering their worn-down troops to withdraw and go home to their families.

Ever since Richmond fell into Union hands and Lee surrendered to Grant, the biggest problem for the fallen Confederacy was to get the soldiers to lay down their arms and pick up their ploughs. Getting the word to the troops, and convincing them that the Confederacy was now a lost cause, was the biggest task for both the Rebels and the Yanks.

The most difficult part for the civilians—in Confederate and Union states alike—was getting some normalcy back in their lives. Many homes had been destroyed in both Union and

Confederate states, and generating enough food and basic supplies for the country to run efficiently again was a monumental
task.

John pulled Louise's dark hair down from the bun she'd made
at the nape of her neck when she was baking. Her hair curled
naturally and tumbled down over her shoulders.

"Oh, my love," he mumbled as he buried his face in the silky
strands.

Louise's appetite for sex had increased recently and she had
dearly missed him the other night, spending the night alone in
their bed, fantasizing about making love to him. Now she was
pressed against the full length of his body, and she could feel his
erection against her leg. Louise began to undo his pants with an
urgency that they both felt. Although they knew each other's
bodies well, Louise had yet to grow tired of exploring John's
lanky form, running her hands down his broad back, down to
his narrow hips, holding him inside her for as long as they both
could stand it, until they finally came as one.

She sank to her knees and took him in her mouth, running
her tongue around the ridge, his hands clutching and unclutching
her hair, his gasps so close together—

"No!" he whispered hoarsely, "not yet."

He gently pulled her back up to her feet and kissed her
deeply, his tongue exploring hers as his fingers playfully unfas-
tened the top few buttons of her bodice. Louise felt herself getting weak, the space between her legs growing wet with anticipation. John's hands slipped inside her dress, cupping her breasts
and stroking her nipples. Her breathing became quick. She was
frantic to have John inside her, and he knew it. But he teased
her by slowing everything down.

He slid the dress down her shoulders, freeing her breasts so
that he could flick his tongue lightly over her nipples.

"Oh," she moaned softly, arching her back and sliding her
hips onto the kitchen table. "Oh, John, don't tease me any
more." She parted her legs, ready to receive her husband and
lover. His hands pushed her skirts up, running the length of

her smooth thighs, slipping under her buttocks to cup them and rocking her forward enough to slip inside of her. She felt her breasts brush up against the stiff wool of his uniform, and then he was inside her, both of them working as one toward the ultimate pleasure.

The moment was interrupted by the sound of a rider and horse. They stopped what they were doing, almost as if they thought the rider would hear them. Louise and John held their breath in unison, both hoping that the horse and rider would keep on riding past their house. But they knew otherwise, and John reluctantly withdrew, Louise giving a deep shuddering sigh. Duty called at the strangest hours. John buttoned up his trousers to look presentable as the heavy knock came to the door.

A quick kiss between them, and Louise slipped into the bedroom to fasten the buttons on her dress, leaving John to answer the door.

She heard the insistent voice of one of General Grant's men—it sounded like Sergeant Parmenter. Louise checked her image in the bedroom mirror and smoothed the lines of her dress.

"Louise, my dear," she heard John call out. "Would you please come to the parlor?"

Both men stood when she entered. The sergeant had his cap in both hands and looked respectful, but she could see the light in his eyes. Louise was aware that she was considered beautiful, and it was gratifying in these troubled times to be looked upon by a man, other than her husband, with desire in his eyes. The sergeant wasn't as sharply handsome as John, but Parmenter was a large man with a full mustache, curly fair hair and ruddy good looks.

"Sergeant Parmenter has been asked to escort us to the general's quarters." There was no question which general had done the asking—it was General Grant with whom they were going to keep the impromptu appointment.

John and Louise lived ten minutes from the general's house. John had saddled two horses, and the threesome was soon on their way. Grant lived in a big slab of a house with few windows, big enough for the general to live in and have a set of offices away from Washington.

Julia Dent Grant came out to greet the visitors. She was a small, energetic woman. She would not be considered a beauty, but when she smiled, her face lit up and highlighted warm eyes.

Louise had only met the general's wife a few times, but she enjoyed the woman's company. Now Mrs. Grant greeted them like old friends, kissing Louise's cheek affectionately. "Please forgive my husband's swinish manners, making you travel all this way in the middle of the night. I just returned from New Jersey, where the children are still staying, and I'm afraid I wasn't able to get much of a meal together for you."

"It wasn't necessary for you to feed us at all, Mrs. Grant," John said graciously.

Mrs. Grant turned slightly and smiled. "Oh, but a good hostess must always prepare something for guests whose dinner was interrupted."

The three travelers followed her inside to the den, a large airy room with whitewashed walls and spare furnishings. A massive oak desk and chair sat at one end, bookshelves and leather-bound books filled the wall across from the double doors, and a loveseat and two easy chairs were arranged before a cozy fireplace. A small table was set with a platter of bread and roasted chicken and a pitcher of water.

"Please help yourselves," their hostess said. "The general has already eaten."

At the mention of food, Louise had felt hungry. Now, at the sight of it, she felt queasy.

John tried to get Louise to eat something, and she finally had a crust of bread, no butter, just to please him. The men ate silently. Louise looked around the den, taking it all in as the three of them waited for the general. Grant entered the den fifteen minutes later. Louise had always thought that Grant was a handsome man with a magnetic presence. She was used to seeing him about once month, sometimes showing up at her house with John. He'd even had dinner with them a few times, sharing their small rations, and thanking her graciously for her hospitality at the end of the evening. It was a habit of his to send a bag of onions or flour to her house the next day as payment for the meal. It had been over a month since she had last seen him, and she was shocked by his appearance.

Now, Grant stood before her, a man who had not slept well in a very long time. The war had certainly taken its toll, but she had seen him not longer than a month ago, and he looked as if he had aged ten years in that scant amount of time.

She glanced at her husband, who looked concerned, but was certainly used to the way the general looked these days, having worked in his presence every day for the last year.

"There is unrest in the capital," he began, dispensing with the greetings. "A very unstable situation has arisen, and I need people I can trust to handle it discreetly." He looked first at Louise, then John. "You two are the ones I trust the most. You are in a good situation to investigate without causing too much suspicion." He looked back at Louise. "You, my dear Mrs. Ames, are in the position of being able to get information from others in a way that a man is not able to. If I had not seen with my very eyes the miracle you performed during the early days of the war, something few women would have attempted, I would not request this favor of you." He turned to John and bowed. "I am aware that it is unusual to ask a married woman this favor, but your wife is an unusual woman, Colonel. So forgive me for what I am about to ask of her."

"My wife has my blessing to serve in whatever capacity you require," John replied.

"How may we be of service, General?" Louise asked.

Grant gave her a half-smile. He seemed to pause for a moment to think about it, then returned to his frowning countenance as he continued. "We are all aware of the conspiracy to kill the president, which was successful, and the unsuccessful attempts that were made on other key members of the Union government, including me, on the same night. If I, and many of my fellow victims had not been out of town that night, who

knows how many funerals would have taken place in the following week? Although we were able to crush the plot, another,
more insidious plan has taken its place."

He stopped and looked at the Ameses.

"Please tell us how we can help," John said.

"Houses are being robbed," Grant said, "in the District of
Columbia. But these are not simple burglaries. The culprits gain
entrance, rob the place, and smash whatever they cannot take
with them. Then the thieves destroy the house by fire. It is sav-
agely done, and almost always takes place on a night when the
master of the house and his family are away."

Louise had heard that there had been an unusual spate of
house fires lately—at least one a night. "You say almost always.
Has someone been hurt lately?"

Grant sighed and nodded. "Yes. That is why I've come to
you. The house of Presidential aide Harrison Weller was set on
fire last night. The fire department has been vigilant ever since
the second house fire about a week ago, and got there in time
to put out the fire before it destroyed more than a room. But
they found Weller's secretary, Edward Crosley, in the library. He
had been viciously attacked."

John spoke up. "Mr. Crosley was saved, then?"

Grant got up from his chair and paced. He shook his head.
"The secretary was dead. He hadn't died from the flames or the
smoke—someone had put a knife in his back." He stopped pac-
ing and turned to both of them. "The word is out that some
Confederates will stop at nothing to break down the morale of
the Union, even after peace has been declared. First the president, now this—"

"What was Mr. Crosley doing in the house anyway?" Louise
asked.

Grant nodded. "He had come to deliver some important pa-
pers to Mr. Weller. Edward Crosley had permission to enter the
house, even when the Wellers were out for the evening."

"And he knew that the Wellers would be unavailable," John
said.

Grant nodded.

"How are we supposed to find the culprits?" Louise asked. She was intrigued, but apprehensive. "My work for the Union grew out of my love for John. Why would you think I am qualified for such work now?"

Grant smiled. "You and John are much respected here in Washington. John is my aide de camp, so I trust him. And I believe you have an intuition, Mrs. Ames, which transcends your gender. What you did during the war required great ingenuity and an ability to put disparate pieces of a puzzle together. Someone had to know that the Wellers were out for the evening, as with the other homes. But this time, Crosley must have surprised the burglars and they panicked. I would like you both to ask around, investigate, find out who is giving information to the robbers, giving them a way to gain entrance, to know when the owners will be away from their homes."

John and Louise looked at each other, then back at the general.

"So you believe there is a Confederate sympathizer who hides behind the mask of Union sympathizer," John said.

"Yes. Will you do as I request of you?"

Louise stood, as did John. "Tell us everything you know about who was robbed, and whom you suspect."

It was late at night when Louise and John returned to their home, escorted by Sergeant Parmenter. The moment Louise opened the door and turned one of the oil lamps up, she gasped. Their home had been burglarized. The kitchen table and chairs had been upended and smashed with an axe. Crockery was shattered on the stone floor.

The sergeant moved them out of the way and went through the entire house to make sure the vandals were gone. When he returned, he was shaking his head.

"I don't know what to tell you, Colonel Ames. They must have heard us returning and slipped out the kitchen door." The sergeant told them he would stay nearby until they had gone through their house.

It looked as if the vandals had been caught in the midst of the destruction because two rooms—the guest bedroom and the parlor—hadn't been touched yet. It was fortunate that the meeting with the general had taken only a short time. Their house might have been burnt to the ground if they had stayed longer at General Grant's.

John moved into the bedroom and Louise followed, disbelief making her cry out as she took in the slashed feather mattress and quilts, wedding gifts from John's family. Their clothes had been taken, and as they walked through the house to take inventory, it was clear that the silver and food had been taken from the kitchen. She and John moved into the bedroom. Her clothes had been taken, as well as her jewelry. She wouldn't miss much of the jewelry, but a pretty little cameo brooch that had been her mother's and a garnet ring and necklace, a wedding gift from John, were gone, and she would sorely miss them.

"The corncakes are gone as well!" Louise cried. "I baked them specially for you, John." She sighed.

John took her into his arms, and they stood in the midst of destruction, holding onto one another for dear life. The tears that trickled down her cheeks had nothing to do with the purloined corncakes.

Sergeant Parmenter escorted them to a nearby inn for the night. Louise slipped beneath the sheets to lay naked next to her husband. She could feel the heat of his skin where it touched her arm and her hip. Her thoughts turned to all that had been destroyed.

"How could this have happened to us?" she said. "Who knew that we were going to visit the general?"

John pulled her close to him. She felt his warm naked skin along the length of her body. "Parmenter. Mrs. Grant. I doubt the general told anyone else. Parmenter is known for his ability to keep a secret. Mrs. Grant would never talk to someone she didn't trust."

Louise pulled slightly away to look at her husband's face. "So that leaves only one other possibility."

"What?"

"Someone has been watching the general and followed Sergeant Parmenter."

"Well, then, having been victims of this crime will make it all the easier to find the culprits," John pointed out.

Louise wavered, feeling helpless with the rage that was building inside of her. Then she remembered Grant's words: "...the Confederates will stop at nothing to break down the morale of the Union..." She took a deep breath and swallowed her anger. She had been through worse when John was missing. She had to think without letting her feelings take over. The war was over—a declaration had been made to that effect only a few weeks ago—yet it appeared to her that the war wasn't truly over. Still, she had to put it out of her mind for the night. There was nothing she could do until morning.

Louise turned toward her husband and reached for him. "Let's finish what we started earlier tonight." She felt him growing hard with the insistent pressure of her thigh against his groin. He kissed her neck, fluttering kisses down to her breasts and flicking his tongue over her nipples until they were hard and sensitive to his touch. She stopped him and rolled on top of him, straddling his hips. He sat up and held her close, her hard nipples pressing against his firm, smooth chest. They kissed, then her tongue found the sensitive spot on his left ear and she lightly played her tongue along the inner shell until he made her stop. He rolled on top of her and, with one knee, parted her legs. She stopped him, both breathing hard. "Let me turn over," she whispered, and slid out from under him, positioning herself until her buttocks found his belly. Then she guided him inside her and they moved together.

His hands slipped under her, sought out and found her breasts, caressing them, teasing her, moving fluidly over her breasts to her hips. She threw her head back in abandonment as she rode the wave of ecstasy, John joining her shortly after.

They lay panting, curled into each other, part of each other, and finally, Louise found the time right to tell John the secret she had been reluctant to share until now.

"John, I'm with child."

He sat up in bed. "You are?" Slowly, it dawned on him what she had said. He grabbed her hands and kissed them, then took her face in his hands and tenderly kissed her on the lips. "We're going to have a child!"

She laughed, and he joined in.

As they lay back in bed together, he gently placed his hand on her flat belly. "We're going to be a family soon."

And that, more than any other reason, made Louise feel the importance of finding the men who had broken into their house, violated their lives and the lives of other families as well.

In the early morning, John and Louise went back to their house to sift more carefully through the wreckage of the kitchen and the bedroom. A soldier had been sent to guard their house all night, and now John gave the soldier orders to report back to Sergeant Parmenter, with his thanks.

When Louise stepped inside, the wreckage didn't look as harsh as the night before, but then she noticed that someone had come in and cleaned up the broken crockery. And in the corner on the floor, provisions had been sent for them so they wouldn't go hungry. She opened up the bag and found dried apples, eggs, a sack of flour, some smaller bags of coffee, sugar and cornmeal, dried venison, a slab of bacon, and lard. A note promised to bring two chickens, a bottle of milk, and a pound of butter once Mrs. Grant finished churning it. It was signed by General Grant. Louise blinked fast to keep the prickly hot rush of tears from spilling over onto her face. She held her breath to keep from crying.

"Louise? Are you feeling well?" her husband asked.

She stood up slowly to get her feelings under control, breathing deeply and letting it out a little at a time. Oh, how she felt for the other families who had gone through much worse than this! To have to take this necessary charity, to know she couldn't live without the butter and the eggs and the flour for bread, and the pemmican for stew-—and the cornmeal for corncakes. She knew that the general and his wife were tightening their belts to share this food with John and Louise. How did the other families manage? She turned, putting a smile on her face, and handed the note to John.

"Yes, John, I'm well enough to do what we must for the general."

He quickly read the note, a slight smile on his face.

"He is a good man, John, and his wife is a good woman," Louise said quietly. "How did the others live without these necessities after their homes were ravaged in much worse ways than ours?"

John tucked the note away in his jacket and pulled her close to him. "I don't know, but I am grateful to the general for thinking this highly of us."

Later that same morning, Louise took a carriage over to the Weller house. Harrison Weller came from a prominent family in the wealthy part of Washington. He lived in a Georgian-style house, common in the residential area, but beautifully appointed with a wrought iron fence and ornamental trees in the front. From the outside, it was hard to tell that the house had been vandalized and almost lost to fire. The Wellers had suffered little fire damage. Louise could see nothing from the outside.

The woman who answered the door was the lady of the house, Jane Weller. Louise was surprised, and it must have shown on her face.

Mrs. Weller was slender to the point of emaciation, and she wore a reddish stain on her cheeks to give the illusion of health. Many people had suffered during the war, including the wealthy women who didn't move west or go overseas. Louise knew of Jane Weller's sacrifice—she was one of the privileged women who had stayed behind to be with her husband, an aide to the President. She rolled bandages and cared for the infirm at a local hospital.

Louise introduced herself to Mrs. Weller, told her what business she had come on.

"I must say," Mrs. Weller replied, "it is unusual for a woman to be acting as an investigator."

"General Grant asked me to help by talking to you. He believes that I might be able to help," Louise said.

"And how do you know the general?" Mrs. Weller asked, her eyebrows raised in amusement.

"My husband is an aide to General Grant—Colonel John Ames."

"Oh! Then I do know who you are from your exploits, which provided hours of entertainment here in the capital," Mrs. Weller exclaimed. "You are the young woman who went in search of her betrothed and infiltrated the entire Confederate Army!"

"Well, it didn't happen exactly the way you describe it," Louise said modestly.

Mrs. Weller laughed and stepped aside to let Louise into the foyer. The faint smell of wet smoke was detectable once she was inside. The lady of the house led the way to the parlor. "Maybe not," she replied, "but by the time the story got here to our city, that was how it was told!" She laughed, and Louise joined in.

Louise took a moment to take in her surroundings and to ponder what she would ask of Mrs. Weller.

"Please forgive the state of our house," Jane Weller said as they passed from the large foyer into an almost barren parlor. One chair and a crate sat in the center of the room. The crate had been hastily assembled into something resembling a chair with pillows that served as upholstery.

The chair had been mended, but all four legs appeared to have been spared the ax. "Apparently this chair was missed by the men who broke in here," Mrs. Weller told Louise in a dry tone of voice. "May I fix you some tea?"

"Oh, really, I—" Louise began to protest.

"I was already in the process of making a pot, so please stay for a while." Mrs. Weller disappeared for ten minutes, enough time for Louise to ponder what she would ask, and returned with a pot of tea, two cups, and a small plate of sweet biscuits.

"I bought this teapot and these cups and saucers yesterday," Mrs. Weller explained. "Everything else was smashed. We have nothing." She explained all of this matter-of-factly, and Louise felt comfortable telling her what happened to their house the night before. When she was finished, Jane Weller leaned over and patted her hand. "My dear, how awful for you!"

Louise smiled and gestured around the room. "Oh, we only had two rooms destroyed, and apparently the vandals had no time to set a fire or—" She cut herself off before she said more, but Mrs. Weller picked up where she left off.

"Or leave the body of a dear friend in the library." She shook her head, a troubled expression on her face. "I think that was the worst of it. If setting fire to our house would have saved Edward's life, I think we would have gladly given up our home in exchange. He had only been with Harrison one month, but he was proving invaluable."

"Please tell me the events of that night," Louise said as she gingerly sat in the chair.

"It happened two nights ago. We were out having dinner with President Johnson and his wife—it was a banquet—and when we returned home, we found the firemen here, and we were told all that had happened while we were gone. The news of Edward hit Harrison especially hard."

"Was it possible," Louise even hated to ask, "that Edward was a Confederate sympathizer?" It was possible that he'd had second thoughts about his Confederate friends pillaging the house of the man he thought highly of.

Jane Weller's eyes widened in horror at the thought. "No. Not at all. Edward fought at Manassas. When his regiment went south, he contracted malaria. He recovered, but the malaria slowly weakened him. Fort Stedman was the last battle he fought. After the Union took the fort back, his regiment leader discharged him because he collapsed. He was grateful to work with Harrison and help in the cause of the Union."

"What items are missing from your house?"

"Our silver is missing, most of my jewelry, except that which was locked in a small safe in my husband's office, and everything was—" She swept a hand around the near empty room, then abruptly stood up. "Please. Let me show you."

No room had been left untouched, even the nursery. Jane Weller lingered in the empty room that had once been the nursery. "It is fortunate that my children are grown," she said. "We kept the baby things because we thought our son and his wife, who is with child, might want the cradle and some of the clothes worn by my son when he was a baby." Louise noticed Mrs. Weller blinking rapidly to keep tears back.

"...to break down the morale of the Union..." The words echoed through her mind.

The lady of the house quickly moved to other rooms and gradually regained her composure. The kitchen had gotten the worst of it. The walls were black, the outer wall was reduced to ashes. Outside in the yard, broken furniture and crockery had been piled together.

The women went back to the parlor and Mrs. Weller turned to Louise. "So you see, we are without a stick of furniture or clothing."

Louise looked around. "I noticed you have no servants—"

She waved her hand dismissively. "Harrison insisted on letting them all go. I told the maid and cook yesterday."

"Your servants weren't here when you were out?"

Mrs. Weller shook her head. "They don't live in with us."

"Did they know you would be gone?" Louise wasn't sure where she was going with this. It didn't seem to make sense that the servants would allow themselves to be put out of work by providing information that would destroy their employers' homes. Then again...

"You had just a cook and a maid?"

"We used to have a cook and a butler, but James, the butler, died recently—he was quite old. My cook, Amelia, asked if her sister Cora could work in his place. Cora had just moved to town."

"From where?" Louise felt her pulse quicken at the thought of maybe a connection.

"Amelia said her sister was from Pennsylvania." She told Louise where Amelia and Cora lived.

The maid and the cook were sisters who lived in a less glorious part of Washington. Amelia and Cora Scruggs occupied two rooms on the ground floor of a boarding house. Amelia was home.

She was a small, round woman in her early forties. A strand of hair had escaped from her messy bun. Good yeasty smells emanated from the kitchen in the back.

Louise introduced herself.

"I've never heard of a woman being asked to do anything for the general," Amelia Scruggs commented with a slightly suspicious tone.

"I did some work for the Union a few years ago, and my husband is now an aide to General Grant," Louise explained. "So the general thought I might be able to help with the investigation."

"He must have great faith in you, being a woman and all." There was a twinkle in Amelia Scruggs' eye when she said it. "Please come in. I'm baking in the back."

"I thought you rented a room here. I didn't know it included kitchen privileges." Most boarding houses only rented a room and two meals a day, except Sundays.

"Since I'm out of work, I help the woman who runs the house. I bake bread and cakes for her boarders and get a reduced rent for my trouble." The kitchen was small and well used. A bowl of bread dough sat on a floured wooden counter. Amelia went over and punched it down, then turned it out on the floured counter and started kneading it with a practiced hand.

"Well, you've come to ask about the murder at the Weller home," Amelia Scruggs said. "What did you want to know?" She shaped the dough into a round loaf and put it into the oven. She cut thick slices from a recently baked loaf and buttered them, sat a pot of jam and a pot of tea, with a creamer filled to the brim with thick cream and a mound of sugar in the sugar holder. The silver spoons that she sat on the tray looked familiar. Louise followed the woman into her room near the kitchen. It was cozy— a bed sat in one corner, and there was a receiving area by a small fireplace that was the kitchen fireplace on the other side of the wall. There were double doors that were propped open through which Louise could see another bedroom. This must have been Cora's room, and her sister kept the door open to share heat in the winter and cool breezes in the summer.

Amelia Scruggs set the tea tray on a small worn table and poured tea. Louise picked up her spoon and put some sugar in the tea, then stirred.

"You seem to be getting by despite being let go from the Wellers' house." Louise took a small bite of the hot, crusty bread. It was heaven. "What do you know about the burglary?"

Amelia shook her head. "Nothing. I feel terrible about what happened to them. And poor Mr. Crosley! But my sister and I were here that night. Mr. Weller blames us, thinks one of us left a window open, but it was clear as day that the thieves broke the door in. Thank the Lord Mrs. Weller has sense. She's still paying us half wages until she can talk some sense into that husband of hers. Mrs. Weller promises that we'll be back in service to them before the month is out. Mrs. Weller, she's a good woman."

"You recommended your sister to Mrs. Weller. Where did your sister live before this?"

Amelia Scruggs suddenly looked down at her cup of tea. "Cora is my sister-in-law. My brother Nat was killed in the war. She came to live with me. When Nat died, it was a sad day for all of us, but the soldiers are just now returning, and I thought she might be able to help around the Weller place until a suitable replacement was found." It wasn't unusual for many of the wealthier homes to have a servant shortage, and often lower class women were hired to perform duties that a butler would do.

Louise silently agreed. "What about that day, was there anyone suspicious who came by? Anyone who was out of place?"

Amelia frowned. "I cannot say. I'm the cook, so my place is in the back in the kitchen. Perhaps my sister—"

Heavy steps mounted the stairs and stopped outside the door. Amelia brightened. "That's her now."

A thin, gray-haired woman, older than Amelia, care-worn, entered the flat next door, with some bags. She put her burden down, then looked up and peered through the double doors, first looking suspiciously at Louise, then raising her eyebrows to Amelia.

Amelia jumped up and pulled a chair out for her sister. "Cora, this is Mrs. Ames. She is here to ask about the murder and the burglary. She's trying to find out what happened."

Cora looked gruffly at Louise, then sat down with her. Her eyes strayed to the plate of bread and jam. "What is she doing here without her husband? She has no right to come here asking questions."

"But General Grant has given her permission—"

Cora clumped into the room. Her face shut down as soon as the general's name was mentioned. Louise toyed with her spoon, then stopped. She looked at the spoon as closely as she dared without giving away her interest. Yes, this was one of her spoons—it had the same pattern and had the engraved A on it. She wanted to stand up and accuse both of them at once, but she managed to keep still.

"What do you think you're doing, sister, offering these treats to a strange woman who claims to be here at the request of General Grant?"

Louise felt sorry for Amelia, who blushed with embarrassment for her sister's coarse behavior. "Sister, it is clear that Mrs. Ames is a lady, and we treat our guests with respect."

Cora eyed Louise, then nodded shortly. "I have nothing to tell you."

Amelia stepped in again, her attitude nervous. She fairly

fluttered around her sister. "Cora, why do you treat my guest so rudely?"

By now, Louise was anxious to get out of there. She finished her tea and discreetly slipped her spoon into the folds of her dress. She felt bad doing so, but reminded herself that it was her spoon in the first place, and it was now evidence. It was clear that Amelia was the generous, friendly one, but she would get no information out of the sister.

But Cora did the unexpected. "As a matter of fact," she said with a look of cunning that clearly told Louise that she was lying, "I do remember a beggar in a Union uniform coming to the Weller door the same day the house was burglarized, asking for a crust of bread."

"And you sent him away?" Amelia cried. "How can you be so heartless?"

Cora eyed her sister impassively. "Why, sister, should we feed the whole world if it came to our doorstep?"

Louise excused herself, having heard enough. She thanked Amelia Scruggs for her hospitality, and left.

Outside, away from prying eyes, Louise inspected the spoon. Yes, it was definitely her silver. It would take a year for poor Amelia and Cora to save up to buy a set each for just themselves, but Louise doubted it came from their house directly. She thought back to the bread and jam, tea and cream that had been served. Even for a boarding house, it was a lot to serve in these times of rations. Louise had some places to go where she would have some questions. But for these questions, she would need to be escorted by her husband.

Louise visited a few of the other residents whose houses had been destroyed and discovered much the same story. She didn't visit any more of the servants, but asked questions that always pointed to a servant who hadn't been with the house long, and who was from a town in Pennsylvania or Vermont.

When Louise returned home, John was waiting for her. He

had found a couple of chairs and a bed in an abandoned property. Several of their plates had escaped total destruction, and the pots and pans, while battered and bent, were serviceable. While Louise made an evening meal, they talked about the day. Louise recounted her visit with the Scruggs sisters.

"They sound interesting," John said. He took out a small object and held it up for his wife to inspect. "I found this among the destruction."

It was a button, but not just any button—it had come off of a Union coat.

Louise frowned as she ran her finger over the metal button. "A Union soldier did this?"

"Or a Confederate spy who took the coat off of a dead Union soldier. A Confederate coat would have been conspicuous here in Washington."

"Does this leave Cora out?" Louise asked. She told him of finding the spoon and showed it to him. "I don't believe that Amelia Scruggs is involved, else why would she serve me with my own silver?"

John shook his head. "I'll ask around about Cora Scruggs."

"And her husband Nat. If he was a Union soldier, then Cora may just be an unpleasant woman."

"Amelia is Nat's sister. I think we need to visit her together tomorrow," John said. Louise agreed.

Sergeant Parmenter came to their house that evening after dinner. He was amazed at the extent of the destruction. "Please let me know what you need." He clearly meant helping around the house, fixing the furniture, but John and Louise had other more urgent ideas.

"You can help, Sergeant. Do you have a set of civilian clothes?" John asked.

The sergeant nodded in the affirmative and, after discussing it with Louise, John told him what needed to be done.

The next day, Louise and John went out to call on silversmiths. The first one she called on was Henry McCullen. His shop was small and serviceable, but he made beautiful items.

Louise admired a particularly striking silver service. McCullen, a small man with delicate hands, beamed with pleasure.

John had finished explaining why they had come here. "I implore you, sir, to answer any question my wife asks of you to the best of your ability."

Henry McCullen inclined his head and turned to Louise. "How may I be of help to you, madam?"

"How are you able to obtain silver in these trying times?"

He nodded. "I assure you, mistress, that my sources are impeccable. I have bought from the West, raw ore mostly, but since the war, people have brought their silver in for money to buy food and other items, sometimes for passage out of the city, to go out west."

She nodded. She liked Henry McCullen. John had chosen him to approach first because the general knew him and trusted him. He had fought beside Grant at Manassas and lost his leg there.

Now she took him into her confidence, only as far as he needed to know, and asked him to do a favor for his country. He readily agreed.

There was just one more visit for the Ames' to make, and they reluctantly did their duty.

It was late afternoon back at the Ames house when Sergeant Parmenter returned with a scruffy boy caught up by the collar of a Union coat that was much too big on him. Louise noticed that the coat was missing a button.

"Here's one of 'em," the sergeant said. "He'll turn on the others eventually, and we can gather them all up." He hauled the boy, no older than nine or ten, onto a chair and sat him down.

Louise looked at the boy in amazement. "You are the cause of all that destruction to our house and to the other houses?"

A shock of hair hung over the boy's eyes, and he looked up at her, anger and resentment in his eyes.

"Would you like some water?" she asked.

The boy sneered. "I won't take nothin' from a Billy Yank."

"But you took this coat," she reasoned.

"But that was from a dead Yank."

"Dead like Mr. Crosley?" she asked.

He looked perplexed. "Who?"

"The man who was found dead in the Weller house. He had been stabbed in the back," she explained patiently.

The young boy fell silent. He turned away from her, his face pale and his Adam's apple working. This was information he clearly didn't have before now. She tried to question him, but he appeared to be frightened. She showed him the silver spoon. He closed his eyes.

She straightened and looked at the sergeant. He nodded shortly. "You and Colonel Ames were right, madam. I followed Cora, like you suggested, and she peddled your silver to one of the silversmiths. I went in the shop after she left and got the smith to admit it. I don't know about her sister, though."

Louise's eyes met John's in understanding. It had been hard to interview Amelia. She had broken down and told them everything she knew.

Half an hour later, the smell of corncakes filled the house. Louise took it out of the oven and set it near the boy, but not too close. She could see his eyes light up and his tongue moved across his mouth. He was scrawny. She doubted he got enough to eat each day.

Henry McCullen came by, arriving just as John came home.

Louise introduced everyone. They all turned to look at the boy. Parmenter stayed near his charge.

"We don't have a name for our visitor yet?" John raised his eyebrows.

Louise put the corncakes on a platter and set it on her makeshift table. "I don't serve anyone whose name I don't know," she said, looking straight at the boy. "First name will be sufficient."

"Tom," he finally said. "My first name is Tom."

Louise served him a corncake.

McCullen had visited with the other silversmiths he knew, and discovered that a large amount of silverware had been bought by them. Singly, it had not been enough silver to warrant suspicion, but so many individuals, mostly lower class women, were bringing silver to sell to the shops that the overall picture looked suspicious.

McCullen had described Cora Scruggs and several smiths recalled a woman fitting her description coming into their shop to sell silver pieces.

"Nat Scruggs served with the Confederate Army. He was at Fort Stedman. His sister, Amelia, confessed that Cora came up from the south. She felt sorry for her brother's widow and took her in." John turned to the sergeant. "I think it's time for us to bring in Cora Scruggs." The sergeant nodded and began to leave, then turned back to John and Louise. "What about the young one here?"

John nodded. "You handle the Sisters Scruggs, and I'll stay here with young Mr. Tom."

Louise was serving another corncake to Tom, who was eating as if he wouldn't get another meal. Henry remained and sat near the boy. "Where are your parents?"

"Dead," the boy replied. "Killed in the war." He looked up. "My dad fought for the Confederacy." He lifted his head up with pride, daring anyone to say something against his father.

"And your mother?" Louise asked.

"Died of starvation." His shoulders wilted and he pushed away the remains of his cake. "I was an only child, fortunately. Not many of us left to starve or be thrown in a Union prison."

"Why did you make your way up north?" Henry McCullen asked the boy.

Tom paused in his eating to say, "We're starving down there. Not enough food for everyone. If you don't have a family, you join the Army. But there's not enough to go around. I figured the Union could feed me. I didn't want to be a burden on anyone down south."

Louise's heart was breaking. So young and cynical. So full of hatred for "Yanks." He probably cheered when President Lincoln was killed. But there was no true understanding of what the war was all about. Just what his father and mother had told him.

Louise was reminded of Lincoln's second inaugural speech, given just six weeks before he died, in which he talked of pulling the nation together, forgetting and forgiving the differences of the past:

> With malice toward none; with charity for all; with firmness in the right, as God gives us to see the right, let us strive on to finish the work we are in, to bind up the nation's wounds, to cure for him who shall have borne the wounds, and for his widow and for his orphan, to do all which may achieve and cherish a just and lasting peace among ourselves, and with all nations.

With malice toward none, she thought. *Not quite.* The question was, why now?

The sergeant returned later that night with a carriage and bundled everyone, Tom included, into it.

"General Grant requests our presence."

Half an hour later, the carriage stopped in front of a large building. Louise knew that this was Grant's headquarters.

Grant stood behind his desk and greeted John and Louise. "Thank you for your services. As we speak, my soldiers are gathering up the rest of the conspirators." A soldier entered the room, Grant nodded and a moment later Cora Scruggs and several other women were escorted into the office. Cora wore the same mixed expression of disgust and anger.

Louise held up the spoon. "This was your undoing, Mrs. Scruggs."

Cora spat at her. The other women, the sergeant explained, had been servants at the other houses that had burned. Their backgrounds would be checked, and most of them would probably turn out to be widows of Confederate soldiers.

"My sister is a simpering idiot," Cora declared. "I knew you was trouble the moment I laid eyes on you."

"Have you located the sister?" Grant asked the sergeant.

Cora Scruggs' face paled. "Please, sir. No. She wasn't involved. She's a timid mouse. Wouldn't have the mettle to do what I and the others did."

Louise was certain she could pick out which of the women had been involved in the destruction of the houses just from the glares they aimed at Cora.

John nodded. "So my wife was right. The servants in the houses had been Confederate sympathizers. Most of the servants are widows of soldiers for the South who banded together and infiltrated the homes of influential people."

Louise looked over at Cora Scruggs. "What about Edward Crosley? Did he surprise you?"

"I'm not talking anymore," Cora said.

Tom stood up, a look of amazement on his face. "She was there at the end," he said. "She set fire to the house. Usually it was one of us who set the fires, but she said she had unfinished business—"

"Hold your counsel, young man!" Cora said in a sharp tone.

One of the other women turned to her with an accusatory glare. "You told us there would be no killing, that we were just going to steal for the Confederacy to rise up again, to destroy the spirit of the Union!"

Cora crossed her arms and stared straight ahead.

It finally struck Louise—Nat had been killed at the battle of Fort Stedmen, Edward Crosley had fought there. "Was Edward Crosley the man who killed your husband?"

The men looked at her in amazement, but Louise remembered that many wives of soldiers followed their husbands' regiments because they had lost their homes and had nowhere to go and nothing to eat. Fort Stedman had been captured by Lee at the end of March, but General Grant's reserves took it back shortly afterwards."

"Don't be ridiculous!" Cora replied sharply. "How could I possibly know who killed Nat?"

Louise took a guess, tried to sound confident. "You were at

the fort and witnessed your husband's death." She knew that many of the wives of soldiers were the first to be evacuated from a battlefield. But some of them didn't make it out. Cora could have hidden somewhere in the fort.

Cora's eyes widened, but she didn't say anything.

Louise continued, her voice softening. "You saw him die, you saw the face of the soldier who killed him." She paused, then added, "And you saw him again when he came to the Weller house."

Cora's shoulders shook. "I saw him the first week I worked for the Wellers. I knew who he was. And I knew he was going to die for killing Nat. I just had to wait for the opportunity." She looked up at Louise, then at every Yank face in the office. "And when he came to the Weller house that night, it was perfect."

Cora, by now, was stone-faced, but tears ran freely down her cheeks, and Louise felt a small sympathy for this bitter woman. There was nothing else to say. Cora would hang for the murder, and for being a traitor to the Union.

"What about the boy?" Grant asked. "How does he fit into all of this?"

John answered. "He runs with a band of orphaned children who live in the streets. Cora and her co-conspirators came across them when they were begging door to door for something to eat. That was how this group of Confederate widows put together their plan to demoralize the Union here in the capital."

Grant shook his head. "It was a reckless plan."

"But it might have worked," Louise said, turning to the general, "if you hadn't been vigilant. What's going to happen to the orphans?"

Grant looked unhappy. "We will round them up, and if they are of an age to have served as soldiers against the Union, they will be imprisoned or hanged. The younger ones—an orphanage."

Tom was perched on a chair in the corner of the large room, looking forlorn.

Henry McCullen spoke up. "If you please, General, I would like to take the boy Tom as an apprentice."

Grant stroked his beard. "I don't know...he conspired against the Union. He destroyed property."

Louise stepped forward and put her hands on Grant's desk. "General, please."

Grant gave Louise an appraising look.

Grant went over to the boy. Tom looked up at the famous general, awe in his eyes despite the fact that Grant was a "Yank." "Would you like to apprentice to a silversmith, young Tom? Would you be willing to lay down your arms and, in the words of President Lincoln, 'bind up the nation's wounds'?"

"You don't have to answer him, Thomas," Cora piped up. "He's trying to trick you."

"How?" Louise asked her. "The general is generously offering this boy a new life. Are you trying to take his life away from him? Make him sit in a prison or an orphanage until he becomes of an age to make a living? Perhaps he can sell coal, or maybe he'll be able to work on the docks." Louise went up to Cora and looked her square in the face. "Tom is being offered a life, a noble trade. Apprentice to a fine silversmith." She softened her voice. "Do the right thing this time, Cora. 'With malice toward none; with charity for all...to care for him who shall have borne the wounds, and for his widow, and for his orphan.'"

Cora blinked back more tears.

"From President Lincoln's second inaugural speech—he was trying to tell all of us to make peace and to go on. And your General Lee was an honorable man. He knew surrendering was the only way for our nation to become whole again. Else we could have civil unrest for years to come. You can rail against the Union all you want, Cora, but please don't ruin the boy's life for your own end."

Cora held Louise's gaze a moment, then looked away. She turned to Tom and put a hand on his shoulder. "Do as she says. She's right. It's ended. Go on with your life."

She dropped her hand and was escorted out the door.

⟶≡◎≡⟵

If you'd like to read more about the adventures of Louise & John, look for the forthcoming novel, Captured Hearts, *available in April, 2001.*

Firebase Tiger

Stephen Mertz

Stephen Mertz is a military veteran who, under a variety of pseudonyms, has been one of the architects of modern action adventure fiction. His novels have been widely translated and have sold in the millions of copies worldwide. He lives in Arizona.

Vietnam, 1970
Quang Ngai Province
North of Saigon

The Huey gunship banked in over Firebase Tiger, a clearing carved from the jungle hilltop.

From behind the shoulder of the door gunner and his big

M-60 machine gun, the woman, who was calling herself Tara Carpenter, began snapping pictures from the open side door of the helicopter..

The landing zone was a barren five acres. After the stark green carpet of jungle they'd flown over from Saigon, the base was drab and squalid. There were no trees, no color except for the coating of dust that blanketed everything: bunkers, vehicles and personnel. Machine gun emplacements lined the perimeter at intervals. Artillery and mortars were inside the compound. The sun, like an angry fireball seen through the gauze of a humid haze, was arcing low in the west, painting the horizon beyond the tree line a brilliant red.

The view of this remote scene vanished behind a veil of red dust, a sandstorm kicked up by the chopper's backwash as the pilot touched the Huey down gently on the landing pad and initiated systems shutdown.

Tara's fellow passenger stood beside her.

"Getting enough pretty pictures for the war protestors?" he asked.

His name was Cord McCall. He was an investigator assigned to a special operations unit of the Joint Services Criminal Investigation Division detachment in Saigon. Death was naturally commonplace in a war zone, but there were other crimes perpetrated within military ranks—homicide, desertion, robbery—that fell under the CID's jurisdiction. McCall, a major, was forty years old, dark-haired, heavily muscled. His fatigues were sharply pressed even in the three-digit heat and suffocating humidity.

He did not wait for a response, but leaped from the gunship and strode toward a trio of awaiting soldiers.

Tara hopped to the ground and caught up with him. She was seven years McCall's junior, a redhead with intelligent green eyes that could glitter like those of a mischievous cat. Her GI fatigues did nothing to conceal a firm, shapely figure. She chose not to respond to his sarcasm because she well understood and appreciated its source. And McCall knew it.

First off, he was not overjoyed with being assigned the dual task of performing his normal duties and nursemaiding a journalist. But there was another, more significant reason for his displeasure with the presence of Tara Carpenter in Vietnam—and she and he were the only two people in Nam or anywhere else who could appreciate the true undercurrent of tension that had crackled between them since he'd met her, as ordered, at the Saigon airport that morning.

Tara and Cord were husband and wife!

Therein lay one hell of a tale, somehow as simple as it was complex. She'd been Cord's wife for three years before he was sent to Nam. Tara had never been your average military base wife. She'd begun freelancing her photographs to wire services and news magazines before they met. Cord was supportive of her career and, during their separation while he was in Vietnam, she'd continued to rise through the ranks of professional photographers.

He had been dumbstruck when he met her at the airport, not having had the slightest hunch that the photojournalist assigned to him was his own wife! She confided in him right off. It had taken considerable finagling on her part, she told him, including coming up with a cockamamie story for her editor about the need for a cover name, but she'd pulled it off. Wars were the stuff that Pulitzer Prizes were made of. But ambition was not the only reason she had hustled this assignment, she quickly assured him.

She had come because of love. She'd grown impatient, sitting on the sidelines in the States. She wanted to experience her husband's world. She wanted to learn for herself what was going on "in country," as the soldiers called it. She would not have interfered under normal circumstances, she insisted, but this war was hardly normal. As his wife, she well knew of his strength and his self-confidence. Now, she explained, she yearned to know its source.

Cord was anything but happy about the situation, but he tentatively agreed to maintain her secret, that she was his spouse, as much to avoid complications as to avoid appearing the fool. He made no secret of his displeasure during the drive from the airport. He was irritated by her presence. In addition to his concern for her safety, he had to keep his mind on his work, he'd groused. He hadn't bothered mentioning the pure sexual charge he always felt whenever she was nearby, which would be a major distraction during their "assignment" together. He hoped that he could keep his hots for Tara under wraps. But he couldn't deny it, and that in itself could lead to complications...

He protested adamantly, in her presence, to his commanding officer, who'd gone on to not-so-patiently re-explain to McCall how this was part of a PR campaign the Pentagon was waging in the hope that, by providing first-hand reports from Vietnam, they would be able to maintain the morale, hearts and minds of the American people.

That said, McCall was issued this assignment to Firebase Tiger, and Tara accompanied him.

On their brief drive from CID headquarters to the chopper flight out of Saigon, McCall had grudgingly agreed to cooperate with his wife's audacious undertaking. Whereupon she yanked the Jeep's steering wheel with her own hands, steering them abruptly into a narrow, shadowy alley formed by two towering, vacant hangars.

McCall's reflexes were fast, braking safely, and as he turned to give her an angry piece of his mind, she gave him a piece of something else, pressing herself against him. Their bodies melded. His mouth, opening to speak, received her steamy kiss, and he found himself responding with equal fervor, turning in his seat, grasping Tara to him.

When the kiss broke, they gulped in air like two people submerged underwater for too long.

"My God, Cord." Her cover girl features were flushed, flustered. "How I've missed you! I didn't think this would happen. I mean, not so soon. But baby, I need you now!"

There was no one around. He managed to shut off the Jeep's engine, and slipped it into gear. The sounds of the sprawling military complex around them could have been a million miles away.

"You want me, Tara? You've got me."

Their lips locked again. Her tongue darted sensuously, penetrating, caressing his tongue. Her teeth nibbled his lower lip, sending his body temperature soaring, making him rock-hard. Maintaining the clinch, he leaned across her, her back to the seat, and half-mounted her as best he could considering that they were clothed and restricted by the confines of a Jeep. She slumped down to facilitate his maneuver.

He slid a hand to the front of her fatigue shirt, cupping her left breast, palming it with firm gentleness, and he positioned one of his knees at the crotch of her trousers. She gasped. He felt the heat of her against his knee, through the fabric, and began applying pressure with the knee. She clamped her legs around his knee, humping it while she increased the pressure of her thigh against the hardness that was palpable through the fabric of his trousers, shifting her thigh this way and that. Rubbing like this for only seconds made her quiver and tremble. An orgasm shuddered through her.

She moaned. "Cord, I've missed you so much!"

"Guess we both need this," he heard himself admit.

Her body still shaking, she placed a hand over his, guiding his hand beneath her shirt, to the lacy coolness of an unseen brassiere. He knew what she liked, and began tweaking her nipples through the thin material, teasing first one, then the other, with his thumb and index finger. The confines of the alley echoed to her moans and his breathy need. Her hips bucked uncontrollably with another jolt of orgasmic spasms. This, combined with the touch of her lace-covered breasts and the way she rubbed her thigh against his hardness, made him groan. He found himself shuddering with the explosion of his own release; hot, spurting, gushing inside his boxer shorts.

Tara sighed a happy, almost girlish giggle as their bodies began to relax.

"Now that, Cord, is what I call the beginnings of a real reunion between a man and his wife."

McCall kissed her affectionately. "Oh really? You mean making a grown man, a military officer at that, come in his pants like a schoolboy?"

Her green eyes sparkled. "I'll try not to force you to do anything else against your will while we're together." She retrieved a traveler's packet of tissue from a pack clipped to her belt. "Here, hon," she said sweetly. "I think you could use these."

Reality inevitably returned, ending the moment.

After "personal matters" were tended to, McCall backed out of the alley and an uncertain silence settled in between them, unbroken during the flight from Saigon.

When he and Tara had crossed the short distance from the Huey to the three waiting soldiers, their ranking member stepped forward.

"Major McCall, I'm Captain Larson, Executive Officer in charge. Welcome to Firebase Tiger."

Larson was built like a farmer, thirtyish, with a sunburned crewcut and the leathery skin and flinty eyes of a much older man. He did not salute, as was the custom in a combat zone. Enemy snipers loved to disrupt the chain of command, and seeing who was saluted made selecting targets easy for them. Therefore, saluting was avoided outdoors.

"Thank you, Captain, but to tell you the truth, I'd just as soon be somewhere else."

The man next to Larson grunted. He was a big black man with E-6 stripes on his sleeve. "That goes for every mother's son in this hellhole, sir."

"Easy, Top," said Larson. "Sir, this is Sergeant Hines. He's my top shirt."

"I know," said McCall. "I've studied your personnel files."

The third man was a first lieutenant named Grey, and everything about him matched his name. Blond-haired, in his late twenties, there was a paleness to him that was almost albino-like. He exuded jittery nervousness. McCall had seen cases of battle fatigue, and he recognized those symptoms now.

"Captain, Sergeant Hines is only speaking the truth." There was a tremor to Grey's voice. "I wish I'd never heard of Firebase Tiger."

McCall said, "I'm here because you have a fragged colonel."

"Lieutenant Colonel Emmett, 13th Infantry Battalion," said Larson. "Someone tossed a hand grenade into his hooch just before dawn today and splashed the walls with his guts."

"Hooch" was GI slang for makeshift living quarters. "Fragging" was another recently coined term. Bad command decisions by an officer often got good soldiers killed. Sometimes an officer's own men—considering it more an act of survival than murder—would toss a grenade to a hooch, blowing such an officer into itty bitty fragments—"frag" him, in other words—before the officer could get anyone else killed.

"Where's the body now?"

"What was left," said Larson, "was tagged and bagged and returned to Saigon on the daily chopper run at 1700 hours."

Hines eyed McCall speculatively. "One thing you better know up front, sir. Don't expect anyone here to feel too bad about what happened to the colonel."

Grey cleared his throat again. He nodded at Tara. "Uh, if you don't mind, Major, who's she?"

"Her?" McCall spoke offhandedly. "Name's Carpenter. Pretend she's not here. I do. Okay, Captain, show me where the colonel got fragged."

Acting as if she had not heard, Tara commenced taking pictures of the grouped men.

Activity swirled around them; a male world of coarse language, exhaust fumes and the clicking and clanking of engines, equipment and weaponry. Nearly every soldier was toting an M-16 and a wary attitude, eyeing the jungle beyond the cut-down fire zone, outside the perimeter, where the shadows of encroaching night were deepening.

"The colonel got it in his hooch," said Larson. "It's next to the main bunker."

He led them toward a squalid, dust covered pile of sandbags that was somewhat bigger than the other hooches. A strip of field tape ran across the entry as a makeshift barricade.

The colonel's hooch was a low, ten-by-twelve, makeshift structure of timber and plywood beneath a shell of sandbags. Its entrance was charred, misshapen from the outward force of the murderous blast.

McCall crouched for a few seconds to observe the interior. The walls had indeed been splashed with blood. Flies buzzed, thick and loud. He stood and faced the others.

"Did anyone see anything?"

Larson shook his head, negative. "Security was paying attention to outside the perimeter. Everyone heard the blast. The nearest ones to the site were me, Sergeant Hines and the lieutenant."

Hines nodded. "Cap and I were sprucing up the files for the Inspector General's visit day after tomorrow. If it hadn't been for a couple of walls between the colonel's hooch and the TOC, we'd have been hamburger too."

Grey indicated a squad-sized hooch across from the Tactical Operations Command bunker. "Those are the officers' quarters. We compared notes after it happened. No one saw anything."

"It wasn't the VC," said Larson confidently. "They'd never breach our perimeter."

"Any ideas then," said McCall, "on who'd want the colonel dead bad enough to frag him?"

"You mean suspects?" Larson nodded, the flint cold in his eyes. "Yeah, I could think of a few."

Grey cleared his throat, a nervous habit preceding almost anything he said. "You might as well go ahead and tell him, Cap."

Tara lowered her camera. "Tell us what?"

This got McCall's goat. "Not us, ma'am. Me." He returned his attention to the men. "I take it the colonel was not well liked."

Hines chuckled coarsely. "You're saying that just because someone fragged his ass to hell, right?"

"The colonel was assigned here last month. A new CO always shakes up a command to put his own brand on it. The troops never like it, but it usually settles into mutual respect after a while. Sort of a honeymoon in reverse."

Tara murmured beneath her breath, "Now there's a concept."

Hines grunted. "You want a list of suspects, Major? You could start with the roster of every man assigned to this base."

Grey cleared his throat. "There are thirty men who were stationed here who have been dropped from that list. And I should be one of them. I should have been out there with Sergeant Williams and his platoon last night."

"Lieutenant Grey is a platoon leader with Bravo Company," Larson explained. "A platoon from Bravo Company was ambushed last night on patrol. Heavy casualties."

"Fifteen killed, fifteen wounded," said Hines. "Wiped out by one of our own bombs. The VC find our dud shells, rig them up, and use them against us."

McCall next went around the hooch to the entrance of the command center. He glanced inside. Tactical maps were spread out upon folding tables. Rifle and ammo crates served as chairs. A clerk was busy at a typewriter. A radio man monitored mostly static from a small receiver.

McCall turned back to Larson. "Let me guess. Saigon promised you replacements, but night's falling and they're not here yet."

Larson nodded bleakly. "And until they get here, we're way short of manpower. I'm hoping Charlie hasn't figured that out yet."

"Issue me an M-16," said McCall. "You've got at least one replacement."

"Two, actually," Tara volunteered.

They ignored her.

McCall didn't miss the flash of anger that made her eyes a deeper shade of green.

Without clearing his throat, Grey said, "The colonel should never have ordered us into that sector."

"This firebase is assigned two companies of light infantry," Larson told McCall. "One supports the other. The line company conducts recon patrols around the base, and it was Bravo Company's turn on the rotation schedule. The other company provides mortar and artillery support from here."

"Go ahead, Major McCall." Lieutenant Grey spoke fervently. "Check my record. I'd have never sent a platoon down those trails where the Colonel ordered me to. I'm not some wet-behind-the ears cherry! That ambush wasn't my fault. Me and Sergeant Williams always brought our guys home. Right, Captain?"

Larson nodded uncomfortably. "Right, Lieutenant."

Hines said, not unkindly, in an almost paternal voice, "I'd advise you to chill out, Lieutenant, if you don't mind my saying so, sir. You, uh, haven't felt right since, well, since last night. Maybe you ought to lie down in your hooch, sir. I'll have a medic check in with you."

"I don't need a medic," said Grey. "I need to get something off my chest. My father."

McCall frowned. "Your father?"

Tara's knuckles were white around her camera. With one sideways glance, McCall could tell that an impulse within her was trying to dissuade her from capturing, for posterity, Grey's vulnerability and emotional unbalance; a poignant portrait of the ravages of war on even a trained, competent man. Tara grimaced, raised her camera and snapped a picture.

Grey cleared his throat. "The sergeant I just mentioned, the one who died in the ambush."

"Williams," said McCall. "What about him?"

"He was in the Korean war," said Grey, "and until yesterday he was here, keeping alive officers like me and guys who should have been back home drinking beer. Every man on the base respected Sergeant Williams. He was our teacher, our preacher, the one we looked up to. But I owed him a personal debt. That's why I wish to God that I was a dead man, not him."

"Lieutenant," said Larson, "you followed SOP every step of the way last night. You are not responsible for what happened."

"What does this have to do with your father?" McCall asked Grey.

"Sergeant Williams and my dad served together in Korea," said Grey. "He saved Dad's life. Sarge greased a Red Chinese who was about to run Dad through with a bayonet. They stayed in touch after the war. They were both lifers. I must have heard the story a hundred times growing up. I never got tired of it. Cancer got Dad in '68. I was raised to be a soldier. I couldn't believe my luck when I got assigned to Sergeant Williams. I was supposed to be the platoon leader, but we all knew who kept us alive." Grey's lower lip trembled. "And as his platoon leader, sending him and those men on that patrol last night, I am responsible for the death of the man who saved my father's life. I stayed behind to get paperwork squared away for the IG. Paperwork, for chrissake! I should have been out there with my men. God forgive me."

Tara stepped forward and rested a hand gently on his shoulder.

"In no way is that true, Lieutenant. Listen to your captain and to Sergeant Hines. You've been through hell. There is a thing called survivor's guilt. You must maintain. That is what you owe Sergeant Williams and your father and yourself."

Grey's lower lip stopped trembling. His jawline regained its prominence. "Yes, ma'am. You're right." He chuckled self-consciously. "What's the old line about not seeing the woods for the trees? Damn straight. I'm not doing anybody any good, pissing and whining about what happened. I've got to recharge my batteries and get ready for whatever's coming at us next."

She nodded. "I couldn't have said it better myself."

Grey turned to Larson. "Sir, uh, I guess I should try and get some rest."

"I think you're right, Lieutenant."

Grey looked in Tara's direction. "Thanks, ma'am."

He strode off in the direction of the officers' hooch.

"There goes a fine soldier," said Larson, "wearing a hairshirt from hell."

"He'll make it," said Hines. He said to Tara, "Thank you, ma'am. That boy has a lot to offer this man's army, but he was on the verge of losing it. You helped tilt the scales in the right direction."

Tara began to speak.

But McCall cut her off. "Yes, ma'am. That was humane and noble, and thank you for it." Their eyes connected. "But now I will ask you to back off and allow me to get on with this investigation." He glanced back at the XO. "I want a look at Sergeant Williams' hooch."

"This way." Larson started them toward a line of hooches near a row of mortar placements. "Mind if I ask, Major, what you think you'll find in Sergeant Williams' hooch that could shed light on what happened to the Colonel?"

Striding apace, Tara again volunteered.

"I read it this way. The lieutenant said the men on this base looked up to Sergeant Williams like a hero."

Hines nodded. "That's as good a word as any, and that's why everyone really hated the Colonel after the Sarge died." A smile of dawning awareness creased his black features. "And there's your connection. Lady, you're a regular Sherlock Holmes."

"She's also a civilian," said McCall. "I'll thank you, Miss Carpenter, to just zip it and take your pictures."

"Understood, General."

McCall sighed. "Sarcasm yet. I'll be lucky to make colonel with you bird-dogging me." As they drew up before one of the hooches near the mortars, he noted, "Not the quietest neighborhood."

"No such thing as a quiet neighborhood in this sector," said Hines. "We're surrounded by bogey land. It's a free fire zone everywhere beyond that perimeter."

"The first change the Colonel made," said Larson, "was to send out more patrols, and after dark. That was unnecessary and far too risky. Everyone except the colonel knew it. The mission for this firebase is recon. You can't do much recon at night. The ambush last night was proof of that."

Hines spat derisively. "This base has an outstanding record for targeting VC for our flyboys. We do our job. But doing our job wasn't good enough for the Colonel, that is as long as he didn't have to get off his fat ass in the TOC bunker. He wanted the line companies to go right in and get a higher enemy body count so he could get himself a general's star, and he didn't give a damn about sacrificing soldiers like Sergeant Williams to do it."

Tara raised her camera and snapped a picture of Hines' resignation, weariness and anger.

McCall crouched down and stepped into the hooch Sergeant Williams shared with several of the other soldiers who'd been killed during the ambush. Tara lowered her camera and positioned herself between Hines and Larson to observe.

Their grouped presence in the hooch doorway deepened the gloom of its interior. The hooch was of uniform furnishings: several cots, footlockers, a makeshift desk.

"How come you haven't sent all these belongings back to Saigon, yet?" McCall asked.

"Haven't had the time, sir," said Larson. "We just shipped the injured and the bodies out late last night and today. We'll send their stuff along with the next mail run."

McCall dropped to one knee and conducted a thorough search of the lockers. "Uh-huh!" he said triumphantly. He rose, letting the lid of the locker snap shut, and left the hooch, rejoining them, thoughtfully leafing through a bound, leather volume.

Larson tried to see if there was printing on the book's spine. "What did you find, Major?"

Hines guessed, "A bible?"

McCall shook his head, snapping the book shut. "Not even close."

Tara studied the book's dimensions and appearance. "A diary."

"When men keep one," said McCall pointedly, "it's called a journal."

Larson ran a palm across the bristle of his crew cut. "Why would Sergeant Williams keep a journal?"

"Why the hell wouldn't he?" growled Hines. "I'll bet he had plenty of stories to tell, going way back to Korea."

"Too bad he kept them to himself," said Larson. He stretched out a hand, palm up. "Mind if I take a look? Maybe he wrote something about Firebase Tiger."

McCall slid the book into a pocket of his fatigues. "That's what I'm thinking. Sorry, Captain, but first I want to have a look for myself."

Tara studied McCall.

"You think Sergeant Williams' diary—excuse me, journal—could hold a clue to who fragged the colonel."

"I intend to find out."

"I'll show you where the guest billets are," offered Hines, "for what they're worth,"

"And it's past chow time," added Larson. "Will you be joining us?"

"Thanks, but no for me." McCall patted the book in his pocket. "Something tells me that this is going to make for interesting reading. I want to get started."

Tara let herself into one of the guest billets—not her own—without announcing her arrival.

She didn't need to.

McCall sat at a makeshift desk, a slab of plywood resting across two empty oil drums. Remaining seated, he pivoted with incredible speed, a blur of movement, freezing with the .45 in straight-armed target acquisition. He held his fire when he realized that the muzzle of the .45 was inches away from, and aimed at, the center of his wife's forehead.

Tara stood there, lovely mouth agape, her green eyes wide, holding her breath in astonishment.

He sighed mightily, flicked on the safety and returned the .45 to its shoulder holster. "Now there was a temptation." He returned back to the material spread out across the desk. "I thought we were going to avoid personal contact, Miss Carpenter."

She crossed the hooch to stand behind him, resting a hand on his shoulder.

Her touch had always had its intended effect on him, he realized anew, whether it was intended to comfort, arouse or merely share, and now was no exception. He felt that humanizing affirmation borne of the touch of woman, of grace and beauty so uncommon in the harshness of war.

She glimpsed the paperwork he'd been pouring over: three personnel files, a pad of his notations and the slim leather volume, folded open with the spine up. She read aloud the names off the personnel files.

"Captain Larson, Lieutenant Grey, Sergeant Hines. Primary suspects. Motives and opportunities galore. But I don't understand your interest in Sergeant Williams' diary. I'm glad I don't have to guess which one of those three fragged the colonel."

McCall decided that he could either blow up or give up. He turned around to look up at her from where he sat and his exasperation yielded to affection in spite of himself. More than anyone, he could appreciate that this woman he was in love with had a backbone of steel coupled with a tenacity that could wear down stone.

"What makes you think I'm guessing? What I do is called investigating and detecting." He sighed again, allowing himself a chuckle. "What the hell am I going to do with you?"

An impish smile curved her lips and with one graceful, impudent motion, she was straddling his lap, her wrists locked behind his neck, her mischievous green eyes aroused, her glistening, inviting lips only inches away.

She whispered huskily in his ear. "I've got an idea what you could do with me, Major."

He stood without speaking. She held onto him, hugging his shoulders with her arms, his torso with her wrap-around legs. A few paces to the bunk and they fell atop it. She was pinned beneath him, her camera pushed to the side, forgotten. Feverish kissing fueled passion. His fingers went to her trousers, unbuttoning them, the fingers slid inside.

She parted her legs, and his middle finger stroked the cotton of her panties. The cotton was moist. She groaned, then they hurriedly unbuttoned his trousers. Boots and trousers were impatiently tossed off. Touching his hardness with warm fingers, she guided him into her, arching her pelvis, moaning as the full length of him entered her.

Their lovemaking went directly into high gear, with moist sounds as he plunged in and out of her.

His left hand ran through her hair and stroked the back of her neck. The fingers of his other hand moved up under her shirt, this time to beneath the cool silk of the brassier, repeatedly flicking one nipple, then the other, each flick eliciting a tiny mew of desire from Tara, her nipples becoming taut tips of firm breasts that jiggled with the thrusting of energetic lovemaking.

Then he slid both hands down to cup her from underneath. The heat and humidity inside the hooch increased. The heavy breathing of their exertion, pleasure and need built to a feverish crescendo of mutual, lusting desperation for expression, for release. Her fists pummeled his back. She bit into the shoulder of his uniform to muffle the moan of her orgasm, which only served to drive him on with a heightening animal intensity. He groaned against her throat, the lusty, woman-sweat scent of her permeating his senses. They crested a wave of release together and this time when McCall gushed his climax, it was not spurting into his pants but into the writhing, willing body of his moaning wife.

They embraced as tightly as they could, the moment hanging suspended, neither wanting this deepest intimacy to end. When it did, it was with a shared sigh that they relaxed together.

"Wow." She breathed contently in his arms. "Thank you, hubby. I guess we know who the tiger of this firebase is."

"You vexatious wench."

"Vexatious?"

"Sometimes I wish you were more of a nag. That'd be easier to deal with."

Realizing that he was serious, she lost some of her good humor.

"You know something, Cord, you need to brush up on your after-play technique." She remained in his embrace, but shifted her hips so that he slipped from within her. "And since we're dispensing with etiquette, what about that diary? Was it interesting?"

"What diary?"

At that instant, someone outside yelled, "Incoming!"

Then a startling, eerie whistling that decreased in pitch unbelievably fast drowned everything out and was then itself drowned out by a deafening explosion, an impacting blast that shook the hooch. Dust and red dirt powdered down upon the entwined lovers.

They un-entwined, threw on their fatigues, laced up boots. McCall grabbed the M-16 he'd been issued and hurried to the doorway.

A night fog had fallen. A bursting flare overhead cast the base in surreal daylight, as if seen through a mist.

The first explosion had been a direct hit on the Huey gunship that had brought them, now nothing but an unrecognizable, flaming ruin. Everywhere, soldiers were deploying, some firing their M-16s on the run. He heard the steady, throaty hammering of the M-60s. There was continuous incoming fire, winking saffron flickers in the night. He cursed when he saw a GI drop. Artillery and the mortars opened up, returning fire, shredding the night with their thunder and fury. The ground shook.

A round whistled in, chipping off a chunk of the hooch's doorframe. McCall felt a trickle of blood from a flying splinter, razor-thin along his cheek. He absently wiped the blood away.

The next incoming mortar shell struck the main bunker. The Tactical Operations Command evaporated in a copper-red eruption of flame.

Tara was at his side, ready to bolt. "Damn but I wish they'd issued me a weapon. Don't suppose I could borrow one of yours?"

He grabbed her hand. "First, let's get you to cover. They're targeting the hooches."

He yanked her with him and they stormed out into the battle. He led her to a nearby pile of debris, empty oil drums and discarded machine parts; a good place to stash his troublesome wife until this was over. They passed more strobe-like explosions. Shouts filled the air along with the stench of destruction, of burnt gunpowder, of dying and killing.

A round pinged off an overhanging piece of metal. Tara's right, McCall reasoned. He couldn't leave her unarmed. He handed her his M-16, which left him with the shoulder-holstered .45.

"Here. You qualified with one of these on the range back home. Consider this a lesson in practical application. Keep your head down, babe. You are a noncombatant." He unleathered the .45 and flicked off the safety. "I've got to keep moving, to help out."

She took the weapon, comfortable with it. But her eyes were distracted by something behind him.

"Cord. Look."

He whirled, not knowing what to expect. Then he saw it.

Through the disorganized melee, a soldier, whose features were obscured, became centralized in his focus for the same reason Tara had noticed him. Though he fit in, moving through the tumultuous firefight with determined haste, staying low to avoid incoming fire, one hand steadying his helmet as he ran, he did appear to McCall, even from this distance, to be somehow disengaged from the fighting, particularly when he reached the hooch that the McCalls had just vacated.

A shell-burst, much too close for comfort, clearly revealed the man's features in flickering, harsh coppery tones just before he entered the hooch.

"Damn," said Tara.

"Wait here," said McCall, and he took off.

Tara slung the M-16 over her shoulder by its strap as if she were a seasoned vet. She clicked her camera's flash bulb attachment into place.

"Right," she said to herself.

McCall hesitated at the entrance to the hooch, the .45 at his side. His presence went undetected by the man inside because of the ferocious battle raging around them and because the man was preoccupied, in the process of reaching for the slim black book next to the files on the desk.

McCall said, "It's not a journal, Captain."

Larson whirled. His flinty eyes struggled between surprise and panic. "Major, I can explain."

They had to shout to—hear each other above the cacophony from outside.

"I'm arresting you," shouted McCall. "You fragged the colonel."

Larson drew himself up, doing his best to reassert command here, even if he was outranked. "On the strength of what? Every man on this base wanted that bastard dead."

"Yeah, but I smoked out someone with a guilty conscience." McCall nodded to the black book. "That's no journal. It's a notebook I always carry. You wanted a look at it to see if you were incriminated. Williams told you to bite your tongue and take orders when you confided in him that you wanted to frag the colonel."

A shell struck the next hooch over with the thunderous crack of a lightening strike. The ground whumped with its impact. Screams for "Medic! Medic!" came from close enough to sound like they were right inside this hooch with them.

Like a jolt of electricity, this ignited raw, bitter emotion that spewed from Larson. "That's exactly what he told me! 'Let it alone,' he said. 'Follow orders.' Right, follow orders! And look what it got Williams and the men of Bravo Company." When he realized what he'd said, he roared like a gored bull. "Bastard!"

He lunged at McCall.

McCall had hoped that the sight of the .45 would discourage this, but Larson wasn't about to be taken easily. He could escape into the jungle, or die trying. McCall brought up the .45.

The snap of a flashbulb came from close behind his ear.

Tara had crept up from outside, eavesdropping on everything.

The flash filled the hooch, not impairing McCall's vision because it came from behind him. But the blinding flash startled and stopped Larson, who reflexively threw his arms up to cover his eyes.

McCall heard Tara say, "Gotcha!"

He charged the disoriented man, bringing his pistol around in a swipe that cracked the side of Larson's head. Larson's knees buckled. He collapsed to the earthen floor. McCall holstered his .45 and reached for his cuffs, speaking over his shoulder to Tara, who, camera still in hand, looked stunning in her formfitting fatigues even with the beauty of her model's face grime-smudged and her red hair tangled.

"Thanks, hon." He looked down at Larson, whose face, against the earthen floor, was an emotionless mask. "You must have radioed in for air cover as soon as this attack started. We'll hitch a ride back to Saigon when it's over."

"You've got this all wrong, Major. Yeah, I though it was a journal. I came to see if the Sarge thought anyone on base would do it, see if he wrote it down. That doesn't mean I fragged him!"

"Hines will fess up," said McCall. "He's lying to give you an alibi because he hated the colonel, too. You weren't in the TOC bunker with Hines when the colonel was fragged. I'll work Top's conscience and his duty under the Uniform Code of Military Justice, and when your first sergeant talks, I'll have the proof I need."

"What the hell kind of a soldier are you?" sneered Larson. "Whose side are you on, McCall? I'm on the side of our soldiers. That's more important than any VC body count, so some fat-assed colonel can advance his career. You think I could let that go on? Our body count is my concern!" He cooled, his tone reasonable. "Let me go, Major. The colonel got what he deserved. You know that, in your heart."

"Sorry, Captain. It's my job to take you in."

Someone outside yelled, "Incoming!" and again came that fast-approaching whistling.

McCall sprang at Tara without hesitation, yelling to the man on the floor, "Move it, Cap! Save yourself!"

Larson didn't move. "Up yours, Major."

With the incoming whistle growing louder with every heartbeat, McCall plowed into Tara with enough force to knock her off her feet, sending them both airborne, pitching them outside and to ground. They landed together, his arms encircling her. They rolled a few times and came to a stop.

A direct hit demolished the hooch with another loud explosion.

McCall pinned his wife, almost as he had on the cot, but this time to shield her. They were pelted with falling debris. When the shower ceased, they lifted their heads.

She arched her neck for a view of the smoldering remains of the hooch. "Captain Larson..."

"It's better this way," said McCall. "He died like a soldier. It will look better in his file."

"You're not going to report that he killed the colonel?"

McCall said nothing.

She stared up at him. Then she kissed the thin red line of dried blood that crossed his cheek.

The battle was winding down. Three Huey gunships rotored in and began pulverizing the jungle, making the night sky a fire show of tracer bullets, rocketfire and multiple explosions from inside the tree line. The M-60s on the perimeter, and the base mortars and artillery stayed at it.

There was no more incoming fire. The primary activity on the base was centered on tending to the wounded, regrouping, assessing the damage.

And for one stolen moment between a man and a woman, upon the battle-scarred ground of Firebase Tiger, McCall and his wife prolonged their embrace that would appear to any passerby as no more than a soldier shielding a noncombatant after that last explosion.

"Know what?" whispered Tara.

"What?"

"I like being on the bottom."

"You," McCall said, "are impossible."

"And that's only one of the reasons you're crazy about me, right?"

"Yeah, I guess so," McCall admitted. "Crazy is definitely the word. I must be out of my mind." He saw two figures hurrying in their direction. "Here comes Sergeant Hines and Lieutenant Grey. I've got some explaining to do." He got up off of her, extending a courtly hand. She accepted, rising to her feet. He said for her ears alone, "Now stow the personal stuff, okay, hon? I mean it, Tara. For real."

He turned to greet Hines and the lieutenant.

"Right," Tara said to herself, and hurried to join them.

⋆⇒◎⇐⋆

You can read more about Tara & Cord in the forthcoming novel, available in August 2001.

FOGGY WINDOWS BOOKS

Overdrive

The action adventure genre has been around for quite a number of years, from the pulp series of the sixties to the big screen blockbusters of today. Our Overdrive *imprint offers forays into this arena with stories that you might expect to see at your local theatre, tales of men and women whose lives are filled with risk and excitement, and whose bedrooms are just as busy as a hero or heroine deserve.*

Into the Underground Temple

Sean McIver

Sean McIver was born in London during The Blitz and moved to the U.S. with his parents shortly after World War II. He wrote his first story when he was ten, but, authorship not proving profitable, he decided early on to become a professional student, a life for which he thought himself well-suited. Unfortunately, being a student paid little better than his writing had, so, after eleven years of college, he was forced to find another occupation. McIver has worked as a freight hauler, dishwasher, and feed salesman, among other things. Eventually he decided to try writing again and found that it now paid more (though not much) than he had received for his early efforts. He has published poetry, short stories, and fifty novels under approximately ten different names.

1

Joshua Kinkade had once been a strong, powerful man, a rough-neck in the Texas and Mexican oil fields and later a wildcat driller of his own wells both north and south of the border. He had made more money that he ever dreamed possible, but it wasn't enough to save him from the cancer that was destroying him.

He lay in his hospital bed, gray and wasted, fed through plastic tubes, his eyes closed against the pain that racked him. His only son stood beside him.

"Henry?" Joshua said. "Are you there?"

Enrique Kinkade, whom Joshua had always called by the Americanized version of his name, reached out and took his father's hand. As a child, Henry had thought that hand powerful enough to grind rocks to powder. Now it felt more like a loose bundle of sticks.

Henry was tall, a bit over six feet, broad-shouldered, with black hair and eyes. His skin was a golden brown, as if he spent a great deal of time in the sun, though he didn't, and he wore a thin moustache.

"I'm here," Henry said past the lump that had formed in his throat.

"Good." The dying man's voice strengthened. "What about Jeanie?"

Jeanie was Henry's wife, a woman who looked like everyone's idea of the girl next door, that is, if the girl next door had red hair, a light sprinkling of freckles, china blue eyes, and a figure that made strong men go weak in the knees at the sight of her.

"I'm here, Joshua," Jeanie said, taking Henry's free hand and squeezing it.

"Fine. You know I'm dying, I guess."

"That's what the doctor said," Henry told him.

"Son of a bitch could at least lie about it. Anyway, I know I haven't been much of a father to you, Henry, running all over the world and leaving your mother, rest her soul, to bring you up the best way she could. But I didn't know any way to make a living but the oil business, so—"

"It's all right," Henry said. "You were a fine father. I couldn't have asked for better."

"You're a better liar than that damn doctor." Joshua paused for a moment as a spasm of pain passed through him. "Anyway, I'd better get this said before I kick off. I was hoping you might be willing to do your dying daddy a little favor."

"Of course," Henry said. "Anything. Just tell me what it is."

"I want you to find Montezuma's treasure," the old man said.

Henry thought he must not have heard correctly, but then Joshua always did have an odd sense of humor.

"What?" Henry said.

"Find Montezuma's treasure. It won't be so tough. I have a map."

"You're kidding me," Henry said. "Not that old map."

"A dying man doesn't make jokes about treasure. You should know me better than that, even if I wasn't around all the time. Your mama would want you to find that treasure if she were still here. She's the one who gave me the map. You know the one I mean. Got it from her daddy, she said. You going to find the treasure or not?"

"Of course he is," Jeanie said, squeezing harder on Henry's hand. That was Jeanie, game for anything.

Henry sighed. "Of course I am," he agreed.

"Good," Joshua said. "Now I'll tell you the rest."

"There's more?"

"You know how those Aztecs were. They knew all kinds of things, and some of them were about healing. There are some old stories about an amulet that cured wounds. It might work on me."

"But you're not wounded."

"Same difference. It's worth a try, anyhow. It's a gold neck-lace with an eagle's head, and it was supposedly part of the ransom they gathered up for old Montezuma. I want you to find it for me."

"We'll do it," Jeanie said eagerly.

"Right," Henry agreed. Not quite so eagerly.

"Good," Joshua said. "Now get me a drink of water."

2

Five days later, Henry and Jeanie Kinkade were in their room in the Prado Hotel, an eleven-story structure of pink stucco on Avenida Juarez in Mexico City.

"This is crazy," Henry said. "I'm a college professor, not a treasure hunter."

"And a very good college professor, too," Jeanie said. She was wrapped in a bath towel, her red hair damp from the shower. "Do hotels make you horny?"

She opened the towel quickly, then shut it, proving, as if Henry hadn't already known, that she was a natural redhead.

"You're distracting me," Henry said, swallowing hard.

Jeanie twirled, bent over, and flipped the towel up in the back. She grinned at him over her shoulder.

"See anything you like?"

Henry tried to concentrate on the much-folded and quite faded map that he had spread out on the bed. As a child he had been enthralled with the story his mother told him about it, but now he wasn't interested in childish things. He looked back at Jeanie, who was now facing him, opening and closing the towel slowly.

"You're making it very hard for—"

Jeanie smiled wickedly. "That's exactly my intention. To make it hard, I mean."

"I think I'll take a cold shower," Henry said.

Jeanie dropped the towel. "Good. I'll join you. I can help you soap your...back."

⋆⊷═◉═⊶⋆

"That's not my back," Henry said as they stood under the lukewarm water.

Jeanie rubbed her breasts lightly against his chest. The nipples were hot and hard, hard enough to cut glass. At the same time, she tried to look at Henry innocently, as if she didn't know what effect she was having. She was actually quite good at both looking innocent and having an effect, and she was well aware of her talents.

"It's not your back?" she said. "I was going to ask you about that. Do you have a bar of soap in your pocket, or are you just glad to see me?"

"Why don't we dry off and find out?"

"Why dry off?" Jeanie said, giving Henry a few silky strokes. "I need a little more soaping. I have some nooks and crannies that you could help me with."

Henry didn't need any further encouragement. He moved a soapy hand down Jeanie's stomach and into the thick curls below. She sighed and closed her eyes as his slick fingers parted her labia and slid languidly over her clitoris. She moved herself back and forth to encourage him, slowly at first and then faster. With that encouragement, his fingers slid a bit lower, into the hot opening that awaited them. Jeanie sighed with pleasure as they moved in and out. Henry let his other hand move down her back, and her rump moved in small circles as he caressed its taut surface. At the same time, Jeanie kept massaging Henry's penis until he felt the skin might pop from its expansion. He was nearly at the bursting point. His breath came faster and faster.

Judging that the time was right, Jeanie stood on tiptoes, and with Henry's help, she impaled herself on him, moaning with delight as he entered her. She lifted herself up, then lowered herself as hard as she could, forcing Henry's penis deep into her body as the curls of their pubic hair merged.

Henry put his hands on her hips to help, and she began to move on him, faster and faster, her head back, her eyes closed, her wet red hair hanging down, streaming with water from the shower.

"Ah," Henry said.

Jeanie said something similar. As they became more active, they became less articulate, until they were both breathing quite rapidly. Henry leaned forward and licked Jeanie's breasts, and she sank her nails into his back. Finally, with a long, drawn-out sigh, Jeanie arched her back and cried out. Henry cried out too, and, still joined, they slid slowly to the floor.

"Hotels _do_ make you horny," Jeanie said after a while.

"It wasn't the hotel," Henry said.

"And you're panting. Are you all right?"

"It's the altitude," Henry said.

Jeanie smiled. "Sure it is."

The map was still on the bed, and Henry was studying it again when Jeanie came out of the bathroom, wrapped in another towel.

Henry looked up and said, "Don't start that again."

Jeanie gave him the innocent look. "Start what?"

"You know what. Get dressed and help me with this map."

Jeanie threw the towel at Henry and flounced across the room to the closet. He had to admit that when it came to flouncing, she was one of the best. Especially when she was naked.

She got dressed slowly, putting on her bra first, then lingering over her nylons as she rolled them up over her calves to hook them to the garter belt.

"Nylons won't be comfortable where we're going," Henry said.

"But we're not going tonight, are we?"

"No."

Jeanie smiled and continued with what she was doing. Henry tried to look at the map, but it wasn't easy.

"So your grandfather drew the map," Jeanie said. "Is that right?"

"That's the family story."

"And he told your mother on his deathbed that there was a treasure under Mexico City, just before he slipped her the map."

"That's what my mother said. But she was like my father. They both loved a good story. It didn't have to be true. In fact, Joshua likes a good story better if it isn't true."

"But it could be," Jeanie said. "Mexico City is built on the ruins of the Aztec capital, Tenochtitlan. You know that; it's your heritage."

Henry shook his head. Jeanie knew that although his mother had been of Mexican and Indian ancestry, he had been born, brought up, and educated in the United States. He could hardly even speak Spanish, though his mother had told him many stories about the Aztecs and their gods. Still, he didn't feel much of a connection.

"I'm a North American," he said.

Jeanie ignored him. "Cortez captured Montezuma and demanded a great ransom for him. The ransom was gathered but never paid because Montezuma was killed. It could easily have been hidden in the great temple of Tenochtitlan. The ruins of the temple are under Mexico City."

"My grandfather dug sewers," Henry said, trying to bring her down to earth. "He claims he saw this fabulous treasure in 1910. That's more than forty-five years ago. Someone's probably found it by now."

"That's not the question," Jeanie said. "The question is, why didn't he get any of it for himself? He wasn't a rich man."

"He was superstitious, though. He believed that anyone who touched the great treasure of his ancestors would die."

"Don't tell me there's a curse."

"No. But the Aztecs believed in human sacrifice. My mother said that her father was sure the treasure was guarded by the spirits of sacrificial victims. He would never have touched it, no matter how much it was worth."

"Your mother was a believer, too."

Henry thought for a moment of Maria Elena Gonzalez de

Reyes Kinkade. She had been a beautiful woman, and the blood of the Aztecs had run strong in her veins. She had even been able to speak Nahuatl. She died three years ago, during a burglary in her home. Joshua had been in Mexico looking for oil when it happened.

"She believed, all right," Henry said.

"And your father believes in the amulet."

"He didn't exactly say that. He might have been joking. He's not much of a believer in anything."

"True. So are we going to look for the treasure or not?"

"What do you think?"

"I think we're going into the sewers. I think you want to find that amulet for your father, whether or not either one of you believes in it, just to prove you can. But I'll need a new outfit. This one will never do."

Henry looked at his wife, sitting there demurely in bra, garter belt, and nylons.

"Oh," he said, "I think it'll do just fine."

3

The great temple of the Aztecs was built on the marshy land in the middle of the immense Lake Texcoco. Even before the arrival of Cortez, it had begun to sink into the soggy soil. When Cortez conquered the city, he razed the temple and every other building, as if trying to obliterate every memory of the Aztecs. Mexico City grew atop the ancient ruins, and over the temple rises the great Mexico City Cathedral with its tall towers and mighty dome, one of the oldest cathedrals in the Americas. It faces the Zocalo, the city's main plaza, where news vendors, flower peddlers, and food sellers hawk their wares to the tourists. The air is usually filled with the sweet scent of flowers and the smell of tamales and beans.

When Henry and Jeanie emerged from a cab in front of the

cathedral, two of the tourists, who were more or less concealed behind a profusion of flowers, took a special interest.

"There they are," Warren Beaumont said. "I told you they'd show up here. If there's a treasure, it will be in the temple, and the way to the temple is around here somewhere."

Beaumont was handsome in an oily way. He was a professor of archaeology at Brinson College, the small liberal arts school where Henry taught English.

"I don't know why Henry brought that washed-out, freckle-faced bitch with him," Modesty Trilling replied.

Modesty was a striking blonde history instructor who exuded childlike innocence through every pore, a perfect example of the way that appearances can deceive. In reality she had the morals and the temperament of a water moccasin.

"You're just jealous because he won't sleep with you," Beaumont said.

"Ha," Modesty retorted, though she had to admit that Beaumont was right. Henry had proved immune to her charms, and she could never forgive a man for that. Not that she would ever have to sleep alone. In a pinch, she'd settle for second-best. Or third-best, if need be. Even fourth-best, which was about where she'd rate Beaumont, would do in a crisis. It wouldn't do to tell Beaumont that, however.

"Anyway," Modesty said, "you're the jealous one. Henry is going to make a find that will relegate anything you ever did to a footnote in an appendix. I wonder if he knows that you tried to get that map?"

"Of course not," Beaumont snapped.

He didn't like to think about the night he'd tried to get his hands on that map. Maria Kinkade had told him about it at a faculty gathering she'd attended with her son. He'd asked to see it, but she'd refused. She said that she was sorry she had mentioned it, that she should never have let it slip. It was a priceless memento of her father, a private thing. She would never have said anything about it except for Beaumont's evident interest in Mexico and the Aztec people.

Beaumont had known from the beginning that he had to have the map, and if stealing it was the only way to get it, steal he would. The old woman wasn't supposed to be at home, but there she was, and she hadn't been afraid of Beaumont one bit. Still, he regretted having pushed her down the stairs. It had been an accident, more or less; he hadn't meant to kill her. And even worse, he hadn't been able to find the map.

Finally, after several years of waiting, Beaumont got another break. Henry Kinkade, after a visit to his dying father, had asked for a leave of absence from the college to take a trip to Mexico. When Beaumont asked him the purpose of the trip, Henry was evasive.

"Going after that treasure, eh?" Beaumont said.

Henry was obviously taken aback.

"What do you know about that?"

"Quite a bit, old man. Your mother told me all about it."

"That's not true," Henry said.

"Oh, but it is. Aztec treasure and all that."

Henry had simply walked away, but Beaumont was convinced that he was going after the treasure, for whatever reason. So both he and Modesty had arranged a leave as well. Beaumont liked to have company when traveling in a foreign land, especially if the company was as lovely and unimpaired by morals as Modesty.

"What are they getting out of the back of that cab?" Modesty asked, breaking into Beaumont's thoughts.

"A box of some kind," Beaumont said. "I'm sure they have their supplies in it."

"They're just lucky they're alive," Modesty said. She wasn't easily frightened, but her one cab ride in Mexico City had been enough to put her in fear for her life. "Do *we* have any supplies?"

"Never fear," Beaumont said. "I stowed them nearby. If Kinkade finds his way into that temple, we'll be right behind him."

"Oh goody," Modesty said in a little-girl voice. "I can hardly wait."

ч

"You're sure about this?" Jeanie asked, looking up at the imposing facade of the cathedral.

"I'm not sure of anything," Henry told her. "The public works department wasn't exactly cooperative, and their records aren't in the best order. And, as I mentioned, this map is over forty-five years old. If that's not enough, it doesn't show the entrance to the sewers."

"But it's near here?"

"If there's any truth in the story my mother told me, it is, and unlike my father, she wasn't much of one for jokes."

"We'll find it then," Jeanie said.

There was an alley beside the cathedral, and Henry led the way into it. It was dark and quiet and cool, shaded on one side by the massive walls of the cathedral.

"Isn't that box heavy?" Jeanie asked.

"We might need this stuff," Henry said. "You never know."

"The rope and the battery lanterns I can understand. But a pistol?"

"Have you ever been in a sewer?"

"No."

"Neither have I. They say there are alligators in the sewers of New York. So who knows what we might run into."

"You're not scaring me a bit. Can you shoot a pistol?"

"Joshua taught me. That's one thing I can do well."

"I can think of at least one other thing," Jeanie said, standing close to Henry and whispering breathily into his ear.

"Don't start that, or we'll just go back to the hotel and forget the treasure."

"I'll be good," Jeanie said, though Henry doubted she would. "Look over there. Isn't that an old iron grating?"

Henry looked into the deep shadow near the base of the building and saw what she was talking about. The old grating could have been there since 1910. Or even earlier. Henry set his box down and brought out a pry bar.

"Be prepared," Jeanie said. "Were you a Boy Scout?"

"I was never much interested in scouting for boys," Henry said, working the pry bar under the edge of the grating and levering it upward. "Keep a watch, will you? We don't want to be seen."

Jeanie looked back down the alley. She thought she saw something move at the entrance, but it was gone so quickly that she couldn't be sure.

"I think we're alone," she said.

The grating made a screeching noise as Henry pried it away from the concrete, then clattered down as he shoved it aside. A faint but unpleasant odor reeked out of the opening.

Jeanie looked down into the blackness. "We're going down there?"

"Unless you know a better way."

Jeanie shrugged and said, "I don't."

Henry took the leather holster from the box and belted it on. Then he checked to see that the .38 revolver was loaded. It was. He gave a lantern to Jeanie and took one for himself, then looped the rope over his shoulder. Shining a lantern into the hole, he saw that there was a rusty iron ladder leading downward.

"Me first," he said, and climbed down into the opening.

"There they go," Beaumont said, peering around the corner of the alley. "We'll give them a minute and follow."

"Where's your pistol?" Modesty asked.

"Don't you worry," Beaumont said. "It's right here."

He dug around in a mound of colorful blossoms that hid them and exposed a cardboard box. He opened it to show Modesty a .45 automatic.

"Mine's bigger than his," Beaumont said.

Yeah, right, Modesty thought. *You wish.*

5

Henry and Jeanie had to climb down several levels to reach the sewer. Each time they went lower, the air got cooler and the smell got worse.

"Are we climbing through the temple ruins?" Jeanie asked.

Henry wasn't sure, but he said he supposed they were. "Archaeologists will have a field day here sooner or later," he said.

"Then it shouldn't be too far to the treasure room," Jeanie said.

"The map isn't to scale, so I'm not sure. We'll just have to see."

"We won't be able to see much. These lanterns don't give a lot of light."

Jeanie shined the beam on the wall and moved it around to show what she meant.

"I know," Henry said. "But at least we can see well enough to get around. According to the map, the treasure room was on the lowest level of the temple, pretty well hidden, and it's probably sunk even farther into the ground after hundreds of years. I just hope we recognize it when we find it."

"Treasure's pretty easy to recognize," Jeanie pointed out.

"But the room won't be. It's walled up. According to the story my grandfather told, he accidentally opened a hole, saw what was inside, and covered the hole with a stone."

"Your father should have come looking for the treasure instead of you."

"He preferred black gold. And I don't think he really believed the story. If it weren't for that amulet he mentioned, I'd still think this is his idea of a joke."

When they reached the lowest level, it was obvious that they were in a sewer. The odor was almost overpowering, and they found themselves sloshing in sludgy water over their ankles.

Darkness stretched before and behind them, and water dripped from the slimy stones above them.

"I'm glad we wore waterproof boots," Jeanie said.

Henry didn't answer. He was studying the map in the lantern light.

"We go straight for a little way past the first right-hand branch, then take the one to the left."

He slogged forward. Behind him Jeanie stopped and said, "Did you hear something?"

"Nothing. Did you?"

"I'm not sure. It was sort of a splashing sound, I think."

"There can't be anyone down here," Henry said, thinking of those alligators in New York and hoping they hadn't moved south. "We'll keep going."

They went on through the foul water, both of them trying not to think what might be in it and what kind of creatures might thrive on its pollution.

They came to the right turn, then to one that went to the left.

"This must be it," Henry said, and they took the turn.

They hadn't gone far when ahead of them something glittered in the dim light of Henry's lamp. Then something moved.

"Rats!" Henry said, as a chittering furry mass began to slosh toward them, gaining speed with every step.

The rats choked the tunnel from side to side. They scampered and scrambled over Henry and Jeanie's boots and brushed their legs, tumbling over one another as they ran.

Jeanie gripped Henry's arm so tightly that she almost cut off his circulation, but she didn't cry out or move. The rats kept on coming, hundreds of them, their fur slick with scum, their ears back, their eyes straight ahead. After several minutes they were gone down the tunnel.

"Where's the Pied Piper when you need him?" Henry said.

"What could have scared them and made them run like that?"

Henry didn't know. "Maybe they weren't scared at all. Maybe they were just moving from one place to another."

"They should have been scared of us, but they weren't. And they were moving awfully fast. I'm beginning to wonder if this was a good idea after all."

"Too late now," Henry said, and led the way forward.

The rats surged across Beaumont's feet, and he felt goose bumps on his arms. He wasn't fond of rats.

Neither was Modesty, who whispered, "Shoot them! Shoot the little bastards!"

Beaumont didn't want to make any noise. He shook his head and left his pistol stuck in his belt.

"You son of a bitch," Modesty said when the rats were gone. Her voice was shaky and her hands trembled.

Beaumont smiled. "I didn't know you'd met Mother," he said.

"We should be about there," Henry said. "But I don't see anything that looks like a hole with a big rock in it."

"Maybe we've already passed it," Jeanie said.

"Maybe. Wait a minute. Shine your light over there."

Jeanie directed her beam where Henry's was already picking out a large bulge on the wall ahead.

"That has to be it," Jeanie said.

"If there really is an 'it,'" Henry said. "Hold my light, and I'll see if I can pry something loose."

He moved to the bulge, which was indeed a large rock, and worked the pry bar into a small crevice on one side, then began to work the bar with as much force as he could muster. The volcanic stone beside the big rock began to crumble, but Henry was able to move the rock forward. He jumped back as it fell from the hole and splashed into the water at his feet.

"Who gets the first look?" Henry asked Jeanie.

"Me," Jeanie said, holding up her lantern and peering into the hole. After a second she said, "My God. It's true."

Henry stepped up beside her. He could hardly believe the sight that greeted his eyes. He started to hack at the rock with the iron pry bar. The going wasn't too difficult, and soon he had made quite a large opening. He and Jeanie stepped through.

Although Henry had been convinced at first glance that the treasure was real, he wasn't prepared for what he saw now. The room was full of turquoise sculptures of jaguars and eagles. A golden mask grinned down from one wall along with priceless feather shields. A dancing monkey of stone, Ehecatl, the wind god, sported a necklace and bracelets of pure gold. A statue of Xipe Totec, the god of spring, crouched in a corner, wearing the ragged remnants of what Henry was certain had at one time been a complete human skin. There were stone knives and golden faces that Henry couldn't name.

And then Henry noticed the bones. There were also boxes of gold and turquoise ornaments, some of which spilled out onto the stone floor, but what caught Henry's eye was the bones. The Aztecs had believed strongly in human sacrifice, after all, and apparently someone, several someones, judging by the bones, had been left behind to guard the treasure, or had been killed to ensure that one of the gods would guard it.

"Does treasure make you horny?" Jeanie asked. She was already taking off her shirt. "It makes me horny, if you want to know."

"Everything makes you horny," Henry said, looking around for anything that looked like the amulet his father had described.

Jeanie tossed her shirt over the face of a golden jaguar, kicked off her boots and slipped off her pants.

"We can find that amulet later," she said, removing her bra.

Henry looked at her, the perfect breasts, the rounded hips, the lovely, apparently innocent face. She was more beautiful to him than all the treasure in the room. Her red hair shone like spun gold in the dim light, and he felt a stiffening in his groin.

"I guess we can, at that," he said, beginning to undress.

"So much for the idea that yours was bigger than his," Modesty said in an awed whisper to Beaumont as they watched through the opening. "And it looks hard enough to sharpen a knife on."

"Quiet," Beaumont breathed. "Do you want them to hear you?"

"Right now, I don't think they'd hear a rhinoceros if it ran through there."

"We'll wait, nevertheless," Beaumont said.

The two of them had reached the opening just as Jeanie had begun to disrobe, and Beaumont was elated. He'd been a bit worried about how to get the upper hand with Kinkade, but now it would be simple. He would just wait until both Kinkades were too distracted to notice anything at all, and then he'd announce his presence. He could afford to wait a while. After all, he liked to watch.

"That floor looks awfully hard," Henry said.

"That's not the only thing," Jeanie said, admiring the thrust of Henry's penis. "Come here."

Henry went to her and they embraced. His penis was pressed tightly against her, and he could feel the heat of her stomach along its entire length. The hot hard nipples of her breasts nearly singed his chest. He grasped her hair in his hands and pulled her mouth to his in a searing kiss.

When they finally broke apart, Jeanie knelt down and took his penis in her hand. Then she began to lick it slowly up and down. Henry buried his hands in her hair. After a few seconds, she took the tip in her mouth and began to move her head slowly up and down, each time taking in more of him. It seemed impossible that she could get all of it in, but she was determined, and when Jeanie was determined, as Henry often said, she could do anything. And she did. The sensation was so powerful that Henry's knees trembled.

Just when Henry didn't think he could last any longer, Jeanie released him. She smiled up at him, then took the tip of his penis into her mouth again, licked it slowly, and then stuck her tongue into the hole at the end. Henry's body convulsed, but he held back. Barely.

Jeanie released him again and stood up.

"As you said, the floor is awfully hard," she told him, and she swayed over to the statue where her shirt hung. With her back to Henry, she planted her feet and leaned over, resting her hands on the statue. Then she looked coyly back over her shoulder at him with a come-hither smile. "Well, what are you waiting for?"

Henry didn't need another invitation. He walked over to her and began rubbing his penis up and down the soft crack that began at her sacral dimples. He moved it slowly up and down, then let it drift teasingly between her legs, where it found a slick heat that practically pulled it in. Jeanie thrust herself backward, but Henry pulled away. She had tortured him. Now it was his turn.

He reached around her and began to caress her breasts, letting his fingers linger on the rigid nipples, fondling them idly as his penis advanced and then retreated, advanced and retreated again.

"I want it now," Jeanie said. "Now, Henry."

Henry would have waited if he'd been able, but he wanted it at least as much as Jeanie, and maybe more. She was so slick and ready that he slid into her easily. She came almost instantly, contracting around him and squeezing him like a fist.

"Don't stop!" she said. "Don't you dare stop now!"

"Who could possibly make me?" Henry panted.

"I believe that would be me," Beaumont said, stepping out of the darkness and shining his lantern on the love-locked couple.

6

Henry spun around as Modesty was removing his pistol from the holster that lay on the floor.

"Shoot him if he moves," Beaumont said. He looked at Jeanie appreciatively. "Her, too, though it would be a waste."

"Her maybe," Modesty said. "I don't think I could shoot Henry." Her eyes were honed in on Henry's penis, still rigid and pointing now in her direction. "I'd love for him to shoot me, though."

"Please, dear girl," Beaumont said. "Keep your mind on our business."

"I'd rather keep something else on Henry's business," Modesty said.

Jeanie made a move, and the pistol in Modesty's hand jerked toward her. It was clear that she was quite familiar with firearms and not quite so distracted by Henry's anatomy as she had appeared to be. Jeanie glared at her.

"I know this is a bit embarrassing for you two," Beaumont said to the Kinkades, "but look at it this way: it won't last for long."

Henry was disgusted with himself. He should never have let himself get distracted.

"What are you doing here, Beaumont?" he asked with as much dignity as he could muster under the circumstances.

"Why, I'm making the biggest find that anyone has ever heard of. I'll be immortal in the literature, and of course I'll keep a bit for myself. And for Modesty, of course."

"You won't get credit for anything," Henry said. "I'll let the world know the truth."

"Ah," Beaumont said, "but that would mean you'd have to be able to tell. I'm afraid that you might disappear down here in the sewers and never be heard from again. The rats will pick your bones as clean as these." Beaumont kicked idly at a nearby ribcage, which collapsed into a disorganized heap and considered Jeanie, who stood defiantly, her nakedness not seeming to bother her in the least. "Such a waste, really."

"You bastard," Henry said.

"I didn't know you'd been talking to Mother," Beaumont said. "But at least I allowed you a glimpse of your treasure."

"And me a glimpse of it, too," Modesty said, with an admiring look at Henry's now flaccid but still impressive penis.

"Keep your eyes to yourself, you slut," Jeanie said.

Modesty was framing her retort when there was a rustling sound on the farther side of the treasure room.

"What was that noise?" Modesty asked.

"We'll have a look," Beaumont said, shining his lantern in the direction of the sound.

What the light revealed froze everyone in place like the other statues in the room.

There was a woman in the shadows, and her pendulous breasts hung down nearly to her skirt, which was made of writhing rattlesnakes. Another rattler crawled through her hair. Their serpent eyes glowed. The woman's neck was ringed with a necklace of withered human hands and what must have been shriveled human hearts.

"Coatlicue," Henry said reverently.

And who better, he thought, to be here guarding the treasure where the sewer flowed by. Coatlicue was the devourer of filth, and she feasted on human corpses. She must have been quite hungry by now, since the supply of corpses had long since been eaten. Though there was plenty of filth of another kind just outside the room.

"She's moving!" Modesty said, and indeed Coatlicue seemed to take a tentative step forward. Modesty fired three shots into her without effect before Jeanie took advantage of the diversion and slammed a small fist into Modesty's wrist, causing the pistol to fall to the floor.

Henry alertly scooped it up and pointed it at Beaumont, who was still distracted by Coatlicue.

"Advantage, Kinkades," Henry said. "Time for you to leave us, Beaumont. You, too, Modesty."

Modesty stood rubbing her wrist, but she was too preoccupied with Coatlicue to glare at Jeanie.

"Just lay your pistol on the floor," Henry told Beaumont. "We'll let you take one of the lanterns. Now go."

Beaumont seemed to want to argue, but there was another rustling from Coatlicue, and he changed his mind.

"Whatever you say, Kinkade. But I wonder if you'll live to brag about this."

"I won't be doing any bragging," Henry said. "Now get out."

Jeanie picked up Beaumont's .45 and prodded Modesty in the back.

"Out you go," Jeanie said. "Don't let the sewer rats get you."

"Bitch," Modesty said, but she went.

Beaumont followed her with only one regretful backward glance, and Henry heard them sloshing away through the dark tunnel.

"She's coming for us!" Jeanie yelled, and the sloshing became quite rapid before fading away altogether.

"She's not really coming," Henry said. "You're such a liar."

"I know," Jeanie said, shining her light on Coatlicue. "How are we going to deal with her?"

"Very carefully," Henry said, walking toward the god. As he approached, rats swarmed away from the figure. One climbed down from her head. Others poured out of the skirt and ran from between the legs. They skittered past Henry and Jeanie and out the hole Henry had made.

"Where did they all come from?" Jeanie asked.

"There must be another opening," Henry said. "Probably a very small one."

"Then she didn't really move. She's only a statue. It was just a trick of the light. And the rats."

"Believe what you want to," Henry told her. "I know what my mother would have said."

"Well, we know she was superstitious."

"That's right."

Henry looked around the room. "But my father wasn't joking about the map after all. I wish he were here to see all this. My mother, too, and my grandfather. But my mother most of all."

"What about the amulet?"

"I don't see it, do you?"

"That doesn't mean it's not here. If it is, we'll find it. But what about all the rest of this stuff? What are you going to do about it?"

"Turn it over to the Mexican government. It belongs to the people, especially the ones with the Aztec blood. I'll ask that they name the exhibit for my parents."

"They'd be proud of you," Jeanie said. "And so am I. I don't suppose we could keep just a little bit for ourselves? Just the amulet, of course. And a little bracelet, maybe?"

"I don't think anyone would miss it," Henry said. "But as the discoverer, I'd have to exact a payment."

"Do naked women with guns make you horny?"

"You're damned right they do," Henry said, his penis beginning to grow rigid again.

"How much would the payment be?"

"As much as you could stand."

"Oh, I don't know about that," Jeanie said. "I can stand quite a lot. As you may recently have noticed."

She looked at some of the bracelets on the floor. She put down the .45 and chose a golden band in the shape of a snake, slipping it on her wrist. She held it up for Henry to admire, but he was looking at something else.

"When would you require payment?" Jeanie asked.

"That would be up to you," Henry said.

"How about right now?"

Henry smiled. "Do you think the rats will mind?"

"They didn't before." Jeanie said. "I do have one suggestion, though."

"What's that?"

"Let's leave the lights on."

"Personally," Henry said, "I've always liked it better that way."

Jeanie smiled at Henry and started toward him.

"Me too," she said.

-⊱═◉═⊰-

Henry & Jeanie will be back in Desert Heat. *Available in April 2001!*

Sand on the Beach

Colin Vincent

Colin Vincent is the pseudonym of the son of an internationally bestselling British spy novelist. A Sandhurst graduate, Mr. Vincent followed his late father's example and served in British Military Intelligence. After seeing action during the Falklands Island War in 1982, Mr. Vincent returned to England, where he has since been at work compiling the adventures of British secret agent John Sand. Mr. Vincent and his wife maintain homes in Egham, Surrey, England, and Jamaica.

The desk clerk, a slim shapely blonde, whose Caribbean-colorful blouse displayed a tantalizing touch of cleavage, looked at him with obvious interest as she asked, "Name?"

She had managed to turn that one simple word into several promising syllables, her blue eyes riveted on him.

The tall, dark-haired, well-tanned, cruelly handsome man standing opposite rewarded her interest with a small grin; his athletic build was somewhat concealed by his casual vacation attire—pastel blue sport jacket, yellow banlon, white khaki trousers. There had been a time—not long ago—when the comely young woman's flirtation would have been a gauntlet thrown that he'd have gladly snatched up.

Not now.

He merely responded with the small grin, then in an aristocratic British baritone replied, "Sand—John Sand."

Amusement touched the corners of the desk clerk's full lips. "You have a reservation, Mr. Sand?"

"I do."

She was flipping through her card file. "That sounds like a marriage vow."

"If you check my booking," he said, "you'll find you're not far wrong.... I'm here on my honeymoon."

"How wonderful," the desk clerk said, but her tone conveyed disappointment. "Ah, here it is." She withdrew a card. "But where is Mrs. Sand?"

"Doing her wifely duties—spending money." Sand turned to nod across the lobby toward the gift shop where Traci, his bride of barely twenty-four hours, was already fingering the Jamaican trinkets.

"Why, she's lovely," the desk clerk said, and it was almost a gasp.

Sand arched an eyebrow at the young woman, as if to say, "Would you have expected less?"

Five foot four, one hundred ten perfectly arranged pounds, her auburn hair rolling in waves to the midpoint of her spine, Traci might have been the long-lost sister of the woman many Americans thought would be the next First Lady of the United States.

No pink pillbox hats for Traci, however—far too tame. If the two women were indeed siblings, Sand had married the one born in the wild. Jackie would be far too sophisticated, too pristine to go scuba diving among the ruins of a sunken city like Port Royal.

For Traci, however, such an adventure seemed the perfect honeymoon activity. So, here they were, checking into the opulent Mayfare hotel overlooking Kingston Bay.

Turning back to the desk, Sand signed the register and glanced at the curvy desk clerk.

"Beautiful as she is, Mr. Sand," the young woman brazenly said, "I'm surprised you'd settle for one woman."

"You would be surprised, young lady, at how mundane much of my life has been—don't believe what you read in popular fiction, or the press."

"I do hope you'll have a lovely stay with us, Mr. Sand," the desk clerk said, licking her lips, sending a glistening message of a missed opportunity. "And I trust your honeymoon will be anything but 'mundane.'"

Such personal comments coming from a stranger like the comely clerk had become common occurrence in the life of John Sand, and represented, in fact, one of the primary reasons behind his early retirement from MI6.

Ever since his former colleague, Fleming, had started writing those thinly veiled novels based on Sand's exploits—and *Life* magazine had done that article labeling Sand the "real" what's-his-name, hero of JFK's favorite adventure series—the secret agent had been unable to perform his duties with any sort of anonymity. A secret agent, after all, must remain, well—secret.

And Sand's secret was out.

A hand touched his back, and Sand turned to find Traci standing next to him, a small brown bag clutched in her left hand.

"See anything you like?" he asked her, nodding toward the gift shop.

Traci's pretty, puffy lips turned into a pouty kiss of a smile as her green eyes took in the pretty receptionist. "Why, did you?"

Traci's faint but distinct Texas accent seemed incongruous beside his cultured British tones.

The desk clerk, far more businesslike now that Traci was on the scene, handed Sand a pair of keys. "Room 721, Mr. Sand."

Sand nodded.

"I'll have your bags sent up immediately."

"Good." As the couple walked to the elevators, Sand noted the tiny brown bag clutched in his bride's left hand. "Something for me?"

Her contagious laugh bubbled up, then receded like a wave. "In a way."

Sand arched an eyebrow.

"New earrings," she explained, hefting the tiny bag importantly.

"I'm sure I'll look smashing in them."

As soon as they were in their room, Traci disappeared into the bathroom leaving Sand to deal with the black bellman who brought up their bags. After putting their suitcases in the bedroom, the bellman, a stocky man of maybe thirty-five, discreetly accepted the five-pound note Sand slipped into his hand without meeting Sand's eyes.

Though blacks made up a staggering majority of the population, they held down mostly menial jobs such as bellman, busboy or maid. Sand knew the day when his countrymen would be forced to deal with this inequity was near.

Closing the door behind the bellman, Sand turned and took a good look at the sitting room of their suite. Not long ago, his next act would have been to thoroughly search the room for bugging devices and other nasty surprises. But that was the past—and this was his honeymoon.

With its wallpaper of white flowers on a sea green background, the suite had the feel of a garden. A wide white sofa occupied one wall, a low mahogany coffee table in front of it. At angles facing the sofa were wing chairs covered in a light green brocade that matched the walls. Sand strode past the small wet bar to the French doors on the wall opposite him and opened them onto a balcony that overlooked Kingston Harbor.

Bright sunshine kissed the cool blue bay, reflecting white off the gentle wave tips as they meandered to the alabaster beach on the soft breeze. Across the busy Kingston Harbor, barely visible in the afternoon glare, lay Port Royal, once considered the wickedest place in the known world, two-thirds of it now beneath the sea. Tomorrow, they would hire a small boat to run them across so they could dive among the ruins of the once mighty town that had been swept away in the earthquake of 1692.

Behind him, Sand heard the bathroom door open. *Finally,* he thought. Though retirement had been forced upon him by his colleague's novels—as well as the fact that Sand's body carried more lead than a crate of number two pencils—he relished his new freedom and the time it would allow him to spend with Traci.

"How do you like my new earrings?"

Turning to face her, Sand felt his breath catch in his throat. Traci stood before him, two long jade cats dangling from her ears.

She wore nothing else.

A smile creased Sand's face as he took in her tanned, unblemished beauty: the firmness of her full, conical breasts thrusting toward him, the sweet puffy pinkness of her nipples with their generous aureoles daring him, the smooth supple belly with its tiny navel that winked at him when she laughed, the strong thighs, well-turned calves, the tangled tuft of her pubic triangle. She was adjusting the earrings, not a trace of nervousness or self-consciousness in her demeanor.

Crossing slowly to him, jade cats dangling from her lobes, she drawled, "What's wrong, you big bad man? Cat got your tongue?"

They embraced. She was strong for her size, her arms draping around his neck drawing his face to hers, her lips finding his with a hunger he relished. They kissed for a very long time, softly at first, then with increasing passion as their urgency rose.

Breaking away, Sand made his way to the bedroom door, Traci not far behind him.

"Splendid earrings," he commented, finally, blandly.

She smiled up at him, green eyes flashing. "Is that all you have to say?"

"Such a pair of pretty pussies," he said, and he disappeared into the bedroom, barely murmuring, "Here kitty, kitty..."

She strode in after him, stripping him of his jacket, shoulder holster, shirt and tie; then Traci trailed her fingers over his hairy chest, his rippling muscles, the scars of bullets and blades recording his checkered history. Gently, she began kissing each scar.

It took a while.

Her lips against his chest, her words were muffled: "I can't believe you still carry that awful gun. You're retired, John, you're on your honeymoon—and you should start acting like it."

"I will," he said, sweeping her onto the bed. "Right now."

As she helped him out of his pants, Sand smoothed her hair, so soft, so radiant, and so fragrant, minus that stiff spray so many women used. They sprawled on the king-sized bed, making an upside-down V as the young woman propped herself up on an elbow, studying her new husband's handsome, character-grooved face. He was studying her full breasts, hypnotized by them as they swayed gently, like full ripe fruit.

Then he leaned forward and kissed her hard, his hands roaming over her back, around her sides, cupping her breasts, and then she was on her back, moaning with delight as his mouth replaced his fingers, his tongue making tiny circles on her breasts before he nipped at their tips. He worked his way down her chest, over her stomach, stopping to kiss her navel, eliciting a slight giggle before he moved on, his tongue probing, exploring, and devouring every inch of her. When his tongue cleaved through her private jungle to touch the core of her, Traci arched her back and let out a long gasp as she grabbed handfuls of his hair and forced him deeper inside her.

Her body convulsed once, twice, three times, each seizure punctuated by a gasp then a small moan. After the fourth time she let out a long purr of contentment and gently eased away from him.

He grinned at her. "Had enough?"

Traci looked down over the slopes of her breasts at him, quizzically. "Have you?"

"I am an old man, my love."

"Put out to pasture?" she asked, as they both sat up, her finger playing lightly across his leg. As her hand move lazily up his leg, Traci leaned closer, lips brushing his ear, his chest, and then his stomach. "Or to stud?"

Sand tried to speak but no words came as Traci's kisses moved down his body, as she pushed him almost roughly back against the bed. He managed only a slight moan as she eased him into her mouth, lips slipping down and down his shaft, then up, then down, down, down, sucking, nuzzling, returning the favor he had done her only moments before....

Just as it seemed he could stand no more, Traci gave him a moment to regain control before she mounted him, towering over him as she guided him inside her, his hands moving automatically to her bouncing, pendulous breasts, as she rode him, rode her private stud until their passion exploded. The two of them achieved release simultaneously, rocking back and forth, their world reduced to only the space they occupied as wave upon wave crashed over them, even as waves crashed on the beach beyond their open window...until finally Traci rolled off him, both of them spent.

The warm Jamaican breeze wafted through the window, sheer curtains whispering, as the honeymooners whispered their love to each other. They kissed tenderly, passion spent but love unceasing, kissed like young sweethearts, reminding Sand of their very first time, back in her father's home on the outskirts of Galveston, Texas.

Sand had met the young woman while investigating her father, Dutch Boldt, suspected by the spy's superiors of trying to corner the world oil market through terrorist means. Digging into the case—during which time romance had developed between the secret agent and the oil tycoon's daughter—Sand had discovered that Dutch Boldt actually had tried to stop his longtime business partner, Jake Lonestarr, the real criminal mastermind in the affair. Enraged when Dutch wouldn't go along with his plan, the lunatic Lonestarr had kidnapped Traci and held her hostage aboard his yacht, the Cuba Libre.

In a daring midnight raid, accompanied by Dutch Boldt, Sand boarded the yacht. Lonestarr and his chief henchman—a hulking American Indian known only as Raven—had been lying in wait for the pair. Lonestarr gunned down his former partner, and Sand shot the evil tycoon in the chest, sending the bastard tumbling over the rail into the Gulf of Mexico.

Sand had raked Raven across the face with a gaffer's hook, leaving him to go down with the yacht. Then the agent rescued Traci and scuttled the Cuba Libre, escaping in a motorized launch.

Now, many months later, he lay watching Traci sleeping, her head resting on his shoulder, her full pink lips pursed slightly, her body warm against him causing a stirring deep inside him. Slowly, as if anticipating his need, her eyes opened. He kissed her softly, and then she smiled up at him, a hand caressing his cheek.

"As I was saying, splendid earrings," he said.

She laughed deep in her throat. "They're about the only things you didn't touch. I guess that means you like them."

"They're the cat's meow."

Groaning, Traci pulled away from him and slapped him playfully across the chest. "You're shameless."

"Let me show you how shameless," he said, once again taking her into his arms.

And this time he rode her, taking the man's time-honored position on top—no foreplay. His sheer brute passion was gratefully accepted by the sweating, panting, fine young animal beneath him, the globes of her breasts trembling, her nails clawing his back, her eyes huge, her nostrils flaring as she came to a quick, shuddering climax, and he did the same.

It had taken all of sixty seconds—but in those sixty seconds, they had gone on a journey of infinite passion.

Still gasping for breath, she leaned back on her elbows, her fine smooth body beaded with sweat, and said, "Short but sweet...."

He arched an eyebrow. "Short?"

"Well...I was referrin' to duration only, darling. You have... remarkable recuperative powers."

"For an old retired workhorse?"

"Yes," she said, suddenly snippy, "for an old retired work-horse," and she sprang from the bed and ran bareass to the bathroom, where he soon heard the shower.

Thinking of her in there, under those needles of water, naked in her steamy cubicle, Sand considered showing her just how remarkable his recuperative powers really were.

Then he shrugged, and said to himself, "No need to be a showoff," and went looking for his cigarettes.

An hour later they sat for a late dinner in the hotel's lavish restaurant, a pleasing tacky display that was all pastels and sea-shells. The tuxedo fit Sand like a second skin, an elegant outfit that reminded him of more elegant days when he played chemin de fer—and other games—with far greater stakes than mere money.

Across the table, Traci's strapless blue gown showed enough of her ample cleavage to draw glances from the male diners at nearby tables. Her sun-highlighted dark hair piled on top of her head, the effect accentuated her elongated neck.

Sand smiled approvingly at his wife. "You're being stared at," he said, careful to keep his voice low. Grinning back, showing just a hint of even white teeth through bright red lipstick, she said, with that faint Texas lilt, "How do you know they're not staring at you?"

"Because," he said, lighting up a cigarette with a match, "they are presumably not insane."

"Perhaps they are lookin' at me—I have that certain glow that only a honeymooning bride can achieve." Traci's green eyes sparkled. "Jealous?"

Sand chuckled. "Why should I be jealous? Let them dream. I already have you."

"You sure do." Traci's hand stretched across the table toward Sand's...but just before she reached it, something behind him caught her attention and her eyes went wide in fear.

Spinning in his chair, Sand quickly scanned the room...

...but saw nothing, nothing but the door to the kitchen swinging back and forth.

He turned back to Traci. Her hand had gone to her mouth and the color had drained from her face.

"What in hell is it?" he asked.

"I could've sworn..."

Coming around the table to her, Sand put an arm around her. "Traci, my love—what is it?"

The maître d'—a thin shiny-headed man of perhaps fifty—approached their table. "Is everything all right, sir? Madam?"

Sand nodded automatically and looked down at Traci.

"I'm fine," she said more to the maître d' than to Sand. "I was just a bit faint for a moment."

The maître d' appeared concerned, but nodded and strode back to his station. As Traci sipped from her water glass, Sand resumed his seat.

"You look as if you'd seen a ghost."

She shivered, then nodded. "You're more right than you know."

"What?"

"I...I could have sworn I saw Raven across the room."

He sat forward. "Raven?"

Traci was shaking her head. "I know it's not possible. I saw you sink the Cuba Libre with him still on board."

Nodding, Sand said, "That's right."

But suddenly he doubted his own words. Too often a resilient foe had turned up again, with a grudge that had festered into an obsession. Could that bastard Raven have survived? Had the rat abandoned the sinking ship?

After a good night's sleep, and fine morning romp, the couple rented a boat to take them out over the ruins of Port Royal. Fracas, the vessel's skipper—a tall, wide-shouldered Jamaican with espresso colored skin and close-cropped ebony hair—had worked with Sand on more than one occasion.

The former agent didn't want his wife to know how on edge he was after last night's incident in the restaurant; but hiring a boat captained by a frequent MI6 collaborator seemed like a prudent decision.

By the time the boat anchored over the sunken city, Traci seemed to have put last night behind her. Sand couldn't help but want her yet again as he watched her slipping the straps of the scuba tank over her shoulders. Her one piece white bathing suit left very little to the imagination, flattening out her full breasts in a fetching manner, and Sand noticed that Fracas went out of his way to keep himself busy with work around the tiny boat that kept him close to the beautiful young woman.

Smiling to himself, Sand couldn't blame Fracas for wanting to stay near Traci. He couldn't think of another place in the world he'd ever want to be but next to her—tanned and lithe, her dark auburn hair hanging loosely down her back.

"Aren't you ready yet?" she asked, looking over at Sand. "And why are you grinning like the cat that ate the canary?"

More like the canary that ate the pussy... he thought.

Sand shook his head. "It's nothing. Be ready in a moment."

Hefting his own tank, he slung it over his shoulders, snapped the strap across his chest, slipped on his flippers, and followed Traci over the side. He filled the mask with seawater, dumped it out, and then snugged it down on his face. Traci did the same and gave Sand a thumbs up. He returned the gesture as she disappeared into the lapping waves of silty green. Adjusting his mouthpiece, Sand somersaulted and followed his wife into the warm water.

They had been down for nearly half an hour when Sand lost sight of Traci as she swam off to investigate a huge piece of a brick wall that seemed to have sunk mostly intact. He trailed her by maybe three hundred yards as he cruised toward where he'd seen Traci round a corner of the sunken wall.

At the corner, Sand's heart jumped into his throat as he

looked down at the seabed and saw the small cloth bag Traci had been using to collect relics. There also seemed to be just a shadow of red in the murky water!

Looking around wildly, Sand scoured the area for any other sign of her. Examining the area near the wall carefully, Sand finally picked up an old brick and noticed a smudge of blood along one edge. Struggling to control his breathing, Sand swam in ever widening circles around the fallen wall as he combed the area for his wife.

On his fourth circuit, Sand caught a glimpse of fins kicking away from him maybe twenty feet above him and ten feet to his right. Kicking after his target, Sand swam as hard as he ever had in an effort to catch the fleeing swimmer. As he closed in from beneath his target, he realized that it wasn't Traci....

...It was a man—a muscular, black-haired man wearing white trunks that emphasized the reddish-brown cast of his skin.

Raven!

Adrenaline surged through the former agent as he kicked upward, catching the man around the waist just as they broke the surface. The swimmer howled in terror as Sand wrenched him out of the water, then gurgled as Sand rolled him over and shoved him beneath the surface. Traci might be gone, but Sand would exact his revenge right here, right now. Even as the diver struggled, Sand—his rage colder than the water lapping around him—could feel the man's strength beginning to ebb as he started to drown.

"John!"

Traci's voice behind him! Echoing across the water....

"John, what in the name of God are you doing?"

Releasing his grip, Sand spun to find Traci and Fracas standing on the deck of the boat only twenty feet away. Traci's face was twisted in terror, her left arm wrapped in gauze.

Sand turned back to Raven and met the gagging, horrified countenance of a man he had never seen before.

Reaching out to help the stranger, Sand was rebuffed as the swimmer fought him off and stroked toward Fracas's boat. The

Jamaican helped the man aboard while a mortified Sand was left to climb over the side on his own.

"I cut my arm when a brick broke loose from the wall," Traci explained. "I looked all over for you, but I couldn't find you and I decided I'd better get to the surface so Fracas could patch me up." She held up her bandaged arm, displaying it like a trophy.

It took a lot of explaining to persuade South Dakota businessman Leon Whitefield not to press attempted murder charges against John Sand. Had it been left solely up to Sand's brand of diplomacy, the former agent most likely would have been sitting in the Kingston jail at this very moment. Traci's Texan charms, however, had gone a long way toward assuaging Whitefield's anger and, eventually, she had convinced the businessman to allow them to pay for the rental of his diving equipment...and buy the man a nice dinner.

As night settled in on the city, Sand—walking along the harbor, Traci's arm looped in his—finally felt nearly at peace, if somewhat naked. For the first time since he'd been recruited into MI6, he walked the streets unarmed, the tuxedo—tailored to allow room for a shoulder-holstered automatic—feeling loose, uncomfortable. Even retirement hadn't convinced Sand to stop carrying the Walther beneath his jacket...but almost killing an innocent man this afternoon had.

Traci's yellow gown had only the tiniest spaghetti straps holding it in place, her bosom constantly threatening to make a break for it. She also wore a sheer canary shawl over her shoulders to ward off the slight evening chill, carrying a small matching purse with just enough room for a lipstick, a compact, and a short comb.

"That was quite a performance today," she said without looking at him.

Next to them, the harbor lapped against the cement walkway; it was as if they were walking along beside a vast swimming pool. Shaking his head, Sand said, "I couldn't stand the thought of losing you. I..."

She squeezed his arm a little tighter. "You aren't going to be makin' a habit of attacking strangers, now, are you, darling?"

Sand forced a grin. "Not a habit."

Just ahead, swerving through the darkness, a drunk wearing a large, lightweight overcoat tottered into the shadow of one of the benches that lined the harbor every fifteen yards or so. Seeing the figure ease down on the bench, Sand eased Traci closer, nearer the water's edge, as they moved along the narrow sidewalk.

She said, just a little teasingly, "Maybe I should take you back to the hotel and help...relieve your tension...release some of that excess energy."

Motion from the bench caused Sand's eyes to roam from his wife toward the drunk...

...who leapt forward, snatching Traci away from Sand!

A jagged scar ran from the corner of the attacker's right eye to his jaw line; it glistened in the moonlight like a luminous pink worm against the dark, coldly crazed face.

Traci screeched as she tumbled onto the bench, carrying him over onto her back as she crashed to the ground.

"Raven," Sand growled, dropping into a combat stance.

The Indian stepped forward, a nine-millimeter pistol in his right hand. "This is for you," Raven said, in that low rumble of his that passed for a voice, pointing the pistol at Sand's face.

Then the massive Indian pulled something from somewhere inside his large, loose coat. A gaffer's hook glinted in the moonlight, like a jewel winking. "And this...this is for your new wife."

Sand pitched sideways, off the walkway and into the harbor, disappearing down into the deep cold water, Raven getting off one wild shot that screamed into the night. The Indian looked once into the swirling waters of the harbor, then turned his attention to Traci who was climbing to her feet, her shawl gone, the small purse still clutched in her hands.

"Coward of a husband ran out on you," the Indian said, a tight smile crossing his face, as he took a step toward Traci, as her eyes searched the night for an escape route.

Playfully, like a lion taunting its kill, Raven swished the hook back and forth, the blade whistling nastily through the air with each stroke. "Time for you to pay for his sins."

Sand exploded from the water, a baseball sized rock from the bottom in his right hand. Hearing the splash of Sand surfacing, Raven spun and aimed the pistol Sand heaved the stone just as the Indian fired.

The rock smacked into Raven's forehead—the sound was a thick crack that echoed off the water, reverberating into the night like another gunshot.

Traci screamed as Sand again slipped below the surface of the water, like an apparition that had come and gone.

Staggering, the Indian dropped both the gun and hook as he slumped to the sidewalk, on his knees, as if praying to some god or other. Then he flopped onto his face and went to sleep.

Traci picked up the pistol and aimed it awkwardly at Raven, even as her eyes scoured the surface for her husband.

"Where are you," she muttered, "where the hell are you...."

Finally, a hand extended out of the water and grasped at the edge of the sidewalk. "If...if you please...."

Ignoring the unconscious Raven, Traci helped Sand pull himself out of the water, his left arm hanging uselessly at his side, flopping onto the cement walkway like a big fish onto a boat deck.

"He shot you?" she asked, aghast.

His sopping tux slick and sleek and black as a seal, Sand shrugged one shoulder. "It would seem so."

"Where the hell is your gun?"

"You told me not to carry it."

"What kind of marriage are we going to have, if you listen to everything I say?"

Sand grinned. "A wonderful one."

"Good answer," she said, hugging his wet carcass to her.

Sand was about to kiss his wife when he saw something reflect in her green eyes.

It wasn't the moonlight: Raven had erupted into motion. Snatching the gaffer's hook from the ground, the brute dove toward the couple as they clutched each other. Sand grabbed the pistol from his wife's hand and, as the Indian brandished the hook, Sand fired twice.

The first bullet caught Raven in the chest, standing him up straight. The second entered through his left eye, exiting just behind his right ear in a spray of bone and blood and brain, and the Indian slumped into a heap at their feet.

It was morning before they walked wearily from the constable's station back to their hotel. The police had grilled them both pretty hard even as a doctor from the British governor's office was patching up Sand's shoulder. Eventually, the Home Secretary had phoned the governor, who phoned the police chief, and the couple was released.

Sand's face remained a mask of barely concealed anger.

"What's the matter?" Traci asked as they neared the hotel.

"It's over! We've won. We're safe again."

"I'm afraid Raven wouldn't have come after us on his own steam."

Traci seemed confused by that. "What are you saying?"

"I am saying," he said softly, meaningfully, "that his employer—Jake Lonestarr—might still be out there."

Terror froze her eyes. "Is that possible?"

Seeing that, Sand tried to minimize what he'd said with a shrug. "Possible."

"Probable, you mean. John—what does that mean to us?"

"That until I ascertain whether Lonestarr is indeed dead, my dear, we're not going to be completely safe—and that I'm not as retired as I'd hoped."

They entered the hotel and rode the elevator to their room.

"Maybe I was wrong," she said, "about you not wearing that gun."

He smiled. "Well, you Texans do like packing a shooting iron. Shall I put it on now, when I get out of this poor tux? It is almost time for breakfast."

Wrapping her arms around him, she said, "No. I've got other plans for you now."

"Such as what?"

"Such as breakfast in bed."

Stepping back, she dropped the straps off her shoulders, allowing the gown to pool at her feet, full breasts thrusting forward, relieved at last to be set free. With her standing there naked before him, his thoughts of Lonestarr faded for now.

"You know, Traci," he said, stroking her breasts tenderly, "we do make a smashing team."

Leading her wounded husband gently to the bed, Traci whispered, "Nobody does it better."

Look for more of Agent John Sand in late 2001!

FOGGY WINDOWS BOOKS

Flintlock

The frontier of America was filled with dangers, both seen and unseen. In a moment, you could be faced with deadly weather conditions, mad desperadoes, or hidden assassins looking to make their mark on the West. The tales in our Flintlock *imprint bring to life the passionate stories of the men and women who conquered this land—and each other.*

A Lie for Love

Daniel Ransom

Daniel Ransom has worked in several confidential capacities as an investigator and decoder. Ten years ago, he decided to give up the "spooks" of the investigative world and deal full-time with the spooks of horror fiction. He has written a dozen nov-els and more than two-dozen short stories. Publisher's Weekly *noted: "Ransom certainly gives horror readers their money's worth!" and* Booklist *said: "(Readers) looking for something beyond Stine and Pike will find plenty to captivate them." In a departure from his work in horror, Ransom chose to develop this Western tale for Foggy Windows Books.*

The barrel of his Winchester fit perfectly between the slats of the boards. Killing Governor MacReady was going to be no problem at all, but they had a tight time limit. The governor was scheduled to leave soon for Europe.

The hour was near midnight. The horses in the livery were long settled in for the night. So was the old man who watched over the place at night, a pint of rotgut sending him into a reverie of ancient memories.

The young man's name was Blake, Jeff Blake. He was twenty-five and a city fella. The sharp cut of his dark suit and the tilt of his derby spoke to that. His face had the softly handsome look of a man long spoiled by women.

The older man was Paul Conrad. He was the opposite of Blake in all respects. Fat, his suit cheap and wrinkled and dusty, there was an air of cold permanent anger about him. His dark eyes rarely showed anything but disapproval and contempt.

Jeff crouched on the second floor of the livery—the night air sweet with the scent of hay and horse droppings—and guided the Winchester to the exact spot where the governor would be standing two nights hence. Wade City was the county seat of Abner County. The livery opened on an alley across from the Royale Hotel, its restaurant being the governor's favorite place to eat. He always came and went the back way, so he wouldn't have to spend time shaking hands with all the people filling the front of the hotel.

Blake and Conrad had been in town a week. They'd watched the governor carefully, and his pattern never varied. Just around nine, finished with dinner and riding the crest of his vanity and not a few good whiskies, MacReady would come out the back door of the hotel and stand there talking with his cronies while he lit a cigar. He'd look up at the starry night sky and hook his thumbs in his vest pockets and seem profoundly satisfied with himself. Then he'd take a brisk stroll back to the Colonial-style house the Territory provided the governor and his invalid wife.

Blake and Conrad had no real idea of who had hired them. In the war, they'd been assassins for the North. They'd been good at their job—and they'd liked their job. It sure beat the hell out of plowing up rock-hard soil on a no-account farm in Missouri, as Blake had been doing; or tending bar for a bunch of boomtown rummies, as Conrad had been. So, naturally enough, they'd continued their calling after the war. There were always men who wanted other men killed and were willing to pay for it.

And so, they'd ended up here, another job. The fact that this target was a sitting Territorial governor meant an extra fee, and the girls and the menus in a county seat like Wade City were just fine. They had no idea why someone wanted him killed, and it didn't matter to them. All they knew was that at eight o'clock, forty-eight hours from now, they needed to give the old soak who watched over this livery some sleeping powder with his whiskey, and have two horses saddled and ready for their getaway. There was a riverboat leaving exactly at ten, and they planned to be on it.

Now, they parted company. They were headed for whorehouses, but while Blake proclaimed a "hankering for white meat," Conrad made it clear that he "preferred dark."

It had been a fine way to start the morning, Sam Hodges thought, smiling at his wife across the table. It was a good thing the hotel restaurant served breakfast late, because Sam and Kirsten had spent nearly two hours in bed together after waking up.

She had been lying down resting when he finished up shaving, covered only with a white sheet that revealed the shape of her breasts and her pubic thatch. He was a morning man. An explosion of vitality and need impelled him toward the bed.

"I was hoping you'd stop by for a visit," she smiled. She was a fine, clean woman; one he both loved and lusted after even more than when he'd first met her.

He demonstrated this now by leaning over to kiss her tenderly on her naturally pink, erotic mouth. And as he leaned, her hand went up and found his desire, freeing it from his underwear. She used it to guide him down to the bed. Soon her breast filled his mouth. His tongue made them both a little crazy with the tattoo it made on her nipple. Their bodies arched against each other, her jutting hips under the control of his big hands. He kissed her mouth, her chin, and lingered on the elegant angle of her neck, working his way down again to the sensuous perfection of her breasts. He continued to trace the shape of her body all the way down to the beautiful, clean hair atop her legs.

Then he eased himself between those long, perfectly shaped, ivory limbs to find the moist warmth of her womanhood. She was guiding him again; and he was sliding his hands beneath her to raise her up to him. He found her buttocks very arousing and had learned how to use them to enhance her pleasure, squeezing then releasing them, squeezing then releasing them until she pitched and writhed in a pleasure very close to pain.

They almost always made love twice in the morning. The first time with great urgency and frenzy, the second time tenderly and slowly, him finding depths and sensations in her that startled and pleased them both. And then, at the very end of the second time, he would ride her so hard, the bed threatened to fly apart, and they would delight in all the noise they were making. They were no doubt scandalizing the other hotel guests....

Lovemaking always left both of them calm and relaxed. It was both an exorcism of various anxieties and a celebration of their love for each other. They'd met when Sam, badly wounded from his service in the war, chose to recuperate in a place outside Denver. She'd been a nurse at that particular hospital, and they'd soon fallen in love. One of his constant visitors was the man who'd been his commanding officer, Stephen MacReady. Though he could be a somewhat stuffy and pompous man, he'd been a damned good and very clever commanding officer. He lost few men and had taken each loss and injury personally.

Sam and Kirsten were in Wade City to attend a dinner for some of the men under MacReady's command. It would be good to see everybody again, and good to get away from the small helltown where Sam was the sheriff. Kirsten had started having the nightmares again. Sam being back-shot by an outlaw. Sam being lynched when he wouldn't turn over a prisoner to a mob— as had happened in a small, nearby mountain town recently. Or Sam being overpowered by a prisoner and being stabbed— as had happened to a lawman friend of theirs recently. The knife had cut the spine in such a way to leave the lawman paralyzed from the waist down for life.

So Kirsten had begun hinting. She took every opportunity to show Sam advertisements in the Denver paper about possible new careers. The trouble was, Sam liked being a lawman, even given the low pay, the long hours and the danger. He could honestly say that when he awoke each day, he looked forward to going to work. And how many jobs could you say that about?

He was just finishing his coffee, and thinking about lighting his pipe, when Kirsten said, "Why, gosh, look who's across the street! It's Jeff!"

Sam saw him, too. At first he wasn't sure the man was actually Jeff Blake, his wife's brother. The other side of the street was some distance away. But then the man turned to look back at something, and they had a clearer look at him. It was definitely Jeff.

"I'll go get him." Sam was up and out of his chair, hurrying out of the toney restaurant with its sparkling crystal china and silverware and its rather chilly waiters. But that was life in the big city.

This time of morning, the city streets were packed with commerce. Streetcars, stagecoaches, farm wagons, and carriages of all kinds clogged the street. Jeff disappeared around a corner.

Sam caught up with him a few minutes later.

"Hey, stranger."

He caught Jeff by the elbow and turned him around.

"Oh, God, Sam!" Jeff said. "What're you doing here?"

Sam expected the younger man to be happy to see him. Even though they rarely saw each other, they'd always gotten along fine. And Sam knew the pride and love Kirsten felt for her younger brother, too. After leaving the farm, Jeff was now a successful sales representative for a firm that made specialized wagons back east. He made a lot of money. They just wished he'd find a girl and settle down.

Instead, he saw fear in Jeff's face. But why should Jeff be afraid of seeing him?

Jeff struggled for words. "This is a real surprise, Sam. Is Kirsten with you?"

"Right back up the street. We're here to see my old commanding officer. He's the governor of the territory now."

"MacReady?" Jeff said. His voice sounded choked. "Stephen MacReady is your friend?"

"Sure. It was because of him that most of us made it through the war. He can be a pain in the ass sometimes but he's a good man. So some of us from his command are getting together at the Royale Hotel. He'll be there, too."

Jeff looked pale. The fear had faded somewhat. But he seemed a bit dazed. "That'll be...nice...for you."

"So, c'mon, let's go see that beautiful sister of yours."

Jeff shook his head. "The truth is, I've been traveling so much, that I'm a little under the weather. I was just heading back to my hotel—the Stanton—to get a little rest. Why don't I plan to meet you in the dining room there for dinner tonight?"

Sam studied him carefully. Something was wrong. He had the sense that he was talking to an imposter. A very good and very clever imposter. The man looked like Jeff but sure didn't act like him. Where was the smooth, affable, almost arrogant young man that the ladies liked so much?

"Everything all right with you, Jeff?"

"That's a hell of a thing to ask," he snapped. "After I told you I was feeling sickly." Then, "Gosh, I'm sorry, Sam. I guess I'm so worn out, I'm just cranky. Some rest'll help me. I'll be better by tonight." He smiled and he was almost like the real Jeff for that moment. "And I won't be so cranky."

Sam tried to joke along with the mood. "You promise?"

The smile again. "I promise, Sam. It's great to see you. And tell Sis I love her."

He was composed again. More relaxed now. The fear gone. Still, there was a tension remaining that puzzled Sam. Something was clearly going on with his brother-in-law...but what?

He spent the afternoon finding out what. He told Kirsten the story about Jeff being under the weather and then excused himself as quickly as possible. He wanted to get to the Stanton Hotel. He didn't tell this to Kirsten. He just said he wanted to see some of his old lawmen friends. She said fine, wanting to go shopping anyway.

Having been raised in a South Dakota soddy, Kirsten had never gotten over her thrill of being in an actual city. She loved dawdling in front of store windows, imagining all the fine things she'd buy if she had the money, how this hat would look on her, or that dress, or how their tiny sitting room would look with that couch in it.

But today she couldn't enjoy herself the way she usually did. She just kept thinking of her brother Jeff and how strange it was that he hadn't come back with Sam to see her. That wasn't like Jeff at all.

Their father had died of cholera when Kirsten was eight. Their mother had died when a wagon tipped over on her one rainy afternoon, crushing her head. Twelve-year-old Kirsten had pushed Jeff away so he wouldn't see the condition his mother was in. Kirsten didn't want that picture haunting him the rest of his life.

Kirsten had raised him until he was fourteen, taking a small room in town and working in a café. She cooked for him, sewed his clothes, made sure that he got to school, and talked to him about what a good future he could have in a town.

Then the war came, and Jeff enlisted. He was barely fifteen. Somehow he survived. And prospered. The few times they'd actually seen him, he was every bit the dandy you'd see strolling down a street in Chicago. And he had money, too; he was always sending them expensive gifts. His life as a salesman was even more than she could have hoped for him. Now, if he'd only find a woman and settle down.

Then this morning...not coming to see her.... Normally, Jeff would've come, even if he had to get there on two broken legs. What was going on with him?

It took Sam twenty-three minutes to find out what was going on.

He went up to Jeff's room. No answer. He went back downstairs. The desk clerk said he'd seen Jeff leave not ten minutes ago. Sam knew better than to ask for the key.

One thing a lawman learns fast is how to pick a variety of locks. He was inside Jeff's room within a minute of reaching the door.

The room was well appointed with a large bed with a carved wooden headboard, new bureau and a closet big enough to run around in. Sam went through all the drawers, and then through the closet. Finally, he rummaged through the large war bag sitting next to the bureau. Nothing untoward there. Not until he came to the newspaper stories, anyway. They'd been carefully cut out.

MINE OWNER SHOT
STATE SENATOR DROWNED
POLICE CHIEF STABBED
SALOON OWNER BURNED ALIVE

Twenty stories in all. Each one detailing a different—usually prominent person—meeting a violent end. The methods were all different and so were the locations—all over the Midwest and West.

Then there was another batch of clippings, all these concerning Governor Stephen MacReady.

"You're a nosy bastard, Sam."

Sam had been so caught up in reading the story of a

minister who'd fallen down a well and broken his neck that he hadn't heard Jeff come in.

As Sam turned toward him, Jeff laughed. "You've got to admit, I do pretty nice work for someone with a limited education. I killed men in the war, Sam. I don't see a whole hell of a lot of difference, to be honest."

A lot of men felt that way. They'd learned that taking another life didn't bother them as much as they'd feared. To them, human beings were animals no different from squirrels or dogs or rats. No big deal killing them.

They'd spent an hour talking in Jeff's hotel room, passing a bottle of good whiskey back and forth to fill their glasses. It would have been a decent time if Jeff hadn't confirmed the fact that he was a killer for hire and that his job here was to kill Governor MacReady.

"I won't let you do it," Sam said. The funny thing was, both men spoke in civil, mostly friendly terms. No arguing. No bickering. No shouting. "He's a friend of mine."

"I'm not alone in this, Sam. If I don't do it, my partner will."

"Then I'll go to the local law. They'll figure out who your partner is."

"That what you want? For Kirsten to know everything about me?"

This last point brought a lot of silence from Sam. That's what had to be avoided here. Kirsten finding out about her brother. She'd never get over it.

"Plus, it wouldn't look real good for my future business, brother-in-law. Me finking out on a killing I'd already contracted for. But if you want to go to the law and have my sis learn about me..."

Sam cursed. "Pride. It's your pride, isn't it?"

"I'm known as a man you can rely on. I don't miss when I go after somebody."

Jeff was the imposter again. The decent kid Sam had known and liked was gone. The imposter was the real Jeff now. Hard and cocky, the cold light of a killer in his eyes.

"I guess it's up to you, Sam. But right now, I've got to start getting ready for dinner. Got a date with a very fancy lady. I'll be bringing her along when I hook up with you and Sis."

Sam stood up and said, "Somebody ever told me a man could change the way you have, I wouldn't've believed them."

Jeff stepped up to Sam and said, "I wish it could be some other way, Sam. I really do."

Jeff hadn't been exaggerating about his lady friend. Red-haired, beautiful, elegant, she dominated the entire dining room. Men got whiplash stealing glances at her, and women put permanent frown lines around their lips from sending signals of disapproval. The lady friend, whose name was Marla, wore an emerald-colored silk dress cut so low that the top edges of her aureoles were visible.

Kirsten saw immediately that Jeff had changed. There was an anxiety in him now. He seemed distant, distracted. His humor, which had once been gentle and boyish, was now harsh and cynical. He rarely let anybody else speak more than a few sentences before butting in, as if his opinion alone mattered. And there was no love in his eyes. That was what hurt the most. He looked at Kirsten no differently from the way he looked at this Marla. What could have happened that changed him so?

When Jeff and Marla got up to dance to a tune played by the six-piece band, Sam and Kirsten followed them to the floor. But Kirsten led Sam to the other side of the floor so they could talk quietly while they kept time to the sad ballad "Lorena," so popular during the war just past.

"He's changed."

"He's just tired, honey," Sam said. He didn't want her to worry about her brother. She was always concerned that she hadn't raised him well. If she found out the truth about him, she'd blame herself. Forever. Nothing Sam could say would change her mind.

"He's—different. Haven't you noticed that?"

"Not really," Sam lied. "He's got a lot of responsibility on his shoulders, and I think it just wears him down a little from time to time. Nothing to worry about, hon. Really."

"I just want him to be the way he was."

Sam grinned. "You just want him to be a little boy again so you can mother him."

She laughed. "You know, you just may be right."

Paul Conrad didn't like complications. You had a job and you did it. It was that simple. Most of the time, anyway. Now, there was a hitch. Blake's brother-in-law, a nosy hick sheriff, had discovered what Jeff really did for a living, and what he was doing in Wade City. Conrad didn't like this feeling of helplessness. His fate was in the hands of this rube lawman. If he went to the local law, there was no way they could pull off the assassination. And their reputations would suffer. It wasn't just pride, it was business. In the underground world of hired killers, Conrad and Blake were known as the most daring and the most reliable. If a nosy family member was allowed to mess up their plans...

Conrad, making sure he wasn't being followed, had gone to Jeff's room late in the afternoon. Jeff was getting all fancied up in his best new duds. He always irritated Conrad when he got gussied up like this, maybe because the fancy clothes and the merry attitude reminded Conrad that he didn't have much of a life of his own.

Jeff was finishing up with his string tie, appreciating himself in the mirror.

Conrad sat in a chair with his stogie, watching. Finally, he said, "I thought I'd better tell you that I've decided to kill that brother-in-law of yours."

Jeff snapped around, glared at him. "Are you crazy?"

"Are you? He knows all about us. He's got our ass in a sling, Jeff, whether you want to face it or not."

"I told you, there's nothing he can do. He goes to the law and Sis finds out about me, it'd kill her."

Conrad shook his head. "Not good enough. Any time he wants to inform on us, he can. Maybe he won't do it right away, but somewhere down the line, this rube's gonna feel like he's gotta tell *somebody*. He'll go to someone somewhere and eight months later, a guy with a hood is pulling the trap door open."

Jeff said, "Damn."

"What?"

"I know you're right. I know we can't just leave him wandering around out there. Why the hell'd he have to break into my room, anyway?"

"Because that's how lawmen think. They have the least little suspicion about somethin' and then they break into your place to find out what's going on." Conrad spoke with some bitterness. His little brother had been trapped by a lawman in this manner and sent to prison, where two older men had beaten him to death.

"I don't want her hurt."

"Don't worry about that. I know how you feel about her."

"And you have to make it look like a robbery."

"It's all handled," Conrad said, standing up, setting his derby back on his head. "It's all handled and there's nothin' to worry about."

So now Conrad climbed the fire stairs to the third floor, savoring the smells and sounds of the night. The stink of cigars and callow beer and sweet perfume. The grunts of sex. The hacking cough of a smoker. The ungodly stench of used chamber pots. The backsides of hotels had always fascinated him. You got to see little private glimpses of other lives by peeking into the windows as you climbed the stairs. The couple that didn't get along, him pounding away on her, threatening to hit her even harder if she screamed. The couple that couldn't keep their hands off each other, doing it right by the breezy window like dogs. The solitary salesman at the writing desk, composing a letter to a wife or a child or a grandchild.

...then he was on the third floor and climbing into the window of the room where Sam and Kirsten were staying.

It happens all the time.

A couple comes back to their room from a night out, and surprise—a burglar. And the burglar does something absolutely unnecessary and unwise. He gives into panic and shoots the man of the couple. An unfortunate death.

It happens all the time...

Conrad crawled through the window and waited for Sam and Kirsten in the darkness.

A few minutes before they concluded dinner, both Sam and Marla excused themselves to go the restrooms. While Kirsten was glad she had the opportunity to be alone with her brother, she wasn't quite sure what to say. He was a stranger now.

"You look great, Sis."

"Thank you."

"Things have turned out pretty darned well for both of us, I'd say. You have Sam, and I've got my job. Couldn't ask for much more than that."

Babble is what it is, she thought. *Babble*. What you said when you really wanted to avoid saying anything of meaning. She looked at him and said, "You've changed, Jeff."

He smiled. "I have?"

"I don't mean to pry. But is everything all right?"

"Everything is just fine, Sis."

But even as he spoke tenderly to her, she saw that the hard cold expression in his eyes had not shifted any.

"I pray for you all the time, Jeff."

The smile again, false and bright. "Maybe that's why I've had such good luck."

He was like a bank vault she couldn't open because she didn't know the proper combination. Inside was the truth. The truth of what had changed him.

Then Sam was back, and a few moments later, Marla. All four of them were doing their best to sound and look festive. The waiter came with the check. Jeff grabbed it before Sam even saw it. He left a large gratuity, making sure everybody saw it, and then he held Marla's chair for her to stand up.

It was a late-night city. Cabs and carriages still filled the streets. Top-hatted men and fine-dressed women laughed gay wine laughs as they strolled along the lamp-lighted streets. Here and there dark-uniformed coppers strolled, too, occasionally twirling their brutal nightsticks. Thieves and pickpockets would be fools to operate around these fellows.

Jeff was all hugs and kisses with his sister. "I'm going to surprise you two and just stop through town one of these days."

"We'd love that, Jeff. We really would."

Then she saw the strange way Sam was staring at Jeff. Anger, even contempt, was in his expression. Suddenly, Jeff's voice fell away—he was still babbling, but she wasn't hearing anything—and she concentrated on her husband's face. What was going on with Sam and Jeff? They used to be so friendly. She'd seen the cold way Jeff had regarded Sam earlier in the evening. But it had been nothing like this. Sam looked as if he genuinely hated Jeff.

"I've had a lovely time," Marla said.

Then it was time for Kirsten and Marla to babble for a few minutes. But all the time she talked, she noticed how her two men made a point of neither looking at nor speaking to each other.

Then Jeff was making a show of kissing and hugging her again.

And then Kirsten and Sam were walking alone back to their hotel.

A couple of times Paul Conrad heard people coming down the hall. He gripped his Navy Colt, ready. He was almost angry when they walked by.

"You sure everything's all right between you two, Sam?" Kirsten asked as they approach their hotel. "You and Jeff barely spoke tonight."

"He just seemed to have a lot on his mind, honey. You make the kind of money he does, you've got a lot of responsibilities."

"It's just you two seemed so—distant."

Sam was thankful for a sudden burst of drunken laughter. A small group of drummers were just leaving the hotel. A couple of them had open bottles of whiskey, something that could get you arrested in a town like this. But drunken salesmen were drunken salesmen and they seldom worried about such vagaries. Their noise ended the uncomfortable conversation Sam had been having with Kirsten.

They eased past the drummers—all of whom turned to stare lustily at Kirsten—and entered the hotel lobby. It wasn't often they got to see a place as fancy as this one, all the leather couches and chairs and discreet lamps. The atmosphere was like that of a wealthy man's den. It was tempting to just sit down here and read newspapers and pull on a stogie for several hours. But they were tired and went straight to their room.

Sam was just opening the door when he heard it. A country sheriff gets used to small warning sounds. The best ears can hear a snake slither. Sam wasn't *that* good but he did hear something that sounded like a man shifting his weight slightly in response to a noise, maybe a man coming alert because he'd heard the door opening. The first thing Sam did was gently push Kirsten back out of the doorway. Then he put his finger to his lips for quiet.

The sound of movement came again.

The visitor was getting impatient, maybe even a little nervous. Good.

Sam dove inside the room without any warning. He rolled across the floor, his Colt in his hand, his eyes adjusting as quickly as they could to the darkness. They had help. The man stepping out of the closet shot three times and each round was accompanied by a jab of flame as it left the gun.

Kirsten screamed. She was standing in the doorway, a clearly outlined silhouette. The man fired in her direction, Kirsten screamed again, and then slowly slumped to the floor.

Sam fired twice himself. But the visitor was already moving toward the window, which is how he'd gotten in. And at this moment, Sam didn't give a damn about him anyway. Kirsten was his only concern.

He knelt next to her, and took her in his arms. "I told you to stay out of that doorway."

"I know, honey. I was just so worried about you when I heard those shots—"

The hall was quickly filled with sleepy, curious residents. Then a short, stout man in a black suit pushed his way toward them. His black Gladstone bag marked him as a doctor.

Kirsten had been wounded, all right.

"Just a solid scratch in the upper arm," Doctor Devers said, after tearing the shoulder from her dress. "She probably won't live longer than another seventy, eighty years."

Kirsten smiled at his joke. But when she looked at Sam, she found him over by the window, staring angrily into the night. It made sense that he'd be angry about a burglar who'd broken into their room and then shot her, scratch or not. Sam's usual response to a situation like this was anger. He had a quick temper. She was always telling him to calm down. But this was a strange reaction, this brooding. It matched the mood she'd sensed in him while they were at dinner with Jeff. Almost as if there was something he wasn't telling her. He'd made quick work of the deputy who'd come up to investigate, too. Just a routine burglary, he'd explained to the young man. Couldn't identify the intruder. The big thing was that Kirsten was all right. Though Sam was most appreciative of the deputy's interest and concern, he'd practically pushed the kid out the door.

Doctor Devers, being a city doctor and far more up to date than his country brothers and sisters, used an array of tools, wound cleansers and healing ointments. They had to be good because they stunk like hell. Surely nothing that harsh smelling could be ineffective.

He worked on her for nearly an hour. The way the shoulder of her dress had been torn exposed the side of her breast. She kept covering it. She secretly felt that the doctor was having himself a harmless peek every once in a while.

When the medical man was done, Sam paid him five dollars.

"Now I should work on you."

"On me?" Sam said.

"Your nerves, man. The way you've been pacin' around, I've seen men more relaxed on the mornin' they were to be hanged." He touched Sam's elbow. "I know you love her. And it's perfectly understandable that you're worried, but she's gonna be fine. Nothing to worry about. The bullet passed right through the flesh, and the wound will heal just fine. I'll stop back in the morning to check on her. Now, you just relax."

"Thanks," Sam said. "I appreciate it."

Only a scratch, Sam thought. *If Kirsten ever finds out about Jeff, it's going to be a lot deeper wound than that.*

He walked the doctor down the hall a ways and said good night. When he returned, Sam saw that Kirsten was sleeping, lightly snoring. He took off his clothes and eased into bed next to her. She needed her rest, and he didn't want to wake her.

Sam tried to keep from moving around. He lay still, hoping for sleep. Fury wasn't something you could settle in with, though. He wanted to get his hands on the man who'd shot Kristen.

"Your jaw is grinding." Her voice surprised him in the darkness.

"You should be sleeping," he replied softly.

"So should you."

She gathered him up and kissed him. His anger waned soon after. He was completely alive to her kisses and caresses.

"You sure you want to do this?"

She laughed. "Fortunately, he didn't hit any vital areas."

He helped her ease off her dress. They lay naked, pressing against each other, even the gentlest movement stirring and stiffening him. He explored and teased, explored and teased, the way she liked him to. And she clutched his manhood vigorously, teasing its tip in return, so that he began to move to the rhythms her hand dictated.

He moved up on her body, putting himself between her breasts. They both liked this very much. She filled her hands with her breasts and then used them to massage his erection. By now, he was thrusting, gasping, and she was taking him into her mouth, getting him ready for melding with her.

And then, almost as if by magic, their mutual hungers blinding them to time and movement, he was inside her and they were riding their way to the ecstasy that only got better the longer they experienced it.

Slamming into her, his legs running with her juices, he felt her lift to him so that he was in as deep as this position would allow. Her moans melted into his gasps as they reached their blinding pounding shrieking pinnacle together...

Sam wrapped his arms around Kirsten, and waited as her excited breathing slowed and eventually gave way to sleep.

Jeff had been so scared when Conrad told him what happened, he went to the hotel immediately and questioned the desk clerk. He didn't want to go upstairs and see Kirsten and Sam.

Satisfied that his sister was going to be all right, Jeff left the hotel and found a quiet saloon where he drank his way through two angry hours. Then he went back to his own hotel and went straight to Conrad's room. Conrad was asleep. When he finally, groggily opened his door, Jeff hit him with a roundhouse right that drove Conrad seven or eight feet back into his room. He'd given the older man a seriously bloody mouth.

"What the hell you doin', Jeff?"

"That's for shooting my sister."

"I told you. It was an accident."

"Not the way the hotel clerk told it. She screamed and you shot her."

"Shot in her direction, Jeff. *In her direction*. That was all. Just so she wouldn't scream no more."

"Shooting at her wouldn't make her scream even more?"

Conrad had turned the lamp up. Now he sat in his nightshirt on the edge of the bed, his fingers delicately touching the split lip Jeff had given him. "I admit I wasn't thinking very clear, Jeff. But I sure didn't mean to hit her." You could see Conrad was uneasy playing the supplicant. He was usually the one in charge.

Jeff poured himself some of Conrad's whiskey. "This damned thing has been jinxed." Like most men who made their money on violence, he was very superstitious. He frequently saw fortunetellers. "Maybe we should forget it."

Conrad said, "Sure. Forget it. And we might as well forget our reputation, too. We have an agreement to kill him by tomorrow night or the deal's off. He leaves for Europe." Then, "I can always do it again, Jeff. I won't miss this time. Go after your brother-in-law, I mean."

"That's all we need, isn't it? You try again—and have him waiting for you."

Conrad scowled. But he knew Jeff was right.

And Jeff *was* right. Once Kirsten had fallen asleep, Sam quietly got up and spent the rest of the night sitting awake in a chair. She moaned and twice screamed. Nightmares.

Sam had but one thought. He couldn't let his old commanding officer Stephen MacReady be assassinated but he couldn't let Kirsten know what Jeff had become, either. And just how was he going to go about that?

He worked the dilemma over and over in his mind but by pale dawn, no solution had come to mind.

After cleaning up and shaving, Sam decided there was only one way to handle this. Kirsten was still asleep. Sam walked quickly to Jeff's hotel room and knocked on the door.

Jeff, rubbing his eyes, was irritated when he saw who it was. "You've had your say."

"The hell I have."

And he stormed inside, forcing Jeff to back up.

Sam slammed the door closed behind him and said. "I want you to pack and leave town. And I mean right now."

"Get out of here, Sam. You're starting to make me mad."

"You've got one hour to clear out. I watch you get on a train and leave town. Otherwise, I go to the law."

"And let Sis find out about me?"

"If that's how it has to be."

Jeff smiled. "You won't do it, Sam, and you know it. Sis'd never get over it. And you don't want one of those wives who sits in a shutup house all day long and takes nerve pills, now do you? That's how she'd be. She'd blame herself. The way mom did when our brother got killed that time." Kirsten's older brother had died when a horse fell on him. Her mother had never really recovered. In some ways, her own death had been a blessing to her.

When Sam stayed silent, Jeff continued, "You want a healthy, young woman like Sis. And I sure don't blame you." He shook his head. The sarcasm was gone from his tone. "Sam, listen, the war changed me. That's not an excuse, just a fact. And this is what I do now. I'm good at it. Maybe one of the best. I like the money and I like the respect I get. The fear, too. I know that's probably not what you want to hear, but it's the truth. It gives me a real sense of power, having people fear me. I grew up with nothing—and no talents or skills that anybody wanted. I sure as hell didn't want to go back to the farm and I sure as hell didn't want to go to work in some shop somewhere. So I decided to do the only thing I was good at. Conrad and me killed a lot of Confederate officers in our war days." The smirk returned. "I never was much of a hero, Sam. But I make a pretty damned good villain."

Sam just stared at him. He didn't feel that Jeff was insane. He just had a different, and very cold way of assessing his job prospects. And that's all killing was to him, a job.

"Now I've got to get fixed up for the day, Sam," Jeff said. "So I'd appreciate it if you'd excuse me."

⋈

Sam hurried back to the Royale. He told Kirsten that he'd met some old war friends who'd just arrived for the dinner tonight. He said he'd like to spend the day with them if she didn't mind. She said fine. She'd do some more shopping—and resting.

He spent the day following Jeff. Nothing of note happened for the first six hours. A couple of leisurely meals, an hour at a horse barn where some excellent equines were being shown, and then nearly two hours at a very elegant whorehouse. These were the kind of women who probably took actual baths once in a while.

Around five, though, Jeff's demeanor changed. His body seemed to stiffen, tense. He began glancing back over his shoulder, as if he suspected someone might be following him.

Then he slipped into the livery shop, the back of which opened onto the back of the restaurant where Governor MacReady would be dining tonight. And the whole plan became apparent to Sam.

The governor would come out the back way, and Jeff and his partner would be waiting on the second floor of the livery. There would be horses saddled and ready nearby. It was not a very dashing or daring plan, but then assassination was a simple game. You got as close as you could and opened fire. If you were a lunatic, then you didn't care about getting away so you walked right up to your target and opened fire. But these were professionals. Escape was part of the plan.

Sam was waiting for Jeff when the younger man got back to his room.

"Make yourself at home, Sam."

Sam said, "There's still time."

"Time for what?"

"To leave town. To forget about tonight."

"Too late to forget about it, Sam. I've already explained that."

"Your pride is all it is."

Jeff looked at him. "Maybe you're right, Sam. I guess I've got the kind of pride that just couldn't ever settle for being a small-town sheriff."

"I'm trying to help you, Jeff. Even if you insult me."

Jeff took off his suit coat and hung it up in the closet.

"I hope your friend is a better shot tonight than when he tried to kill me."

"Things don't always work out." Jeff faced him now. Smiling. Smirking, really. "I notice you haven't gone to the local law."

"Not yet."

Jeff laughed. "Not yet. Not ever, you mean."

Sam stood up. He felt tired, old. "I won't let you do this, Jeff."

"I guess you'll just have to kill me, brother-in-law."

"That's what I've been thinking."

Jeff put his arms over his head. "Then get it over with, Sam. Right here, right now. A lawman like yourself, they'll believe you. You knew I was going to assassinate the governor and this was the only way you could stop it. The law'll probably buy it. I guess all you've got to worry about is convincing Sis. You think she'll buy it, Sam?"

"For the last time, Jeff, I'm warning you. Don't go ahead with this."

Jeff smiled again, and lowered his arms. "Give my love to sis."

The dinner was enjoyable. The men and their wives posed for pictures, danced, talked over old times, even had a teary roll call of the men they'd left behind in the war. Three or four times, the night seemed to wind down. The men, while not old, no longer had the stamina of youth to get them through a full night of drinking. Yawns started replacing calls for more drinks. Governor MacReady made a point of spending private time with every one of the twenty-seven ex-soldiers who'd come here to-night. He'd always been an emotionally generous man, and they appreciated that.

Sam knew he was doing a good job of hiding his anxiety

because Kirsten was having a good time. If she'd sensed his unease, she would have said something.

After three couples said their goodnights to everybody, Sam knew it was time to move. And quickly.

He leaned over to Kirsten and said, "Duty calls."

She smiled and kissed him on the cheek. "Duty calls" was their term for needing a restroom.

As soon as he reached the corridor outside the private dining room, Sam walked over to one of the governor's aides and said, "I need to talk to the governor in private. It's extremely important." He paused. "There's going to be an attempt on his life tonight."

If the aide had had any reservations about Sam's request to see the governor, that last statement had pushed them aside. In this day and age, assassination was something everybody took seriously.

A few minutes later, Governor MacReady joined Sam in the corridor. "I don't have time right now to explain anything more than to say that I need you to lend me your clothes."

"It's a good thing I know you don't drink too much, Sam," the governor said, "otherwise I might think you're drunk."

Jeff kept thinking of his sister and Sam. Good people. The kind of person he'd been once. He couldn't keep blaming everything on the war. Sure, it had changed him but he'd *let* it change him. The only thing he could say for himself was that the only people he'd killed were people who'd badly needed killing—other killers, slave traders, child merchants.

Governor MacReady was the first decent man he'd ever been hired to shoot. And he didn't like the feel of it.

"He's gonna come out any time now," Conrad said. "Get ready."

Jeff slotted the barrel between the pieces of wood. Sighted down the barrel. You couldn't ask for a clearer shot. And with some twilight lingering for light, too.

"Never seen you like this," Conrad said. "Somethin' the matter?"

"Just shut up, all right. Your jabber's makin' me nervous."

"I don't think it's my jabber," Conrad said, eyeing Jeff carefully. "It's something else."

And then the back door of the hotel opened. And two of the governor's aides stepped out, looking around to make sure that nobody was hiding in the shadows.

"You got a clear shot, kid," Conrad whispered. "Take it."

He said this just as the governor himself came through the back door, strutting into the evening with a stogie in one hand and a walking stick in the other.

"Now," Conrad hissed, "Shoot him now!"

A single shot from the top floor of the livery. The governor and his men pitching themselves to the ground. The echo of the gunshot seemed to reverberate for many minutes.

A couple of city police officers rushed from the governor's side to the livery stable. You could hear them pounding up the wooden steps inside. Then: "Halt! Come out of there with your hands above your head!"

A minute later, one of the officers shouted: "All clear!"

Over the course of the next five minutes, with Kirsten by his side, Sam stood in the governor's clothes and watched as Conrad's body was brought down from the livery. Then Jeff came down.

"The dead man was the assassin, Governor," the police officer explained to the real governor, who looked a little uncomfortable in Sam's clothes. "This is the man who stopped the assassin."

Jeff stepped forward and said, "He was drinking too much last night in a saloon where I was playing cards. I told Sam here about it, and he told me to keep an eye on him. We were staying at the same hotel. I followed him after dinner tonight, and he came right over here. I told him to put the rifle down, but he tried to shoot me. I had to kill him."

Kirsten walked over to him and slid her arm around his waist. "How's it feel to be a hero?"

Jeff grinned. "Pretty darned good, actually."

Later that night, Sam joined Jeff in the hotel saloon.

"Sis asleep?"

"Yeah. She was exhausted from telling me what a hero you are."

Jeff smiled. "I recognized you right away. I knew it wasn't the governor, I mean."

"I was hoping you would. And that you wouldn't be able to shoot me."

"I couldn't, but Conrad could. That's when I shot him. He wouldn't put his rifle down even when I told him it wasn't the governor. He thought I was lying, and turned his gun on me. I didn't have any choice."

"I appreciate what you did."

They were silent for a time, and then Jeff spoke softly. "Maybe I can start all over again, Sam."

"You can if you want to."

"Find one of those nice, safe, boring jobs I'm always making fun of."

Sam smiled. "I'm told that heroes almost never have a hard time gettin' a job."

"Yeah," Jeff said, "I guess I've heard that somewhere, too."

Coming in 2001, a brand new novel from Daniel Ransom—his first Western novel, ever!

Shotgun Wedding

Lindsay Hart

Lindsay Hart, a seventh-generation Nevadan, has worked as an exotic dancer in the Lake Tahoe area for five years. In winter, she volunteers on the Ski Patrol. Ms. Hart lives in Incline Village with her Samoyed, Ivan, and her twin Jack Russell terriers, Cisco and Pancho. Her grandfather was a member of one of the search parties sent out to locate the Donners, and his diary remains in the Hart family.

It would have been much more of a storybook wedding if only they hadn't had to shoot anybody.

To be fair, the wedding part of it was more or less uneventful in terms of actual gunplay. The former Grace Hill, late of St. Louis, had worn a lovely white dress, with a lacy veil that cascaded from the crown of her shimmering red hair to the floor of

129

the Calvary Presbyterian Church. Her groom was Hunter Jedediah McKenna of Laramie. Looking at her in that dress, admiring where it clung to the swell of her breasts and displayed, when she moved just so, the turn of her ankle, Hunter was put to thinking that the day's events were really going to begin that night, after the reception was out of the way, all the guests thanked and sent home, and he and Grace had retired to their room at San Francisco's Palace Hotel.

The past year and a half, working with Grace had proven to be a lusty combination of heaven and pure torment. Hunter had not been alone in this, of course. All the other men in the Secret Service had been just as thunderstruck by the presence of the beautiful young woman in their midst. But just as she knew how to defend herself with a gun, a knife, or her own two fists, she knew how to defend against unwanted advances, how to ward off the interest of those whose interest she didn't return.

Hunter didn't ever claim not to be interested, but neither did he make a fuss over her. It was, he knew, in many ways a tactic—but one didn't rise as quickly in the Secret Service as he had without being a bit of a tactician, especially when he had the disadvantage of not having been brought up in an important Eastern family.

And as a tactic, it seemed to work.

One night when they were holed up in the tiny fishing village of Dundee about two hundred miles up north, he had come into a room he thought was empty, only to find her taking a bath.

He didn't leave immediately, as he ought to have done. Instead, he stood in the doorway and took off his hat, saying, "Beg your pardon, Miss Hill."

Her masses of glorious red hair were piled on top of her head, several curls tumbling over her bare shoulders in a most fetching way. She had the most pert smile and the biggest blue eyes he had ever seen. Her neck was swan white and long, and her shoulders just ached to be covered with kisses.

She looked at him and slowly put down the sponge she had been using. Surrounded by bubbles, she was no more exposed than she would have been in a ball gown. And yet, knowing that she was naked beneath the foam set his body to straining against his trousers, and his face was hot.

Then she slowly rose. The bubbles clung to her body, then began to slide downward, exposing her heavy, beautiful breasts and large, dark nipples. She let him look, standing perfectly still as the bubbles sluiced down her curvaceous legs, to reveal a perfect, delicate triangle of copper between her thighs.

He took a step forward; she halted him with a wave of her hand.

"Mr. McKenna," she said, "you may know that I was raised by my uncle, who is a physician. He has fully explained the nature of relations between men and women to me, including the fact that performing these relations is pleasurable to men but strictly a necessary duty for women."

"No, ma'am—" he began, but she cut him off with a grin.

"Your practiced and deliberate lack of interest in me—combined with stories I have heard about your tastes and habits from some of our co-workers—have only succeeded in making me exceedingly curious about you. And I know, in spite of your attempts to disguise it, that you've been very curious about me. *However...*" She gazed at him sternly as he took another step toward her, and he stopped.

"However," she repeated, more softly, "I can't believe my uncle is telling me the truth. The fact that so many women have enjoyed your attentions gives me hope that it's a bald-faced lie that I would not enjoy them."

"It is, it is," he assured her, his voice hoarse.

"Well then," she said, reaching for the towel that lay folded neatly upon a chair next to the copper tub. "What is it they say? No time like the present?" She began to dry herself off. Hunter could see her breasts move under her towel. "You do want me, don't you?" she continued.

He knew he'd hate himself later for what he was about to do. But if he took the other path, he would hate himself still more.

He took his hat off and cradled it against his chest. "Miss Grace," he said, taking the liberty, under the circumstances, "you're the most desirable female I've ever seen naked, and may God strike me dead if I'm lyin'. I want you more than anything—but not here, and not now. You're a woman who should have everything just so, includin'—maybe especially—this. Save it for your marriage bed, and could be I'll join you there."

God had not struck Hunter down. In fact, God had rewarded him for his honesty. Generously. God had allowed him to kiss Miss Grace Hill on several occasions. And when Hunter proposed, God had given him permission, from that moment until their actual marriage night, to fondle and cup her clothed breasts and slide his hands beneath her hips, exciting her until she found the release her well-meaning uncle had told her was reserved only for men.

Now, just after the ceremony, as Hunter watched Grace move through the church, smiling her carefree smile, touching her long neck the way she did when she was lost in thought, greeting friends, he could hardly stand to wait for nightfall. One smoldering look from her told him she felt exactly the same.

Once during the reception at the Cliff House, he was so aroused he considered trying to find a closet or private nook where he could pull her aside, hike up her skirts and pull down whatever it was a woman wore under such an elaborate construction, and give it to her right there. But such a first time would not be good enough for his Grace.

And besides, that was before the president started to vomit.

Grace and Hunter were Secret Service agents, and highly regarded in the Treasury Department. It was rare that a woman was allowed to work in such a field, even in the enlightened year of 1872, but Grace had proved herself on many occasions, and there were times that a woman could go undercover in places where a man couldn't. Hunter, too, was one of the department's top agents. So when they married, it was a big affair. President Grant had come out for it, leaving Vice-President Colfax to run things back in Washington. The First Lady had accompanied the president, too. The head of the Secret Service, Charles Throckton, was there, as was the Secretary of the Treasury, George Boutwell, and various other Cabinet members. All in all, there were two hundred guests at the wedding and reception.

They had been partaking of the lavish lunch of beef, chicken, hams and salmon prepared by the Cliff House staff when the first guest got sick. By the time the president fell ill, more than two-dozen people were weak, pale, vomiting, or just rolling on the floor clutching their stomachs. Doctors were called in from all parts of the city.

And then the first guest, a San Francisco society widow named Mrs. Dorothy Canton, died.

It was less than an hour since she'd begun to eat.

The president and Mr. Throckton had eaten about twenty minutes after she had.

Someone had poisoned the reception food in an attempt to assassinate half of the federal government.

And, on their own wedding day, Grace and Hunter found themselves on the job.

The doors of the entire building were being sealed off and guarded—no one else in, and no one out. The president's own special detail had already keeled over like so many three-legged mules on a windy day, so now Vice-President Colfax's proxy, Mr. Dunbar Fitzgerald, was dogging Grace and Hunter's boss, ordering him to send the agents who could still ambulate to grill the guests and staff.

"Everyone must be questioned," Fitzgerald announced, with a twirl of his mustache. "Even the ladies."

"Yessir. I'll get right on that."

Charles Throckton had not risen to the top of his profession by being impolitic. He was as polite to horse's asses as he was to the president himself, always had been, which is why Hunter had stayed on even after the scandal that broke his twin brother, Ethan. A man like that was intelligent, and intelligence was hard to come by in these United States. Or so Hunter figured, anyway.

—◦—

The first man Grace and Hunter tried to question made a run for it, until they caught him.

"Well, Mr. McKenna, I'd allow that married life is proving to be exciting," Grace said, as she whipped out her handcuffs and smiled at her brand-new husband. He held up two wrists, and Grace clapped on the cuffs.

"Darlin', that was awe-inspiring," Hunter said. "You ever need a new calling, I'd suggest a Wild West show. Reckon you'd be the main attraction."

After hiking up her skirts and petticoats, Grace had leaped over the nearby table—narrowly missing the elaborate wedding cake topped with a bride and groom—and landed on the floor beside her husband. The heels of her white kidskin, high-button shoes made a clack on the wooden floor. With one swift motion, Grace pulled her Derringer from the lacy blue garter around her thigh and pointed it at the man her husband held pinioned. She'd been a good shot before, but Hunter had been teaching her some trick shooting, and even with the Derringer she was a deadly aim.

Now she winked at him, her gaze sweeping from Hunter's broad back down to the smooth curve of his saddle-hardened rump as he bent over the struggling man. Hunter was as dark-headed as an Apache, with a trim beard and sideburns. His eyes were a wonderful blue-green that changed with his moods...and they just about glowed when he was giving her pleasure. At the memory of Hunter stealing into her hotel room this morning, a thrill flared at the base of her spine and shot like a powder trail through her body.

"You want to talk awe-inspiring, Mr. McKenna..." She let her words trail off suggestively as she slipped her right forefinger around the trigger of her Derringer and pointed it at the man on the floor. With her left hand, she did her best to cover up her bloomers with a few dozen of the yards and yards of the embroidered French satin of her wedding gown. Her bustle was all clumped up behind her, and she figured she was just about as indecent as a gal could be in public without getting paid for it.

"'Ey, 'ey," said the man on the floor. Judging by his uniform, their subject was a Cliff House waiter. Just like everybody else, the man had halted when instructed to and joined a clump of employees in the back of the ballroom. Then, when the employees were being separated for questioning, he had tried to make a run for it, not realizing he'd dashed headlong into McKenna territory.

Et voila, as they said in Paris, France.

"I *innocente*, I *innocente*," the man babbled at the two of them. He had a thick foreign accent. *Italian*, Grace presumed.

"Then why were you trying to sneak out of here?" Hunter demanded.

The man rolled his eyes in exasperation. *"Mamma mia,* you are a foreigner and a rich *signora* dies. Do *you* stay?"

"If I'm *innocente*, I do," Hunter shot back.

"Ah, but you are American," the waiter persisted.

"Actually, he's from Wyoming," Grace offered. "And I'm not sure that counts."

"Or what that has to do with tryin' to light a shuck out of here," Hunter added. He helped the man to a sitting position as he said to Grace, "Your underwear's hangin' out, honeybunch."

Grace punched at her bustle. "I think it's bent," she grumbled. "I swear, Hunter, I look like a cornbread muffin."

"No, no, *signora*," the waiter assured her. "It's not so bad." He appraised her hind end. "A most tiniest *gnocchi*, perhapsa."

Grace fumed and batted at the wires. Finally she gave up and held a hand out to her husband. He steadied her as she got to her feet and then she helped him pull the Italian to his feet. He looked from Grace to Hunter and back again.

"Ah, but this is the night of love for you, is it not? And you must discover murderers. Alas!"

"Don't worry, friend," Hunter said. "We're resourceful."

They walked their new friend over to a chair and had him sit down. Grace managed to push her skirts back over her bustle, only to discover that in all the excitement, her décolletage had shifted and her breasts were straining against her bodice. The waiter's eyes were spinning like pinwheels, which she figured for a good thing—all modesty aside.

So she flashed a glance at Hunter and leaned over just a little farther, and cooed, "*Paisano mio*, would you by chance have noticed anything odd about the meal fixins back there in the kitchen?"

He swallowed and shook his head. His eyes did not leave her breasts. Hunter's own gaze ticked admiringly in the same direction, and Grace took a nice deep breath, all the better to entice and tantalize.

"Was anyone new working in the kitchen?"

"My Angelina, my, how you call her, fiancée, she'sa work inna the kitchen. She tell me about a, what do you calla him, Gianni?" The Italian placed his forefingers at the corners of his eyes and pulled upward.

"A Johnny?" Grace whispered. "You mean, a Chinaman?"

"*Si, si*." Beads of perspiration formed on his forehead. He slipped his finger into his tight collar and tried to find some breathing room. Grace took the opportunity to gently lay her hands on either side of his chair back, so that her face pressed close to his. She heard him gasp, then exhale, his warm breath caressing the tips of her nipples.

Good Lord, is everything on display? she thought. "This Chinaman. Did he go near the food?"

The Italian snaked one hand between her upper arm and his forehead. "It'sa so hot in here," he mumbled.

"How near?" she asked seductively. "The food?"

"The food," he said slowly.

"The food." Her voice was honey-sweet. "That I ate."

"Ah. He..." He closed his eyes. "I must think."

"That'd be a good idea," Hunter said, breaking the spell. "Thinkin', I mean. Not whatever else you might be considerin' right about now."

It wasn't that he wasn't enjoying watching what his wife was doing—one peek at a comely ankle of Miss Grace Hill's could drop a desperado at twenty paces, and that was a good thing in the Secret Service; and besides, he had personally assisted her in discovering her secret weapon. Not to mention that Hunter was the only man alive who had title to the claim, and nobody liked to jump it, not if he wanted to live.

But the man was beginning to lose his handle on the English language. Pretty soon he'd forget everything he'd ever learned except "Would you care to order?" and Hunter had already taken Grace's order. He knew exactly what she wanted, how much, how hot, and in what order the delectables were to be served. He'd had her fill out the menu this morning, whispering her requests in his ear while she smiled and sighed and caught her breath and he forbade her the main course until they were churched proper.

Right about then, Grace's uncle, Dr. Oral Increase Hill, reappeared from the kitchen with a grim look on his face. Hunter thought about all the sharp knives in there and the fact that it would be a wise thing to autopsy Mrs. Canton as soon as possible, if that would help save the president's life. Her uncle was one of the best doctors in these United States, not to mention the kind of man who would take in his dead sister's only child and raise her like his own. He was still gussied up in his morning coat with his rosebud boutonniere on his lapel, lately of the Calvary Presbyterian, where he had walked Grace down the aisle.

"It's poison, all right," Uncle Oral announced. "Not a natural sickness or influenza of any kind."

"Can you tell what kind of poison?" Hunter asked. "Or what the antidote might be?"

"I'll need to do some more testing before I can know for certain," Oral replied. His square face was set in a serious expression, his mouth a thin, pale line. "Attempting the wrong sort of antidote could just complicate matters."

"I'm sure you're doing your best, Uncle Oral," Grace told him. "You just keep on with whatever it is you're doing, and we'll do the same. We'll find the poisoner, and you'll know what poison it was."

"I have every faith that you will, Grace," he said. "And you as well, lad."

"Thanks, Uncle Oral."

"Poison inna the kitchen," the waiter moaned. "Captain Foster, he'sa not gonna be happy 'bout this." Captain Foster, Hunter knew, ran the Cliff House, and had taken it from relative obscurity to its current standing as one of the city's most popular restaurants. Plus, the Secret Service had done him a favor or two in the past, and he was returning those favors, with interest, by giving them a special price on the plentiful feast that had been prepared today.

Of course, if President Grant died, Hunter had a mind to demand the return of his deposit.

He looked around to see Grace soothing the waiter by brushing the backs of her fingers across his forehead, wiping away the perspiration that had beaded there during his interrogation. Even this glimpse of her cleavage, disappearing into the depths of her gown, was nearly enough to make him forget the business at hand and whisk her away someplace. *Or just let the waiter watch*, he thought. *The man must have seen stranger things in his employ here.*

"You don't worry about Captain Foster," she was telling the man. "We'll talk to him. You just point us toward the Chinaman you mentioned, and we'll take care of the rest."

The man—reluctantly, it seemed—pushed himself to his feet and led the way toward the kitchen. "He should'a be in here, with my Angelina, but I don' know where everyone'a went after the people started getting'a sick."

Hunter moved in front of the waiter. If the poisoner was by any chance still in the kitchen, odds were he—or she—would be armed and anxious. Hunter didn't want the Italian waiter to be the first through the door. He drew his own gun, a Walker Colt that was never far out of reach, and pushed the door open with the toe of his boot. It swung wide.

There were only two people in the kitchen. The one Hunter recognized was Dunbar Fitzgerald. In one hand, he held a napkin, and he was dabbing at his full lips with it. In the other hand, held low and almost behind the bulk of his body, as if he were half-heartedly trying to hide it—he gripped a chicken leg by the bone. Fitzgerald was evidently a man who enjoyed a bite now and again—he was so round that his clothes were tight against the curve of his belly. Even the outline of his pocket flask was clearly visible against his waistcoat.

The other was a raven-haired, dark-eyed beauty whose uniform strained to confine a lush figure that rivaled Grace's own.

"Angelina!" the waiter cried out when he saw here.

She crossed the kitchen to him, throwing her arms around him. Tears had streaked her lovely cheekbones. "My Antonio," she said. "I am so frightened." The waiter spoke soothing words to her in Italian.

"Mr. Fitzgerald," Hunter said, gesturing toward the chicken that the man held. "Isn't that a little dangerous?"

"Why, not at all," Fitzgerald assured him.

"Why not?" Grace asked. "What if the chicken's poisoned?"

"It couldn't be," Fitzgerald replied. "I had three pieces of it before anyone took ill. If the chicken had been bad, I'd have been right down there with the lot of them." As if to prove his point, he lifted the leg to his teeth and tore off another chunk.

"Wouldn't say the same for that plum pudding, though," he added. "A bit gamey, if you ask me."

"Hadn't noticed," Hunter said. The truth, he and Grace had both been too busy greeting guests to sample so much as a bite, or even to take a sip of water or wine. Which, in fact, probably went a long way toward explaining why they were still upright, when all about them people had fallen over.

"Plum pudding?" Grace said slowly, and Fitzgerald cocked his head.

"Yes, ma'am," he said, "plum pudding."

"You haven't, by chance, seen a Chinaman in here?" Her

voice was full of charm and delicate phrasing. Fitzgerald cast an appreciative eye at the way her gown had become disheveled.

"Seems likely that I'd recall, if I had," he replied. "No, I believe the kitchen was empty when I arrived. I did, however, assign Kelton and Fisher to interview the kitchen staff, so they may have taken them all somewhere."

Leaving you free access to the grub, Hunter thought. But the man outranked him, and was in charge of the investigation, so he held his tongue.

"What about him, there?" Fitzgerald demanded. He waved the drumstick at the Italian waiter.

"We're fairly certain he's clear," Hunter said. "*Innocente* as a newborn babe."

"Right, then," Fitzgerald humphed. "Well, we can't just have you two standing around doing nothing," he went on. He stroked his chin with the napkin hand, pulling his gaze away from the tops of Grace's breasts long enough to cast it ceiling-ward and appear lost in thought for a moment. "But you know, it seems like a few of your wedding guests hailed from below the Mason-Dixon line. I wonder if this isn't some kind of South-shall-rise-again conspiracy."

"We'll have a talk with the Southern contingent," Hunter assured him. "I believe they're relatives on the Hill side of the family."

"That would be my Aunt Letitia and her brood," Grace agreed. "Powerfully built boys, but not the smartest geese in the flock, I'm afraid."

"Thanks for the insight, Mr. Fitzgerald," Hunter said. He gave a small bow and left the kitchen, holding the door open for Grace to follow. She brushed against him as she passed, her eyes locking on his. Her smile was warm and full of invitation. *The sooner we get this over with*...it seemed to say.

In the corridor, she stopped and waited for Hunter to catch up. The passageway was deserted, as the kitchen had been, save for the presence of Fitzgerald and Angelina.

"My Aunt Letitia's boys are no more longing for the return of the Confederacy than they are for the return of Letitia's husband

Casper," she said in a hushed voice. "Took their best horses, all their cash, and a pie that she'd made for the church picnic when he left. They weren't but boys when the war ended, and they haven't the faintest interest in politics."

"That gives them something in common with me," Hunter told her, a rasp in his voice. "Only thing I'm interested in is under that dress you're almost wearin'."

"Why, Mr. McKenna, you'll make me blush," she said, batting her eyelids at him.

He touched her cheek. "That ain't all I'm fixin' to make you do."

They shared a moment, and then she sighed and said, "First things first, my love."

"So what do you think we should look at, then?" Hunter asked. "If your aunt and cousins aren't trying to overthrow the land?"

She thought a moment. Then she said, "Did you order plum pudding to be served?"

Hunter looked surprised. "Not sure I've ever even heard of plum pudding. Sounds kind of sketchy to me. Figgered maybe it was somethin' you wanted."

"In June?" She narrowed her eyes. "It's a winter dessert. Hunter, it seems to me that Fitzgerald has kept awfully busy, sending agents investigating this way and that while he blithely eats chicken. The only person who hasn't been investigated, as far as I can tell, is Fitzgerald himself."

Hunter laughed.

"No, I'm serious," Grace insisted. "What do we know about him?"

Hunter shrugged. "He didn't like the plum pudding that we didn't ask for in the first place."

"Exactly."

"If the plum pudding is even at fault," Hunter pointed out.

"Plum pudding is never totally innocent," Grace said. She touched her stomach protectively. "At any rate, we could ask Uncle Oral to test it."

"Let's do that," Hunter said. "I'm still not sure that's grounds enough for us to accuse the man."

"Perhaps not," Grace agreed. "But combine it with this. Mr. Fitzgerald is the vice president's man. And Mrs. Grant told me last night—in strictest confidence—that General Grant is none too happy with the vice president. In fact, he's considering withholding his support from Colfax in the coming election."

Hunter looked surprised. "You weren't plannin' to tell me about this?"

"Not at my wedding, no," she retorted. "If Grant does decide against supporting Colfax, he might back another candidate. Probably Henry Wilson, is the First Lady's guess. There's no guarantee of anything, of course, but the president maintains a certain popularity, and if he's behind Wilson, then we'll probably have a new vice president."

Hunter gave a low whistle. "And Colfax will be out of a job, with no hope of attaining the presidency. She actually told you all that?"

She gave her head a toss. "You'd be surprised what we women talk about when you men are smoking your cigars and drinking your brandy. It's not all just French fashions and bedroom adventures."

"You talk about bedroom adventures with the First Lady?" Hunter asked, astonishment ringing in his voice.

Grace chuckled. "Let's just say General Grant's soldier is rarely at parade rest."

"No foolin'," Hunter said. "You've got to fill me in, darlin'. Later. But for now, how do you expect we ought to confront Mr. Fitzgerald?"

"The best way," Grace suggested. "Walk up to his face and talk to him."

They both turned and went back to the kitchen, Hunter's boots clomping on the hardwood floors. He shoved open the kitchen door.

Fitzgerald looked up at them with surprise, and maybe a little fear, clouding his face.

"I thought I gave you an order," he sputtered.

"You did," Hunter replied. He and Grace moved in closer. "But we have a couple of questions for you, first."

"What is the meaning of this? You dare to disregard my authority? Why, I—"

"I'm blamed terrible about authority," Hunter told him. "Ask anyone in the Service, and they'll tell you the same thing. Just no good at all with followin' orders."

"I'll have your job, McKenna."

"Chance I'll take."

"And by the way, Mr. Fitzgerald," Grace spoke up. She stepped right up to Fitzgerald, tapping at the telltale bulge in his jacket. "I'd be most interested to see what's inside that flask in your pocket there."

"Are you suggesting I'm the only man here carrying a flask?" he demanded.

"Not at all," Grace said. "But you are the only man here representing the vice president—a known teetotaler who is infamous for only employing the same. Isn't it true that the president's drinking is one of the main sources of contention between them?"

"I don't discuss politics with ladies," Fitzgerald said. "And I won't dignify this line of questioning with any further discussion at all." He started to turn and head for the kitchen's other exit, into the dining room. Angelina and Antonio had to disengage and turn sideways to let him pass.

"Not so fast, Mr. Fitzgerald," Hunter said before he had taken more than two steps. "As Secret Service agents, we have the right to detain anyone we choose. And I, like Mrs. McKenna, would be very interested in seein' that flask."

Fitzgerald moved surprisingly quickly for a man of his bulk. His eyes flicking this way and that like a cornered animal, he drew a revolver from a holster hidden beneath his arm, and pointed it at Angelina's ravishing head. The woman let out a scream, but Fitzgerald silenced her by clapping a hand over her mouth, wrapping his arm around her head.

The waiter watched in horror. "Don't let him'a hurt her," he cried. "My poor Angelina!"

"Don't worry," Hunter assured him. "He won't do anythin' to Angelina. He knows if he did he'd be dead 'fore she hit the ground."

"You're all such fools!" Fitzgerald announced. "No wonder you don't recognize that Schuyler Colfax deserves to be president. You aren't intelligent enough to recognize genius when it's staring you in the face. Grant's afraid of him, that's what it is."

"If you're any indication of the sanity of his supporters, could be he's right to be afraid," Hunter observed.

"No more talk from you, McKenna," Fitzgerald spat. "And I want that Colt you carry on the floor, now. Or this girl will never cook another dish."

Hunter complied, lifting the Walker Colt from its holster with two fingers and setting it gingerly on the floor. "It's down, Fitzgerald," he said. "Now, how about yours?"

"I want passage out of here," Fitzgerald said. "There are coaches outside. I want one of those, with fast horses. I'll let her go then, and not a moment before."

"Fine," Grace promised him, with a low curtsy that ruffled her disordered petticoats. "You can go to the coaches. We'll make sure no one stands in your way. Just tell us what the poison is."

"Ha!" Fitzgerald roared, his face become even redder. "Just how stupid—"

His voice was cut off by the muffled bang of Grace's Derringer, fired from beneath her petticoats. A round hole in the fabric still smoldered, and a smaller hole had appeared in Fitzgerald's head, centered between his eyes. The man fell to the floor, releasing Angelina as he did.

Hunter knelt down next to Fitzgerald's body and pulled the flask from his jacket. He opened the lid, sniffed the contents. Almonds. "Arsenic," he announced. "Let's tell your uncle the poison is arsenic."

"There's an easy antidote for that," Grace replied. "Antonio, fetch as much milk as there is in the building. And send for more if you have too. Milk counteracts the arsenic, some-how."

"Milk," the waiter said. He smiled broadly, and took Angelina's hand in his. "Let'sa go get some milk, *mia cara*."

Hunter left the flask on Fitzgerald's ample belly. Then he rose, turned to his new wife, and looked into her blue eyes. "I love it when you shoot straight," he said.

"And speaking of shooting straight," he said huskily, as she turned to him in her wrinkled bride dress, her veil askew.

They were in the bridal suite at last. The president and all the other survivors were resting comfortably. Fitzgerald's body had been taken away. The case was closed.

It was time to conclude all other unfinished business.

Lamplight cast the room in romance and shadow; the brass bed gleamed with welcome. A half-consumed bottle of cham-pagne sat in the cooler, and beside it, Grace's bridal bouquet of pink roses and lilies lay in a sea of white satin ribbons.

The room was filled with gardenia perfume and the musky odor of lust. Grace inhaled it, wanting it on the tips of her fin-gers and inside her mouth. Hunter's aroma, strong and masculine...she was filled with a desire stronger than any she'd ever experienced in her life.

She let her eyes half-close as he threaded her wedding veil from her tangles of red curls. The stiff netting trailed across her arched neck as it slid to the floor. Hunter kissed his wife, his lips pressing gently against her smooth mouth. She wanted him to be a little rougher, so she returned the kiss harder, pressing her lips against his, tasting him with small flicks of her tongue. She already wanted him so much she was trembling.

But this was her first time. This night would set the tone for all the other nights—and dawns, and sunsets, and high noons—to come. He had pleasured her without crossing her boundaries, and with each rocking climax she had enjoyed beneath his touch, he had promised her that this night would feel more amazing than all those times combined. So she knew he was trying to go slow, and to pay close attention. This was not just some woman who had come into his room for a few hours of fun. This was his wife, and she knew he would treat her as such.

Slowly he ran the tip of his tongue over her lips; she parted them slightly, and he touched his tongue with hers. She heard his breath catch, and then he surrounded her with his powerful arms. She moved toward him, exploring his mouth. Her nipples were so taut she was convinced he could feel them through her satin bodice and his own white shirt.

Hunter splayed his hands over the small of her back, easing her hips forward slightly, and centering his erection so that, if she were naked, he would lie between the folds of her sex. She moaned softly, deep in her throat, and undulated against him.

"I can't wait any more," she said huskily. "Hunter..." As their tongues searched each other's mouths, her hands began to roam over his body—his shoulders, his chest—and she tugged at the tucked-in hem of his shirt. He squeezed her hands and brought them against his chest, holding her as he kissed the corner of her mouth, each closed eye, her forehead, her temple, and just beneath her jawline. He breathed into her ear, and she jerked, making the soft little whimpers that had always tantalized him so.

"I can't wait," she murmured again.

He bent over her and ran his mouth to her collarbone and trailed his lips along it. There was a pulse in the hollow of her throat. He kissed it, then brought his head down to the swell of her breasts. She pressed against them from the sides, cradling his head between them.

"Just give it to me, Hunter," Grace said. "You know what I want."

She pressed her hand against the fullness of his erection, feeling the heat and the hardness. She fumbled slightly with the opening of his trousers, then caught his shaft in her hand and closed her eyes as it bulged in her grasp.

"Grace," he blurted, perhaps shocked, or just surprised; but Grace had waited long enough. She did not need to be gentled like a frightened virgin, even though she was a virgin.

She slid to her knees and took him in her mouth. For a

moment she was afraid she wouldn't be able to get it in—it seemed so big, the bulbous, purplish head so round. But she did. It slid into her mouth, pressed against her cheek, and then she pushed it down farther, into her throat. She heard his gasp and closed her eyes as the large, stiff shaft pulsed. She ran her tongue over the head, exploring it, then around the ridge. Her fingers followed the thick vein.

"Grace, Grace, stop," he was saying. She kept sucking, then tasted the first drop of her husband's seed. She thrilled at the taste, honey-like, and took her mouth away. She leaned back and smiled up at him.

"Take me," she said.

"Grace, I want you to be satisfied," he said. "You've waited so long—"

She laughed and stood up. She opened her arms and said, "I love you, Hunter."

As he moved to embrace her, she pushed him backward, onto the mattress. Lifting her skirts, she climbed onto the bed, then lowered herself over his member.

She braced herself for a jab of pain, which came, but it was much less intense than she had anticipated. She was slick and excited and all her muscles—the ones Hunter had taught her that she had—gripped him as she straddled him. She slid down his full length; it was like a column of fire rising up inside of her, hot and hard and thrilling like nothing she had ever known.

"What are you doing?" he nearly shouted, but she knew he was loving it. His hands gripped her waist and he held her as she rode him, up and down, increasing the pace; her breasts were heaving and she heard herself grunting like an animal. As she pushed down against him, taking every inch, he rose up from the bed and thrust into her. She realized she could feel his balls slap against her ass with every thrust, and the realization sent a shiver of excitement coursing through her.

"Come in me, Hunter. I'm your wife," she managed, before the room stopped being a room and all that everything was, was *good*; a good that went right down deep past words and thoughts and people and everything else; it was raw and wild and fiery.

She was coming; she knew what it was but it had never been like this, with something inside her; with her husband's penis throbbing hard against the seat of her womb. With his seed—she felt it! She could feel him coming—with the whole thing happening to both of them at the same time, so fast, so hard, so wet, so good.

He groaned as if he was dying; and she knew he was done. But she had more inside her; she wanted more, with him still hard. And he knew it, somehow—he always knew—and he rubbed the nub of her sex with his wet fingers and gazed at her with more love and more animal heat than she had ever seen on his face. It was like she didn't even know who he was, but she didn't care; he was the pleasure-center and he was the huge, rock-solid core inside her.

She came.

He kept at her.

She came again.

And when she began to droop over him in a half-faint, he got hard again, and he came again.

When she could finally open her eyes, her bride gown lay in tatters all around her. The sheets were on the floor, and Hunter's upper arms bore scratches from her nails. She shifted, half-expecting some pain, but all there was, was the deepest, most satisfying sense of being filled and loved.

She draped a tender hand over his cheek. To her surprise he caught it and brought it to his lips. He lifted his head.

He had been crying.

He said to her, "There are tears all down your face."

She felt her own cheeks, and laughed, because there were tears there after all.

Hunter began to laugh, too. Then he rolled over on top of her and said, "Good morning, Mrs. McKenna."

She held out her arms. "Good morning, Mr. McKenna."

And a very good morning it turned out to be.

Hunter & Grace will be returning in June 2001 in, the first of two action-packed novels, featuring these sexy characters.

FOGGY WINDOWS BOOKS

Undercover

Whether you're interested in a heart-stopping thriller or the challenging puzzle of a good mystery, our Undercover novels and stories are the place to go. These are the stories that claim your attention, keep the pages turning, and often make you wonder if the bad guy is ever going to get captured. Of course, when you get a husband and wife involved in some of the darkest passions of society, things are bound to get a little bit more tangled.

Breathtaking

Tim Waggoner

Tim Waggoner is the author of The Harmony Society, *forth-coming from DarkTales Publications. In addition, he's published close to sixty short stories in various magazines and anthologies. He teaches creative writing at Sinclair Community College in Dayton, Ohio.*

⊰⊱≡◉⊂≡⊰⊱

You can never identify a murderer just by looking at him. After all, given the right circumstances, anyone is capable of murder.

Liana Mallory kept this thought foremost in her mind as she watched Roman Gullatte—their host—wield a large clear plastic dildo with all the mastery and grace of a conductor's baton. Roman knelt on an oriental rug before a crackling fireplace, fingers wrapped around the lube-slicked dildo, sliding it in, drawing it out of the masked brunette lying on her back. Liana had no

153

trouble imagining him as a murderer. He operated the dildo as if it were a weapon instead of a sexual aid. Not clumsily, but with the dexterity and confidence of a fencing master handling a foil.

Liana felt her husband growing soft inside her. She turned her head to look back at Justin and whispered, "Hey, how about keeping your mind on your work?"

Liana was bent over, hands gripping the back of a leather couch, her husband behind her. They were both naked, as was everyone else in the house—at least two-dozen people, perhaps more, though of course not all of them were down in the basement den. And not all were completely naked; about half the partygoers wore masks to conceal their identities. Some chose anonymity for the fun of it, others because of their standing in the community—standing which they wished to keep.

Surrounding Liana and Justin were maybe ten people in various stages of coupling, tripling, quadrupling and other mathematical combinations. Justin was holding tight to Liana's slim, well-muscled hips, screwing her from behind. Well, trying to. As much as having sex during a case turned both of them on (and Liana was a little embarrassed to admit this, even to herself), Justin was having trouble focusing on the task at hand. Not that his hand was the body part in question.

"Sorry," Justin mumbled, and focused his attention on Liana once more, though she had no doubt he continued to keep an eye on Roman. That was, after all, why they were here.

Justin was a sweetheart, but he had trouble multitasking sometimes. Liana put it down to a man thing, a legacy of single-mindedness passed down from caveman days. Me hunt food, me find food, me kill food, me eat food. Ug! Still, his "focus," as he preferred to call it, was one of the things that made him a good detective, she supposed. Liana, on the other hand, had no trouble doing several things at once. As she was thoroughly enjoying her husband boffing her from behind—to the accompaniment of the throaty moans and moist movements of the other lovers in the room—and building satisfyingly toward orgasm, she was watching Roman Gullatte like a hawk. Well, a hawk in the throes of wild, frenzied mating, but a hawk nonetheless.

Roman was in his mid-fifties, but he looked like a man ten, maybe fifteen years younger. Tanned, with broad shoulders, thick arms, and large hands, he had hardly an ounce of fat on him. His curly hair was silver at the temples, but still mostly jet-black. Liana wondered if he colored it, leaving a touch of silver behind for effect. Probably, she decided. He was handsome, though he looked more Greek than the nationality his name implied. He was the owner and head chef of Roman's Holiday, not only the best restaurant in Knighton, but the best this side of Cleveland.

Liana watched as Roman used the dildo on a cute little brunette who was young enough to be his daughter. Behind her half-mask of feathers and sequins, the brunette's eyes were closed, head tilted back, hands clutching double fistfuls of the Oriental rug beneath her. She was making little *huh-huh-huh* sounds as she panted, every muscle of her lean body taut, and Liana knew she was getting close to orgasm. Liana imagined she could smell her sweat mingling with Roman's, imagined that Justin's penis—which had become firm again—was a dildo just like the one Roman was using, only bigger, harder, so she barely had room for it within her. It was all she could do to keep from crying out as Justin jammed it in, yanked it out, jammed it in —

And then Roman reached out with his free hand and stroked the brunette's hair, trailed his fingers down toward her neck, caressed it gently. The brunette squealed and arched her back as she came. Roman's hand tightened on her neck, not too much, not enough to hurt her or scare her—hell, Liana doubted she even noticed as hard as she was climaxing—as he worked the dildo so fast, it became a blur.

Ordinarily, it might have been a real turnon, might have sent her over the edge into a nerve-jangling orgasm herself. But not tonight, not when they were investigating the strangulation death of one of Roman's former lovers. Evidently, Justin felt the same way, for he began growing softer inside her. That was okay; she'd lost the mood, too.

One thing Liana noticed: from the first insertion of the dildo to the final spasm of the brunette's climax, Roman's penis never became erect, never even so much as twitched.

"My sister was murdered. I know who did it, and I want you to get the proof so the bastard who killed her doesn't get away with it."

Liana was impressed by how calmly Cecile Pitner spoke. If it had been her sister who had been murdered, she would be howling for the killer's blood—and then she'd go spill it herself. Liana glanced at Justin, and he arched his left eyebrow to let her know he was more puzzled than impressed. There was no obvious grief, no anger. Just a cool, reserved calm.

"We're private investigators," Justin explained. "Despite what you see on TV and in the movies, we don't solve murders. That's a job for the police."

Liana nodded. "Justin knows what he's talking about. He was a cop for close to ten years before he became a PI. Not only don't we have the manpower or the legal authority that cops have, they aren't too damn thrilled when a couple of PI's start poking around in one of their cases." She gave their prospective client a half-smile. "That doesn't exactly make them inclined to play nice with us." Liana knew this as well as her husband; she'd been an army M.P. for about as long as he'd been a cop.

"I don't have anyone else to turn to," Cecile said. Earlier, she had shown them a picture of her sister, Moira, and Liana was struck by the resemblance—both were lovely petite blondes in their twenties; almost twins, though they'd been born four years apart. But where Moira looked like a model, Cecile was somewhat mousy—she wore glasses and her hair was pulled back in a spinster's bun.

"I can't go to the police," Cecile said. "Their theory is that Moira was killed by a 'drifter'—maybe even a serial killer. Not only wouldn't they believe the truth, I can't tell them, not without risking damage to my sister's reputation. But I know who did it, and I want to hire you two to prove it—without tarnishing my sister's memory."

Liana was the more intuitive partner of Mallory and Mallory Investigations, Justin the more logical. When it came to deciding whether or not to accept a case that sounded kind of "iffy," Liana usually made the call. Justin glanced at her, giving her a chance to indicate she wanted to step out of the office (which was in their home—forget the ubiquitous seedy downtown office of most PI fiction; what client with a sensitive matter to discuss wants anyone to see them consulting a PI?). Liana didn't feel the need for a private conference, though, so she gave Justin a nod so imperceptible she doubted their client had noticed. A nod that said, *Let's go on.*

Justin turned to Cecile and smiled a professionally understanding smile, one that Liana knew he'd worked for years to perfect. It was just like Goldilock's favorite porridge—not too warm, not too cold, but just right.

"All right, Ms. Pitner," he said. "Why don't you tell us what you know?"

Cecile took a deep breath, then began. "Roman has this . . ." She struggled to find the right term. "Sex club, I guess you could call it."

Liana glanced at Justin. He had the look he always got when things started to get interesting, like a hunting dog that had scented its first whiff of prey. It was a look Liana was always glad to see, because Justin didn't just get enthused by a good case, he got excited. Liana, too. She could feel herself beginning to get wet as Cecile continued with her story.

Cecile told them about Roman's biweekly orgies at his big house outside town. It wasn't quite a mansion, but it was close enough for little Knighton, Ohio. She told them how her sister Moira had been a waitress at Roman's restaurant, how he had asked her out, dated her a couple times before ushering her into his secret world.

"She was shocked at first," Cecile said. "Most people would be, right? But she went along with it; I'm not sure why. Maybe because she thought she loved the asshole. Anyway, she kept going to his parties for about a year. He'd occasionally see her on the side. Not often, just enough to keep her thinking she was special, you know?"

She sounded quite bitter as she divulged this last bit of information, and Liana didn't blame her a bit. She felt like hunting Roman down herself and administering a good, swift kick to his manhood.

"Eventually she got tired of it, and she decided Roman had to make a choice—his lifestyle or her."

"What happened?" Justin asked. He sounded caught up in Cecile's tale, as if he were waiting to discover a plot twist in a particularly juicy novel.

Cecile answered in a small voice. "I don't know. The last time I spoke with Moira, she said she planned to tell Roman that if he didn't quit having his parties and commit to having a relationship with her and her alone, she'd expose him—go to the police, the town paper. He'd be ruined."

Despite Knighton's seamier side (or perhaps because of it), the town also had its conservative elements. Liana had no doubt that Moira's plan would've worked.

"Several days later, a policeman showed up at my apartment to tell me that Moira's body had been found by some hunters in a patch of woods off the interstate. She was naked, and she'd been...been..."

Liana and Justin always made sure to keep a box of tissues in their office. Clients don't seek the help of PI's when they're happy. Liana picked up the box and held it out to Cecile. She took a tissue, blew her nose, and then held onto the wadded tissue as if she somehow might draw strength from it.

"She'd been strangled. And the police said there was evidence she'd been engaged in sexual activity, maybe even—" a breath—"been raped."

"You didn't tell the police about Roman, did you?" Justin asked.

Liana thought of how fast Justin's mind worked.

"You're right; I didn't. I was sure Roman killed her, to prevent Moira from exposing him, or maybe out of anger at her trying to blackmail him like that. Maybe both. But I didn't want to drag her memory through the mud. We have family in town. Our mother is still alive, and our brother has three kids.... Besides, I figured if the police found out Moira was into a kinky scene like Roman's, they'd start to think she was into all sorts of bad stuff. Drugs, prostitution...And Roman's a prominent citizen in town; it's not like he doesn't have friends, you know? Hell, I'd be surprised if a few of Knighton's cops, city council and school board members haven't been to at least one of his parties."

"More than one, probably," Liana said cynically. And Knighton's government officials and employees weren't above taking the occasional bribe—not to mention regular ones.

Cecile went on. "I thought I'd wait and hope that the cops would find some clue linking Roman to Moira's murder. You know, like they do on TV. Some hair, a bloodstain, whatever. But they didn't. It's been almost six months since Moira was killed, and I think the police have given up." She dabbed at her eyes with the wad of tissue. "That's why I want to hire you. I want you to prove that Roman murdered my sister."

Liana and Justin usually turned down murder cases and tried to convince people to go to the police if they already hadn't, or to have more patience if they had.

But Liana could tell from the way Justin was looking at Cecile, like a safecracker eyeing a particularly challenging combination lock, that they were going to make an exception this time.

In order to get close to Roman without his becoming suspicious—and hopefully gain an invitation to one of his parties—Liana and Justin had approached him as "security specialists" and said they were offering a discount on security consults. Roman, who had been having trouble for years with supplies going missing—especially fine wines—took them up on the offer.

They examined his restaurant from top to bottom, interviewed his employees, and helped revise his security procedures and update his alarm system. In the process, of course, they learned a great deal about Roman Gullatte and Moira Pitner from the gossipy staff. And when they hinted to Roman that they'd heard about the special parties he threw, he invited them both to attend.

Liana wasn't sure exactly what they'd hoped to gain by attending. Maybe a deeper insight into Roman's sex life, maybe a few bits and pieces of information about him and Moira from the other partygoers. Maybe it just sounded like a turn-on, one that she and Justin couldn't pass up. Whichever the case, they would go and poke around to see what, if anything, they could turn up. And if they happened to have some great sex in the bargain, so much the better.

Roman finished with the brunette (who was now lying in a drowsy aftersex coma on the rug), and then went to the den's bathroom where there was a bucket of bleach for depositing used and no-longer needed sex toys. By this time, Liana and Justin had given up any pretense of making love and were cuddling on the couch, doing their best to look as if they were as much awash in the afterglow as the brunette. Roman didn't bother to close the bathroom door, and they saw him place the dildo in the bucket and check out his reflection in the mirror before leaving and heading upstairs.

Liana nuzzled Justin's neck, then nipped at his earlobe. "What now?" she breathed.

"Roman's conquest looks as if her defenses are down," he whispered back. "Maybe I should talk to her, use my preternaturally sharp interrogation skills to see what information I can pry out of her."

Liana nipped his earlobe again, hard enough to make him yelp. "The only naked woman you're allowed to interrogate in this place is *me*, mister. You got that?"

Justin grinned. "Can't blame a guy for trying. How about you talk to her then, and I'll go see what Roman's doing, maybe try to strike up a conversation with him."

She nodded. Between the two of them, Justin was the better planner—not that she'd ever admit to him. He already had a high enough opinion of himself as a detective.

He frowned. "You know, there's something about that woman..."

"What?"

He shook his head. "I can't quite put my finger on it, but there's something familiar about her."

"It's hard to tell who she is behind that mask. Maybe it's her body that's familiar to you." Liana smiled. "Maybe it's one of your legion of ex-girlfriends."

Justin sighed. "I don't have that many exes."

Justin was a boyishly handsome man who was so often caught up in his own thoughts that he had a tendency to look a little lost. The combination tended to draw women to him like flies to road kill.

"Whatever," Liana said, "but you're definitely not allowed to talk to her now."

Justin grinned and gave her a quick kiss, accompanied by a squeeze of her breast. He then rose from the couch and headed for the stairs. Liana watched him go, enjoying the easy, confident way he moved. Both Justin and she worked out—he ran several miles every day and played tennis while Liana studied jujitsu— and overall, they were in pretty decent shape. Evidently the masked brunette thought so, too, because she watched through drowsy, half-closed eyes as Justin headed up the stairs.

Liana stood and walked over to the woman and sat down next to her.

She opened her eyes wider, gave Liana a once over, and then favored her with a sleepy smile. "You're sexy and all, but I'm kind of worn out right now. Why don't you try me again in about a half hour or so, after I've had the chance to take a little nap." Liana couldn't decide whether to be pleased the brunette had called her sexy, or irritated that she automatically assumed

Liana had approached her for carnal purposes. She and Justin might be more adventurous than some couples, but they were completely dedicated to their marriage, and to them, that meant staying monogamous.

Liana glanced around at the men and women who were still going at it wildly—sweat-slick bodies writhing, the air filled with the sound of moaning, the musk of sweat and sex.

Not that it's going to be easy staying monogamous in this place, she thought.

Liana decided to act pleased with the woman's response, at least for the time being. "No problem." She smiled but stayed seated. After a moment more, she said, "Roman's very handsome, don't you think?"

The brunette opened one eye and looked up at Liana. "Honey, the way he can work a toy, he could look like a pig with leprosy, and I wouldn't care." Her voice was throaty and sweet, like wood-smoked honey.

"Still, it doesn't hurt that he's easy on the eyes. Or rich. He must make a lot of money with that restaurant of his."

She opened her other eye then. "Don't tell me you're thinking of making a play for him." She sounded more amused than jealous, though there definitely was a little of the green-eyed monster in her voice.

Liana shrugged. "He certainly seems open to trying new experiences. You're the second woman I've seen him with tonight."

"Third," she corrected. "And believe me, I won't be the last. Roman is single and he likes it that way. He has an insatiable appetite. Why else do you think he throws these little parties? He has two, sometimes three a month."

"I take it you're a regular."

Now it was the brunette's turn to shrug. "I get invited more often than not. It's your first time, though, right? I haven't seen you around before." She looked Liana over again, her gaze edging a little too close to a leer for comfort. "And I'd have definitely remembered you." She reached out a delicate hand and rested it lightly on Liana's foot. She began tracing a little circle on Liana's skin with her index finger, the motion sending electric shivers up Liana's leg and into her sex.

Liana didn't want to discourage her. She and Justin had worked too hard to wrangle an invitation to one of Roman's parties to spoil things now. That was the only reason she didn't draw her foot away—at least, that's what she told herself.

"You know, suddenly I don't feel so sleepy anymore." The brunette sat up and leaned close to Liana. She was afraid the masked woman was going to try to kiss her, and a little afraid of what she might do in return. But instead the brunette whispered, "I'll tell you a secret about Roman; it doesn't work."

"What?"

"His dick. He can't get it up." She breathed softly in Liana's ear. Now electricity was shooting down her neck and along her spine. "Prostate cancer. Happened a little over a year ago. Viagra doesn't work for him, least that's what I heard. But he still has his sex games. Whatever gets you off, right?"

That was interesting. So Roman was impotent. Liana had noticed he hadn't achieved an erection while he was working his magic on Little Miss AC/DC here, but she'd assumed it was because he'd come earlier with another partner, or because he was so jaded by all the orgies he'd thrown that it took more than regular sex to excite him.

But if he really couldn't get hard...

The brunette put her hand on Liana's knee and began sliding her fingers along her thigh, moving toward her vagina that was, despite her best efforts, becoming increasingly wet.

"Got a few minutes to spare, honey?" she said. She parted her lips and leaned in close to kiss Liana.

"So I told her I had to pee. Pretty smart, huh?"

"Not exactly the most elegant solution," Justin said smiling, "but as long as it kept you from succumbing to her charms, I can't complain." He frowned. "You did get away before anything happened, right?"

Justin and Liana trusted each other, and she knew he knew

that she would never do anything to betray their relationship. Still, Liana gave him her best mock-innocent smile. "Of course I did, honey." She patted his hand. "Before anything worth talking about happened, that is."

Justin scowled, but he didn't take the bait.

By coincidence, they had met at the same time outside the downstairs bathroom. When they were fairly confident no one was looking, they went in together and locked the door. Liana sat on the wooden toilet seat and Justin leaned against the sink counter. They both did their best to ignore the dildo soaking in the bucket of bleach on the floor. It wasn't easy—Liana couldn't help thinking what she and Justin might be able to do with it once they'd rinsed it off...

Liana shook her head to clear it, then told Justin what she had learned from the brunette.

Justin's brow furrowed slightly, and his eyes narrowed. Liana recognized the expression: it indicated the wheels in his head had shifted into overdrive. "Cecile said Moira was killed six months ago, right after she tried to blackmail Roman into making a commitment to her. Why would a young woman go to such lengths to force an impotent man to agree to a monogamous relationship?"

"The brunette said Roman's a whiz with toys. Maybe Moira didn't care that he couldn't get an erection. Or maybe she cared more about his money."

"Maybe," Justin said, but he didn't sound convinced. "Cecile gave the impression that her sister confided in her. Why wouldn't Moira have told her about Roman's impotence? Surely Cecile would have mentioned it to us if she had."

"Maybe Cecile held that back for some reason. It wouldn't be the first time a client has lied to us."

"True. But there's something about it that bothers me; I just can't figure out what it is."

"Well, while you're thinking about it, why don't you tell me what happened upstairs?"

Justin did so. He'd followed Roman to the kitchen, where

their host made himself a drink—scotch on the rocks, which didn't surprise Liana; Roman seemed like a scotch man to her. Justin got Roman talking, and during the course of their conversation, he learned about Roman's "special room."

"He has a private chamber on the second floor which is stocked with his favorite 'implements of pleasure,' as he put it. What's more..." Justin trailed off.

"Yes?" Liana prompted.

"He said that he'd noticed we'd kept to ourselves downstairs. I told him it was because we were new to this sort of thing and needed time to adjust. He said he understood, and then he added, and I quote, that my wife is 'a most beautiful woman.' And should she be interested, she is more than welcome to join him upstairs in his private 'playroom.' "

Justin grimaced as he related this last bit of information. He looked as if he'd accidentally bitten down on a particularly crunchy and foul-tasting bug. "Jealous?" Liana asked.

"Who, me? I'm a professional private investigator, and we're here on a case. I'm perfectly capable of managing my emotions..."

Liana gave him a skeptical look.

Justin sighed. "Well, all right. Maybe I am a little jealous." He changed the subject. "You know, now that I think about it, maybe Roman can get it up. Prostate surgery doesn't always result in impotence. For that matter, he might not have had surgery at all, only told people he did."

Liana frowned. "Why would he do that?"

"To set up an alibi for himself. Moira's murder certainly looked like a sex killing, but if Roman was impotent—or at least people thought he was—who would believe he did it?"

Liana shook his head. "I'm not sure that would work. An impotent man might kill because he's impotent. Out of anger and frustration, or maybe as a way to get a different kind of thrill."

"True, but that doesn't mean Roman thought it out that far. After all, love, you know as well as I that criminals aren't usually geniuses."

"I suppose." Liana thought for a moment. "So what do we do next?"

"I think you should take Roman up on his offer," Justin said.
"What?!?"

He grinned. "Not literally. I mean that you should go up to his 'special room,' whatever that is, and see if you can't get him to admit he's fully functional."

"You realize, of course, that I might have to do more than talk to prove that Roman can still get it up."

Justin's jaw muscles tightened. "As long as you don't do much more than talk. Make sure that you're careful; I'm not thrilled with the idea of your being alone with a suspected murderer."

Liana stood, walked over to Justin and cupped his face in her hands. "You're sweet, but I'm twenty years younger than he is, and I know martial arts. I can kick his ass without breaking a sweat."

Justin grinned and maneuvered himself so that their pelvic areas pressed together. "I love it when you talk tough." He leaned forward and kissed Liana, in the process proving that he had no trouble at all getting hard himself.

When they came up for air, he said, "How about you postpone visiting Roman for about fifteen or twenty minutes?"

Liana grinned. "Tempting, but I want to catch Roman before he comes with someone, otherwise I might miss my chance."

Justin didn't look happy, but he nodded. "All right, but what am I supposed to do now that you've got my engine revved up?"

Liana glanced at the bucket. "No one seems to be using that at the moment."

"You're not funny, you know that?"

She shrugged. "Go upstairs, make yourself a drink, and try not to think about me alone with Roman and all those toys..."

He made a sour face. "Definitely not funny."

Liana left Justin in the kitchen making a double vodka on the rocks. She wasn't worried that women would hit on him while she was gone (at least, not too worried). When they had first arrived, Roman had explained that the kitchen and bathrooms were neutral territory, so people had someplace to go if they needed a break from the fun.

"Besides," he'd said, "as a chef, I insist on being able to move about my kitchen without interference."

Liana left the kitchen and crossed through the dining room. The table was loaded with gourmet hors d'oeuvres prepared by Roman himself. Nestled among the food were crystal bowls full of various types of condoms, flavored lubricants, massage oils, edible panties... There were also several bowls containing pills and a wooden cigar box filled with rolled joints. Roman Gullatte, the host with the most.

She moved gingerly through the house, weaving among groups of lovers engaged in various sexual activities, some of which she'd only read about before, and some that seemed more like acrobatic maneuvers or medical examinations than sex, all set to the strains of a Mozart aria emanating from the sound system. More than half the partygoers wore masks—from simple domino half masks that didn't really conceal the identity to far more elaborate disguises that wouldn't have been out of place on Bourbon Street during Mardi Gras. The whole effect was more surreal than sexy, and Liana was glad when she finally reached the stairs leading to the second floor.

Once she was upstairs, it wasn't hard to find Roman's private room. On the door was an engraved brass plate that read ROMAN'S EMPIRE. Cute. She paused outside, listening. She heard a loud smack, followed by a low moan. A second passed then another smack, another moan. She debated whether to interrupt or not—Roman might get annoyed and take back his invitation— but she decided to plow ahead. Liana was a firm believer that sometimes you had to stir things up if you wanted to make any headway in a case.

She knocked.

The smacking and moaning ceased, and a moment later the door opened to reveal Roman in all his au natural splendor—

sans erection, Liana noted. He was holding a leather-covered paddle in his left hand; she glanced over his shoulder and saw a plump, matronly woman wearing a half mask kneeling on her hands and knees atop a large, round bed covered with black silk sheets. Liana recognized the woman as the town's head librarian. She tried to keep from smiling; she knew she'd never be able to check out a book again without remembering this moment.

Roman smiled. "Liana! So you decided to take me up on my invitation! Wonderful! Come in, please!"

"I don't want to interrupt anything —"

"Nonsense! Bethany and I were merely breaking in one of my new toys." He held up the paddle for Liana's inspection. "It's covered with the finest leather, but I don't think it delivers as satisfying a blow as plain old wood. Do you, Bethany?"

"No," she giggled. "But it certainly feels more decadent."

"I'll concede the point." He turned to Liana. "Would you like to give it a try?" He waggled the paddle for emphasis.

Liana thought of the feel of that rich leather striking her buttocks—the sting, the sound, the anticipation of the next blow, never knowing for sure when it was going to fall..." Maybe later."

The librarian crawled off the bed. "Speaking of later, that's when I'll see you, Roman. There's a young stud downstairs that does landscaping for the library. I've been dying for a chance to put him through his paces, and now that you've got my pump primed, so to speak—" she giggled—"I'm ready to make my move." She kissed Roman on the cheek, then gave Liana a wink. "Enjoy, darling." Then she flounced out of Roman's Empire in pursuit of her landscaping stud. Liana doubted the boy had a chance.

When she was gone, Roman closed the door. Liana noticed there wasn't a lock, and told him she was surprised, given the nature of what went on in here.

"There are no locks on any of the doors inside the house," he explained. "I want my guests to feel comfortable to come and go as they please. This way, people can join in with a group if they wish, or depart without anyone trying to force them to stay.

In my home, while we hope you'll say yes, it's quite all right to say no, and no hard feelings."

Such a considerate attitude didn't seem to fit a man who was supposed to be a strangler, but then again, Liana had met cold-blooded killers with impeccable manners before.

"Would you like me to give you the grand tour?" Roman asked.

Liana said yes, and he took her hand and led her to a polished cedar cabinet on the other side of the room. On the way, she noticed that there was a large round mirror over the bed; she wasn't surprised. Roman opened the cabinet and proceeded to show her enough "marital aids" to stock several sex stores. There were dildos of every shape, size and variety, along with vibrators, paddles, fur-lined handcuffs, whips, riding crops, masks and gloves (in both leather and rubber), dog leashes, nipple clamps, candles for wax dripping, enema equipment, and a pair of rubber pants with straws protruding from the knees. Liana did not want to know what those were for.

"Choose your poison," Roman said.

Liana frowned. That struck her as a strange—and sinister—turn of phrase. She could handle Roman if it came down to a physical confrontation, she was sure of that. Still, she couldn't help but feel a little creeped-out by what he'd said.

Liana had watched Roman closely the entire time he was going through his catalogue of toys. Not once did he show even a sign that he was getting hard. She decided that despite the increasingly strange vibe she was getting from Roman, it was time to take the bull by the balls. With a mental apology to Justin, she reached out and grabbed Roman's penis.

"I thought we could do it the old-fashioned way," Liana said in her huskiest, sexiest voice.

Roman gave her an apologetic smile and gently removed her hand. "I'm sorry, my dear, but I'm afraid the old boy's closed for business these days. An unfortunate after-effect of my prostate surgery. I can't complain, though; after all, it did save my life." He gestured to his toys. "And I still have these, and my parties. They aren't the same, but they're better than nothing."

Liana watched his face closely as he spoke, listened intently to his tone of voice. But she didn't detect any bitterness, any anger. He seemed perfectly well adjusted to his condition—at least, as well adjusted as any man could be.

And then it hit her. Of all the equipment in his cabinet o' fun, she hadn't see any ropes, any scarves. Nothing that could be used for bondage. Or for another specialized sexual technique.

"Actually, Roman, there is one thing I've always wanted to try, but I've never been able to work up the courage."

His eyes lit up. "Really? What is it?"

"I've always wanted to try breath control play." Otherwise known as erotic asphyxiation or asphyxiophilia. One partner suffocates or strangulates the other, bringing about a euphoria that intensifies orgasm. Breath control play is supposed to stop short of serious injury or death. Supposed to.

Roman's face went pale. "I...I don't do that. It's too dangerous." He closed the cabinet. "I beg your pardon, but I really should go downstairs and see how the rest of my guests are doing."

He turned and began to walk toward the door. Liana decided to take a chance.

"Tell me about Moira Pitner, Roman."

He didn't stop. "I don't know who you're talking about." He opened the door and stepped into the hall.

Liana followed. "Did it happen in here, Roman? In your little 'Empire'?"

Roman didn't answer; he reached the stairs and started down, Liana close behind.

"You've lived with Moira's death for six months, Roman. That's a long time for something to gnaw at a man's conscience."

Roman hesitated at the bottom of the stairs, his hand on the railing. Suddenly he turned, his face a mask of grief and anger.

Liana, on the stairs above him, tensed her body, ready in case Roman was going to lunge at her.

"What do you want me to say?" he shouted. His voice cracked on the last syllable and tears welled in his eyes.

"Just tell me the truth, Roman," Liana said softly. "That's all."

Roman looked at her for a long moment. People began to gather on the landing behind him, drawn no doubt by his raised voice. Liana saw Justin toward the back of the crowd; she also saw the masked brunette from the basement. It was strange, but the woman looked almost as if she were fighting to hold back a smile.

Something wasn't right. Liana caught Justin's eye and nodded toward the brunette. Justin nodded in return and starting making his way toward her through the naked revelers.

"Yes, I killed Moira Pitner," Roman said. He sounded small and defeated, his shoulders slumped and he showed every one of his fifty-five years. "It was an accident. After my surgery, when I realized that I couldn't achieve an erection anymore, I turned to playing sex games, the kinkier and more extreme, the better. But as my games became more dangerous, fewer women wanted to play with me. Not Moira, though. She was willing to try anything. During a party one night, she suggested we do erotic asphyxiation. I had never done it before, but it sounded so exotic, so on the edge, that I couldn't resist."

Tears were streaming down his face now, but he made no effort to wipe them away. He didn't even seem conscious of them.

"We used a satin rope and various toys...Moira's orgasm was intense, stronger than any she'd ever had with me before, but right after she came, she passed out. I tried to revive her, but I couldn't. I panicked and ran out of the playroom. One of my guests that night was a doctor. It took me a few minutes to track him down—the man was wearing a mask—but by the time we got back to the room, it was too late. Moira was dead."

Justin had almost reached the brunette. Her eyes glittered as she listened to Roman tell his story. Liana remembered what Justin had said about the woman seeming familiar . . .

"I paid the doctor off—" a sad smile—"I'm quite a wealthy man, you know, and then when the party was over and everyone was gone, I dressed Moira and took her downstairs to the garage. I put her in my car and drove off. I had some vague, ill-formed plan about taking her back to her apartment and putting her in bed. I suppose I hoped whoever found her would think she had died of natural causes." He gave a derisive bark of laughter. "Idiotic. Halfway to her place, I came to my senses. I knew no one would ever believe she had just died: there were marks on her neck from the rope, and a simple examination would show that she'd had sex that night, even if only with dildos and the like. I knew it was too late to go to the authorities. I had bribed the doctor to keep quiet about Moira's death, and I had removed her body from my house. I was scared that I would lose everything—my restaurant, my friends, my place in the community..." He shook his head. "It sounds so petty now, but that's how I felt then."

"So you drove to the woods and left Moira's body there," Liana said.

Roman nodded. "I hoped the police would think she was murdered by a serial killer or something, and they did."

Roman's guests began speaking at once. Some were clearly shocked and outraged; others were stunned and disbelieving. Justin stood directly behind the brunette now; he frowned as he closely examined her mask. The woman wasn't bothering to hide her smile now.

When Roman resumed speaking, the crowd quieted down. "I don't know how you found out," Roman said, "but in a way it's a relief." He looked at Liana and smiled weakly. "You were right; six months is a long time to live with something this horrible." He frowned then. "I really should be telling this to the authorities instead of you, shouldn't I?" Roman turned to the crowd behind him, and in an apologetic voice said, "Would someone please be so good as to call the police for me?"

No one moved. No one, that is, except Justin, who took this opportunity to yank the brunette's mask off her face, along with her brown wig.

Liana suddenly understood why the woman had seemed so familiar: it was Cecile Pitner. She wasn't wearing her glasses, and her blonde hair was pinned up, but it was unmistakably her.

"My God," Justin said. "I'm in an X-rated Scooby Doo cartoon!"

Instead of reacting with surprise or anger at being revealed, Cecile laughed delightedly.

"Is this the part where I say I would've gotten away with it if it wasn't for you darn kids?" She giggled.

Roman was clearly perplexed. "Cecile? What are you doing here?"

"What do you think? Watching you finally get yours, and I'm loving every minute of it! Why do you think these two—" she pointed to Justin, then to Liana "—are here? I hired them to expose you, you bastard!"

Liana was having trouble processing Cecile's sudden appearance, let alone the fact she was in attendance at one of Roman's parties. She hadn't come across to Liana as the type. "How did you know we would be here tonight?"

"I used to be a cook at Roman's restaurant, and I still have a few friends on the staff. One of them overheard Roman invite you and told me. I had to come, just on the off chance that you'd catch him tonight. I wore a mask and wig so none of you would recognize me. After all, I didn't want to mess up your investigation." She looked at Roman and smiled a snake's smile, sly and completely without warmth. "Having you do me downstairs and then having her—" she nodded at Liana "—question me without either of you knowing who I was...well, that was just icing on the cake, wasn't it?"

Cecile turned to Justin. "What are you waiting for? He's confessed; go call the cops."

Roman's other guests began to look nervous. A few started

sidling away from the crowd, no doubt headed in the direction of the nearest exit.

"I don't think we're quite ready for that just yet," Justin said. He glanced at Liana. "Are we, love?"

Liana shook her head. "No. Cecile's not exactly acting like a grief-stricken sister, is she?"

"Nor is she behaving as someone whose long-awaited quest for justice has finally ended."

Cecile frowned. "Why are you two talking about me like I'm not here? Don't do that!"

Liana came the rest of the way down the stairs and put her hand on Roman's shoulder. "When Liana hired us, she gave the impression that she knew nothing about your parties until her sister was invited to them. But that's not true, is it?"

"No, she was a regular," Roman said. "For a time. As she said, she was one of my cooks. A good one, too. In fact, I hired her sister as a server because Cecile asked me to."

"Funny," Justin said. "Cecile omitted telling us that." He turned to her. "Any particular reason? And please don't bat your eyes and say, 'I didn't think it was important.' You can do better than that."

Ceclie seemed amused. "I left out all sorts of things—about working for Roman, knowing he's impotent..." She looked at Liana. "Though I told you about that last part tonight, cutie. I like to play all sorts of games, not just the sexual kind. Besides, I figured the less you two knew about me, the better." She looked at them each in turn, then shrugged. "What the hell? Roman's confessed; why shouldn't I? If nothin, else, it'll make good theatre, right?

"It's true; I was once a regular at Roman's parties. But I wasn't just another slut in a mask looking to play naughty once or twice a month. I was his favorite. He spent more time with me than anyone else. Time alone. I was the one who helped him through his cancer, went with him to doctors' appointments, sat in the waiting room while he had surgery, nursed him at home." Her hands had balled into fists, and her jaw was clenched tight. "And then he throws me over for that little bitch, Moira.

"She was always a copycat, ever since we were kids. Everything I did, she wanted to do. Everything I had, she wanted to have. After I got the job at Roman's restaurant, she pestered me until I got her one too. And then she caught Roman's eye, and he invited her to one of his parties. When she saw I was special to Roman, she decided she wanted him, too. What was worse, he wanted her just as much. Before long, he forgot all about me. I wasn't special anymore, just another stupid whore.

"I decided to get even with both of them. Roman was into kinky stuff even before his operation, and after his dick stopped working, he got into it even more. Moira did anything he wanted, especially if she thought he and I had done it. Moira had a little secret, though. She had a heart condition. Nothing real serious, but she had to take medicine for it. So I researched sex toys and games on the Internet, hoping to find something that would be dangerous enough that it might set off Moira's heart. I came up with erotic asphyxiation. I told Moira that Roman really got off on it, that we'd done it lots of times. I knew she'd have to try it after that."

Roman stared at Cecile as if she'd suddenly sprouted horns and fangs.

"By that time, I'd stopped attending Roman's parties, but I made sure to come to the next." She gestured to the mask and wig Justin was still holding. "In disguise, of course. I watched and waited until Roman took Moira upstairs, and then I made sure to hang around the stairs so I could find out if my plan worked."

She grinned. "It wasn't that long before Roman came flying back down the stairs like someone had set his dick on fire. When he was gone, I couldn't resist; I hurried upstairs and went into his playroom to see if Moira was really dead." Cecile made a disgusted face. "She wasn't, though. As I walked in, the little bitch started to come to. She was still groggy, though, and the satin cord Roman and she had used was lying on the bed next to her..." Cecile smiled. "I decided to go ahead and finish what they'd started. When I was done, I got out of the room before Roman could come back with his doctor friend."

She looked up at Roman then, and it seemed to Liana that her face was more of a mask than what she had been wearing before—a cold, inhuman mask, better suited a for reptile than a woman. "You fool. All these months you thought you'd killed her, when it was me all along!"

Roman, trembling, sat down on the stairs and buried his face in his hands. Liana moved past him, walked up to Cecile and before the woman could react, hit her with a hard roundhouse right. Cecile's head snapped to the side, her eyes rolled white, and she fell to the wooden floor, her naked body making a loud SMACK! as she hit.

"What did you do that for?" Justin asked, not that he sounded terribly upset about it.

Liana shrugged. "Just because."

Justin nodded. "Good reason."

It was nearly three in the morning by the time the police finally took Cecile and Roman away and finished getting the Mallorys' statements. As it was, Liana and Justin would still have to show up at the station tomorrow and answer more questions, but at least they were able to go home.

As they got in their Accord, Liana thought that it felt strange to be wearing clothes again after spending so much time running around Roman's house naked.

Justin started the car and backed out of the driveway. When they were on the road heading home, he said, "Another case closed, eh, love?" He sounded tired; Liana knew just how he felt.

"Do you think Roman will have to go to jail?" she asked. "I mean, he wasn't responsible for Moira's death."

"Probably not, unless they decide to bust him for the drugs he was serving at the party. Even then, as Cecile pointed out, Roman has friends in town, so he might get off scot-free in the end."

"I hope so. He's a nice man, and he's been through a lot."

Justin frowned. "What exactly happened between you two in 'Roman's Empire'?"

Liana smiled. "A girl has to have some secrets, doesn't she?"

"I suppose." He reached over and put his hand on Liana's leg. He slid his fingers along her thigh, until her reached her crotch. He began gently massaging her vagina through the fabric of her slacks.

"You know," he said softly, "despite having attended our first orgy tonight, we didn't manage to complete a single sex act. Maybe when we get home..."

Liana reached out and lightly touched his cheek. "After everything that happened tonight, I think I'd rather just be held, you know?"

Justin smiled. "I understand, love." He withdrew his hand and placed his arm around her shoulder. Liana cuddled close to her husband and stayed there all the way home.

⊹⊱═◉═⊰⊹

Dying for It, *a novel featuring the private eye team of Justin & Liana, will be available on Valentine's Day, 2001.*

Who Killed Natalie?

Billie Sue Mosiman

Author of eight novels of suspense, nominee for both the Edgar and the Stoker Awards, and story author with over 150 stories in print, Billie Sue Mosiman lives in Southeast Texas on a ranch and is writing a big Texas vampire novel titled Red Moon Rising.

Jane Sloan had not yet dressed for the day. She sat at the dining room table in a red satin short-sleeved nightgown that came to mid-thigh. Dressed in red, her dark hair shining down her back, she made the entire room brighten and sparkle. Her husband, Jim, walked into the room after showering. Brushing thick black hair back from his forehead, he paused in the doorway assessing his wife's mood. Then he saw the typewriter.

Jane was struggling over the words she typed on the old portable Remington. "Is it that time again?" He expected he looked as resigned as he sounded.

Jane raised her head where she was hunched over the machine at the dining table and winced, a slight furrow forming between fine dark brows. "You know I have to do this, Jim."

"It's been four years. If a letter to the editor of the local newspaper was going to make the killer confess or bring out a witness, don't you think something would have happened by now?"

She lowered her hands from the typewriter, and Jim took the opportunity to pull up a chair next to her. He stared into her haunted eyes. They were a silvery blue, a color he'd never seen on any other woman or man. Every time he looked in them, he fell in love all over again.

But looking into those silvery blue depths now, he knew, as he'd known for the last four years, that she'd never let it go. Natalie's death was killing her. It was killing them. Their marriage had always been strong, but when Natalie had been murdered four years ago, the night after graduation, Jane fell into a million pieces. For months she was like a zombie, walking through the house touching things as if to remember their function and reason for being. She began to sleep in Natalie's room, on her bed, Natalie's favorite stuffed teddy bear held tightly in her arms. Jim lay alone in their queen-sized bed wondering when his wife would ever come back. After a few months she did return, but she seemed no more interested in Jim's touch than if he'd been a stranger lying at her side.

In the second year after their daughter had died, Jane suddenly announced one day that they needed Natalie's room for overnight guests. "We need to move everything out so I can redecorate."

Jim felt some relief at first, believing Jane was putting the past behind her, but once Natalie's furnishings, her clothes, all her personal items—except for the teddy bear—were gone, Jane fell into an even deeper slump.

"I miss her bed," she would say, and wander off to the newly furnished guest room to stare at the new sleigh bed they'd installed there. Or she'd turn to Jim while watching television at night after dinner and say, "What did we do with Natalie's notebooks from her senior year?" He would have to remind her they disposed of them along with the old dolls, the Tony Lama cowboy boots, and the hair barrettes.

Then Jane decided to write a letter to the editor. Now it was the anniversary of Natalie's death, and again Jane was writing a heart-wrenching recital of her daughter's unsolved murder to the newspaper. She might say it in different words, but the story was the same. A teen party. The murder. The burned Camaro. The lack of a suspect.

Jim was the Sheriff of Matagorda County, Texas, and he hadn't been able to find enough evidence to indict anyone in his own daughter's murder. The letters were a rebuke not only to the murderer who walked free, but to the county that had investigated the murder and come up with zip. And most of all, it was a reminder to Jim of his ultimate failure.

The whole thing was killing them. Some days, Jim thought the loss was going to kill him first.

"You have to do this, don't you?" he asked now, putting his head close to hers at the table and an arm around her shoulders.

"You know I do, Jim."

"I keep searching for something," he said in his own defense.

"I know. I know that, honey. I just can't not do this." She lifted her fingers to the typewriter and began to type. "I know he's out there. Her killer."

Jim sat nearby, helpless, and his mind began to wander. The strangest thing happened to him when he was near his wife, smelling her slightly sweet floral cologne, feeling the warm heat radiating from her body, listening to her breath as she breathed. He was always inundated with sexual thoughts. How he wanted her, now, at this moment. How she aroused him with nothing more than a glance. How he ached for her like he had never

ached for another woman. He could try to wipe his mind clear
and think of innocuous subjects, but when near Jane his mind
turned to sex. It wasn't just that he wasn't getting enough. It
was because being near her always aroused him, always, always.

She could pass by him where he sat on the sofa, and he
wanted to reach out and stay her, slipping a hand beneath her
skirt to feel the warm depression between her legs. She could lie
down in bed at night with him, and if she made no indication
she was interested in sex, he would lie awake in torment. Finally
he would rise stealthily when he thought her safely asleep, go to
the bathroom and, in the dark, with moonshine shimmering
through the window over the tub, he would relieve himself by
thinking of her and masturbating. He never needed a dream
woman or a *Playboy* centerfold, since he could fantasize about
the woman he loved.

He fantasized about their years of sex, sometimes finding a
very old sexual memory popping to the fore, and sometimes a
memory of more recent vintage. He'd close his eyes, a cool night
breeze wafting through the open bathroom window, bringing with
it the scent of night-blooming jasmine planted at the back of the
house. He'd wait, his hand on his member, stroking himself carefully, slowly, and the memory would surface. Like the time he
and Jane went camping with her brother. Their own tent was
placed close to her brother's tent, so Jane, not long married, was
reticent about having intercourse as her brother might hear them.
Jim had a brainstorm. He was very hard. He had to find a way.
"Let's go out in the woods. Let's get off by ourselves, Jane."

She fell into the adventuresome mood instantly, grabbing for
her sandals and the flashlight. "No," he said, taking the light
from her. "In the dark. So no one will know we're out there."

They wandered down a path of leaves sodden with night
dew, listening and flinching when an owl hooted, giggling like
children, holding hands. He was searching for a clearing, a spot
with soft grass where he could lay her down and get his hands
on her breasts, her hips. But the woods crowded the path and
it seemed to go on forever, mostly inky darkness with some

spots of star shine dappling down over their shoulders. Finally, unable to hold back his lust any longer, Jim turned to her and pulled her to him roughly, his hands sliding under the back of her pink babydoll pajamas.

"Here?" she asked, startled.

"No," he said, walking her backward and to the side of the path, right up against a tree so big around it was like a wall. "Here."

He tore the elastic on her pajama panties and let them drop around her ankles. She laughed up into his face, and in the low light her eyes were like silver medallions. He thought he was about to make love to a forest nymph or some angelic being who had replaced his wife.

"Oh, Jane," he whispered.

He lifted one of her legs, placing it just above his own hip, and inserted himself. Neither of them felt the roughness of the tree bark, the damp of the ground or the occasional drip of dew from low-hanging leaves. They felt nothing but one another, moving in perfect rhythm. Jim was transported into a place that was not earth, but a world of pure sensation. He couldn't get enough of her. He rocked against her body, pushing her against the tree, holding fast to her buttocks to keep her steady. He thought she might have called his name in ecstasy, but he was lost in his own warm, building, blinding moment of release and he was coming...

...coming into a towel in the bathroom, wishing it weren't so, wishing she had wanted him tonight. He leaned back against the sink edge and waited for his breathing to slow. *Jane,* he thought, *what's happened to us? How did a monster invade our lives and take our child and leave us alone this way? Who let that happen?*

Now, he sat by her at the dining table, the typewriter keys clacking away in his numb brain, and instead of thinking of his failure as a detective to solve his own daughter's untimely demise, all he could think about was how he might maneuver Jane back to the bedroom. He thought of the soft curve of his wife's breast beneath the red satin as it pressed against the table edge, the sheen of her shoulder-length dark brown hair, and how she felt beneath him when he pushed into her. He thought he would die if she didn't return to herself and love him again.

He rose abruptly from the table, took his hat, and said, "I have to get to the office."

"Okay," she said. "I'll see you tonight."

See me and not really see me, he thought. The way she loved him without loving him. For he did know she loved him. She'd simply lost herself in a maze of sorrow so convoluted she couldn't find a path back to him.

On his way to the small town police station, Jim decided the anniversary of his daughter's death was as good a time as any to re-question the kids who had been at the party. He'd hound them, year after year, until he got a shred of a clue about what happened. He had to. His marriage—no, his whole future— depended on finding a resolution.

He picked up the car radio and called in to Sheryl, the dispatcher, telling her he'd be in late this morning. In fact, he said, modifying his arrival time, he might not be in until after lunch.

This would be the fourth time he had interrogated Ralph Bandy. It was Bandy who had called in the first report of something burning on Shepherd Road. "It's like a freaking bonfire," he had said on the dispatcher's tape. "Something bad's happened."

Bad, indeed. One of Jim's deputies took the call and went out to Shepherd to see about the problem. Jim was at home that night with Jane. Natalie, of course, was out, attending a graduation party four miles from Shepherd Road in a woodsy clearing off Ringling Lane. It was to be a big blowout. Six of the graduating class's brightest students, all of them, except Natalie, from the wealthiest families in town, had taken six packs of beer in coolers, a few joints of marijuana, and a quart of Jim Beam down to the clearing. Natalie had been invited because she was quite a popular girl at school. She wasn't rich, but she was beautiful. They needed her around to make the whole picture of perfection complete. She'd been with the in-crowd since elementary school.

If Jim had known there was going to be drinking and drugs, he never would have allowed it, but who would have told him that? He suspected Natalie didn't even know until she got there.

Tad Kerritt, the deputy, drove down Shepherd Road that night and came on the smoldering wreckage of a sports car. It sat in the center of the dirt lane, burned right down to the wheels, a skeleton of a car, melted and stinking. He called for a wrecker and had it hauled. He didn't check over the car carefully. No one did. They all thought it had caught fire and been abandoned.

Until Jim and Jane didn't hear from Natalie. Until the next morning when Tad mentioned the burned car looked kind of like a Camaro.

Jim turned white and sat down heavily in his chair in the sheriff's office. Then he stood shakily and drove to the impound lot. He was chain-smoking and trembling so badly he could hardly hold onto the wheel of the car. He had recognized the burned hulk of his daughter's car at once. And in the back of the wreckage, behind what would have been the back seat, the crumpled and blackened body. He felt his world come apart, flying off into space. Nothing would ever be right again.

Natalie was identified by two rings she wore that her mother had given her and by her dental records. It was Natalie all right. No one knew what happened. It wasn't a wreck. She didn't crawl into the space behind the rear seat of her own volition. All they knew for certain was that the death was a homicide.

Jim questioned the kids. Natalie had left alone, they said. They knew nothing about the fire, they said, and some of them cried, and some of them couldn't meet his eyes. Then he called in the Texas Rangers. They sent specimens from the car to Austin, and it was determined a highly volatile fuel was poured over the vehicle and set fire. Searching the surrounding area where the car had been found on Shepherd, Jim discovered a pipeline where a key lock had been broken and fuel siphoned off. Someone had stolen gasoline from the pipeline, deliberately poured it over Natalie's Camaro, and that person had killed her. It appeared Natalie had either been dead or unconscious when the fire was set. Other than that, there wasn't enough left to tell them anything.

His Natalie. His bright beautiful child. Only a few bones and teeth left and two melted gold rings.

"How're you doing today, Bandy?" Jim said, moving onto the porch of the old man's place. He lived a half mile from Shepherd Road and had seen the fire in the distance.

Bandy came out onto the porch from the cool interior and sat in a porch rocker. "I'm fine, Jim, how're you?"

"Fine as pig's feet."

"That's fine indeed." Bandy spit tobacco juice into the wild grass growing near the porch steps.

"I was wondering about something, Bandy..."

"Yeah?"

"Yeah. That night. The fire. What were you doing up that late anyway?"

"What time was it?"

"Past midnight. Close to one in the morning according to the time of your call to the station."

"It's been four years, Jim."

"I know. And Natalie's still gone."

Bandy nodded his head, understanding. He frowned, thinking back. "You probably asked me this before, but seems neither of us can remember it. I believe I had a stomach upset that night," he said.

"What from?"

"Beans? I ate some beans for supper that night, I remember. Always tears up my stomach. I was up getting some Pepto and saw a light out the window in the distance. Stepped out here on the porch..." He pointed across the land toward the road. "...saw it was some kind of fire. A big one."

"You see any headlights out there?"

"Nope. Not saying there weren't none. I just didn't see any. All I saw was that big damn flaming fire."

"You go out there after you called in?"

"Nope, my stomach cramped me too bad. I sat right here in the rocker, waiting for somebody to come see about it so the whole woods wouldn't catch fire."

"So you saw Deputy Kerritt's headlights when he got here?"

Bandy seemed to think it over. "I guess so."

"Why do you guess?"

"Cause I got a calm feeling and saw the fire dying down and I went on inside to bed."

Jim moved down the steps. He never got anything new or any insight. He might ask questions ten different ways and none of it gave him a clue to follow. "Well, sorry to bother you again, guess I'll be going."

"You come around this time every year. I'm getting used to it."

"Do I? I came out here last year?"

"Yessir, you did. May. Graduation time."

Jim nodded, admitting to his obsession, and went to the car. He felt Bandy watching his back. He had to think him crazy. In some ways, Jim admitted to himself, he was that too.

The next person Jim wanted to question again was Brad Folsworth. His father owned the largest car dealership in town, and it had been Brad's idea to hold the party in the woods that night.

He found Brad at his father's dealership in the finance office, having coffee with the manager there.

"Talk to you a minute?" Jim asked, hooking his thumb at Brad.

Brad cast an aggrieved look at his finance manager and stood, placing the coffee cup on the other man's desk. He followed Jim down the hall to the customer waiting room. It was empty.

"How old are you now, Brad?"

"Sir?"

"Nearly twenty-three?"

Brad nodded.

"And you're the vice president of Folsworth Motors, thanks to your dad, right?"

"There a law against that?"

"You know what, I don't think I ever liked you," Jim said, his tone stern now.

Brad shrugged. He said, "Look, is this like last year? This about Natalie?"

"It will always be about Natalie."

Brad stuffed both hands into the pockets of his expensive gray slacks. "I don't know anything else! I've told you a million times."

"It was your idea, the party."

"Yes, yes, you know it was. We were kids, Sheriff. We wanted to celebrate."

"And who wanted to kill Natalie?"

"I don't know!"

"Brad, someone killed my daughter. I'm going to find out who. If it was you, I'll find it out. Sooner or later, if not this year, next year. Five years from now. Seven. But I'll find out."

"Jesus Christ, this is worse than harassment. You think I did something, prove it, okay? Otherwise this is getting monotonous. Every May you do this."

"Every May is another May the killer is loose."

"Look, we didn't do it, Sheriff, I swear to God. We've told you and told you. She left early. She'd had a couple beers. I don't know what happened down that road when she was leaving. We never even knew about it until the next day. The rest of us turned down the other way, on Walker Road, to head back home."

"Anyone leave with her, anyone from the party?"

"No. She left alone. I told you that."

"Was she with anyone at the party then? A boy?"

"Oh, her and Josh Handlin were talking and stuff, drinking, you know, but he didn't leave with her. He was with us."

"You think of anything new, call me." Jim turned on his heel and left the dealership. He thought Brad a very spoiled rich boy who wasn't worth the powder to blow him away, but he couldn't see him as a killer.

Josh Handlin worked the car wash. He had never gone to college like the rest of the others who had been at the party. His family, once wealthy, had lost all their money when Josh's father invested in some bad stocks. Before Natalie was dead half a year, Josh was knocking around town looking for work.

Josh sat in a little office and made change for car wash customers who either used the drive-through automated wash or the stalls for washing their cars themselves. For this he was paid below minimum wage and given Sundays off. It seemed to Jim that Josh lacked all initiative. He didn't seem to care what he did with his life.

"You again," Josh said, seeing him come through the office door.

"Me again."

"It's May," Josh said.

"It's May. Kids are graduating. Like you did four years ago. Going to be the oldest car wash attendant in the county, aren't you?"

"That's not nice, Sheriff."

"I don't feel nice. My wife's at home writing her annual letter to the newspaper and about now she's crying while she seals the envelope. My daughter is still dead. Her murder's still unsolved. I don't feel nice at all."

Josh turned up the palms of both hands. "I can't help you. I didn't do it. None of the kids at the party did it. It was someone else. Maybe a stranger."

"A stranger on Shepherd Road? No one goes down there unless he's heading for the clearing."

"Maybe the stranger was lost."

"And came upon my daughter in her Camaro and flagged her down."

"I don't know! Maybe."

"Then he disappeared."

"I guess so."

"He had no motive. He didn't rape her or steal anything. He just killed her and set the car on fire." Jim stated all these supposed facts in a dull voice. It made no sense, and he knew Josh knew it.

Josh put his head down on his arms on the desk. Jim noticed he'd been doodling on a pad of paper. He picked it up and his heart began to race.

"You've been writing Natalie's name." He held the pad up to Josh. "Why?"

"I can't get her out of my head."

"Why is that, Josh?"

He raised his head and his eyes looked like Jane's—haunted. "I don't know. Every year when May comes I get a prickly feeling and I can't stop thinking about her. That night we...we talked."

"Tell me what you talked about." Jim took a seat in a plastic vinyl chair across from the desk.

"She was happy, laughing, but she was a little pensive too..."

"Pensive? Isn't that like a college word?"

"Do you ever give anyone a break?" Josh asked, anger inflaming his cheeks.

"Okay, forget I said that. Go on."

"She was talking about going to college, but she said that for a while she'd have to put it off. She said...she said she was leaving town in a few days."

"Leaving?" Jim felt his heart do a flip. "She didn't like the town?"

"Hated it. That surprise you? Most of us hated it. We all wanted to get out and most of us knew we wouldn't—or we'd be back."

"But Natalie had plans? And you never thought to mention this to me before? Not in four years?"

"Yeah. Plans. Listen, is this important? I didn't think it was important or I would have told you. It's only lately I think about our conversation back then. I hear the sadness in her voice when she's telling me she's going to leave town. She's going to put off college for a while."

"These plans have to do with you?"

"Hell, no! I only wish. She was just a friend. She never knew that I...I..."

"What, Josh? Say it."

"I was in love with her."

"In love enough you'd do anything to keep her from leaving?"

"Oh God." Josh dropped his head to his arms again. In a muffled voice he said, "I never would have hurt her. I loved her, don't you understand? I loved her."

"Okay, then who might have hurt her, Josh?"

"I don't know."

"If you could take a wild guess, even if it's way off the mark, who would you accuse—off the record, of course. Help me, Josh. Help me find her killer."

Josh raised his head again, and there were tears on his cheeks. "I just don't think anyone at the party did it. But a couple left right after her. Brad. Then Cathy, in her own car. They both left a couple minutes after Natalie."

"They told me that before. But they said it was maybe fifteen-twenty minutes later."

Josh shook his head. "Not that long."

Jim sat for a few seconds and then he left the office. He sat in his cruiser a minute, running the air conditioner. Josh had never admitted he'd loved Natalie before. What could it mean? And he'd never known his daughter had been so unhappy she wanted to leave town. But most of all, what had she been talking about when she told Josh she had to put off college? Why would she have to do that? This seemed as deep a mystery to him as her murder.

He couldn't believe Josh had killed her, but why hadn't he ever said he'd loved her before now? He was someone who had kept a secret for four years. He had married a girl who worked at the Burger King, and they had a baby on the way now. And still, he couldn't get Natalie out of his mind and admitted that he'd loved her more than anything.

Why hadn't Josh told him the truth before about Brad and Cathy leaving so soon after Natalie? He tried to remember if he'd ever asked the question in a way he might have gotten that kind of answer, but couldn't think. He'd asked so many questions. None of them led him anywhere but to hell and back.

Cathy Pimpkin lived in a mansion in the best residential district. She'd gotten a degree from A & M in liberal arts and came home to write romance novels. She'd inherited the mansion and all the money to go with it in her freshman year, when both her parents were killed in an airplane crash over Denver.

She'd never married. Jim didn't know if her novels were published or not. People just said she "wrote." She had become a recluse and hardly left the mansion except to grocery shop.

He knocked on her door and waited while two little poodles barked at the leaded-glass door. She came finally, dressed in yellow slacks and a white tank top, her hair piled high on her head. She was gorgeous. That was the only word for her. Slim, yet curvy in all the right places, almond shaped dark eyes, lips that were full and sensual. Jim wondered how she'd be in bed and immediately chastised himself. She was just twenty-three or so. She was his daughter's age.

"Hello? Can I help you, Sheriff?"

He hadn't talked to her last year, he remembered now. He'd stopped short of speaking to her after questioning several of the others. He'd been so depressed he just couldn't go to see the last two names on the list.

"Can I come in for a minute?" he asked, taking off his gray felt hat and holding it in front of him to cover the start of an erection he couldn't seem to control with willpower.

"Sure." She stepped aside and ushered him into a marble entrance. "I was working. I'll have Barb bring coffee to my office if you want."

"That would be nice." He hadn't had a shot of caffeine since leaving home. He studied her office as he was led into it. A large L-shaped mahogany desk sat in the corner, bookshelves climbed to the ceiling on all the other walls, books overflowing them onto the floor. Vases of flowers graced the desk and two small tables. There was a computer with a monitor the size of a picture window, and on the screen he could see sentences.

She sat in the desk chair and swiveled around to face him. He perched on an easy chair covered in shiny pink material. Cathy pushed a button on an intercom on her desk and said, "Barb, coffee please, for the Sheriff."

There was a squawk from the box that Jim expected was the servant affirming her mistress's request.

"It's graduation time," Cathy said. "It's about Natalie again?"

Jim caught himself staring at Cathy's breasts. They were held snug in the white tank top and he could see the impressions of large dark nipples. Her skin showing between the top and yellow slacks was tanned and smooth. He forced his gaze away to the bookshelves.

"Yes, Natalie. Josh told me you left the party that night soon after my daughter. Brad left. Then you."

"A few minutes later, yes. But both Brad and I took Walker Road home. I saw his rear lights ahead of me."

"And neither of you saw the fire?"

"No. We would have, if there'd been one. Shepherd Road isn't that far away. But we didn't."

"How's the writing going?" he asked, changing subjects, putting her off guard. She seemed too studied to him, everything too pat. But God, she was gorgeous.

Surprise showed in her dark eyes for a moment, and then she recovered. "It's going okay. I'm working on my third novel."

"You've been published?"

"Sure. Two others. One came out when I was at A & M."

"Hey, that's impressive. You're pretty young to be a celebrated author."

She laughed, throwing her head back, and he thought about the lovely lines of her throat, the cleavage between her breasts, how long her legs were, how tan and smooth and...

"I wouldn't say I was celebrated." She rubbed at her eyes, still smiling. "I just write romances, Sheriff. It's something to fill my time. There are about a zillion romances coming out every month. It's popcorn. It's candy. I'm a candy-peddler."

"Really?" He now looked for the first time at the wall above her desk and saw two framed book covers. "Those your books? You don't use your name?"

She glanced back and nodded. "Not many of us use our real names." When she returned her gaze to him, she had the tip of her little finger in her mouth and was looking at him beneath long lashes in a sultry manner.

He sat still for several seconds, trying to read the message. Was she coming on to him? A man twice her age, a man who could be her father? Again he felt blood rush to his groin and he began to grow. He shifted his hat on his lap, uncomfortable. Goddamn her. She knew he was attracted and she was playing him.

Barb entered the room with a silver tray and set it on one of the tables near the center of the large office. She poured two cups of steaming coffee, smiled at Jim, and retreated without having said a word.

Cathy rose and handed him a cup. He took it, mumbling his thanks. He gulped at the coffee, burning his tongue, trying to wrench his mind off sex. He felt like a traitor to his wife. He'd never cheated on her, even these last years when she hadn't been as willing a bed partner as he would have liked. She'd suffered enough hurt; he wouldn't add to it.

He sat the cup down on the edge of Cathy's desk and when he turned back he saw Cathy still stood nearby, her hands empty. He glanced up at her and his gaze lingered on her breasts a half-second too long. He wanted to kick himself.

Cathy took his look as an invitation. She came closer. Jim put both his hands on her waist, holding her off. Another two inches and her breasts would be in his face and he didn't think he could resist smothering himself between them. He pushed her a little, and she stepped back. He dropped his hands.

"You're a handsome older man, Sheriff. Anyone ever tell you that?" Her look was coquettish and alluring. She smelled of baby powder. He looked away then he stood. His hat hung at his side now, his desire dwindling rapidly. "Cathy, who killed Natalie?"

She turned her back and went to the desk chair, sitting again. She wouldn't meet his eyes.

"Look at me. Who killed Natalie?"

"What makes you think I know anything about it? I've told you I don't know."

"The come-on was a diversion, wasn't it? You don't like my questions, do you Cathy? You know something."

"I know nothing. I write romances. I get carried away with my own imagination, looking for my white knight, so I gave you a flirt. I'm a foolish girl, is that what you want to hear? Well, I've said it."

Jim didn't think so. He thought Cathy was probably the most intelligent woman in town, and she knew exactly what she was doing every minute of every day.

When he left the mansion, he drove to the bookstore. He found her novels under the name Kaitland Katerra, which he thought a silly nom de plume.

They carried both her novels in stock, simply because she was a local author, he supposed. He bought both and drove to the station. Until lunchtime, he read her first novel. It was truly terrible. There was an annoying ranch owner who raised prize stallions. A woman came to town to be the veterinarian. She didn't like the rancher. Then later on she loved the rancher. He had a secret past. She helped him work it out, and he began to love her back. They got married.

By the time Jim had eaten a burger at the local pharmacy counter, he closed the short novel and sighed. *What a crock of shit,* he thought. She was right. Popcorn. Mind candy. It didn't seem to fit the intelligence of the woman he'd interviewed that morning. What could she possibly be doing writing things like this, he wondered? She was definitely an enigma.

Back in his office, he wrote up the duty roster, called back a couple of people with complaints, and finally began the second novel.

Within the first chapter he was hooked.

This novel was very much like the first one except for the details. And the details made him sit straight up in his chair, his brow furrowing in concentration as he read. The hero wasn't a rancher, he was a detective. The villain was the successful owner of a car dealership who had gotten a high school girl pregnant during a brief affair. The heroine was the detective's sidekick, a lowly patrol officer in love with him. Together they solved crimes.

Pregnant high school girl who comes up dead.

The car dealership owner is the culprit.

He goes to jail, and the detective marries the patrol officer. End of story.

It was five P.M. when Jim closed the book's last pages. He sat back in his chair sweating. There was a look of permanent horror etched on his face. If his dispatcher had stepped into the office, she would have thought he was having a coronary and called for help.

He pushed the little paperback away from him with the tips of his fingers as if it were a deadly snake that might bite him. His heart was thudding in his chest in a slow, painful rhythm. From the trash, he fished out a McDonald's hamburger paper bag and pushed both novels into it.

Cathy knew the truth. She'd written about it, doctored it up with fiction, and put it into print. What had kept her quiet so long?

Jim picked up the phone and called the judge. "I want a court order to check bank records of two people," he said.

Within an hour he was down at the town's only bank going through computer printouts on Don Folsworth and Catherine Pimpkin. Just as he suspected, once a year, in May, Cathy made a huge deposit to her account of two hundred thousand dollars. She didn't earn that from romances. Even he knew that. Folsworth's personal account was debited two hundred thousand every May. For four years.

It all figured. Don Folsworth, Brad's father, had gotten Jim's daughter pregnant. It made Jim want to weep and gnash his teeth.

That was why Natalie mentioned she was leaving town after graduation, the reason why she was putting off college. Cathy knew about the pregnancy. Natalie might have confided in her, asked for advice. Maybe Natalie was going to keep the baby. Maybe she was never coming back to town. Maybe Folsworth couldn't take the chance she'd come back. He'd be ruined in town. His marriage would dissolve, his business would go in the dumpster, his reputation soiled forever.

So he killed Natalie.

One day, soon after the murder, Cathy Pimpkin must have gone to him with what she knew. He paid her off, year after year.

One thing Jim couldn't figure. Why did she need the money? She'd inherited everything. The big house. The money. Or was there any money?

Early the next day Jim contacted the Pimpkin attorney, and with another court order from the judge, he'd had Cathy's parents' will released to him. Except for the house, they were destitute when they died. The family fortune had petered out. They'd even cashed in their life insurance policies. And then they'd died in an unfortunate accident, leaving their only child broke to the bone.

It all fell together.

That night Jim didn't sleep. He'd gotten up as soon as his wife was asleep and sat at the kitchen table drinking coffee and smoking cigarettes. He had Cathy Pimpkin's books before him, their lurid covers shouting at him every time he looked at them. She was intelligent, all right, and cold-blooded, but she took one too many chances. She never thought people in her little town would read the books. After all, they were Texas ranchers and farmers. Who read? And even if they read them, who would really put it together? But what infuriated Jim the most was how she'd used his daughter for a plot mechanism. She was beyond cold-blooded. She was as evil as Don Folsworth, a murderer who thought he'd gotten away clean.

And now they'd both go down because she hadn't depended on her imagination quite enough. She'd dipped into reality and used it for a popcorn romance.

Now Jane could stop writing letters to the editor.

Natalie could sleep peacefully, her killer found and punished. Though the evidence was circumstantial, he'd make sure the DA would make it convincing to a local jury. Cathy might even confess her part in it. One way or another, Natalie's killer was going to pay.

When daylight broke through the kitchen windows, Jane wandered in sleepy-eyed and found him at the table. He was haggard, but there was a spark of triumph in his eyes.

"What are you doing up?" she asked, coming to him immediately and taking his head to press against her chest.

He nuzzled the fullness of her left breast, leaned back his head, and smiled a weary smile.

"I found the killer," he said. "I found him, finally."

Jane's legs turned to jelly, and he had to support her. He stood up, taking her into his arms.

"Is it true? You've found him?" Tears stood in her eyes.

"Yes, my darling. It's almost over. We'll prove him guilty, and he'll pay."

"Oh, Jim, oh God, I can't believe it."

"I'm going to arrest him this morning. Believe it. Listen to the radio, it'll be on the news."

"Who is it? Why did he do it, for God's sake, why?"

"Don't worry about all that. He's caught. That's the important thing, remember that."

On the way into town Jim called into Sheryl and said, "Send Tad over to Folsworth Motors. I'll meet him there at nine."

In the dealership's shiny show room, Jim stood around smoking and looking at a new Cadillac SUV. *Jesus,* he thought, *either you want a Caddy or you want a big bush-hog vehicle to run in the woods and through the mud holes. Who the hell would want both in one and pay a hundred grand for the privilege?* He consulted his watch, saw it was 8:30.

A salesman approached cautiously. Jim waved him away. "I'm not shopping. I'm waiting for your boss."

"Brad?"

Jim frowned at him as if he were stupid. "Mr. Folsworth. The freaking owner of this place."

"Oh! Well, he should be in soon. I'll tell him you're waiting."

"Do that." Jim walked to the glass door and threw out his cigarette butt. Probably he wasn't supposed to smoke inside the dealership, but he'd like to see one of the little pipsqueaks stop him.

Folsworth was fifty-four years old, but he could pass for forty. He kept in shape, Jim supposed, with some kind of exercise machine. He had muscles a man much younger than forty might admire. His hair was blonde, no gray in it at all, and cut short, almost a military burr cut. Jim could imagine what his young daughter had seen in the man and had to admit there was a sexual charisma about him that nearly consumed you as you got closer. But his eyes were green and mean. He hadn't built a huge dealership, biggest in the county, by being a softhearted grunt with sex appeal.

"Sheriff!" Folsworth's greeting was animated and fake-friendly.

"Folsworth. I need a few minutes of your time."

"Absolutely. Come to my office."

Once they were inside in the luxurious office, the door closed, Jim touched Folsworth on the arm before he could make for the desk and get behind it to the large gray velvet chair there. "Hold up."

"What's going on?"

"You have the right to remain silent..."

"What?"

"You have the right to an attorney..."

"Jim, what's this about, man?"

"If you cannot afford an attorney... Shit! You can afford an attorney, Folsworth. You can afford young girls. Two hundred thousand dollar annual payoffs. You can afford any damn thing you please, can't you?"

Folsworth fell back from Jim's touch. His face had blanched and he seemed to be holding his breath. There was a look in his green eyes that reminded Jim of a scared rabbit.

"I don't know what the hell you're talking about."

Jim wagged his head and finger at the same time. "No, no, no. That's not the right response. You're supposed to tell me how a man like you could hurt a little girl like Natalie. That's what you're supposed to do."

Jim pulled back his coat jacket and rested his hand on the gun in the holster there. He didn't give a rat's ass if he was intimidating the suspect. If he got one more ounce of back talk from Folsworth he thought he might pull the revolver and shoot the bastard dead.

"Don't go pulling a gun on me, Jim. I've got enough money to have you sent to prison for a good long time if you try something."

Jim pulled the gun. He'd hoped not to. The gun in his hands felt too good. It felt like four years worth of pain and endless lonely nights. It felt like it wanted to blow good and hard. It felt like it had Natalie's name imprinted on it.

"You don't want me to pull my gun? What would you say if I said I might shoot off this son of a bitch right in your lying-ass, lowdown, evil, murdering face? What would your attorney have to say to that, Folsworth? What would your money do for you then?"

"You wouldn't do that." But the man was shaking now, his hands flipping about in the air, gesturing at nothing.

"Why'd you do it? She was leaving town. She wouldn't have told. You didn't have to kill her."

Jim was in his face now, pressing the business end of the gun barrel hard against Folsworth's cheekbone. He had him by the lapels. He towered over him four inches, and if this wasn't intimation, by god, he didn't know what the word meant.

Folsworth stuttered, "She wanted to keep it. She couldn't keep it!"

"Oh. My. God." Jim let him go and twirled around, the gun aimed high in the air. All the blood left his face and he thought he might pop a vein in his head or break off his molars he was grinding his teeth so hard.

"Look, Jim, I didn't mean to..."

Jim totally lost it. He came around and swung the gun with enough power to down an elephant. Folsworth hit the floor so hard the gold plaque awards on the wall shook and threatened to fall.

Jim stood over him. He hadn't knocked him out. He sort of wished he had.

"You didn't MEAN to get a teenager pregnant. You didn't MEAN to break the seal on the pipeline and haul gasoline over to the Camaro. You didn't MEAN to burn her alive!"

"She wasn't alive," Folsworth whimpered, wiping blood from the corner of his mouth.

The door banged open, and Tad Kerritt came into the room, his revolver drawn. "What's the ruckus, Sheriff?"

Jim thanked his lucky stars Tad had showed up on time. If he'd been about ten minutes late Jim believed Folsworth would have been ready for the coroner.

"Get this fuck out of here. Cuff the bastard. I want his people here, especially his son, to see him humiliated."

"What's the charge, Jim?" Tad asked, confused and stunned at the scene of one of the most powerful men in town lying on the carpeted floor, bleeding like a gutted deer.

"Murder. The charge is murder. When you get him to the station and in the cell, go pick up Catherine Pimpkin. Use the cuffs on her, too. She's being charged as an accessory."

Jim stomped from the dealership slinging open doors, glaring at employees who stood around gawking, and shaking a cigarette from the bent package in his shirt pocket.

He lit up just outside the door and stood still a moment, letting the sweat dry from his forehead. He'd almost killed Folsworth.

To hell with that. Let the state of Texas kill him. They were real good at it.

In his office, he called the DA and gave him the details. "God almighty, it was Folsworth?" the DA shouted.

"You got that right." Jim hung up after the call and walked out to Sheryl. "I'm taking off the rest of the day. Think you can handle it?"

"Sure, Jim." She'd heard the news. She knew what a victory it was. She was smiling from ear to ear.

Heading up the walk to his home in the middle of the morning felt extremely odd. He almost wanted to knock at his own door to keep from frightening Jane.

Instead, he opened the door carefully and found her standing, waiting. She hadn't dressed yet. She was still in her favorite sleeping attire, the red satin nightshirt.

"You hear yet?" he asked.

"Folsworth."

"Yes."

"He'll get high-priced legal help."

"Let him hire the goddamn pope, it won't matter. He's fried."

"And Cathy. She was Natalie's friend."

"Yeah, wasn't she?"

Jane came into his arms and laid her head on his shoulder. He threw his hat across the room to the sofa. He eased out of his jacket and then, stepping back a little, got the holster off. He began to unbutton his shirt.

Jane watched him. She'd been crying, but he knew it wasn't like before. These were tears of closure. It would take a while, but she'd get over it now.

"I knew you'd come home," she said, smiling just a little.

"You know me too well."

"You've never stopped loving me, have you, Jim?"

"Absolutely not."

"I don't know why you stayed. I just couldn't help myself. I couldn't..."

He had his shirt off and pulled her against his bare chest. "Hush. I know you couldn't."

"And you still loved me." She was crying now.

"Oh yes, always." He leaned down and licked the tears off her cheeks. He lifted her into his arms and carried her to the bedroom to the unmade bed. She'd showered while he was gone and put on the floral cologne. He almost swooned as he pressed his face down into the crevice of her neck. He put her down and pulled the blinds closed. By the time he had his pants and boots off, she was disrobed and lying in the center of the mattress, holding out her arms for him.

"We haven't made love in the morning in a long time," she said.

"It's time we started."

He crawled into the bed beside her, pulling her into his embrace. He was already hard and needing her so much he thought he was going to die.

She took one of his hands and guided his fingers until one of them was inside her. She sighed against his chest.

"Do you remember that time we camped out with your brother on Lake Livingston?" he asked, thinking of the dark woods and the hot sex they'd shared.

"I remember."

He kept moving his hand until he felt her tremble and come against his palm. She kissed his cheeks, his nose, and finally, his lips. "I remember all the times, Jim. I remember the night we made Natalie. I remember the vacation in the Montana mountains. I remember we always loved each other enough to overcome anything. It's my fault you've been alone and needing..."

"Hush," he said again, taking his fingers from her and putting them against her lips. God, he loved the scent of her. He moved on top and slipped effortlessly inside. He caught her gasp with a quick kiss, swallowing her fine breath, searching deeply with his tongue.

It was going to be all right, he knew that. Or as right as it could be without the child they'd loved so dearly. Their love was back and whole and healthy. His life was back. His wife was back.

And he'd never have to ask anyone who killed Natalie again.

He thought he felt a coolness brush up against his shoulders as he began to move above Jane. He paused, and Jane opened her eyes, questioning.

He smiled down at her, thinking that Natalie's spirit might have come through the room, greeting him, thanking him. It wasn't something he'd ever talk about. He didn't think he could explain it.

He began to move again, his desire swelling and blotting out the world. Jane closed her eyes, her hands tightened on his arms, and Jim Sloan fell into a bliss unmarred by sadness and worry and grief.

He really never had to ask the awful questions again. Life was almost good.

FOGGY WINDOWS BOOKS

Afterburner

Science fiction is an ever-changing medium, and technology races to catch up with the imaginations of the best writers in the world—to create something that before existed only as a dream. Our Afterburner imprint takes the imaginative technology of science fiction one step further...and puts a husband and wife into a mix already filled with the potential for danger, and laughter.

GALACTIC EMISSARIES

David Bischoff

*David Bischoff was born in 1951 in Washington D.C. He gradu-
ated from the University of Maryland in 1973 and spent many
years at NBC Washington. He's been a professional writer for
twenty-five years now and has published numerous novels,
short stories and articles. As a teen, Bischoff was a great fan
both of the humorous stories of Keith Laumer and the funny,
erotic art of Vaughn Bode. He'd like to dedicate this story to
both of these fantasists. Bischoff's new books include:* Philip K.
Dick High, *a novel, and* Tripping the Dark Fantastic, *a short
story collection, both from Wildside Press.*

⊷══◉⊜══⊷

Her torso was like a cello.
He played chamber music upon it with his erect bow.
"Oh stars! Stars!" she moaned.

"Betelgeuse tonight my love?" he answered.

His tongue was ready and wet, ready for the taste of her slip-pery flow.

"Oh ...oh... No."

"No?"

"The Planets!"

"Holst?"

His hard instrument thrummed a chord of pleasure across her strings.

"God—Yes. Mars! Be my Mars."

"And you, my moons."

"Oh, yes... the moons."

Bare and right angular, he raised his thruster—and settled down deliciously slowly upon the smooth round tight Martian mound. His bow played a new song here, and sobs at its beauty rose up from her red, open lips. The earthy smells of her wafted in a gentle perfume as he ground his bow across her stiffening redness. And the taut, tight nipple rubbed along the underside of heaven, straight to hairy bliss...

"Sir?"

"Careful," she said. He shuddered and gasped. "I want you inside me before this is over!"

The very thought of the inside of his love, and his liquid song almost reached cacophony. But he drew back, and the score unwound like statistics in his head, and the urgent crisis was delayed—

"Sir! You're daydreaming again, sir!"

Thomas Diadem, Galactic Emissary for the Human Neo-Conglomeration, blinked. With a ruffle of his proud platinum-thread epaulets, he turned to his attaché, Appleby, his trained diplomatic mind instantly shifting into overdrive, easing through the context that surrounded him.

Attaché Appleby was dressed in a simple but elegant Victo-rian ensemble: Joinville bow tie, tails and handsome black pants. His shoes were as shiny and black as his long slick hair. Sarah Diadem, Thomas' wife, always said he looked like a Victorian prime minister in this get-up. When Appleby was so dressed, Sarah called him Disraeli Gears.

Appleby was an android that could not understand the nature of the daydream Thomas Diadem had just had. In fact, Appleby rather disapproved of the strongly erotic connection that existed between Sarah and Thomas Diadem.

At the moment of this contextual rundown, Sarah Diadem was up on the N.S.S. *Mercury*, now in orbit above this great planet of Brouhaha III, their current mission.

Brouhaha III was a tough diplomatic nut to crack. Thomas Diadem knew this because he'd been on surface duty for a whole week—a week without Sarah, a week without the sweet sex that made this long galactic journey that they dubbed a "Mission of Emissions" bearable.

"Yes. Sorry, Appleby," said Thomas Diadem. "What have I missed?"

The attaché pointed a discreet pinky. "The governor is currently enjoying a filibuster in the assembly on the subject of the AckBack Trade Board's certain doom should any outside trade be allowed with our ilk."

"Hmmm. Daydreaming was much more fun."

"Doubtless in this daydream you were engaged in a disgusting act...sir."

"I'm not sure. You know, Appleby, human sex is only truly disgusting if done correctly."

The attaché shut his mouth, which was the desired result of Thomas Diadem's comment. Diadem took the opportunity to lower his ocular augmentation and click through spectrum settings to enhance and focus the ever-startling image of the ReekReek congress in session. The translator hanging on his ear was giving him a low drone of half-decipherable verbiage. He adjusted a vernier, and the speech speaker, one Totally Enhanced Governor, MikMik Thingbot, became understandably semi-Englac.

"I dance the Dance of Alarm," the tall, awkward exo-bio cried out in a vibrato that might excite Queen Victoria, dead or not, if used properly, "I sing the Song of Warning!" This was exactly what MikMik Thingbot had been saying for almost a full day's worth of session. It was some sort of refrain for the musical tantrum the politician was throwing, and frankly, Diadem was getting sick of it. Although the AckBacks seemed at first like peaceable descendants of the human race, there were times in this last week when Diadem wondered if they didn't have more subtle methods of attack. Like wholesale boredom, for instance.

"Item Number Two Mach Gingold Fourth Tier, Tertiary Quadrant. I hold in my mandibles evidence that, should economic and trade relationships be established with certain members of our erstwhile ancestral contemporaries, the Sungmung Fields of SweetDung continent may well be exploited improperly for sexual lubrication oils for Primate Humans! This will do us no good in our relations with the UgBug—who not only disapprove of sex, of course, but who have found biological ways around it. Our relations with the UgBug are always tense at best!"

"My ears are pricking up," said Diadem to Appleby. "So to speak."

"The weight on your mind would be so much easier if the one thing that weighed upon it were lifted—sir," said the prissy and dignified android.

"Are you implying, my dear Sub-Ordinate, that the one thing that I think about is sex?"

"Sir, if I may remind you. Our duty to the Neo-Conglomeration is to spread the light of civilization, the beacon of knowledge, the joy of human harmony and cooperation. Our position in the galaxy is that of Reason's missionaries."

"I love missionary positions!" said Diadem. "Sorry. Couldn't resist. You're right though. There's a duty to be performed here. Unfortunately, it looks as though these particular descendants of the human race are not particularly eager for Enlightenment."

The android sighed, an expression that he'd perfected only recently, but now used quite often. "Too true, Captain, sir. However, we may certainly attribute this reluctance to the fact that for all intents and purposes, the genetic pool from which they spring is more alien than human."

Thus, the android had succinctly placed a primary digit upon the dilemma.

Once upon a time, beyond the far reaches of memory and somewhere upon a misfiled and almost-forgotten planet called Urtha, had sprung up a race called homo sapiens. These "humans" had stunk up their planet and rearranged their ecology so much that for survival of their species, they were forced to settle nearby planets—and then make the jump through Faster Than Light Travel to neighboring stars. This latter seminal event, as Diadem liked to call it, was millennia ago. Even when branching out, humans had remained in touch through e-mail (an abbreviation for ether-mail) a subspace FTFTL (Faster Than Faster Than Light) communications. However, after Earth was forgotten and galactic storms shut down this e-mail and the empire that had been born of human travel fell apart miserably, humans often as not forgot their origins and went native, as the British Library Node would have it. For all the whining and nay-saying of the exo-biologists of Earth before they'd even looked at any alien life form, the human genome turned out remarkably adaptable. The human genetic code mixed quite freely with many different forms of alien life. And thus, over these tens of thousands of years, on many separated oases of Self-Awareness, humanity absorbed—or was absorbed by—native civilized species.

Upon several planets, however, planets close enough to continue communication, there was no other intelligent life. The human gene pool had remained essentially the same. After a Revival of Technology, as well as a huge discovery of Ancient Tech Caches in neighboring deserted space stations and planets, the Galactic Empire was reborn. However, for an empire it was pretty damned tiny. In honor of the true purpose for its existence, the empire became a neo-conglomeration. Still, most other worlds contacted had no interest in joining. Each world had its own peculiar starfish to fry.

Thus began the fleet of Galactic Emissaries.

This was the esteemed mission of this Galactic Emissary Team, the trio of Thomas Diadem, his wife Sarah Diadem and their android attaché, Appleby. To go forth and discover old life and talk them into being friends.

Unfortunately, all too often, supposed human cousins on the exotic alien planets they visited had forgotten they had any kinship with the planet Earth.

"I play the Orchestra of Agony! To think, our precious Planetary Fluids could be exploited to satisfy the perverse pleasures of immoral decadence," said MikMik.

"You know, he does have a point," observed Appleby.

"So does your head—Esteemed Colleague."

In fact, that was a gross exaggeration. Appleby the Android's head did have a bit of a taper to it, but nothing to speak of. Otherwise, he had the rather narrow, pinched look of the denizens of EngPlanet, who had created him. His nose was narrow, his chin was narrow, and his cheekbones were high and effete. The point of his long nose was easy to stick way up into the air because its natural position was halfway there.

Diadem himself had more the ruddy, healthy look of a human from IrePlanet—his hair was reddish and his nose was squat. His brow was low and looked like a Karnarkan caterpillar had chosen it for permanent residence. He had a big mouth—sensual and active—and his blue eyes glittered with mischief.

Diadem and Appleby might have continued to bicker, which was something they were actually better at than diplomacy, if Diadem's fingerphone had not tinkled.

The emissary brought the fingerphone up to his ear.

"I was just thinking of you, my love," Diadem said, watching as MikMik raised a triple jointed arm above a large, pointed ear.

"I'm naked," Sarah Diadem said huskily.

"I'm not."

"My finger is moving down slowly," growled Sarah. "It's right between my legs now, hubby. It's right on my love button."

It looked as though a week of solitaire up there on the N.S.S.

Mercury, while the natives did their Songs and Dances of Debate, was boring Sarah as much as it was as him.

"Is it wet?" whispered Diadem.

"Soggy."

"Squish it around a bit," he suggested lightly. Then he gave her a pause to execute. "Better?"

"I can't do it as well as you, sweetie-comet!"

"It's all in the fingernail brush, moon-cutie!"

"Perhaps if I had some intimate mouth-to-receiver glandular-secretion-promoting-instructions."

"Sir?" said Appleby. "Is that Madame? Is everything all right?"

"Yes, Appleby. She's just having a maintenance problem with that clankety old ship. Plumbing problems."

"But I just fixed the evac tubes!" said Appleby.

"Look, maybe I'd better head back for the little ET's room in the back and give some hardcore instruction to the little woman," said Diadem, standing up and shaking his legs awake. "Come and get me if anything planet-shaking happens on the killing floor, won't you, Appleby."

"I will indeed...sir."

Diadem lifted himself out of his oddly tilted chair. He walked up the balcony through a wisp of green <u>pottah</u> smoke, a weed the AckBacks seemed to enjoy smoking through their secondary hydro-oxy exchange gills. It smelled like burnt peanut butter.

The latrines were pretty much like most latrines he'd seen around the universe. Holes with attachments. Water. Graffiti. Still, it was quiet enough if you ignored the gurgling noises of the sewers through the holes. And not only could he hear Sara better here, he could not hear MikMik at all.

Alas, there were no stalls.

"You know, you could be formulating a diplomatic coup of the first caliber instead of playing with yourself," he admonished. "We're kind of dying down here."

"I'm ambidextrous. You talk, I'll play."

"Can I play too?"

"That's up to you."

"I'm up," said Diadem. "There's just this zipper thing in my way."

"Hmm. You'll have to describe your plaything. It's been so long, I forget what it looks like. Is it still big and beautiful?"

"Only to you, sweetie."

He leaned against a gumgum swisher by a rack of drying mantises, which immediately began to glow red and blow out warm air. Diadem moved over to where it was safe and undid himself. He brought out the Galactic Emissary's Little Helper. It seemed a bit alarmed by the insectoid drying system, but with a couple of strokes and the image of his wife's spread legs, and her garden of dark goodies being troweled, he could feel it begin its remarkable biological star trek enterprise.

"I'm so hot for you, honey," she told him.

"I want you so bad," he told her. "You're all I think about."

"I hope you're thinking about the mission. By the way, I am getting cold. I think I'll put on my spiked heels."

"The political factions are amazing here. Appleby and I are presenting suggestion after suggestion of variations for regulated contact with continued difficulty. I'm about to give up on any notion of trade. The AckBacks are just too paranoid about their precious planetary juices. Speaking of juices..."

"You know these spiked heels," breathed Sarah. "I'm standing up and they're already squooshy and wet."

"Would you put those black strap stockings on?"

"Don't you remember? We broke them."

"And we were just supposed to break them in. So it goes. Anyway, I'm coming up with an excellent idea. You see, per previous reports, sweetie, it would seem that the AckBacks haven't even got a united biological front. There's a whole race here I haven't seen. I don't know what the hell they look like, and they are supposed to be religious fundamentalists."

"Oh darling. I get religious about your fundamentals all the time," Sarah replied. "My nether parts worship you. I believe I even feel an alleluia or two coming on right now."

"Can you wait till I finish before you finish?"

"Darling—you're usually so considerate...."

"No, damn it. With the report. So get this: there's supposed to be a faction in Stunkee City. Right now. I saw some big saucers come in this morning. Geez, they looked like pregnant Boonza cigars with lower intestine inflations. Anyway, the boys at AckBack HQ are setting up a meeting, and I just hope that we can agree to something, because I'm about ready to give up and head off to the next outpost of humanity and let the Doom Squad deal with these Bozo-oids."

"So you're just standing around now with your dick in your hand, is that it?" said Sarah archly.

"It would rather be elsewhere, I assure you."

"I'm wearing my Junian lipstick, sweetie."

"Oh god. That tingles so much when your lips suck on me."

"In my mind, I'm sucking on you right now."

"In my mind, I'm doing math!"

"Math? Are you holding back on me?"

"No. I'm looking for the square root of sixty-nine. I've found just the root so far."

"Let's look for the sixty-nine."

"Did you trim your bush, you hot devil?" Diadem asked. Sarah usually let him do that with a little pair of scissors, and he found it enormously gratifying and artistic. Lately, he'd made her pubic hair look like a Galactic Astro sign. He collected Astrolabes and wanted to have one by his side.

"I am a vision of loveliness. A little while ago, I was dressed in an evening gown. I was sitting by a rose from hydroponic. C-R had a nice Bach air on audio. The perfume from the flower drifted over my glass of champagne and touched my erect nipple, which had come through the top of my gown. I could feel the smell, Thomas."

Diadem shivered. He could feel the smell of the flower as well. His fingertips drifted over the silky smooth underside of his shaft and the beauty of the flower shuddered up his spine.

"I want this to be a good one, cowboy," she said softly and

lovingly. "I want this one to make you remember how much I love you and always will love you."

The gentle sound of her voice touched his heart. His hand pulled down hard on his penis, pressing against his scrotum with all the memory of love and hope and commitment eagerly pushing him toward his goal.

"Oh," he said. "Oh."

The power of the climax shook him. He throbbed and bobbed, and the huge supply of seminal fluid, generated not just by the Solar Company sexual potions this husband and wife shared, nor just by abstinence, but by the magic touch of passion, gushed forth. It spurted and spurted like white spray from a garden hose. With velocity and power it rammed toward the latrine door.

The door opened, and contingents of the UgBug faction walked in.

"Oh," said the tattered radio skin. "Ohhhh!"

"Yes!" said Sarah.

She yanked an invisible chain in the air, just as she had yanked Beloved Hubby's chain from a distance of oh, Five Thousand Kilometers, give or take a few meters. In the Vu-Screen, the bright blue, orange and red orb of Brouhaha III hung like a pregnant painter's palette in the thick black stuff of space.

Sarah leaned over and turned down the volume of the Ship-to-Planet connection. She leaned a head full of curlers toward the microphone.

"Oh...oh... honey.... I'm coming too. I'm coming."

She smiled to herself. It was so flattering that he thought of her all the time, even if she was the only normal human female within a hundred light years. It did a girl's confidence wonders. She picked up her clipboard with her scribbled calculations and walked over to the Input Station at the far end of the room. A monitor twirled with color. She stabilized it, pulled up a density screen, adjusted the code dimensions, found the hub routine she needed and began to program.

"Oh," said C-R. "Oh... I'm coming!"

"Shut up, douche bag. At least Thomas's vital programming is not broken."

The computer, called "C-R", accepted the reformulaic fractals, as well as the rebuke, in silence.

Then the artificially intelligent computer's voice smoothed out from the speaker that had previously been tweaking a Bach chamber music piece, "You know, Sarah. You'd think that adorable Appleby would realize that we machines are every bit as wired for sensuality as biologicals. I wonder if he's down there on that planet cataloguing species or something inane." The computer sighed. "Love hurts, Sarah."

"Tut tut, Putt-Putt. . If you didn't break down so much and could actually function properly so that I didn't have to let the men in my life go down on their lonesome and spend lonely time with a cranky algorithm-and-blues monstrosity, fixing her, maybe you could work a little bit on your seduction techniques."

"I asked you never to call me Putt-Putt!"

"I asked you not to break down! When you start giving us a few weeks of uninterrupted function, then I will call you by any name you like."

"Marilyn! Marilyn Monroe! I like that name. Data banks show she was one hot dame!" C-R's lights and monitor colors flickered excitedly.

"Look. Right now, Marilyn, I just want you to ingest the programming and let me know if you detect any misalignments in the mainframe. Hardware is so much easier to adjust or replace than fucked-up software!"

Sarah Diadem was a sturdy, compact woman. She was no longer young, but she was far from old, and she wore space jeans and a T-Shirt that read "Daddy's Girl" stretched out over big, firm breasts. She was a scientist, a computer programmer, an astrophysicist, a starship pilot—and now, she was a diplomat. She half-wished that her husband hadn't convinced her to join the Corps Diplomatique Neo-Conglomeration.

She had a firm chin, a cute nose, and eyes the color of

ecstasy. The tilt of her dark black eyebrows could turn a sunny day stormy, the dark of space golden and bright. Her hair was brunette, and the curlers were to put a little more bounce in it. Thomas liked his wife with bounce, so she was experimenting with her hair.

As she walked, her jeans felt a little tight. Gravity fluctuations—or...oh dear. Heaven forbid!

"Putt—Sorry. Marilyn? Have I put on some weight?"

"There's a scale in the toilet, sweetie."

"No. Do I look fat?"

"You look.... perfect."

"Damn it! You're not going to take a page from Thomas' dialogue. You're not going to wiggle out of this, computer!"

"Can you still wiggle into your jeans?"

"Sure."

"You're not fat, sweetie."

She smiled. "I'm sorry I called you Putt-Putt."

"We girls have got to stick together. Say, looks like those new numbers did the trick. I can feel the Z Plus Plus kicking into a pretty subroutine and erasing the backup. The blown buss fuses in my rear are another problem."

"I'll just get out my wrench —"

However, the squawking on the radio interrupted her mechanical odyssey.

"Goodness. Is he still having an orgasm?" she said. She went and turned up the volume.

"Human foulness," cried a rachety voice. "Put that biological weapon back into your hip-cloth immediately, or I will be forced to use this gunpowder-projectile-device!"

There was silence for a moment on the messy and ramshackle bridge of the N.S.S. *Mercury*.

"Oh-oh," said the computer who now called herself Marilyn Monroe.

The gun was mean and deadly looking.

The Diplomat's Little Helper, expended, had shrunk to an

abnormally small size, making it an easy matter for Diadem to slip it back into his pants. He did so with as much dignity as he could muster under the circumstances.

He squared his shoulders, assumed a relaxed attention, smiled, and raised his left arm in AckBack Greeting.

"I dance the Dance of Warm and Hospitable Encounters!" Diadem said in his best diplomatic tone. "I am Thomas Diadem."

There were two intruder UgBugs. Both held guns. They were much more humanoid than their brothers. They both wore dark robes and strap-on hats that looked like World War I German pilot helmets. One was slender and the other was heavier, mostly by the addition of what seemed to be numerous mammoth mammary glands pushing out the front of her cloak. Male and female, presumably, this duo.

"You ToeDirt Worm!" said the male, wiping off the stuff that Diadem had inadvertently squirted upon him. "This fluid—is it toxic?"

The male of the duo lifted his free hand to his face, which was also spattered with recently rocketed stuff. It dripped down white and gelatinous.

"I have just honored you with the Ancient Human Jism Salute," said the diplomat, always quick with his tongue, whether on the job or in bed. "Please, I refuse any monetary rewards or beach condos. I only seek peace between our planets."

"Raise your manipulative digits high above your brain-pan!" said the male UgBug. "In the Name of the Lord God HoHoHo, I abduct you for the purposes of interrogation as to your true evil purposes—and to prevent our beloved planet from infection from the filth of your ilk. Bracka! Intone the Sacred Kidnapping Benediction."

The female, however, seemed distracted. She was wiping her face, which had a wad of white human reproductive fluid upon it. She sniffed it and a curious expression lifted over her big oddly tilted face. She started licking her seven fingers and her bright chartreuse eyes went wide.

"I sing the Song of Curious Gustatory Discovery," she said.

Her colleague furiously spun upon her. "We are UgBug! We worship the Great God HoHoHo. We sing no songs! Songs are blasphemous! Wipe yourself off immediately, woman vassal. We must hurry. There is much torture and interrogation to be accomplished."

"Yes, OverGuy RubDub!"

For his own part, the male UgBug pulled a gray piece of cloth from his robe and delicately dabbed off the dripping stuff from his own twisted features, careful to keep his gun on his victim.

"Now. With digits remaining motionless in that position you will—What is that?" asked the UgBug.

"What is what?"

"The item on your finger. It is beeping."

"Carbuncle," explained Diadem. "Little skin problem I get, noble friend."

"That is not a skin blemish. That is technological. It is some sort of radio. Take it off and give it to me, immediately."

RubDub must be a quick study, thought Diadem wearily. He pulled off the finger ring and made to toss it to his captor.

"No, Treacherous Primordial Ooze," said RubDub. "Place it on the counter."

Diadem obeyed.

"Bracka. Retrieve the device."

"But OverGuy—I might be killed!"

"Then so be it. Silence! You are a female. Do your bidding. For the Great God HoHoHo hath sayeth in The Book of FlipFlop, Verse 3:19—'The Female Shall Obey The Male'!"

The woman trudged forward. She looked up at Diadem with what the emissary thought would be fear. Instead there was a sparkle in the large and luminous eyes, and a thick, slimy tongue ran along her lips.

She grabbed the fingerphone and hurried back.

"Now, MuckBeing," said RubDub. "Proceed to —"

The door opened and in walked another being.

"Sir, I believe that..." Standing there was Appleby. His jaw dropped. He looked from Diadem to the two natives in their black robes and his eyes went wide.

"Pardon me! This appears to be a private parlay. Perhaps I should wait outside—far outside, by our shuttlecraft. In fact, perhaps I should warm it up for a spin."

The gun swung around to address the newcomer. "I dance the Dance of Enforced Welcome, Alien. Come and join your fellows.

Another gun emerged from the lumpy and voluminous robes of the female.

Sarah said, "Something went wrong!" She could feel her heart pounding in her chest. For all her levity and brightness, deep down, the fear that Thomas would be hurt or killed on one of these missions was always there. However, even as terror hit her, that faithful friend, adrenaline, the champagne of glandular liquors, whisked through her. She remembered a time in her life when she needed comforting. Now, she needed action. If Thomas was in trouble, she needed to save him.

"Transmission's been cut off," said the computer.

"Damn!" She wheeled around. "Look. Just how 'fixed' are you?"

Lights blinked on the console.

"How fixed do you want me to be?"

"Planet-fall fixed."

"Allow me one moment to check systems!"

Blast and double blast, thought Sarah. Why had she read that novel last night? Yes, the candle and the faux-apple and pseudo-cheese had been sweet too. But if she had been down with the computations and the wrenches, this boat would be in landing trim now, and she could go down and haul her hubby's ass out of trouble.

"Systems checked," said the computer. "I'm afraid a landing with that kind of 1.1 gravity and the severe atmospheric winds would be extremely hazardous at this point. I should also like to point out that it may well be that the natives are restless."

"Honey. If Thomas is in a dinner pot, I'm going down to get him out." She went to a closet. She pulled out her gun. It was an old heavy-duty blaster, and Thomas made fun of her for using it. But carrying it around not only gave her a workout, it gave her a sense of security. Yes, sure, Thomas called it her Battle Penis, but she'd noticed on several occasions that when diplomacy had turned ugly, one sight of Big Papa turned the opposing side a bit more malleable in negotiations.

"Oh ho. Heavy artillery," said the computer.

"Damned straight." She clicked it into place in ready phase, goosing up the energy supply some.

Then she jumped into her webbing harness.

"I assume we are still in synchronous orbit over Stunkee City."

"My components weren't *that* screwed."

"Geronimo."

Lights went dark, and the planet wobbled as the jets and anti-gravs kicked in and the N.S.S. *Mercury* tilted down for a good old-fashioned rescue mission.

The hovercar jerked to a halt. Diadem couldn't tell where they were because of the blindfold over his eyes, but it didn't smell like a very nice place at all. He felt himself being picked up and hustled down a long corridor. Then he felt a blast of damp cold as he heard a door open. He was thrust down hard stone steps. He rammed against something and grunted in pain. Behind him, he could hear Appleby's non-biological parts clump against cement and stone.

It smelled like someone's cold breakfast, regurgitated.

Diadem's own breakfast was acting up. He wondered if Appleby was right and that the long flights between planets had turned him into a sex addict. If he hadn't been strung out and getting a fix in the bathroom, he wouldn't be in this fix.

They were jerked down a hallway. Diadem was shepherded through another doorway and alien-handled into a room. His bonds were pulled off his wrists. The door banged shut.

Footsteps thumped away.

Diadem took off his blindfold.

Appleby stood facing him in a dim room, hands on his hips. "Well, this is a fine mess you've gotten us into, Stanley," he said.

"Oh god," Diadem rolled his eyes. "Why, oh why, did I bring that twentieth-century culture vu-cube with us?"

"For the porn? Oh yes, your fixation on Bettie Page."

Diadem sighed. There was a mat of straw-like stuff on the floor that smelled odd, but looked safe enough. He sat down in it and thought.

His annoyance at the android buoyed his mood. They weren't dead, and they were here for a reason. Where there was life, there was diplomacy. Thomas Diadem lived and breathed negotiation, and his mouth was free. Thomas Diadem solved problems waking and sleeping, and his hands were free.

"So. I'm waiting," said Appleby. "What are we going to do?"

"Let's check the door."

The android examined the door. "There are possibilities here for manipulation using my hidden tool appendages. However, the gears seem rusty, and a great deal of noise would sound—surely the sort of noise that would attract attention. Better to wait a bit."

"Very well. I'm tired. I'm going to take a nap."

Thomas Diadem put his head down. He dreamed of solutions.

"Psst! Awaken!"

When Diadem awoke, the cell was darker. He blinked and looked around him.

Standing there beside him was Appleby. And beside him was the form of Bracka, the female UgBug.

"I believe," said Appleby, "that we are in a negotiation position with a corollary power conduit in the distaff faction."

Diadem got up. He brushed off the straw-like stuff.

He smiled and showed the rich magnetism of his diplomatic energies, measurable on all known energy meters in the universe.

"What an honor! I hope that we can be of service to you, mademoiselle!" he purred.

He would have kissed her hand, but in strange cultures he was very careful about that kind of thing.

"Yes! I sing the Song of Aid. Service-Service! Yes! Yes! Please, Service-Service. I am Bracka, and I sing the Song of Imprisonment. Might we not liberate one another?"

As Diadem's eyes adjusted to the dimness, he saw that Bracka was still wearing a dark, floor-length robe. There was a veil about her face now. Something was different, though, and he abruptly realized that she exuded a musky odor, like perfume in heat.

"I am welcome to discussion of any or all suggestions. Of course, I should like to know you better, and I might have my own suggestions."

"I sing the Song of No," said the female flatly. She held out her hand. In the smooth large palm behind the seven fingers was the fingerphone. Diadem reached for it, but she pulled it away. "I sing the Song of Request!"

"At your service, mademoiselle."

She pocketed the fingerphone, then immediately reached out and grabbed his crotch.

"Withdraw Biological Weapon. Fire Creamy Ecstasy Juice." Her eyes glittered wildly and she opened her mouth wider than any even vaguely human mouth had the right to go. "Aim well!"

When Diadem managed to get his breath back, he reached down and gently removed the hand. "Please, mademoiselle. The—er—Biological Weapon you speak of—and for your information, it is called God's Gift to Sarah—is full of nerves and therefore quite sensitive."

"I sing the Song of Pardon. I hope I did not damage it!" She looked more concerned for herself than for Diadem. Despite his alarm, he could not help but notice her reverence. Power to a diplomat was vital, not necessarily for egotistical purposes but for leverage.

"Oh, dear. It has a delicate ganglia array. Perhaps if you left it alone for a few hours and we have a good talk, it might heal."

She seemed very alarmed. "Will the Sacred and Mighty Weapon never rise again?"

Diadem was a diplomat, true. But first, he was a man.

"Unlike the South, yes."

Noticeable relief flooded her rapidly human features. "I should be damned to the Seventh Lower Shade of BurpHell should I have permanently damaged the Sacred and Mighty Weapon of SpurtJuice!"

"Well, we certainly don't want that!"

Talk. Talk was as important in diplomacy as it was in seduction. His mind spun. He had to shift over to diplomacy, and fast.

"Perhaps I should apply the heeling Tongue Langour of Trollopa!" said Bracka. "I assure you, although I have never actually engaged in such an action, I am told by my sistren that it is a natural instinct, quite contrary to what the Domar Males proclaim."

In some other time, in some other space, this odd alien woman might have succeeded in her ardent pursuit. Quite simply, she was becoming more attractive by the moment. However, Diadem was mindful, as ever, of his Soul Commitment with Sarah. This was not something he took at all lightly. One of the reasons he had grabbed at the chance for a couple of years out among the stars and the aliens was that he thought this would bring him and his wife closer. And also that there would be no temptation to veer from the course he knew was true and good and intimate with the female who was, after all, the love of his life.

His diplomatic mind slipped into overdrive.

"Appleby. Front and center!"

"I live to serve, Your Highness," said Appleby. His voice dripped with sarcasm.

"Now that we have a moment to talk, before we do any kind of resuscitation on the Sacred Spurter.... Perhaps you might tell me your name!"

"My Secret Name!" she seemed alarmed and also charmed. "Why—my name is Pie of Honey."

"Oh my! What a delightful name. Don't you think so, Appleby?"

"It touches my soul, my lord."

"Now tell me, Appleby. Have you ever seen a more splendid female in the universe?"

"I was impressed from the instance I laid orbs upon her, Your Awesomeness. Females by nature are splendid, but surely this one was born with the stars in her heart."

"Oh... You sing the Song of Beauty. And to a Wretched and Damned Female of the UgBug Sub-Species. Oh, HoHoHo forgive me —- but I delight!"

Although the Appleby was the artificial one in the room, Diadem could feel gears click in his head. Everything fell into place. He understood. His mouth, always somewhat ahead of his thoughts, but never a stumbling block, already was engaged.

"Your feelings! Oh, how I understand them. I suspect that HoHoHo understands them as well, praise be his glorious name!"

"You worship HoHoHo as well? Oh how glorious are his ways—he spreads his power through the universe and all its planets!"

There were times like these when a diplomat had to take a leap of the gut, and with his life at stake, and the fortunes of the Neo-Conglomeration on the line, Thomas Diadem did just that.

"HoHoHo... praise his name...Of course, we call HoHoHo by a different name, because we come from a different world with a different language. But I am a bit confused. We call the Glorious Shining Godhead of the Universe HaHaha."

"HaHaHa? Some kind of vowel difference in language?"

"I don't think so. All languages of Earth-derived civilizations are similar. But you have to understand that we worship the female aspect of the Great Godhead of the Universe."

Bracka—aka Pie of Honey—stepped back. Her magnificent sets of cleavage jiggled mightily.

"Female!" She seemed awestruck.

"Well, yes, of course. I'm sorry. I don't wish to intrude upon your sacred culture."

"No! No! There are giggles and whispers amongst my sex within the harem scarums of our peoples," said Bracka. "In truth, I come tonight in selfish thrall to the taste I felt today. However, now that I speak to you, there are resonances in what you say... Say on!"

Bingo!

"Please! I implore you!" said Diadem, "My task here is for understanding and mutual peace. I do not wish to trouble you with Truth and Discovery. I only wish the best for all peoples of the Universe."

"This is not what the Patriarchs say! They say you are here to destroy the sacred trust of the Kingdom. That is why you are being held. They wish to discover if there are large BoomShips that might Blaspheme the Sacred Patriarchs should they send you on to be with HoHoHo."

"BoomShips!" said Appleby. There was a chuckle of contempt in his voice.

"Then there *are* BoomShips?" said Bracka.

"Only that serve our Lady, HaHaHa," said Diadem, shooting an angry glare at Appleby. He resumed his mild and solicitous tone. "Now then...I am most concerned for your soul, Sweet Lady. For there are rumors of planets who worship Our LordHead, but where Males have subsumed the glorious female aspect of HaHaHa from their worship, which displeases the entire universe."

Bracka was silent. She said nothing. Her eyes were wide with fear.

Risk was necessary again. Diadem stepped forward and put his arms around the female and held her close and with fervid sympathy. The sensation of numerous breasts against him was very odd indeed but far from unpleasant.

"Please. Forgive me," he said. "You must be safe. You must save yourself. It is dangerous for you to be here. Go now, that your Males may destroy us so that your Society may be safe and your Males may rule, however misguided that rule should be."

"No! I must savor your essence. My heart sings the Song of Want!"

She grabbed him and pulled him even closer to her. Her musk was overpowering.

"Perhaps, if I allow this, Bracka, you will then help us escape!"

"I will sing the Song of Slavery at that time."

Diadem gently pushed her away and stepped back. He slowly began to unzip his fly. "Very well then—But you are not ready!"

"I am ready for anything."

"Let me guess. There's no actual touching of any kind between the males and females of your race and religion."

"It is forbidden! The Book of HoHoHo tells us so. The Rite of Reproduction is inducted artificially!"

"I don't suppose there's a Secret Book stashed somewhere in a temple run by males, is there?"

"Why yes! The Manuscript scribbled by HoHoHo's own hand. Every year we receive new laws and proclamations from it. How did you know?"

"Wild guess. Now then—if you are truly desirous of the full impact of my Joyous Juice, you must sing the Song of Foreplay. I don't think you're quite ready for anything yet."

"Anything! Anything!"

"My servant here is a wonderful creation. He will perform special massages and osculations upon your person that will prepare you for my Liquid Bounty. And if you are lucky, you will discover what your biologies are for!"

"What!" A horrified Appleby stepped back.

"It's a Song of Ife-Lay and Eath-Day, after all, so a servant must serve his Master...eh?" said Diadem. "Just sing the Song of Uck-Fay!"

The android shook his head. "But I have no Song of Enis-Pay!"

"Songs of Once Referred to Endages-Appay will do the trick, I think...old boy."

"I accept!" The female lunged for Appleby.

"A moment before the Sacred Foreplay begins. You must shed your robe, Bracka," said Diadem. "You must leave it here and go to my servant in your Glorious Bareness."

Without delay, Bracka dropped her hooded robe. Her strikingly Amazonian body's flesh was vibrant with life and filled with odd crevasses. In truth, though, Diadem's eyes were immediately drawn to the three pairs of the most perfect and magnificent breasts he had ever seen in his life.

She stormed over to Appleby, those large and erect breasts jiggling provocatively, arms outstretched. "I sing the Song of Anticipation!"

Appleby shot Diadem a glare and braced himself for the embrace.

As soon as Bracka's back was turned and the amatory action commenced, Diadem grabbed the discarded robe and searched for pockets.

That fingerphone must be in here somewhere!

Folds of vines and murky water and swamp muck gurgled up the vu-screen. Even before the safety light went off, Sarah Diadem unhitched herself from the grav harness. She grabbed her mammoth gun from its mooring and stomped over angrily to the console, behind which the nexus of computer's "brain" worked.

"Okay. This may be the end of this ship and of me, and I must say, I rather hoped for a death with more dignity than getting sucked down into some fetid alien swamp." She ratcheted the huge gun into firing mode. "But I promise you, I will first have the satisfaction of burning your circuits into hell!"

"I feel upset when you say these things, Sarah," said C-R. "We did land safely upon the planet's surface! And I have always warned you that impromptu landings have never been my strong point."

Sarah raised the gun. "I've got two strong bolts here. One for you—and one for me!"

"I suggest, sister, that you use the latter first to make sure the weapon works properly!"

Sarah blinked, then laughed helplessly. She lowered the gun and shook her head. "Perhaps I just might," she said mordantly, looking at their situation.

"Now that your tantrum has passed, let me assure you that I am working on the matter and exploring all remaining rocket devices that might get out of here. I —"

The comm unit buzzed. Sarah hurried to it.

"Thomas!" she said.

"Darling. Sorry for the interruption. I wonder if you might take a moment from your busy schedule, make planet-fall and save us."

"I tried to. We're stuck in a swamp now. C-R says we can get out, but I'm not at all sanguine on the subject." He took a deep breath. "I'm so glad to hear your —"

Over the comm Sarah could hear waves of heavy breathing and gasps. These gave way to moans and screams of erotic tension.

"What the hell is going on there?"

"It's a long story."

"Abridge."

He did, and she got it, quick.

"Geez—Appleby and the native girl. I didn't know that Appleby had ...equipment."

"Well, he doesn't have a penis, but he's got equipment. And it would seem he knows how to use it well enough. But this won't last forever, and I'm surprised that these squeals haven't summoned the guards. Darling—we might be able to get out and back to the Stunkee City on our own, with Bracka *and* a way to proceed with a new tack in planetary diplomacy here. But there's a price."

"Save yourselves!" said Sarah.

"Bracka demands my Sacred Juices. She got a taste when I

was in the latrine, and it's just turned her into in a wild woman."

"What are you saying? She wants to drink your semen?"

"From the tap, so to speak," said Diadem.

"Die, you two-timing bastard!"

"I am faithful!" said Diadem. "I love only you! But this is a matter of life and death. And frankly, sweetie, I have a big problem. I'm supposed to produce a significant amount of sap and then deposit it. However, I'm not confident that this...human-descendant is quite what I'm looking for in the arousal department. Understand?"

"You scum!" said Sarah. "You want me to play phone sex for you while some six breasted hussy gives you a blow job!"

"I wish you wouldn't be so coarse, darling."

The volume of the cries reached a fever pitch. Then they ululated away. There were peculiar fleshy flopping sounds, and a bullish female voice came through the speakers.

"You have shown me the Song of Truth, Great One. It is well that your servant had so many appendages! Now please—I yearn for your Glorious Juice. Allow me to sip from the Pool of Joy— and I will surely see that you are taken back to Stunkee City safely. I swear it!"

Thomas' voice came over the speaker. "Sarah. Do you get what sort of dilemma I'm in?"

"Okay," said Sarah. "She's human and she's a woman, even though there's some exo floating around in her biology."

"Yes. And as you can see, she has been repressed by male religious, cultural and social domination like you wouldn't believe."

Sarah sighed. "Put her on the fingerphone. I think what Bracka needs is some heart-to-primary-blood-pump Girl Talk!"

The ceremony and its attendant parades were magnificent. Thomas Diadem could feel the joy in the bracing alien air of Stunkee City on a pleasant day gifted to them all by the Planet Brouhaha.

Sarah Diadem and Appleby sat on comfortable seats in the reviewing stand beside him, observing all and enjoying large glasses of exotic AckBack LoopFruit wine.

ReekReek the AckBack wobbled up some steps and looked upon the new Diplomatic Celebrities with obvious awe and gratitude. "I sing the Song of a New Era. I did not believe that these old eyes would ever see the end of the fractious regime of the UgBug DeepDug—and in so short a time!"

"Troublemakers, I take it," said Diadem. He squeezed his wife's hand warmly. They'd gotten back to Stunkee City in time to get a crane and a grav-tow, find the muck-bound Mercury and haul her out to safety. Now the beautiful boat was off in the spacefield, polished and shiny and ready to lift off for further adventures.

"These Posterior-Religionists always are, are they not?" replied ReekReek. "In any case, now that there is a different regime in control there, all Inter-Race Board Members unanimously agree that full contact and diplomatic relations should be created with your human Neo-Conglomeration. There are some issues, of course, and major talks must proceed."

"We would have it no other way. We wish to relate—not dominate," said Diadem.

"I cannot tell you how grateful we are!" said ReekReek. "Somehow you have solved a centuries-old problem of our planet. There is no way we can thank you fully. Just know that you two are welcome in our homes at any time. We sing the Song of Eternal Hospitality!" The alien turned. A smile creased his tilted head. "Ah! I believe your other new friends have arrived with their presentation."

Diadem turned. Even years of professional training did not prevent a slight gasp. Proceeding toward them were ten UgBug women. They no longer wore baggy black robes and hoods. Rather, leather and brass bras held their valiant breasts up high, and leather thongs clung around their large hips. Their hair floated behind them, wild and free. Flashing jewelry dangled from pierced eyebrows, earlobes—and doubtless God-Knew-Elsewhere

Lobes. Attached to strong abdominal muscles were chains that led back to a collection of males, bare but for loincloths. On their arms were tattooed symbols that looked to Diadem like a kind of UgBug branding. The UgBug males looked exhausted and drained. But they also had expressions of total bliss on their faces.

Behind this procession, a large float motored. There seemed to be a statue of some sort underneath, covered by a light black tarp.

"I sing a Song of Grateful Worship!" announced Bracka as she stepped up before the couple. She bowed to them both, and her exotic jewelry tinkled. "Equilibrium in our race has returned, thanks to your intercession. The full and correct text of The True Scripture has been restored."

"You found the Secret Book! Excellent!"

The UgBug female's eyes flashed. "Yes. And we have disclosed the True Identity of our Deity. In fact, it is the Book of Ho! And, praised be Her Fecund Uteruses, we have discovered that her wicked priest HoHoHo rewrote the scripture to put himself in his place while she was elsewhere singing other songs of Child Bearing Creatures' Consciousness!"

"The pig-oid!" said Sarah.

Bracka nodded gravely. "Now the priests have been overthrown, and Priestesses have been reinstated. We have restored the Sacred Rites of In and Out, which renders males into the reproductive and political position in which they belong. And all is heading once more into harmony!"

"Now I understand why no guards came down while Bracka was screaming under Appleby's erotic administrations," said Diadem. "Poor sods must have instinctively recognized the mating cry of their female and been paralyzed."

Appleby shook his head with awe. "Four separate vaginas with full hypersensitive nerve clusters. It is well I carry my toolbox with me, wherever I go!"

Bracka pointed back to the float. "Let it never be said that our Songs shall be forgetful, but in order to celebrate your remarkable intervention, we have erected a monument to your growing fame amongst our people!" She spun about. "Sisters!"

Two more very well endowed UgBug women appeared. They grabbed hold of lines that led to the tarp on the float and they pulled.

The tarp came down, revealing a statue.

It was a huge erect penis, grounded by a set of plump testicles and a curly thatch of hair.

The effect on the UgBug women was immediate. Wonder filled their limpid eyes. They fell to their knees and began to bow and cry out in a mild imitation of the sounds that a pleasured UgBug female could not help but make.

Only Bracka remained standing.

"Hmmm," said Sarah, regarding the statue. "You even got the freckles right." She turned to Diadem. "Only a quick flash, eh?"

"Yes! I swear. The woman must have a photographic memory."

Bracka nodded gravely. "The image of the Great Missionary is engraved indelibly upon my mind. And now it shall stand forever to be worshipped as a minor deity in the Pantheon of Truth!"

Sarah rolled her eyes. "Uh oh. Thomas, you're never going to be able to fit your head through the airlock door!"

Diadem shrugged.

"Well, I must say," said Sarah, stretching. "I am so overwhelmed by this display that I must retreat to the ship for a nap before we prepare to take off for our further adventures."

Bracka looked alarmed. "No. We forbid it!"

Two UgBug women quickly hopped to Sarah's sides and locked arms with her.

"Pray—stay one more darkfall and one more dawn. Our sculptors wish to model your four vulvas for a much more important idol. They shall be major deities in our pantheon."

Sarah still did not look particularly pleased. "I'm afraid there's only one."

"One? O benighted female, we pity you." The UgBug women wailed. "But nonetheless, it must be a perfect and truthful one!"

"Look, you have fun, dear," said Diadem. "Appleby and I should get back to the ship. There's some more fitting that needs to be done, and I've promised him a game of chess for services rendered."

The diplomat and his attaché began to walk away.

Two more UgBug women, even more muscular and breastier, hurried to Diadem's side, grabbed his arms and held him in place. "No, no! Please! We ask only one more simple request," said Bracka. "Tonight, when the Three Moons have risen, we wish the two of you gods to illustrate the finer techniques of In and Out."

Diadem blanched. "Really! What an honor. But Sarah and I are quite a private couple."

"Please. Should you do so, we shall sign an immediate trade proposal with your Neo-Conglomeration. And we shall immediately build, in our capital of Foogah, an embassy for your diplomats!"

"Er—well..." Diadem looked at his wife, who smiled and shrugged in a "what's the harm?"" kind of way. "Just as long as you don't put those statues on the back lawn."

Well, he supposed they would still be doing pretty much what they'd be doing on the Mercury. They'd just be getting applause for their exertions.

"Appleby, it looks as though you're the only one who can go back..." Diadem looked around. The android was already disappearing in the distance, tails flapping.

Appleby cycled the door closed. If he breathed, he would have breathed easier. He wasn't sure it would have happened, but he didn't want to stick around to wait and see if those wild biological extremes would need more of his appendage services. He'd had his fill of quivery flesh—for a lifetime.

Yes! He could now relax and engage his mental facilities in other pursuits. A good book? A game of Memory Chess? Oh, the possibilities of mental challenges! Sublime!

He pushed through the door and stepped into the main area of the starship.

A table stood there, with candles, an array of sparkling crankcase cleaners, and a gleaming dish of Android Stims.

"C-R! What is going on?" he said.

The door slammed behind him and locked.

The voice of C-R oozed from all over, pure aural seduction. "Welcome back, Apple Sapple, my love! And please, call me Marilyn!"

"What? Look, C-R. I explicitly stated to you that —"

The voice turned sultry with algorithmic silicon anticipation, and the computer stations on the sideboards quivered and jerked, their disk drives oozing an odd oil.

The computer, who now called herself Marilyn Monroe said, "Hidden appendages, eh, Appleby?"

⋅⊶⚬⊷⋅

Diadem & Sarah will be back with more hilarious adventures on Valentine's Day, 2001! Look for the forthcoming novel, The Diplomatic Touch.

Surfacing

Allison Lawless

Allison Lawless is a junior at Sitka State College in Oregon. She is majoring in Japanese History and Photojournalism. On weekends, her idea of a good time is singing at jazz clubs. She also plays the clarinet.

⊷══◉══⊶

"Hey, Ki, the gills are great." Tikka Fen gently stroked the new frills low on her neck. Soft and extremely sensitive, they could drop down to look like regular skin or open like exquisite flowers. "But what's with the hair?"

She frowned at her image on the wall. Usually this wall showed a real-time flatcast of a forest on Verify, the planet where Tikka had grown up. At the moment, the spaceship had turned the wall into a temporary mirror so Tikka and her husband, Shom Pirelli, could check their latest body modifications.

237

Usually Tikka's hair was short and black. Now she had a huge purple castle on her head. She touched a tower. Solid as an asteroid. She leaned her head forward, and almost fell over from the weight of the structure. How could she think with this thing on her head?

"I've been monitoring cultural broadcasts from Sewassa since we got this assignment," said Ki, the ship. "You want to blend, don't you?"

Shom touched the six-inch blue spikes that now crowned his head. "Ouch! Ki, you have to stop sneaking extra bodymods in without asking."

"I think you look lovely," Ki said in a soothing voice.

Even after three missions with Ki, Tikka couldn't tell when the ship was kidding. Ki had to be kidding, right? Tikka and Shom looked ridiculous.

Tikka gripped her new crenelations. "How am I supposed to sleep in this thing?"

"I wondered about that myself," said the ship. "I've been watching the ads and the soaps, but I don't see anything about people sleeping. Maybe they don't."

"Forget sleep," Shom said. He came up behind Tikka and slid his arms around her waist, leaned into her—and got a face full of castle. He sneaked his head around the castle to peer over her shoulder. "This thing could poke my eye out."

Tikka stared at the image of herself and her new husband. His beautiful dark long-fingered hands crossed over her pale stomach, warm and firm against her skin. She relished the feel of his strong arms around her, reveled in his spicy scent, enjoyed the thought that she could lean on him. She had spent most of her life standing up for herself.

It was all new: they had met last mission, and married only a month ago. She wanted to be always touching him, and she didn't like how the new hair would change that any more than Shom did. She reached up behind her and felt Shom's spikes. "I don't want punctures, either. Are you sure this look is supposed to be so hard?"

She bent her head forward so the castle wouldn't hurt him, and he responded by pressing closer to her, as she had hoped he would. Skin to skin, his body heat against hers.

Their reflection disappeared, replaced by a live-action drama. Everybody in the story had monuments on their heads: one woman had a green-and-yellow house; another sported a sculptured grove of red trees; a man wore a black speedboat on his head. They all talked to each other normally, as though their head sculptures didn't exist. The topic of discussion was someone's unborn baby, and who might have fathered it.

"You can't tell from those pictures whether the hair is actually solid," Tikka protested. "Maybe their hairstyles are held together by shaped energy fields, like Sewassa water architecture."

"It's the look that matters," Ki said.

Shom's hand wandered up to cup Tikka's breast. He frowned. "Listen to their Universal. We'll never get that accent right. I think we should go in as tourists, and keep our own hair." As he listened, Shom kneaded her breast. Her nipple rose and bumped against his palm as heat bloomed under his hand, spread through her. She clamped her thighs together, then relaxed.

"Hey. You feel different," he murmured.

She ran her hand down the outside of his thigh. Warm, smooth, muscular...and somehow slippery.

Shom gripped both her breasts, squeezing and relaxing. She felt his erection growing against her.

"You're slick," he whispered. His hands slid over her, skated down across her stomach, cupped her mound. He pressed his body closer against her back, hot and hard and perfect, then leaned forward to nuzzle her shoulder. "What's this new smell? You smell delicious. Raspberries? Violets?"

She ran her hands up and down his thighs. The oil on his skin warmed. He, too, smelled even better than usual. In addition to his usual musky scent, something vanilla and hot from the oven. She lifted one of his hands to her mouth and licked the back. Yum! Buttery and hot. She wanted to taste him everywhere.

"That's another mod I made," Ki said. "So you won't get dehydrated underwater. I gave you extra skin oil, but it's only supposed to activate when you're actually in the ocean, and...you're not listening, are you?"

Shom smoothed his hands over her thighs, eased one hand between them, explored with his fingertips, waking waves of heat at the source of her pleasure. She jerked and squirmed in response. Her breath came faster. She wanted him inside her.

"You're so ready," he whispered.

"Come in." She was panting and heard his breath go ragged. She could bend forward. But he closed his hands tight around her breasts, his palms against her hard nipples, and pulled her back against him. Heat flushed along her skin. She could feel the shudders coming.

She leaned her head on his shoulder.

"Aaiiieee!"

His scream shocked her out of arousal.

Shom gently pushed Tikka's head up and stepped away from her. He sucked breath in a harsh hiss.

Tikka opened her eyes and looked at Shom. He held his hand to his neck, which was bleeding. She had sideswiped his neck with her head castle.

"That's it," she said. "We're getting rid of the headgear right now, Ki. We like the oil. We like the gills—"

"You'll love the extra eyelids."

"What?" Tikka shook her head. "Cancel the hair. We'll come up with a different cover story." She palmed open her medbed compartment and backed into it, took a breath and released it as Ki settled the treatment medium around her like a warm blanket, then tightened it until it was as close as another skin. Spots of warmth and wet bloomed here and there, and she felt, or thought she felt, tiny manipulations as Ki took control of her outermost self.

Ahhh. Dropping into the medbed was always chancy; here, Ki held complete control of what happened to Tikka and what she would emerge looking like. Yet there was something primally comforting about it. She was being taken care of in a way that she had never been while she was growing up. Ki might play practical jokes on her, but Ki would not hurt her.

Ki had no sense of dignity, but she had an absolute sense of safety.

The space station-to-planet surface shuttle dropped to the landing strip with a faint jar. Everyone piled off.

The sky was brilliant blue above the ocean that stretched in every direction away from the floating city. The kelp beds, the primary industry and export on Sewassa, stained the water yellow-brown. The air smelled of salt water, iodine, and scoot fuel, and it was thick in her mouth. Local gravity was light enough to make her feel as though she floated. She loved planets where that happened. It happened often; Ki kept shipboard gravity high so they would stay in shape.

Scavenger flyers cried and swooped low over fishing boats in the near and far distance. The yellow sun struck them with light so harsh it felt sand-papery, though the breeze off the water kept the temperature down to warm instead of scorching.

Tikka would be glad to get into shade.

The other passengers must all be locals, Tikka thought; they all walked off the landing strip and took the floating road toward the city. Only Tikka and Shom were stopped and led to a customs shed, where their bags and persons were scanned three different ways.

Beyond the edge of the bobbing landing strip, Tikka saw the great blue walls of Sewassa water architecture, a floating city made of water.

"Explain those machines on your wrists," said the customs official.

"These?" Tikka said in her best bright chirpy dumb voice. "They're the latest tech from the Clusters. Personal shields! Check it!" She pressed a bump on her steel-and-black-metal wrist cuff, and a forceshield shimmered into place around her. "You guys don't have these yet? Everybody does in the inner systems! Also it's got a mini autodoc in it, so if I get sick from something, it can medicate me right away!"

The customs man ran his scanner over the wrist cuff again. "That's all it does? No weapons?"

"Oh, no. We don't carry weapons, do we, honey?" She turned her thousand-volt smile on Shom.

"We're just here to collect news, customs-sir," said Shom. "We're doing a feature on sport fishing on ocean worlds for TourNews Network."

"What can you tell me about *this* machine?" asked the customs man, hefting a curved-edged silver cube the size of a human head that was the only thing in their duffels he'd actually taken out.

"That's our three-D camera!" Tikka said. "Watch the lens, please. They cost a fortune to replace."

"Show me how it works."

Tikka slipped one hand through the strap, tapped a fingercode on the side of the cube. An eyepiece telescoped out, and the lens zoomed out of the other side. "Smile." She aimed the camera at the customs man, who smiled, then frowned. "See!" She lowered the camera, tapped another code, and a three-D image of the customs man appeared beside her. First he smiled, then he frowned. Tikka coded the camera and the image disappeared.

"Ach!" said the real customs man. He ran a hand over his head, smoothing down his hair. "How long has my hair been like that?"

"Your hair looks great," Tikka said. "We're curious, though. When we dropped out of hyperspace, we watched some of your entertainment on our way insystem. The players wore hairstyles we've never seen in the Cluster. We thought everyone here would have them." She glanced around. Nobody in the shuttle terminal had a castle on his head, or a forest, or even a velocipede.

"Oh! That's the second story," said the customs man. He smiled, this time condescendingly. "The actors tell the first story, and their hair tells the second one. It's a local artform."

Tikka blinked. "Fascinating," she said in a toneless voice.

"Thank you for showing me your devices. You are free to go," said the customs man.

Shom picked up both their duffels.

As they walked away, Tikka held the camera, Ki's planetside body, up to her face, the lens aimed toward her. She muttered into a tiny mike set in the collar of her shirt, "Nobody here has castles on their heads! You would have sent us down there looking like that?"

"Not really," Ki's mobile component said through her earpiece. "Well, maybe. You looked so cute! You would have been treated like stars."

"TourNews? TourNews?" said a dark-skinned, big-breasted woman. She waved a sign at them. It said: TOURNEWS.

"Yes," Shom said.

"Hi! I'm Bic, your government-assigned guide to Sewassa. Welcome to our planet!"

Tikka blinked again. "We have a guide?" she murmured, more weary than surprised.

"Our wonderful world offers many dangers to the unwary, and we want to make sure you have a great time and avoid trouble," Bic said. "What can I show you first?"

"How about our hotel?" suggested Shom.

"Where are you booked?"

"The Seaview."

"Oh, no, no, no! Much too close to open water! Why, they even have a corridor out to the ocean, right in the middle of the bathing rink. Dangerous! You don't know about the indigenous life around here. Known to come up through the floors of some of our less substantial buildings and eat babies out of their beds. We'll book you into a very nice totally downtown central hotel. How about the Cloud Castle?"

"Guide-sir, we chose the Seaview because we're doing a feature on open water fishing, and the Seaview has access to the boatways," Shom said.

Also, their contact worked there—their secretive, elusive

contact who had presented Interstellar Business Machinations with an option on a product everybody would kill for: Pearl, the ultimate aphrodisiac. To get an exclusive license to merchandise and distribute the product, all IBM had to do was overthrow the planetary government and change the Cooperative status of the planet from colony world to partner world.

Pretty big stakes, Tikka thought, but she'd done it before.

"The Seaview isn't even listed in the guide books," said Bic, pouting. "However did you wind up there?"

"Our research division is thorough," Shom said.

"Thoroughly misguided," Tikka whispered to the camera. Then she aimed the camera at Bic. "Smile!"

Bic smiled. Ki ran an intense body scan on her. Tikka watched the dataflow through the eyepiece. Hmm. Bic was armed with two stunners with extra charge packets, some food additives that, added to food and eaten, would make people fall asleep, possibly die, several small throwing knives in strategic places, and an elaborate surveillance system that was embedded in her shirt. Nipple cam. Clever, thought Tikka. Put the camera where men will focus so you can get a good shot of their faces. Maybe I should get me one of those.

"What's your favorite thing about living on Sewassa?" Tikka asked, still filming Bic.

"I love everything about it. Our fabulous water architecture, famous throughout the Allied Systems. Our brief but glorious history. Our kelp farms, which supply six systems with nutrients! And just wait 'till you see our fabulous sunsets! We had enough undersea volcanic activity last year to blast a lot of particulates into the atmosphere. Our sunsets are orgasmic!"

She's really selling it, Tikka thought. *Maybe she's actually happy here.*

"Would you like to sample our local cuisine? We have some great restaurants that specialize in the preparation of local sea life unavailable offplanet. If you're fond of Steka-style, char-grilled, drizzled, water-cured, we can accommodate your tastes."

"Guide-sir, you make my mouth water," Shom said, staring straight at the nipple cam.

Tikka kicked her husband gently in the shin.

"Aren't you hungry after that long flight?" he asked her.

"We ate at the space station an hour ago. I really want to check into our hotel and make sure our boat rental arrangements are in place so we can get to work on our story right away."

Shom's beautiful forehead wrinkled with worry. "Guide-sir, my camera person is correct. Would you lead us to our hotel so we can confirm our arrangements? Perhaps afterward we could eat together."

Bic deflated. "Oh, all right."

Tikka couldn't figure out how the Seaview could look dilapidated. Like all the other structures in the city, its walls were made of water held in place by forcefields. The water was stained opaque rosy pink on the facade that faced the street. The architectural style, which could be changed anytime by reprogramming the fields, was up to the minute, including ridiculous furbelows and gewgaws that were just now fadding their way into more solid buildings in the inner systems, that hive of current culture.

And yet, somehow, the Seaview managed to look...seedy.

Tikka loved it.

"Are you sure, sure, sure you want to stay here?" Bic asked. "Their kitchens keep getting closed down when inspectors find waterfleas and ratsnake turds in the food."

"We must stay here, guide-sir," Shom said. "Our company demands it."

Bic scowled, but let them check in. She listened while they talked to the boat-rental desk and made plans for tomorrow. She followed them up to their room, too.

The infacing walls, ceiling, and floor of their room were stained opaque blue and green. The wall that faced toward the ocean was clear, giving them an unending view of sky, kelp beds, and fishing and farming boats. Far in the distance, a blue-green bump sparkled above the surface: another floating city. Tikka walked to the sea wall and stared out. Somewhere out there, under the surface, secret activities were going on. Soon, she hoped, she and Shom would head out and discover what they were.

Bic joined Tikka at the window, shaking her head the whole time. "Shoddy architecture." She patted the wall. "Look how thin the walls are! One good storm—and we have the mothers of all storms here—and this whole place could blow over. Did you see the joins between the wall and your room door? This place is riddled with faults. Now that you've seen it, doubtless you'll want to move someplace safer."

"We can only pray we will survive," Tikka said, with her best fake smile.

"Please, guide-sir, allow us a little time to settle in. We will find you in the lobby in half an hour." Shom held the door until Bic walked out of the room.

Then he collapsed onto the bed, which quaked and surged under him. More water held in place by forcefields, but this time the fields had give to them. Tikka launched herself to lie beside him. She enjoyed the tsunami that resulted and almost bounced Shom off. "Wow." She slid her hand along the surface of the field, pushed down so that it dented the purple-dyed water beneath. "Ki, are you getting this tech? We could have a lot of fun with it."

"Scanning," said Ki in her ear.

"Oh, yeah." Tikka sat up and scanned the room with the camera, watching dataflow. Ki red-dotted a spot on the window. Tikka went over and found that Bic had slapped a microbug there. She isolated it under a whitenoise shield with a chip that would play innocuous, somewhat muffled Tikka-Shom conversation for it.

She sat back down on the bouncy waterbed to finish her scan.

The rest of the room was clear.

Ki did spot a heat outline beyond the water door. Bic, hovering, Tikka guessed. The walls were soundproof, though, unless you leaned right against them and shouted.

"Now that she's gone..." Shom crawled across the bed and wrapped his arms around Tikka's waist, pressed his face to her back.

She leaned forward and set Ki's mobile unit on the floor, then squirmed around in Shom's embrace until they lay facing each other. "How are we going to get rid of her for real? She's outside right now spying on us."

"Once Ki analyzes the forcefield tech, I suspect we'll be able to walk through walls," Shom murmured. "What do you taste like now?" He pulled her closer and tasted her cheek. "Mmm."

She touched her cheek. "Ki didn't get rid of that glitch in the oil stuff? It's still here? No, it's not."

"Just you. Toasty marshmallow you."

She tasted his neck while the bed surged beneath them. He too was back to his own spicy, musky taste, with a little salt from sweat and the ocean air added in. She licked her way up his neck and over his jawline to his mouth. Their tongues dueled for a little while. "I can't get enough of you," he said when they came up for air.

"Mmm. Me too."

"But," he said, "that's a chronic condition. I'll just have to live with it until we have more time. Our contact is supposed to be here by now, isn't she?"

"Perhaps, but I'd back off if I saw Bic sitting outside the room. The woman is bristling with offensive weaponry."

"Really? Maybe we should invite her in and stock up."

"Okay, maybe 'bristling' was an exaggeration. Surveillance, two stunners, little knives, and assorted Mickey Finns."

"Kid gloves."

Tikka sat up, stretched, smiled. "Nobody wants to alienate TourNews!"

"This is a good cover. We should use it more often."

"Plus we could actually file stories and make some extra credits."

He checked to see if she was joking.

She smiled. "You are adorable on camera," she said.

"And off."

"Ahem."

Shom and Tikka turned to find a slender, colorless woman standing against one wall. She wore a maid's uniform and looked invisible even though Tikka was staring at her.

"Hello," said Tikka.

"Welcome to Sewassa," said the woman. Her voice was pleasant and musical.

"We've already been welcomed, and given a government stooge named Bic. She's just outside." Tikka glanced toward the door, then back at the stranger. "I hope you're more interesting."

"That depends on who you are."

Shom nudged Tikka. "Give her a sign."

"Oh. Free the Strethil."

"Free the Strethil," echoed the woman. Her mouth curved into a sharp *V*, and her eyes brightened. Her smile transformed her face so that she did become instantly more interesting. "I'm Arka."

"Oh, good. What if you weren't and I said that? Instant trouble, right?"

"That depends too. Most of the locals only know the Strethil as food, but any agents of the government, overt and covert, would know what you meant, and yes, that would be trouble. What are your plans?"

Tikka retrieved the camera from the floor and aimed it at Arka, who put her hands in front of her face. "No pictures!" she said.

"I'm not photographing you, I'm just scanning you," Tikka said. "Huh. No wiring. No weapons..."

"Normal citizens are not allowed to carry. Only government agents can."

"Unknown machine in your right palm. Unknown substance in your right front pocket."

"Sophisticated scanning!" Arka stepped to the bed, reached

into her pocket. "This is a sample of the product," she said. She dropped three gray-green pearls into Tikka's palm.

Tikka aimed Ki's component at the pearls and watched dataflow. Everything she and Ki and Shom had come to the planet to find was in her hand right now. Was it real, or was this a hoax?

The pearls were made up of many different complex molecules, some of which Ki couldn't decode or replicate.

"Test it," said Arka. "You will be astonished."

Tikka tucked the pearls into a protected compartment of her wrist cuff. "We will test it, but we can't right now. That agent is expecting us to eat dinner with her. She's totally wired. Any suggestions on how to get rid of her?"

"There's no safe way if she's locked into the government web. Any strand breaks and they know instantly. You're supposed to be resourceful. I hope you figure something out."

"We can't just dump her off the boat?"

"They would send out search birds. She probably has a tracking device."

"We'll improvise. You know which boat we've rented?"

Arka nodded.

"We'll be there as soon as we can. Probably this afternoon."

"I'll be on board." Arka went to the wall, pressed her right palm to it. The forcefield split open, lifting the water away to leave a slit in the wall, and Arka slipped through it. It closed behind her.

"Told you that was possible," said Shom.

"Ki, did you get that?"

"Gotten. Analyzing now. Ah. Program acquired and downloaded to your cuffs."

"Excellent," Tikka said in her best gloating villain voice.

The door pinged. The speaker next to it activated with a gurgling, throat-clearing sound. "Are you ready for lunch yet?" Bic asked plaintively.

Tikka thumbed the intercom. "We still have to put on some clothes," she said. "Be with you in a few."

⊶═◉═⊷

Bic managed to get them downtown, away from the sea after all, only by promising she'd take them to a dive where deep sea fishermen hung out so Tikka and Shom could start backgrounding their story.

It proved to be a lie. Nobody fished at the Freak Zone. But there were a lot of very strange creatures of the deep in real-time flatcasts on the walls.

"What *is* that?" Tikka asked when a thing that was all jaw, spike teeth, and bioluminescent eyes flashed toward her, jaws snapping, until it broke some teeth on the camera and veered off.

"That's a sea devil. It's one of the things that comes up through the plumbing in less well-maintained places." Bic shuddered delicately.

The image shifted, showed something in green water that looked like a flying carpet, a flat, shaggy, diamond-shaped thing that swam by frilling its edges and whipping its long thin black tail so rapidly it was almost invisible.

As they watched, a human diver rose up and speared the carpet. Black blood stained the water. The carpet raged and struggled and fought, but ultimately it died.

"Strethil," said Bic. She licked her lips. "Tastes so good. Wish I could afford it."

A chill tingled the back of Tikka's neck. *Don't react,* she told herself.

The image shifted again, back to the depths. Something new approached the screen, a strange spiky thing with glowing worms dangling all over it. Something chased it, trying to bite the worms. Light sizzled off the first thing, illuminating the horror of the chaser, but then the chaser fell away, stunned or killed by the first thing's energy.

"What a friendly place." Tikka selected a small bite of the fish on her plate and placed it on her tongue. Despite its flaky texture, it tasted like shoyu-chicken. So many things did.

"We locals love our world, but it can be very, very

dangerous to off worlders." There was a suspicious edge to Bic's voice.

"Are you saying this isn't a good place for tourists?" Shom asked. "We thought you wanted some promotion, and we heard about the fishing here. Are we wrong? You don't want visitors?"

"Oh, no. We love visitors." Bic's face had gone blank.

"We don't want to direct our viewers to places that will treat them badly," Shom said in his best I-am-a-benevolent-god voice. Tikka loved that voice, especially in the dark, when Shom said some of the most peculiar things as though they were orders from above. She also loved the way his mind worked. He could always surprise her.

"Tourists can have lots of fun," said Bic, "as long as they're properly supervised. Some places are just too dangerous."

Shom turned to Tikka. "Camera-sir, maybe we should leave the planet now."

Tikka nodded. "TourNews hates fake leads. And this fish tastes like chicken."

Bic tried a sickly smile. "Please," she said, thrusting her nipple cam toward Shom. "Give us a day. We could really use some tourism."

"Stop telling us what we can't do and move to what we can," Shom said. "Top of the list, we're going out on a boat this afternoon to take a look at some fish. Correct?"

"Sure," said Bic. "I'll take you straight to the best fishing grounds for the true exotics. Do you have all your equipment?"

"Oh, no. We travel light. We assumed it would all be rentable."

"Excuse me. I'll make a call and set it up," Bic said. She headed for the phone banks.

Tikka scanned their table and found four listening devices.

"Taste my meal," Shom said after she showed him four fingers. "It's actually quite good." He held out a forkful to her and she nipped the white flesh from it.

Smooth, buttery, briny, and somehow wild. "Mmm!" she said. "What is that?"

"Plake," he said. "One of the sport fishes." He glanced around the restaurant, pointed to a flatcast across the room. "Magnificent, isn't it?"

Tikka watched a fisherman wrestling with a heavy line. The flatcast showed both above and below the water. The fish was sleek and silver, with lots of muscle, and dorsal spines as long as a person's arm. It fought being caught until the person on the boat had to call for aid. Three others came and helped the first one land the fish. Even then, one of the spines cut someone on the boat, and he fainted.

"Venom," said Shom.

"Interesting. Our viewers will be intrigued."

"Try some more." He held out the loaded fork again, only this time when she leaned forward, he teased her by pulling back. "My eager fish," he said. "I've found your bait."

"Hey." She grabbed his hand and forced it close enough for her to bite the flesh off the fork, after which she nipped the back of his hand, sucked his flesh up under her front teeth. "I'll get you later."

Bic came back. "It's all arranged."

Tikka got sunscreen and eyeshields out of her duffel. "Do you even know how to fish?" she asked Shom as he slid into his swim trunks.

"Sure. Ki gave me a sleep course." Shom buttoned on a blue shirt.

"Where was I?"

"Taking a course on camera work."

"Oh, right." Tikka looped Ki's mobile component over her shoulder and threw some snacks into her carrybag. She put on deck shoes, something Ki had manufactured for this mission. "What about swimming? Do we know how to swim?"

"Didn't you swim as a child?"

"No. The streams on Verify were infested with parasites. Nobody ever swam."

"I guess we'll find out when we go in the water," he said.

She gave him a look, and he said, "Of course we can swim, honey."

Tikka discovered when they boarded the boat that she had also learned to drive a boat: the controls all looked familiar, and the instructions the captain muttered to his mate made sense to her, even though they were in another language.

Arka was the mate. She was even more colorless than she had been before; she wore clothing so worn you couldn't tell what the original color was, and her pale hair was stuffed up inside a dull brown hat.

The captain was a leather-skinned old man with purple sideburns down to his chin and a sculptured purple parrot on his head. The first person with actual second story art Tikka had seen live.

"We got your stinking gear cluttering up the cockpit," he grumbled as soon as they climbed on board. "It's terrible stuff. Break at the first sign of fight in a fish. Who did your shopping?"

He climbed up to the flying bridge without waiting for an answer, and Tikka and Shom turned to Bic.

Bic looked embarrassed. "The shop told me it was all top quality. I don't understand."

Shom dropped down into the rear of the boat and looked over the tackle. "It's not so bad. Maybe he's just grumpy."

Tikka put the camera to her eye. "Do a demo," she said.

Shom straightened and settled into his new on-air personality. "We're about to embark on a fishing trip," he said in one of his better public voices. "The weather is great, and the sea is quiet. Here's our equipment." He held up each piece and named it, demonstrated how it worked when appropriate. Tikka watched dataflow. A lot of the stuff was rigged, some to transmit sound and sight back to whoever was spying on them, some for actions other than the ostensible. The main rod, for instance, had weakness built in; the captain was right. Nobody could land a fish with it. Terrible stuff indeed.

Bic watched closely too.

"Okay," said Tikka. "Good job, star-sir."

"Cast off," called the captain, and Arka unlooped the ropes from the dock. A motor hummed beneath their feet. The boat moved away from the dock and the city.

Tikka got as much joy as she could out of slathering sunscreen on the available parts of Shom's body and having him do the same to her. Shom respectfully offered to help Bic, but she said, "I live on this planet. I put on all the sunscreen I needed this morning."

Good thing, Tikka thought. *Saves me from punching my husband.*

They cut through miles of kelp beds, passed blade boats harvesting the kelp, floating processing plants, fishing boats. No land broke the line between sea and sky. The vastness made Tikka dizzy. The sun baked them, and the dazzle off the water was blinding. Tikka took refuge behind very dark glasses.

Shom played with the equipment as they traveled. He managed to lose the more surveillance-oriented pieces over the side. "Dear me," he said, as Tikka taped him losing the breakable rod. "I've come down with the clumsies." He smiled his best smile. Tikka filmed it on its way into her heart.

Bic climbed up onto the bridge early on and irritated the captain with helpful suggestions. "Why are you going this direction?" she asked two hours into their trip. "The best fishing is south of here."

"We know a secret place," said the captain. "Now get off my bridge."

Arka, setting up what was left of the gear for fishing in the cockpit where Shom and Tikka were now sunning, whispered, "Take care of her. We're getting close."

"Do you have any cold drinks?" Tikka asked in a voice that could be heard on the bridge. Bic had stayed there, defying the captain's orders.

"Got a whole cooler full," Arka said. "What would you like?"

"Lemonade." Tikka had watched what Bic ordered at the restaurant.

"Oh, that sounds good," Bic said from above.

"Any cola?" asked Shom.

"Lots. We also have wine from sea grapes, water, sparkling water, and beer." Arka propped open the cooler to show bottles nestled in ice.

"Nice," said Tikka. "I'll get you a lemonade, Bic." She leaned in and grabbed two bottles of lemonade and a handful of ice chips. She ran the ice chips over her face, then pressed one sweating lemonade to her forehead. "Oh. Better," she moaned.

As she leaned over the cooler, she popped the top on the second bottle, dropped one of the pearls Arka had given her into it, and recapped it. "Somebody has to test it," she whispered. Ki would hear her; the micromike in her strap was very sensitive.

"The ice will melt if I keep it open any longer," Arka said, dropping the cooler top.

Tikka checked her own drink through the camera. Ki analyzed. Normal. She checked Shom's drink. Normal.

She climbed to the bridge and handed Bic a lemonade. She pressed her own against her forehead again. "Aren't you hot?" she asked.

"Born here," said Bic. "Used to it." All the perky had dropped out of her demeanor. She seemed to realize she sounded surly, because she added, "Guess I am hot. Thanks for the lemonade."

"You're welcome." Tikka lounged on the companion bench seat on the bridge.

Bic drank.

Tikka took a long drink, relishing the shock of cold, the bite and sugar of the taste, the feel of cool liquid flowing down her throat.

"We're coming up on our fishing spot right now," the captain called.

Bic moaned.

"Hey, girl? You all right?" asked the captain.

Bic moaned long and low.

"Is that an answer? I can't look at you now, I got some figuring to do."

Tikka lifted the camera and studied Bic through it. Bic's skin flushed, and all her vital signs shifted.

"I feel so..." Bic whispered. She caressed her own breasts as she stared at the captain with half-closed eyes. "So good," she said. She pressed her thighs together, relaxed them, pressed them together, and relaxed them.

"The air — it smells amazing," Bic whispered, "and I can feel the wind. The sunlight's licking me." She licked her own arm, long strokes, like a cat cleaning itself. "Ohhh. The taste. Ohhh. The feel." She sucked on the back of her wrist, her eyes closed, her face ecstatic. "Oh, what is this?"

"Drop anchor, mate," the captain called down to Arka. "We're here." He cut the motor.

Bic worked her breasts. So much for the nipple cam. She ran her tongue slowly over her lips. "Captain," she said in a low voice.

He turned.

"You busy?" Bic asked him.

"Well, as a matter of fact, I just stopped being busy. You feeling frisky?"

"I sure am," Bic said. She gave him a wide, lazy smile.

"Bic," Tikka said.

Bic glanced lazily at her.

"Shom and I are going fishing now. You coming?"

Bic's eyelids slid closed. She smiled wide. "Not right now," she murmured, and turned back to the captain. "Can I touch your parrot?"

"Help yourself, cutie."

Tikka dropped down into the cockpit.

"You wasted a sample on that?" Arka asked her. Moans and murmurs rose from the bridge.

"How long does it last?"

"Tolerance varies. Three to six hours."

"Is that enough time?"

"Maybe."

"We'll take our chances," said Shom.

"It was worth it," Tikka added.

Arka went into the cabin and got breathers, masks, and swim fins.

"I think we're all right," Tikka told her.

Arka shrugged and bit down on a breather, slipped a mask over her head. She sat on the gunwale and fitted fins to her feet, then dropped over the side.

Tikka strapped the camera to her waist. She and Shom took off most of their clothes and followed Arka into the water.

Cold closed around Tikka, shocking her skin awake. She blinked, and the new eyelids dropped down, just as Ki had said they would, and trapped air bubbles over her eyes. She could see perfectly.

For a moment she couldn't breathe. She almost panicked. Then she thought of her gills, and they rose from her neck, filtered air from the water. She glanced back at Shom, saw that he, too, had activated his gills. He swam to her and took her hand.

She felt air trickle into her lungs. She breathed out bubbles.

She kicked three times, and fins unfolded from her feet, stretched out and stiffened. Shom deployed his fins, too.

Shafts of sunlight dropped from the surface, illuminating a green world. They had left the kelp beds behind. A school of small brightly colored scooting things scattered as the three of them dropped through the water. Submarine sounds chunked and thunked and hissed in the distance.

They followed Arka for what seemed like a long time, until the bottom rose up toward them, sand on the side of a volcano that actually poked its head above water. The water here was warmer. Streams of even hotter water bubbled up from vents and fissures in the mountain's side.

Arka held up a hand. Stop.

They stopped, hovered in the water. Tikka and Shom drifted in tandem, gripping each other's hands. Tikka flipped a fin lazily until they rested above one of the hot-spring vents. She tasted the sulfur and minerals in the water, and felt heat welling up against her stomach and breasts.

The new tastes made her wonder about something else. She pulled herself to Shom and licked his shoulder. There it was again, that lovely slick vanilla cookie taste.

He squeezed her hand and nodded down.

Something moved in the sand below them. Something rose, drifted: something that looked like sandy blankets.

There were three of them. Their edges flickered as they rose, and long thin tails whipped behind them, stirring up sand.

Strethil.

Tikka unstrapped the camera and lifted it to her eye.

Arka had told them, in the first letter she sent to IBM, that the Strethil communicated by changing their skin color. The xenobiology division at IBM had searched records for another known race that communicated this way, and nothing surfaced. But Arka had sent them a dictionary she had written herself, and Ki, who had a lot of experience with first contact missions, had developed a decoding program based on Arka's dictionary and had given Tikka a programmable color plate.

Tikka took the piece of cloth out of her wrist cuff and spread it over her stomach, then lifted the vocal coder and pressed it to her throat. It would interpret her words and shift the color of the cloth to match—if everything worked the way it was supposed to. She peered through her camera at the Strethil.

The Strethil flashed a colored pattern.

"Greetings," Ki translated in Tikka's earpiece.

"Greetings," Tikka said, and the color plate on her stomach flashed an imitation of the pattern the Strethil had just flashed. Pleasure flooded through her. So far, so good.

More patterns. "We are here. We were here before the stars fell from the sky, before the non-plants grew from our floor, before the dirt-dropping, sun-blocking things skimmed across the barrier between air and upper air."

"Yes," said Tikka. Her pleasure seeped away. This was language, conceptual, sophisticated thinking, everything required for non-interference or partner status in a planet. The company she worked for was in business to exploit things.

She lived to make deals. It gave her an almost sexual thrill to get somewhere before somebody else and find something fantastic to lock into a monopoly for her company.

Despite the fact that she had killer business instincts, she also had a major flaw for a businessperson. She felt sick at heart every time she heard this story, the story of how a planet with sentient life was wrongly classified as acquirable property.

"We do not hate the non-plants. We do not hate the sky people. We only hate the dirt-dropping, and the ones who kill our children, our parents, our siblings."

Tikka thought of the scene in the restaurant, Bic talking about how good Strethil tasted. Legally, eating a sentient species was cannibalism, and totally against Cooperative law. "I understand."

"Can you give us the power to make our own laws? Stop the things that hurt us? We have trade product to exchange."

"Will you give my company, IBM, an exclusive right to trade your product?"

The Strethil turned and flashed color among themselves. Ki read it quietly to Tikka. "As the little one said." "It is a noncommunal thought." "Reject some community, accept other." "They are a strange race. It is a hard concept." "We must learn." "Ask the other unthinkable question."

The three turned to her again. "How do we know you will do what you say?"

"If we don't do what we say, you must stop trading with us."

"We would not do what _we_ say?"

"Yes."

The Strethil flashed amongst themselves too fast for Ki to translate. One of the Strethil turned to Arka, flashed a question. Arka didn't have anything like a color plate; she had a set of plastic squares in various colors, and she held three up together. "Best I can do," Ki whispered the translation into Tikka's ear.

"We agree," the Strethil flashed in unison.

"Thank you. Please excuse me." Tikka swam up to the

surface, with Shom right behind her. Arka followed, and so did the Strethil.

When she reached air, Tikka aimed Ki's lens at her own face.

She had turned her flaw into an asset, with IBM's blessing. She had taken a second job with the Cooperative Government as a protector of the common good. She would never rise very high at IBM, because she refused to give up her scruples; but a number of missions called for her special talents. She always had work. There weren't many interdisciplinary people with her particular bent.

She was pleased and astonished to have found Shom.

Tikka spoke for the camera. "As an officer of the Government of the Cooperative, First Contact Division, I transmit this report of yet another planet where the indigenous people's rights have been violated, and ask on their behalf for reclassification immediately." She rattled off her government ID number, then told Ki to transmit the conversation she had just had with the Strethil and specify the planet and peoples involved.

Ki sent the report straight into hyperspace. It would reach the Division Head's desk within the next two days, and a copy would arrive on her IBM boss's desk at the same time.

"Thank you," Arka said. "Thank you. Could you make me one of those stomach talkers?"

"Of course. We'll want to hire you as head of IBM operations here. I hope you're interested."

Arka gulped, then nodded. "You want to see the seed beds?" she said in a small voice.

"Oh, yes," said Tikka.

"We only started them two years ago, but we've been expanding ever since."

"Your idea?"

"Yes. I couldn't get anybody to listen without something to trade," Arka said. "In fact, my teachers, the ones who first suspected the Strethil were sentient, were killed by the government when they tried to contact the Cooperative. I figured I better try something sneakier."

"You were good. You are good. You're going places, and you'll take your friends with you," said Shom.

"That woman wore me out," the captain told them when they returned to the boat an hour later. "She just kept going and going. When I couldn't do for her anymore, she rolled around and seemed to get off just on touching things. And look what she did to my art." He shook his head. The parrot was gone, changed to silky purple strands of shaggy hair that hung in disarray around his head and shoulders. "Couldn't keep her hands off it. I took a nap, and she went on by her ownself. She's still down there rubbing things across her skin and crying with happiness."

Shom and Tikka exchanged glances.

Arka handed Tikka a small waterproof purse. Tikka checked inside, found a double handful of pearls. "That's for the stomach talker, and the job offer, and for saving the Strethil, and just everything," she said. "It's the whole first year crop."

"Arka." Tikka tucked the purse inside her carrybag. "You are so smart, and so naive. You need negotiating lessons. Never give anything away." Tikka kissed her forehead. "You need your own Ki, too. The stomach talker doesn't work without a really good interpreter."

"It can't turn your words into their words?"

"It can do that, but it can't read their—oh, you already understand their language, don't you? Here. This is the easy part." She handed the color plate and the attached vocal coder to Arka. "Form the words in your throat—you don't have to say them out loud. It'll translate them for you."

Arka turned misty eyes to her. "This is great. This is so great. You can't believe how happy this makes me."

"You'll still have to lie low for a while. The orders will take a little time to cut, and no doubt the local government will fight it. The Cooperative will probably have to send enforcers in."

"It's all right. I'm used to living in the shadows."

Shom looked at the sun. It was sinking toward the western horizon. Bic had been right: the sunset was spectacular. "We better head back," Shom said.

Tikka nodded. "We have some more product testing to do."

The first effect Tikka noticed after she took a pearl was that her senses heightened. The stars through the seawall of their hotel room brightened in the dark indigo sky, blooms of many-colored light. She was very conscious of Shom's and her own breathing, noticed how they breathed apart, and noticed when their breathing moved to match each other.

Smells intensified. The room service dinner she and Shom had just had delivered called to her in a symphony of odors, shrimp in spicy butter sauce, savory green hunks of dugo flowers drenched in hot fruit, and the desserts, rich chocolate cake slices drowned in raspberry syrup.

She looked up at Shom and saw that he had lifted his head, too. His pupils were wide. His nostrils flared. He glanced toward the table, but turned back to her. "It all smells good," he said, "but you smell the best." He licked her shoulder. Flame woke in the wake of his tongue as he licked his way down toward her breasts. Answering fire woke in her vagina. She knew she was wet and ready.

Tikka lay back and let sensations wash through her as he stroked and kissed her breasts. His every touch sent delicious shocks through her, and his mouth made her shudder with delight. She could feel her climax building with each stroke, and then it broke over her. She writhed and panted as the feelings swallowed her and rocked her, carried her up into a place where she forgot who and what she was.

At last she came back down, a little at a time. She felt movement in the air that brushed over her skin, and she could smell Shom's spice and vanilla, feel his warmth against her as he held her tight.

"Oh, baby," she whispered, "I went there all by myself, didn't I? That wasn't fair. Now it's your turn."

"I felt it. I felt it too," he said. "It was like I was part of you." He ran his hand down her arm. She shivered.

"Well, but you're still ready for more." She reached for his erection, but he caught her hand.

"That's not going away, honey. I know that for sure. I'll wait for you."

"Hey. I have an idea." She brought the tray of food to the bed. "Do you want to be the main course or the dessert?"

"Let's both be both," he said, his voice rough with excitement.

She lifted a breast, savoring the heat of her own hand against her skin, the fine rough texture of her fingers, the water softness of her palms, the warm weight of her breast. Laughing, she hung a shrimp on her nipple, and Shom dove to bite it. He chewed it, then kissed her so that they shared the spicy taste. It burst on her tongue like an explosion. Tikka and Shom rubbed tongues until all they could taste was each other, and heat had settled under her skin again.

She smashed her hands down on the chocolate cake and raspberry syrup, and then fingerpainted on Shom. He drew spirals in warm fruit on her breasts. They pressed themselves together, enjoying how they stuck to each other, and transferred flavors and colors like Rorschach tests. They tasted each other, all the tastes, chocolate, raspberry, fruit, their own scents and the new ones Ki had left them with. Every touch and taste stoked the fires.

Tikka took his penis in her mouth and licked the tip, then sucked. Shom gasped, and she felt him stiffen even more. She dipped her hand in the spicy butter sauce and massaged him, then slid onto him and moved up and down. He lifted his hips, and their connection was tight and strong. They rocked together until he shuddered and cried out and pumped himself into her. Wave after wave of orgasm swept through her.

Years later she came back down from that place and lay next to him on the bed. Her skin still tingled. She stroked his nipple and watched it rise.

"I'm afraid to sleep," murmured Shom's god voice. "I don't want to lose this."

"Don't worry," she whispered. Her hand drifted down over his chest, settled over his navel. "We'll still be us."

Tikka & Shom will be back in the novel Deep Secrets, *coming in April 2001!*

FOGGY WINDOWS BOOKS

Chimeras

A chimera is an illusion, something unreal or impossible. Yet in our Chimeras *imprint, the characters spring to life with an amazing amount of grace and believability. Whether you're exploring a fantasy kingdom peopled with unheard of races, or the darkest parts of the human mind and imagination, the stories and novels found in our* Chimera *series feature husbands and wives in fantastic situations that will leave you begging for more.*

Baskets and Bandits

Jonathan Morgan

Jonathan Morgan, having wandered for several years through Europe and the Far East, currently lives and writes in Ireland. Before that, he worked at a variety of occupations throughout the United States, including census taker, telemarketer, and combine operator. Born in Wisconsin, his hobbies include rock climbing and mountain biking. This is his first short story.

"Whoa!"

Tristan Rathden flew through the air, turning a complete somersault and landing on his back with a bone-jarring thud. His opponent, a slim, ebony-haired woman several inches shorter than him, shook her head, a wicked smile on her face.

"That's four in a row. You know what that means."

Tristan looked down at his dirt and sweat-covered body. He

was dressed only in a rough pair of breeches, the rest of his clothes, from his boots to his jerkin, lay in a pile a few yards away. "You can't be serious?"

"Hey, lover, a bet's a bet." The woman walked over and stood above him, one leg on either side of his body. Her fine hair cascaded down around her face and spilled over her shoulders, blowing gently in the soft breeze. She was clad in forest green doeskin leggings that clung to her slim, finely muscled legs, and a loose muslin shirt that gaped open at her neckline, revealing tantalizing flashes of tan skin. Tristan was sure she had dressed this way just to distract him. Unfortunately, it had worked all too well.

Her words snapped him back to the present. "Or do I have to tell everyone my husband doesn't keep his promises?"

"Serena, be reasonable, how can I possibly spar with you when I'm nude?"

"Maybe I'll be as distracted by your body as you have been by mine?" Serena said, her smile making Tristan think about sparring of an entirely different kind.

He swung both of his legs up and locked them around his wife's waist. With a twist, he levered her down to the ground. Before she could recover, he had untangled himself and was on top of her.

"Well, if I have to lose my pants, would you give me a hand with them?" Tristan asked before lowering his mouth to hers. He smelled her mingled musk and sweat, sweeter to him than any perfume.

As he kissed her, Tristan thought again about how lucky he was. They had only been husband and wife for three months, and as such were still finding out new things about each other every day. Their wedding vows had been taken amidst blood and fire, and they had both emerged from the siege on the keep where they had been married with an understanding that their life together was precious, something to be savored every single day.

Serena hooked her leg over Tristan's and flipped him over,

rolling with him to end up on top. Her hand spidered down his chest to untie the lacings that bound his breeches. Once done, her fingers crept inside and took hold of his iron-hard shaft.

"Tristan, I thought this was to be unarmed combat, and here you've brought your sword."

Tristan's hands had not been idle, either, going under her shirt to cup her full breasts, gently rubbing her erect nipples. When she grabbed him, he inhaled in surprised pleasure.

"Just...a little steel I like to keep ready for occasions like this," he replied, moving the shirt up over her head and slipping it off her taut body. She responded by gripping him harder and slowly moving her hand up and down, her sweat providing a natural lubricant. Tristan grabbed the back of her neck and brought her down to him again, his mouth questing for hers. His other hand loosened her leggings, and he reached inside to stroke the velvety wetness between her legs, making her gasp and arch her body against his.

"Are you sure...no one's going to see us?" she panted in his ear as she shrugged him out of his breeches.

"We rode...for at least a half-hour. There's nobody...for miles," Tristan said. "Relax." He let his hand trail down the inside of her thigh to her boots, which he pulled off one at a time. Tossing them aside, his fingers crawled up her other thigh, stroking the smooth skin and ending up right back where they had started, at her moist, dripping clit.

"Oh, I am. Well, some parts of me more than others," Serena said as she slipped her leggings down around her ankles. Tristan kissed a trail from her mouth to her neck down to the smooth slope of her breast. Nibbling all the way, he crested the silky flesh and licked her nipple with his tongue. Serena moaned with pleasure and kicked off her leggings, spreading her legs apart and rubbing her entire body against his. When her wet mound touched Tristan's manhood, he almost exploded right then, and only with an effort did he control himself. Reaching down, his fingers again explored her vagina, gently pushing in and out, causing her to buck and writhe against him.

"Oh, by the gods, yes!" she cried. "I want you right now."

"As my lady commands," Tristan said, lifting and positioning her over him. "If you would do the honors?"

"It would be my privilege," Serena said, squeezing him one more time as she began guiding him into her. Arranged as they were, she drew it out for what seemed like hours, slipping around him an inch at a time, withdrawing, then sliding further down, until his throbbing member was buried inside her. Serena wrapped her legs around Tristan's calves and clung to him.

"Don't move...for a bit, lover. I just want to...enjoy being this close to you," she whispered.

"Don't worry, I won't," Tristan said, groaning as the muscles in Serena's loins tightened around him, sending rippling waves of pleasure through his entire body. Tristan's hands roamed over her back, tracing lazy patterns on her skin. They ended up near her firm breasts, which he caressed, rubbing her nipples between his fingers.

After a minute, Serena slowly began moving, up and down, up and down on him. Tristan matched her rhythm, rocking his hips to maximize their pleasure. The rocking grew faster and faster, with Serena rearing back, her hands raking down Tristan's chest. He cupped her breasts in both hands and held her steady while she rode him, her gorgeous body tensing with desire. Finally, Serena threw back her head and opened her mouth, only a ragged exhalation of breath coming from her. At that moment, Tristan felt his own release, and he shuddered as he arched his hips one last time, shooting his seed deep into her. He gathered her to him, and they lay together for several minutes.

"It's obvious we have to spar more often," Tristan said when he had gotten his breath back. "I have much to learn."

"I think you already know plenty," Serena murmured, her head resting on his chest. "You handle your sword like a master."

"Why thank you, my lady. While handling it is good, I find it much more enjoyable to sheathe it," Tristan said, grinning for a moment, and then frowning.

"What is it?" Serena asked.

"Do you hear hoofbeats?" Tristan asked her as he placed his hand on the ground.

"No, why, do you?" she asked, rising off him to look around.

"Yes, horses, and something else...coming closer. We'd better get dressed," Tristan said, easing Serena off of him. He had just found where she had tossed his breeches when a figure burst over the hill, nearly running into both of them.

It was a small boy, about a dozen years old, running as if smoke demons from the firehells were on his heels. He was dressed in a simple roughspun tunic, torn and dirty. His eyes were wild and fearful, and his chest heaved with every breath he took. Although he looked exhausted, he still ran like the wind, his legs pumping as fast as they could.

Upon seeing Tristan directly in his path, the boy gathered his legs under him and bounded over the man, not even breaking stride. Tristan barely had time to register what the boy was doing before he was running off down the hill.

"Hey! Wait!" he called after the fleeing youth, but to no avail. Tristan scrambled to his breeches, heedless of the stickiness on his thighs. "Stop!"

"Tristan!" Serena said, looking back over the hill where the boy had come from. Now the pounding of hooves filled the air, and Tristan saw a dust cloud hanging in the distance.

"Get to the horses," he called, pulling on the breeches as he staggered towards their mounts.

Serena was already dressed, boots and all, and swung up into the saddle with ease. Tristan grabbed his shirt as he ran to his own horse. He was just about to mount when the riders charged over the hill.

There were two of them, and they immediately chased after the boy, barely paying Tristan and Serena a second glance. Their panting horses were lean, almost gaunt, and covered with sweat and lather. The men didn't look much better, dressed in coarse woolens and dirty leggings. They were both armed, one with a sword, the other with a rusty spear tucked under his arm like a lance. Tristan got a look at their faces as they rode by, and that told him all he needed to know.

Off in the distance, the boy had reached the bottom of the hill and had started climbing another. The two men pounded after him.

"Bandits!" Tristan said as he hoisted himself into the saddle. "Come on!" He wheeled his horse around and galloped after them. Serena followed suit, drawing one of her *eksiva* sticks from where it rested on her saddle, then prodding her horse into action.

As their mounts were fresh, they gained on the two men, quickly drawing to within a few yards. Sensing someone behind them, one of the men looked back, then called to his partner. By this time all four were coming up on the boy, who had slowed down, and was laboring up the next hill.

Tristan had chosen to approach the spear carrier, and drew abreast of the man, his sword already in hand. The man thrust his weapon at the head of Tristan's horse, causing the animal to shy away, and throwing him off balance for a moment. The bandit drew his spear back to ready it for another strike.

Tristan regained control of his animal and held the stallion steady until he calmed down. He then cut back over, directly at the bandit's horse.

Too late, the man realized what Tristan was about to do, and attempted to drive his spear into the flank of Tristan's horse. Tristan was ready, however, and his sword flashed downward, lopping the spearhead and a foot of the shaft off before it could hit.

Tristan's horse slammed into the other man's, its superior weight causing the other animal to stagger, then fall, pitching its rider headlong onto the dirt.

Tristan looked over at Serena just in time to see her *eksiva* stick fly through the air and slam into the other rider's head, causing him to slump over in his saddle. His horse, uncontrolled, gradually began slowing down.

Seeing that, Tristan kicked his horse into a run again and went after the boy, who had just crested the hill. He caught up to him and grabbed the boy by his shirt, lifting him, kicking and squirming, up over his saddle.

"Let me go! Let me go!" the boy cried.

"Calm down, son, I'm not going to hurt you," Tristan said as he slowed his steed to a canter. Just in case his passenger was planning anything, Tristan kept a firm hand on the boy's neck and pressed his face into the saddle. He gradually turned his horse around and headed back towards Serena. She had caught up to the unconscious man's walking mount, stopped it, and was keeping it in place by the rope bridle.

The boy had stopped struggling and was lying still; only the rise and fall of his back indicated he was still alive. As Tristan passed the other rider, he saw the man was dead, his neck bent at an impossible angle. Tristan collected the other horse, which seemed to have survived its tumble with only its pride hurt, and went back over to Serena.

"Is he all right?" she asked upon seeing his load.

"Why don't we ask him?" Tristan said, hoisting the boy up so he was looking into the child's face. "Well, are you alive, boy?"

"Y-yes, thanks to you," the child said, glancing from Tristan to Serena and back again. He didn't seem quite as scared now, but was still tensed up on the saddle, looking ready to bolt if the opportunity presented itself.

"What's your name?"

"Conor MacTain."

"Don't worry, you're safe now. You've nothing to fear from us," Serena said while she tied the other bandit's hands to his saddle horn with a leather thong. When she finished, she dismounted and tied the man's feet together, connecting them by running a length of rope under the horse's belly. She finished by stuffing a handkerchief in his mouth. "Why were those men chasing you?"

"I was out hunting coneys, and I heard men talking, I went closer, and saw them men who come to our village every third

moon. I tried to get away quietly, but they heard me, and so's
I ran for it. Thought they'd have me for sure, 'cept you got to
them afore they could get to me."

"These men, they come to your village every third moon?"

"Yes."

"How many are there?"

Conor looked at his hands, then at his feet. He held up his
hands, fingers spread apart. "More than this."

"Minus two," Tristan said with a grin.

"Yeah."

"Well, Conor, I think we'd better get you back to your village," Tristan said. "Can you ride?"

Conor nodded proudly. "My Da taught me on the oxen."

"All right then," Tristan lifted the boy off his saddle and
placed him on the fourth horse, "you ride this one. Serena, if
you don't mind, make sure our other guest stays with us."

"Of course," she said, pulling on the bridle of the bandit's
horse and setting off alongside Tristan.

"Now, young Conor, if you'll kindly point me in the direction
of your village...." Tristan said.

After a few miles, Conor pointed to several drifts of smoke.
"There it is."

"Tristan, we'd better hurry. If the bandits have found the body
by now...." Serena left the sentence unfinished.

"Let's hope they haven't yet, but the point is well taken,"
Tristan said as he clapped his heels to his stallion's flanks.
"Come on, Conor, time to feel the wind in your hair!"

"Tristan, I don't think that's such a good idea...." Serena
began.

"Let's go!" Conor said, prodding his horse into action and
galloping down the hill.

"You were saying?" Tristan said as he moved to catch up,
Serena close behind.

With that, the four took off over the hills and towards the
village. On their way in, they passed several flocks of sheep

grazing on the grass of the hillsides, with shepherds watching in confusion as the group flew past.

As they crested the final hill, Tristan reined in his horse and took a look at the village below. It consisted of about eighteen wattle and daub huts with thatched roofs built haphazardly along what amounted to little more than a dirt path. Most of the huts had tofts, or roughly fenced yards where livestock and chickens would graze, many of them empty. Scanning the yards, Tristan saw only one cow. At one end was the village square, with a common longhouse built of stone forming one side of the square and a well in the middle. Behind the village, Tristan saw a vast field of rushes waving in the breeze, and guessed that a stream ran parallel to the road there.

The others, upon seeing Tristan halt, had stopped their horses as well. Looking back, Tristan saw that their prisoner was awake, but was wisely keeping his mouth shut. The fact that Serena had gagged him helped, too.

"Let's go," Tristan said and trotted his horse down the hill towards the village, with Conor, Serena and the bandit falling in behind him.

As they passed the huts lining the road, faces appeared at open windows or in doorways, watching suspiciously as the small party passed by. Conor was smiling and waving to just about everybody he saw, while Tristan and Serena looked around, taking in the lay of the land.

When they got to the village square, Conor jumped off his horse and ran to a hut that was half as large as the rest of them, neatly fenced. Its toft contained the cow, along with a scattering of chickens.

"Da, Da! Come outside!" the boy cried as he ran inside the hut. He emerged a moment later, followed by a brawny man of about forty summers, dressed in a brown tunic and black leggings. He had short curly hair and an open, pleasant face. When he saw the visitors, he lifted Conor up onto his shoulder and walked towards them with a noticeable limp.

"Here now, Conor, what's all the fuss about?" he asked.

"Honored guests, I am Finnegal MacTain, at your service. If my son has caused you any trouble, then I apologize, and beg your pardon—"

"Sir, I thank you for your greeting, but our time is short. I am Tristan Rathden, son of King Severn Rathden. Your son has spotted a large group of bandits near here, and we think they are going to attack your village," Tristan said without preamble.

The man's reaction surprised them. He bowed at the mention of the King's name, but otherwise showed no alarm or fear. "Aye, it'd be about that time. This one of them?" he asked pointing at the captive.

"Yes, we need to keep him somewhere for now," Tristan said.

"I've got just the place," Finn replied. He motioned to two other villagers and waved them over. "Take this man to the grain room, and keep watch over him."

The two men led the bandit away.

"So, you know of these bandits?" Tristan asked as he dismounted.

"Sure, every third month they come, regular as the seasons. About two dozen of them," Finnegal replied.

"Why don't you resist, if they're stealing from you?" Serena asked as she slid down into Tristan's arms.

"Because they have horses and swords, while we have oxen and plows," Finnegal said. "Oh, don't misunderstand, I've counseled fighting back every time it happens, but these people are farmers, not warriors. They wouldn't have the slightest idea of what to do."

"You said the rest of these people. Do you not include yourself among them?" Tristan asked.

"I served your father for ten years as an Outrider for these parts, until a horse fell on me in the Kaheran hills and shattered my leg," Finn said. "So I retired and came back here, to my home." He ruffled Conor's hair. "Started a family. For the most part, it's been quiet, and I like to think it's my reputation that keeps it that way. But these bandits..."

Tristan knew of the Outriders, groups of men trained by the Lord's Blade, the king's captain of the guard, who rode the roads of the kingdom, searching out trouble and stopping it. Trained to live off the land, they weren't as skilled as a proper Bladesman in a fight, but they could more than hold their own. There were stories, especially about the Outriders who worked on the southern border, near the Ruinlands, a lawless frontier filled with bandit groups and tribes of savage, bestial creatures that often raided human villages. Those riders had earned a reputation for fierce skill and animal cunning. The Outriders were known to use whatever worked to win a fight, and doubtless Finn was no different.

"Well, I don't think the village has a choice this time," Tristan said. He told Finn about the encounter with the bandits, and the result.

"Yeah, I guess they'll be coming here with a hard-on for revenge," Finn said. "Dressed as you are, like as not they'll think the village did it."

"And if they discover that the son of the king and his wife are actually here, assuming they're smart enough not to kill us outright, then they'll try to kidnap us to sell to a neighboring kingdom, or even try to ransom us themselves," Serena said.

Finn nodded and set a squirming Conor down. "Their leader, Ras'alga, is a cunning one. No doubt, if they got hold of either of you, it would just be a matter of time to see who would pay the most."

"Ras'alga? The bandits are being led by a Varbolg?" Tristan asked.

"Sure. In the Ruinlands, only the strong survive. Racial differences don't matter next to living to see another day. And you have to admit, a Varbolg is well-suited to surviving out there, yes?"

Tristan nodded, thinking of his last encounter with the Varbolg. His wedding day and the three days after, to be exact. A large tribe of the tall, gray-skinned humanoids had attacked the keep where his marriage was being held, and the besieged populace had held out for three days until reinforcements arrived. During the battle, the Varbolg had killed his brother as well. He thought of how close they had come to losing everything....

"Tristan?" Serena said, putting a hand on his shoulder.

"Hm? Oh, sorry, lost in thought," Tristan said, shaking his head. "Look, we don't have a lot of time. Once they find that body, they'll be here before we know it. What we need is a diversion...I assume you have a sword, Finn?"

"Of course," he said, and headed back into the house, Conor on his heels. He returned a few seconds later with a broadsword strapped around his waist.

"Da, I want to help too," said Conor, coming out of the house with a basket on his head serving as an improvised helmet.

"Conor! Go back in the house. This is man's work," Finn said. Conor, his shoulders slumped, took off the basket and ran inside, throwing it to the ground near the door, and causing a row of baskets to fall over in the doorway.

"That boy, he's got his mother's willfulness, God rest her soul," Finn said, shaking his head.

"I'm sorry," Tristan said.

"Couldn't be helped. She was taken in the last Sorrow Fever outbreak two winters ago. But we were blessed with Conor, and I am reminded of her every time I look at him." Finn grew quiet for a moment, then turned to Tristan with a forced lightness in his voice. "So, do you have any ideas?"

Tristan nodded, staring at the baskets in Finn's hut. "Yes, as a matter of fact I have. Get everyone together, this is what we're going to do...."

A couple of hours later, the bandits rode into the village, with the Varbolg chieftain, Ras'alga, in the lead. A full head taller than any of his men, he was dressed in what looked like a full bearskin, complete with head and fangs, which he wore as a headdress, with the clawed paws draped over his shoulders. In his hand was a large studded club, Ras'alga's favored weapon.

His horse was a massive, barrel-chested animal with huge hooves, and they made a fearsome sight riding down on anyone.

When they reached the outskirts of the village, Ras'alga raised his hand, halting the rest of the bandits. The entire place was silent, with no sign of human life anywhere. Every hut was closed, every window covered with blankets or cloth of some kind.

Ras'alga sniffed the air, his broad, flat nose questing for the scent of his prey. His eyes were large and red, and with his gray skin, bald head, and pointed ears, he resembled a demon in humanoid form.

"They have fled, or they cower in their hovels like women," he grunted to his men. He rode his horse down the path among the huts until he saw the village square and what was in it.

In the center of the grassy clearing were baskets of all shapes and sizes, stacked in a six-foot-tall wall that stretched from one side of the square to the other. The Varbolg examined the unusual barricade, trying to see if anyone was hiding behind it. Reaching behind him, he unslung a massive crossbow. Grabbing an arrow that was as half as thick as a mace handle, he cocked the bow, even his huge arms straining to pull back the string, and loaded the weapon. He took aim at the center of the basket barrier and let fly.

The arrow carved through the bottom of the wall and into the ground several yards beyond it. The basket tore open and fell over, bringing several more with it as that part of the wall collapsed. There was no one behind the wall, no archers, no soldiers, nothing.

Ras'alga threw back his head and laughed, an eerie keening that echoed through the village.

His second-in-command slowly approached him, a grizzled survivor with only one eye, dressed in stinking furs. "Do we attack now, master?"

"No, not yet," Ras'alga shouted. "Do you hear that, village of Tyrne? I am being merciful to you. I have come and taken only what my men and I need, and you repay us by killing one of my own? Hear me now. Give to me the one who killed Sarne, and the rest of you shall live. Defy me, and I shall put all of you to the sword, burn every hut, kill every last animal that walks the earth, and salt the ground so that even the memory of this village shall no longer exist!"

Only silence greeted his threats, save for the occasional clucking chicken. At the far end of the village, the door to the longhouse swung open, then a small hand reached out and hastily pulled it shut.

"Ah, they're hiding in the hall," Ras'alga said, tossing his crossbow aside and hefted his war club, raising it above his head.

"Kill them all," he said. The rasp of weapons being drawn shattered the quiet.

With a terrifying roar, Ras'alga kicked his horse into a blur of motion, thundering down the path towards the village square, the rest of his bandits right behind him.

"Wait for it," Tristan said as he peeked through a chink in the wall of Finn's hut. "Wait for it."

Every peasant that could wield a weapon was crammed in the huts surrounding the village square. With Finn backing him up, Tristan had made an impassioned plea to the village to save themselves, for this time the bandits would not be content with stealing a sheep or two. This time they wanted blood, and if the people did nothing, then that's what the bandits would take.

And a couple of hour's hard labor later, Tristan, Serena, and Finn watched though the hut walls as the bandits charged into the village.

"If they don't go for this, we're in trouble," Finn said, gripping his broadsword tightly.

"They will, trust me," Tristan said. He felt Serena's hand slip into his, and he clasped it tightly. *Come on, guys, go for it,* he thought.

To their credit, the bandits galloped on, shrieking and howling, and heading straight for the baskets.

"The key will be to break their charge," Tristan had explained earlier. "Once we do that, we'll have the advantage in numbers, and in weapons.

"It will be risky. I can't promise that all of us are going to survive. But if we do, then you'll have something more valuable than land or animals—you'll have earned the right to live freely, without having to worry about who's going to take what's yours away from you."

God, I hope I haven't just sent these villagers to their deaths, Tristan thought as he watched the spectacle unfold before him.

The bandits were seconds away from the barrier, their horses' hooves churning up the sparse grass in the square. Ras'alga was standing in his stirrups, a length ahead of the rest of his band. He whirled his club above his head, ready to charge straight through the flimsy barrier and into the longhouse itself. His horse took another mighty step and burst through the wall—

—and shrieked in fear as its front legs plunged into the reed-covered, two-foot deep ditch that had been dug behind the baskets. The horse slammed into the pit with a sickening crack of bone, sending Ras'alga flying through the air. He hit the ground and tumbled to a stop several feet from the longhouse door.

The half-dozen other bandits in the first wave saw what had happened but had no time to react. In unison, their horses also went down, turning the first wave into a chaotic mass of yelling men, screaming animals, and flailing bodies.

The second group had been a few steps behind Ras'alga and the others, and when they saw what had happened, they tried to slow down and ride around the trap. Just as they were pulling back on their horses' bridles, a thick rope snapped up at chest level. Unable to stop, the bandits rode right into it, sending several flying backwards off their horses, which kept galloping right out of the village square.

In the space of less than a minute, the bandits' charge had turned into a disorganized mess, with more than half of the men on the ground, and the rest milling around in uncertainty. The bellows of Ras'alga could be heard above the din, as he tried to put his scattered men into some semblance of order

Tristan grabbed his sword and clapped Finn on the shoulder. "Now."

Yelling at the top of their lungs, the two men burst out of the hut, signaling the peasants to charge.

And charge they did. Men and women rushed from every building, all armed with weapons, from carved pitchforks to threshing flails, scythes, hoes and crude shovels. The roar they all made as they ran into the village drowned out the cries and curses of the bandits.

Even the children got in on the act, for as Tristan ran to the square, he saw a hail of rocks thrown from the roof of the longhouse into the mass of bandits in the square, hitting several in the head or face, and knocking one off his horse.

Then the villagers were upon them. Many of the bandits had barely recovered from the traps and were easy picking for the villagers. With their flails and pitchfork handles, they managed to drop several before the rest knew what was happening. Their nerve broken, the bandits who were still mounted tried to flee, only to see a solid wall of men and women wherever they turned. The horses shied away from the scythes and hoes being brandished in their faces, and began neighing and rearing in panic, dumping several more riders.

Tristan was standing back to back with Finn, working on taking down the rest of the mounted bandits. Out of the corner of his eye, he saw Serena whirl through a knot of three bandits with her *eksiva* sticks, leaving one unconscious on the ground. She had bound her hair in a long ponytail that flew around her head as she blocked a clumsy thrust from a bandit, then brought her other stick down on his forearm, snapping it. A shot to his knee dropped the man, and Serena turned just as the third one tried to skewer her. She dodged out of the way, and the man's lunge impaled his friend instead. Serena's sticks flashed, and the man staggered backwards, bleeding from the nose and mouth, then collapsed. She looked around for another target, her eyes flashing.

She never looked more beautiful, Tristan thought. He smiled and was about to engage another opponent when a roar from the other side of the square caught everybody's attention.

Ras'alga leaped across the ditch and began laying into the villagers with his club, sending them flying through the air, often crashing motionless to the ground. Tristan and Finn looked at each other and nodded.

Seizing the bridle of a riderless horse, Tristan hoisted himself up on its back and turned it around. He galloped straight for the Varbolg, who saw him coming and screamed in rage, readying his cudgel for the charge. Tristan screamed right back at him and goaded the horse even faster, his sword held out to cleave the bandit leader in two. Or that was what was supposed to happen.

At the last second, Ras'alga ducked and swung his massive club at the horse's front legs, knocking it right off its feet. The scream of the horse as its knees shattered reverberated through Tristan's head even as he sailed through the air much like he had a few hours ago, landing with breath-stealing force on the ground.

Tristan rolled onto his back to see a huge form standing over him, blotting out the weak afternoon sun. He scrabbled for his sword, a stick, any kind of weapon, but to no avail. He threw up his hands in a futile gesture to ward off the quick death above him. The Varbolg raised his club over his head to pulp Tristan's—

—and froze, his face twisting in agony, as the point of a broadsword emerged from his chest like a third arm. From behind the Varbolg, Finn pulled the sword out and backed away, ready to swing again.

Tristan used the distraction to roll out of the way. The Varbolg just stood there for a moment, his club slipping from nerveless fingers. A trickle of yellowish blood dripped at the corner of his mouth. Without a sound, he sank to the ground and fell over.

Finn walked over and extended a hand to Tristan, who was

kneeling on the ground. Tristan took it and let himself be pulled to his feet. He kept grasping the other man's hand.

"You saved my life."

"And you saved my home," Finn said, grinning. "I guess that makes us even. Come on, let's finish off this rabble."

The two men turned to see a group of bandits that had broken free of the battle in the square, and were now heading right for them. Tristan dove for his sword while Finn met the charging group head on. By the time Tristan got back up, two bandits were already lying on the ground, Finn's sword flashing as he cut through the small group. Tristan saw a man trying to flank the ex-Outrider and he leapt to Finn's defense, cleaving the man in half with one stroke. The other two bandits turned and fled.

The two men were about to head after them when a huge hand grabbed Finn by the neck and yanked him backwards, making him yelp in surprise and drop his sword.

Tristan spun around to see Finn being lifted into the air by the Varbolg, who had risen and was strangling the life out of the villager, his gigantic hands crushing the other man's windpipe. Finn clawed at the creature's fingers while kicking at the wound on his chest, but he might as well have been kicking a boulder. His face was turning red, and already his struggles were becoming weaker. The Varbolg growled with pleasure as he pressed tighter.

Tristan grabbed Finn's sword from the ground and charged towards the Varbolg, burying the steel blade in the humanoid's neck, slicing through the bearskin and causing a fountain of yellow blood to spurt over him. He left Finn's sword there and hacked again and again with his own blade. After half a dozen more blows, he severed the Varbolg's head from his body.

Although the bandit leader's body sank to its knees, his hands still remained locked around Finn's throat. Finn was barely moving now, and his face was an ugly shade of purple. He would have fallen if the Varbolg's body hadn't been holding him upright.

Tristan took careful aim and chopped off one of the Varbolg's hands at the wrist, sending more yellow ichor flying. He chopped off the other one, then grabbed the fingers and began prying them off Finn's throat. The bones in the Varbolg's hands snapped under the strain, but Tristan managed to lever one off of Finn and impale it on his sword blade, then went back to the other one, grunting with the effort to loosen its death grip from his friend. After breaking the fingers, he was able to tear them away from Finn, who fell to the ground, choking and coughing. Tristan slammed the Varbolg's other hand, still wriggling in a vain attempt to attack something, onto the sword blade as well. He drove the sword into the ground, then sank to his knees next to Finn, who was vomiting in the grass.

He looked up to see Serena and the rest of the villagers surrounding the bandits, who had completely surrendered. She looked around, saw him, and waved. He waved back, his injured body shuddering in protest of the movement.

Finn had recovered somewhat, and he sat down next to Tristan, trying to get his attention. Tristan held up his hand and shook his head.

"Don't try to talk. Just breathe, ok?"

Finn nodded.

"Did you ever fight a Varbolg before?" Tristan asked.

Finn nodded his head, still unable to speak. He held up three fingers.

"Killed three of them, huh? I'd never seen one do that before," Tristan said. "Just as damned hard to kill as always."

Finn nodded as his gaze went to his broadsword, and the hands of the Varbolg, still writhing on the blade.

After cleaning up the debris of the battle and making sure the rest of the bandits were securely locked up, the village celebrated their victory with a huge bonfire in the town square. Several of the townspeople brought out handmade instruments, and soon a lively party was underway.

Tristan could hear the sounds of celebration from where he was, but his mind was on more important things.

"Ow!" he grimaced as Serena applied a hot poultice to his side where he had landed after being thrown from the horse that afternoon. He was lying on a pallet in Finn's hut, being tended to.

"Sorry, lover. Just keep that there for a while. The heat should ease the pain."

"Right now, I just hurt all over. You got one of those for the rest of my body?" Tristan asked.

"No, but I've got something better," Serena said as she climbed into bed with him, gently kneading his tense muscles.

"Hey, remember what happened the last time you did that," Tristan said, sighing in relief. Despite his pain and exhaustion, he felt himself growing harder as Serena dissolved the knots in his arms and legs. He took her in his arms and kissed her, long and slow.

"You were great today," Tristan said when they finally broke apart. "I was watching you during the fight."

Serena smiled, her hands roaming down Tristan's chest to his legs. "No, you were the one who was magnificent. The plan with the baskets, and the rope connected to the poles that let the villagers unhorse those bandits, that was inspired."

"More like desperate, I think," Tristan said as he kissed the underside of her jaw. Serena's hands were still busy at Tristan's waist, and he looked down to see her unlacing his breeches.

"Honey, I don't—"

"Shh," Serena said," reaching inside for him again. "Just lie back and relax. Physician's orders."

She slid down his body, careful of his bruised chest, and kissed his manhood, her tongue swirling around it, from the head to his bottom of his shaft. Tristan moaned and ran his hands through her silky hair. Serena licked him one last time, then took his rock-hard penis into her mouth. She raked him lightly with her teeth, eliciting more groans of pleasure. She began moving up and down, up and down, her head bobbing on him, her tongue sliding along his length, her lips squeezing down on him, bringing him closer and closer to his climax, until, with a long sigh, he came, and flopped back on the bed, drained in more ways than one.

Serena crawled back up his body to cradle him in her arms. "Now, you just relax and get some rest."

"But what about you?" Tristan murmured, already drifting off.

"Don't you worry, lover," Serena said. "My turn will come when you're fully recuperated."

"That's a promise," Tristan said as his eyes closed.

The next morning, the bandits were lined up, tied together hands to neck, ready to be taken to the keep for trial. Several armed villagers waited patiently on their new horses, ready to escort the procession back.

After a few tries, Tristan climbed onto his horse, trying not to wince with the effort. Serena's horse pranced up next to him with her on it. She had not even been scratched during the entire battle.

"Are you sure you're up to making the ride back, love? You don't look so well," she said.

"I'll be fine," Tristan said, fighting to keep his face neutral. "It's not like we'll be in a great hurry or anything."

"True."

"How's Finn?"

"See for yourself," Serena replied, pointing.

Finn was walking towards them, a steaming poultice wrapped around his neck. Tristan smiled and caught his breath as pain shot across his ribs. The older man stopped at his horse and stuck his hand out. Tristan gingerly reached down and shook it.

"You and your lovely wife are welcome here anytime," Finn said in a hoarse whisper.

"Thank you, Finnegan MacTain," Tristan said. "Our door will always be open to you and your family. And, when he is of age, if your son would like to squire, I would be honored to take him on."

"Shh, not so loud, he'll hear you, and then he'll talk of nothing else," Finn said. "When the time comes, I'm sure we'll be seeing each other again."

"Aye, that we will. But let's see each other before then as well, eh?" Tristan said. "Come with Conor to the keep in a week's time, as our honored guests."

"Done, but first, we've got some cleaning to do," Finn said.

"And I've got some riding to do," Tristan said. *And, if the gods be merciful, a lot of resting to do afterwards.*

"May the gods' breath speed you on your journey," Finn said with a bow.

"And may he watch over you and yours, until we meet again," replied Tristan.

The two men clasped hands once again, then Tristan called to the men at the head of the line.

"March!"

As the line of men lurched forward, Serena rode close to Tristan and put her hand on his thigh.

"I suppose you'll be needing your rest when we get back to the keep, lover?" she asked, her hand moving higher on his leg.

"Well, maybe not that much rest," Tristan said as she caressed him through the leather of his breeches. "In fact, I feel better already."

"We'll see about that later," she said with a familiar wicked grin.

"We most certainly will," Tristan said, holding her hand as they rode down the path. *Ah, well, no rest for the weary. And I wouldn't have it any other way.*

⊹⇒◎⇐⊹

Look for more high fantasy adventures from Tristan & Serena in April 2001.

Only the Dead Can Whisper Love

Gary A. Braunbeck

Gary A. Braunbeck is the author of over 170 published short stories, as well as three short story collections and three novels, *The Indifference of Heaven*, *In Hollow Houses*, and *This Flesh Unknown* (forthcoming from Foggy Windows Books). He has been nominated for both the Horror Writers Association's Stoker Award and the International Horror Guild Award. To quote *Publisher's Weekly*: "Braunbeck's fiction stirs the mind as it chills the marrow."

⋯⇒◉⇐⋯

"When I died last, and, Dear, I die
As often as from thee I go,
Though it be but an hour ago,
And lovers' hours be full eternity."
—John Donne, "The Legacy"

On the day of their wedding, when they realized the reception was going to run much later than they'd planned, David and Lisa decided to leave that same night for their honeymoon. This, despite the weather and the protestations of their friends and relatives; after all, though they had been dating for the better part of three years and though neither of them were virgins, they had not slept with each other during their courtship (David always referred to it as their "courtship," and Lisa found it absolutely delicious), and the waiting for each other was driving them both crazy. That's why they decided to try and make the drive that snowy November night. That's why they were on that particular stretch of I-70 when the snow intensified. And that's why, at approximately 2:47 A.M., just as Lisa leaned across the seat to give her new husband a kiss, they hit a patch of black ice, spun out of control, crashed through the guardrail, flipping the car five times and wound up in the back of two separate ambulances. Lisa had several broken ribs and a severe concussion that put her in a coma for nine days. David suffered so much internal and external damage that he died en route to the emergency room.

Lisa awoke to discover that she had very little feeling in her legs and was now a widow who hadn't even had the chance to make love with her husband.

Though she had been an only child and both her parents were dead, she had visitors for a while. Friends and relatives of David's came to see her. They wept. They held her hands while she wept. They hugged her, told her how she had to be strong, that she was a young woman and had her whole life ahead of her. They reminded her that David had loved her, had provided well for her (making her his beneficiary on a hefty insurance policy, as well as giving her total control over all his assets). They assured her they knew how hard it was, how difficult and painful, but she would *survive*; she would *get better*; she would be *up and at 'em* in no time at all.

She nodded her head, and tried both to look and sound grateful to all of them for their concern. They really were trying to help her through all of this. Still, after a while, when her spirits didn't improve (nor her physical condition), the visits became less and less frequent, until, eventually, her contact with most of the friends and relatives was limited to a few phone calls a day, and then only one or two a week.

By the end of her third week in the hospital, Lisa had all but decided she was going to end her life as soon as she could.

What was the point of going on, after all, now that the man she was meant to spend the rest of her life with was gone?

I know, now, that I was meant to be here for you. Shhh—don't say anything, just listen. It used to be, when I told someone the story of my life, it would stop there. But since I've met you...I have told you the story of my life, and you've asked to hear it again...and I find, now, that when I tell it over, it's no longer my story. It's ours, and I will protect that with sword and shield. How could I possibly live without that story? Without you? Lisa, will you marry me?

No, there really was no other choice for her.

Or so whispered her despair.

That was at the end of her third week in the hospital.

Two days into her fourth week, she was wheeled back from her physical therapy session to discover that she had a new roommate.

"Well, hello, you," said the fifty-ish woman with stunning white hair who was doing a Tarot reading on herself. "My name's Sarah Hempel. I'm your new roomie. I guess I should also tell you that I'm a witch. Any questions so far? Ha! You should see the look on your face— Bo-Bo the Dog-Faced Boy looked happier."

"Hi," said Lisa, already deciding that she liked this crazy— though strikingly beautiful and undeniably charismatic—Sarah Hempel. There was something so warm and friendly and alive about her, Lisa couldn't help but like the woman.

"So, tell me," said Sarah, finishing up her Tarot reading and re-stacking the deck, "how long has your husband been dead?"

⋅⋗⟹◎⟸⋖⋅

Over the next few days, Lisa told Sarah everything; about David's proposal, the wedding, their dance at the reception, the accident, all of it, and Sarah listened intensely, nodding her head in sympathy—and never once offering suggestions or words of false comfort. Lisa found her new roomie to be one of the easiest people to talk to that she'd ever encountered.

It was inevitable that Lisa would eventually ask Sarah about her profession—for she had shown Lisa her business card, and it did, indeed, list "Witch" as her profession.

"I learned the Craft from my late Aunt Clarice—she was always the oddball of the family. But she taught me the Ways of the Goddess. She taught me that there are three Aspects to becoming an Earth-Witch and Joining with the Goddess and Her Magic. The first Aspect is Recognition—to know that something is Magic, that it fulfills the purpose of affecting the manifest through the Unmanifest; the second Aspect is, simply, Belief—to believe that the Magic is out there, even during those times you can't—or won't—see it; and the third Aspect—perhaps the hardest one of all—is Embracing— because when you Embrace Magic, when you allow it to wholly enter your heart and spirit, you will be forever Gifted with full Sight. And...and you can wake up now, I'll stop with the lecture."

For the first time in many weeks, Lisa found a genuine smile crossing her face. "So you cast spells and stuff like that?"

"The preferred term is 'ritual,' rather than 'spell,' but, yes, I can and do."

Lisa looked out the hospital window and remembered David's touch, the scents of his body, the taste of his tongue in her mouth, and suddenly the loneliness overwhelmed her once again.

"What are you thinking?" asked Sarah. "Come on, hon, you can tell me."

"H-how did you know that David was dead? Did one of the nurses tell you?"

Sarah shook her head. "Sorry. Like I said, being an Earth-Witch comes with certain gifts, and one of them is Sight." She shrugged. "I won't try and explain it in great detail. Suffice it to say that I, for lack of a more original term, 'picked up' on the psychic vibrations you left in this room. Grief as recent and as intense as yours has a power that's not too hard to sense or read.

"So, how's about answering my original question: What are you thinking?"

Lisa wiped her eyes and shook her head, angry with herself, angry with David, angry with the season, angry with the Universe. "I was just thinking that...you know that he and I never...we never...."

"Yes, hon, you told me."

Lisa tried smiling again, but this time it felt phony and painful. "I was just thinking that it'd be nice if you could cast a spell that would give him back to me for a night.... Don't get me wrong, I'd rather that none of this had ever happened, that he and I were in Toronto on the third week of our honeymoon, but...we *saved* ourselves for each other, you know? I don't just mean the sex, but all of our best qualities, all of our best moments. If he'd lived, we'd have known...I don't know...real intimacy, the kind of love that the Romantic poets wrote about—"

"—all-consuming, fire-in-the-loins, blinding, crippling, God-I-Can't-Breathe-Unless-You're-Near-Me passion?"

"Yes!"

Sarah grinned. "John Donne and the rest of those assholes have got a lot to answer for."

The two women looked at one another in shocked silence for a moment, then both burst out laughing.

It was much later that night, well past midnight, when, from her side of the room, Sarah said the four words that would change the course of Lisa's life: "I could, you know."

"I'm sorry...what'd you say?"

Sarah turned toward her in the darkness. "The ritual—the spell you asked about. I could perform it for you. I could give you back your husband...and for more than one night."

It took a moment for the full impact of those words to register with Lisa. "H-how is that possible?"

"He's only been dead...what? Three-and-a-half weeks?"

"...Yes..."

"The longer someone has been dead, the more difficult it is to resurrect them. But with someone like David...less than a month...I don't mean to sound flippant, hon, but bringing him back to you would be so easy, I could practically do it in my sleep."

Lisa sat up. "For...for how long? How long could I have him back?"

Sarah shrugged. "Actually, that's up to David."

"I don't understand."

When Sarah next spoke, there was a solemnity to her voice: "You know why it is that the poets like John Donne and William Blake and the other so-called Romantics missed the boat when it came to all of their fine words about True Love? Because the Absolute Knowledge of love does not come from this side of life. True Love isn't declared loudly from the mountaintops with a booming voice; passion isn't something that explodes from the center of your heart like a bomb going off or a sun reaching supernova. None of it can truly be known in life—only after its final moments have passed. Is this making sense to you?"

"I'm not sure."

Sarah sighed. "Love and passion aren't things to be shouted about; they are things to be *whispered,* hon. And I mean 'whisper' not as in muttered low and softly into one's ear, but as in a knowledge or realization that enters the heart in silence and blossoms like the petals of a rose—total, complete, perfect. The living don't know how to express that, how to whisper, oh, no; only the dead can whisper True Love, Lisa. And only someone like yourself, someone who's still in the throes of grief for the recent loss of the person who was destined to be the love of her life, can 'hear'—or *receive*, if you will—that whisper when it's offered.

"The dead are all around us, Lisa, all the time. They exist on the other side of doorways that we can't see. I can perform a ritual that's called 'Lifting the Veils'—veils of perception—that will allow David to come through that doorway and into this world, but there are risks."

"I don't care."

Sarah lifted a hand, silencing Lisa's impatience. "You'd *better* care about the risks, hon, because if there are any consequences, I won't be there to help. You'll have to handle it on your own, so listen, okay? Even though the doorway is open only for a few moments, *many* of the dead can come through. Yes, David will be the first one to enter this world because he's the one summoned, but that doesn't mean that others won't follow him. And because they will have come through the same door as he, they will be linked to him."

Lisa shook her head. "Meaning...?"

"Meaning that I can bring David back to you, but I cannot guarantee that he will be alone."

"I don't care."

"Are you certain?"

A pause, then: "Yes." Then, after a moment, Lisa shook her head and muttered: "This is insane."

"No, it isn't."

Lisa glared across the gloom at her roommate. "You're talking about bringing back a man from the dead, about doing a George Romero and having him claw his way up out of the grave and—"

"—Lisa?"

"What?"

"Shut up for a minute, will you?"

Surprised by the hardness in Sarah's voice, Lisa remained quiet.

"First of all," said Sarah, "I don't appreciate your comparing what I do to something out of a gory horror movie—though *Dawn of the Dead*'s a good one, I'll give you that. I am not going to summon David's body to reanimate and crawl out of the grave.

"What the ritual does, is enable a person's *essence* to re-enter this world. A 'soul,' if you will. Our souls contain everything that we've come to think of as defining ourselves as individuals. The souls of the departed are always somewhere *out there*, Lisa, okay? Formless. What will make David's essence become the David you knew and loved...is you. The way you remember him. *That's* why it's easier to bring back someone who's only been gone a little while—because the memory of their physical selves is still quite strong in those they left behind. The longer it goes on, the dimmer the memory becomes. But in your case...in your case, he's still so much a part of you that his essence will have no trouble reclaiming its familiar physical form, because I'm guessing that you remember every detail about him."

"We never...we never actually...."

"...consummated the marriage?"

Lisa nodded. "We never actually had sex at all. We decided to save ourselves for each other. I mean we'd both had sexual experiences with other people before we met, but we wanted to be old-fashioned about this. Does that sound silly?"

"Not at all. But I'm also going to guess that, even though the two of you never had actual intercourse, you probably had some sweaty nights, naked in each other's arms."

"Yes."

Sarah nodded. "So you remember his body?"

"Every delicious detail. God, how I wanted him." Lisa thought about what Sarah had explained to her, and realized that it wasn't so insane, after all.

"Okay," she said to her roommate. "Let's do it. Bring him back to me."

Sarah nodded. "Very well. But understand something here, hon: only David will know when it's time to be with you; only he will know when it's right for the two of you to make any sort of physical connection. Until he decides that the time is right to 'whisper' to you, you must not attempt to touch him. You must wait until *after* he first touches you, understand? The living tend to be so desperate to hold their loved ones again that the sheer force—both physical and emotional—of their desire is too powerful for those who have only just crossed over and reclaimed physical form. Think of it as trying to grasp a blown-glass figure that has only just been created; it's still pliable, it hasn't dried yet, and your touch could destroy it.

"Sounds a bit silly, I know, but you have to wait for him to make the first move. Do you understand this?"

"Yes."

Sarah's eyes burned bright as embers in the darkness. *"Do you?"*

"I won't try to touch him until he's touched me first."

"And you also understand," said Sarah "that I can only do this for you once, that's all. Opening the doorways between this side and the afterlife is manipulating forces that are the dominion of the Goddess, and the Goddess alone. We do it too many times, and She will leave us—leave *me*, I should say. To put it simply: there is a very limited amount of times that I can do this, then I can't do it any longer, not without risking being deemed Unworthy of my powers."

"Only once, yes, I understand."

Sarah lay back and closed her eyes. "Fine. Tomorrow I'll call my apprentice and have her bring the necessary items. I'll perform the ritual and give you what you need—but remember: you absolutely, positively, without any deviation whatsoever, *must* do everything exactly, precisely as I tell you to. Am I clear on this, as well?"

"Crystal."

Sarah laughed softly. "Funny you should say 'crystal.' One will be involved in the ceremony. I use it to manipulate the natural ether in the atmosphere."

"Ether?"

"Yes. Believe it or not, ether is the 'key' to the doorways I mentioned."

And she proceeded to explain this in great detail to Lisa, who fell asleep before Sarah was four words into her second sentence.

◆➤≡◯⊂◄◆

And so the ritual was performed. Lisa found it both fascinating and confusing, as well as mystic and a bit comical. There were candles of various colors and a makeshift altar, various herbs and spices, handfuls of soil mixed with water, circles drawn on the floor with a mixture of flour and crushed stone, a small sack of bird bones and trinkets she had to wear around her neck, and one drop of her blood mixed in with some wine, which Sarah did not drink, but rather offered to the Four.

"Before me," she whispered, holding high the cup, "is Michael, Lord of Flame, Lion of the South; behind me is Raphael, Lord of Air, Angel of the North; on my right is Gabriel, Lord of Water, the Eagle of the West; on my left is Uriel, Lord of Earth, the Bull of the East. The Four surround me." Her voice was Bliss; her inflections Redemption.

She raised the cup above her head.

"Fire above."

She lowered it to her waist.

"Water below."

She held the cup close her heart.

"I am the heart of the Four; I am the center of the Universe."

She opened her eyes and stared directly at Lisa: "It is done, except for this last part; it will be up to you to complete the ritual." She removed a hollow stick from her pocket and carefully, with a precision that came from years of practice and skill, emptied the contents of the cup into the stick, which Lisa now could see was not a stick at all but a hollowed bone of some kind. After the bone had been filled, Sarah sealed it at both ends with melted candle wax, then slipped it into something that looked like the plastic tube an expensive cigar would come in.

She handed it to Lisa. "When the time feels right, when you've been out of here a few weeks and have your strength back, remove the bone from this container and snap it in two—don't worry, it'll break easily enough—then sprinkle what's inside across the threshold of your bedroom doorway. It will serve as a kind of...welcoming mat."

"Sarah?"

"Yes?"

"I know we haven't known each other for very long, but I just wanted you to know...you're the best friend I've ever had."

Sarah grinned and touched Lisa's cheek. "See if you still feel that way after you've finished the ritual."

It wasn't until Sarah was being released several days later that it occurred to Lisa to ask: "What were you in here for, anyway?"

"I had some tests run on a few fibroid tumors they found in my uterus. Usually, it's an out-patient procedure, but I've had some problems with internal bleeding in the past, so when I show up for tests, they tend to keep me for a few days, you know, just to monitor my condition."

"Are you all right?"

Sarah leaned over and kissed Lisa's cheek. "Turns out one of the tumors isn't fibroid, after all, so, no, I'm not all right, but they've done everything they can for me for right now. Don't worry about me, hon; I've got tons of things I can do to help myself. I'll probably outlive this building. Be careful. Be happy.

"But most of all, be careful."

Three days later, Lisa was released from the hospital.

One week after that, on the first night that there were no phone calls or visitors to her house, she removed the bone, snapped it in two, and sprinkled what was now a fine, metallic-looking dust across the threshold of her bedroom.

And waited.

And waited.

And waited.

Finally, to relax herself, she went into the bathroom, ran a hot bath and gently lowered herself into the vanilla-scented water, covering her eyes with a wet washcloth. Since the master bath was connected to the master bedroom, she decided to leave the door open so she could hear when David arrived.

A little while later—it might have been ten minutes, it might have been an hour—she smelled it.

The distinctive aroma of David's perspiration.

Then an unseen hand—not hers—removed a sponge from the side of the tub, dunked it into the water, and squeezed it over her body.

The diamond droplets of water trickled down her cheek, glided over her chin, slipped down her neck, and slid a moist path between her breasts.

Then *his* hand was there, rubbing gentle circular patterns with the soapy washcloth, moist and creamy, lilac-scented, and Lisa stretched, arching her back, sighing as the washcloth dropped away and *his* lips began trailing down her neck, pausing at her shoulder, then to the slope of her breasts. Then *he* delicately cupped one breast in *his* hand, *his* thumb stroking her nipple until it became firm.

His lips covered her nipple, drawing it into *his* mouth meekly yet hungrily, and she closed her eyes all the tighter, hearing a low growl rise from deep in her throat, emerging as a sigh. The slowly drifting lights behind her closed lids separated, shimmering in rhythm with the spasms below her waist, becoming thousands of bright pinpoints that seemed to surge from somewhere in her center as she reached out to clutch the back of *his* head, to guide *his* wonderful lips to her other breast, feel *him* take the nipple in *his* mouth.

The fire and lights within her intensified, caressing her, moving her, rocking her, tickling, rolling, arching her toward him, and she wanted to feel his firmness inside her, pulling back teasingly before plunging in again. She wanted to hold *him* close, pull *him* into her until she thought *he* was buried up to her throat as she shuddered and pulled her legs against *his* pressing hips, digging her fingers into *his* shoulders, forcing *him* deeper inside her as she threw her head back and—

—and as she reached up from the bathtub to clutch the back of his head, she grasped only empty space.

⊷≡◎⊑≡⊷

Lisa dried herself off, then went into bedroom and made a call.

"Sarah?"

"Lisa? What time is it?"

"He was here, but...but only for a few moments. Now he's gone!"

"Calm down, Lisa."

"*I can't!* He was here and I tried to hold him and—"

"Did you let him touch you first?"

"Yes! He kissed my breasts and held them and washed my body while I was in the tub and—"

"—oh, no...."

Lisa felt her center freeze with terror. "What?"

"Water."

"What about it?"

"Do you remember what I told you about that? How water was partially responsible for his death? The snow and ice?"

"Yes."

"I told you to make sure you weren't near any water after finishing the ritual, remember?"

"Oh, God...."

"I'm amazed that he even tried to touch you under those circumstances. Lord, how that man must love you."

"Is he gone forever?"

"No, Lisa, he isn't. You can fix this. Find any kind of candle that you have not yet lighted and light it. Let it burn next to your bed and leave your door open so you can see the powder you left on the floor earlier. This will be your way of letting him know you're all right and still want him.

"Don't worry; he hasn't gone away. He's simply waiting for you to be in a safer place—what should have been your wedding bed."

When Lisa hung up the phone and turned around, she gasped.

There was a satin half-slip lying on the bed.

She had not put it there.

David had bought it for her to wear on their wedding night. She thought it had been destroyed in the accident.

She reached out for it, hesitated, pulled back her hand, then exhaled a decisive breath and snatched it off the bed, heading into the bathroom.

When she came to the doorway, she was wearing the half-slip, just like he wanted her to, the elastic top barely covering her breasts, the bottom of the slip reaching her thighs. She began to dance slowly, gracefully circling the bed, then she flicked off the bathroom light, and there was only darkness where the dead whisper. "Would you like to d-dance with me again?" she asked, angered at herself for stuttering. But she couldn't help it; the last time they'd danced had been at the reception, and she couldn't think of the reception without thinking about what happened only a few hours later. She took a deep breath and waited, sensing how David was following her voice to get to her, and suddenly he was there in front of her. She could feel his breath and the way he slowly, teasingly slipped his arms around her waist. A moment of awkward hesitation, and then they were moving back and forth, side to side, and his breathing against her flesh was maddening, enticing, making her wet and weak in the knees.

You don't touch him; wait for him to touch you first.

He took hold of the elastic top of the slip, pulled it down, and her breasts sprang free, large and ready for his touch. And touch them he did, kissing her nipples as he struggled to get the rest of the slip off, which she resisted for a moment because she was afraid— afraid and turned on. That must have been all right with him, because he played along with it until she wasn't afraid any more. He began tonguing her navel as if it were all he wanted, all he wanted in the world, and then he said something about her body beneath him in the bed, and before she could say anything he'd spun her around and had her on the bed, on her back, and then—

—sweet Jesus!—

—then he was on top of her, kissing her breasts, and she liked that, oh god she liked it, and he fingered her nipples, and that was good, too. Next his hand found her pubic hair and stroked her there until she moved her legs apart, then his finger was in her mouth and she tongued it, sucked it, knowing all the while what he was going to do with it. *He* pulled it from her mouth and slid his hand down between her legs and was using his drenched finger to moisten her, and she almost couldn't stand it anymore because she could feel how hard he was against her leg, she'd never felt an erection so hard.

He straddled her, spread her legs, and ramrodded home. She made a sound, then, a quick gasping sound as her husband—who did not feel at all like a ghost, not at all like someone who'd crossed over from the land of the dead—put his hands on either side of her body, thrust deep, pulled halfway back, then thrust again, again. And as he kept on, it was wonderful, yes, god it was *fantastic*— "I can't...get deep enough," he kept saying, "...can't bury it all the way up to your throat...."— so he reached up, took hold of her shoulders and flipped her around onto her belly and flung the rest of his weight behind her, took hold of his erection, found her soaked vagina, and plunged himself home again, totally penetrating her.

She cried out, screamed and shrieked and scrambled with her hands until she grabbed one of the pillows and pulled it toward her, sliding it under her face. Biting down, she howled into it as he kept ramming himself deeper. There were several times when she thought they were both going to come, thought she felt him starting to shoot it in her, but somehow he always managed to hold it back, knew just how to ease up on her so she didn't climax too early, either.

He pulled out and yanked the pillow from under her head and pulled her to her knees. Then he lay down and helped her fling one of her legs over his hips. "Ride me...."—and now she was on top, driving herself down, and as soon as he started to shoot, he grabbed her shoulders as hard as he could and pressed her down as he moved his hips into her. Then he was way into orgasm, so he released her shoulders, brought her close, so that her breasts were hanging just above his mouth and he sucked on her incredibly engorged nipples until he was still. He pulled back and kissed her mouth, sliding his tongue between her wet lips and then down to her nipples again as he flipped her once more onto her back.

He knelt on the floor and spread her legs, and before she could say anything, before she could make another sound, his tongue was inside her and her clitoris was between his lips. He was moving his head back and forth, and she was starting to come now, God, yes, she could feel herself swelling from deep, deep, deep. Then he reached up with both hands and took hold of her nipples, squeezing them, not too tightly, oh, no, but just tight enough, and it became a rhythm: squeeze the nipples, move the tongue, nibble tenderly on her clitoris. She gasped and wiggled and arched her back, crying out because she loved it, loved being able to feel herself come all over his mouth. Her body was out of control now, her hips rising involuntarily, but he kept his mouth pressed down, licking, sucking, kissing, and nibbling until her body went ramrod straight and ramrod hard, and the vocal cords stood out against the flesh of her neck and she pulled in a breath and released the loudest scream she'd ever heard, shocking even herself. All the while, she kept thrashing, grabbing the back of his head and pressing his lips into her, "Suck it, bite it, lick it!" And he did whatever she said, until her body bucked and shuddered and became still as she exhaled and relaxed on the bed.

He snuggled up next to her and propped his head up in one hand, resting on one elbow, and she touched his face and tried to tell him how great it was, how she'd never dreamed it could be that good. Christ, she was going to be lucky if she could ever get out of bed again, let alone walk in the morning. Then he leaned down and kissed her gently on the forehead, on each eye, and her lips, then moved his mouth to her ear and whispered, "What makes you think we're finished?"

"Wh-what?"

He kissed her everywhere and endlessly, licking her, a bite here, a nibble there, probing her with his fingers, cupping her breasts in his hands and tonguing her nipples in slow, wet, maddening circular patterns. She pulled back and said, "There's a halo around you," and he stopped for a moment, looking down at himself.

There was a thin beam of moonlight slipping in under the window blinds. Each hair on his body was isolated by that light like a bluish gossamer, a wrapping. "It's just a trick of the light," he replied to her, his hand resting for a moment on hers. His fingers were long and bony but soft, soft as her own supple neck. He ran those fingers up her arms and the little hairs there sprang to attention, then he touched her eyes with his fingertips; they were like pads, responsive to her every pore. Her eyelids fluttered beneath his touch, and she drew her own fingers down his cheeks to the bone of his jaw, then down his neck, leaning forward and kissing his lips.

Lisa's mouth felt larger than human, able to protect his in its clasp. She felt his tongue beating against her lips, opened them and soon felt his saliva in her own. His mouth was crawling down her body again, and she lay back, opening her vagina for him. Soon, her murmurs seemed to fill the room. She arched her back slightly as her knees bent around the small curve at the back of his head, pressing it slowly downward.

They twined around each other as if their limbs had lost their natural form. A moment later he lifted his head from between her wet heat and moved up her belly to her breasts again, at first teasing her nipples, then sucking them deep into his hungry mouth. He trailed his lips across her shoulders, his breath moist and warm against the side of her neck, his erection rigid and hot, his entry smooth and painless. The two of them rocked together, pumping slick and steady, and it was good, it was great, it was heaven, and she grabbed hold of his shoulders and rolled him onto his back, straddling his hips.

Lisa locked her ankles under the backs of his knees as her own pushed out and down, her ass rolling back and forth across his groin, pushing him deeper inside of her as his hand grabbed one of her breasts and his mouth encircled the areola, slurping and sucking and biting as he thrust himself upward with more force, ramming his erection deeper, deeper, and deeper still, and she threw back her head and arched her back, her nails digging into his well-toned pectorals, and she caught sight of their bodies reflected in the closet-door mirror; sweating, glistening, heaving bodies attacking one another, devouring one another, then came the sounds, low, throaty growls, grunts and sighs and strangled screams as their rhythm grew faster, harder, frenzied, bedsprings squeaking, almost causing her to laugh but she didn't, she wouldn't, she groaned instead, driving herself down, pushing him in so much deeper it was starting to hurt.

But she didn't care, she wanted him to bury it in her up to her throat, so she dug her fingers into his chest, tangling them in his sweat-matted hair. God, he felt so good, so thick and solid, pulsing, throbbing, sliding wet and steamy into her slick sex as she doubled her efforts, grinding down with all her strength; he arched his back and groaned, she threw back her head once again and squealed, then moaned, then screamed, her juice-soaked thighs sliding against his own, then he was sitting up again, burying his face between her breasts, his tongue lapping at her nipples, then he was biting them, hard, harder, and she loved it, it was incredible, and now they were moving side to side as well as up and down, the chaotic motion setting fire to her body as she pulled up and slammed back down on him.

Lisa glimpsed the shadow-shape reflections in the mirror, dozens of them that had followed her husband through the doorway, they were standing in the bedroom, moving as one toward her bed, surrounding it, their dead eyes glistening as they watched in silence, their breathing getting heavier and more ragged along with her own, their sighs soft and excited, rising into moans, then squeals, then near-deafening screams of ecstasy—

—"God, yes, do it...do it...*shoot it in me*, in me, in me *NOW! YES! GOD, YES!*"—

—Lisa felt the pressure building up inside of her, roiling around, looking for release, and thought the veins in her neck might burst from the strain, then she felt him explode inside of her, his orgasm blinding, overpowering as he groaned, then grunted, then moaned loudly, ramming his hips upward, burying him even deeper, shooting his seed all the way up to the back of her teeth, and she wanted to come with him, wanted their climaxes to be one and the same, but that wasn't going to happen, *his* orgasm was the point to her now, coming like he'd never came and *god did he come again—how could anyone keep it up like this,* she wondered, and then remembered that he was dead, and the dead could do anything because only they could *whisper—*

—and again, he came hard and strong and endlessly, with such intensity she actually thought she was going to pass out before it was over, but she didn't, she stayed with him, groaning and crying out until he was spent, then, smiling, suppressing a giggle, she leaned down and kissed the side of his face, lifting herself slowly off of him, his still-throbbing erection sliding out of her, the head giving one last spurt before the whole thing flopped to the side, something that made them both laugh, then he rolled her onto her back and took his hand and began massaging her vagina.

"What are you trying to do?" Lisa asked breathlessly, her heart trip-hammering in her chest, as if trying to squirt out through her rib cage. "Fuck me to death?"

He smiled at her, tenderly, lovingly, then *whispered* as only a dead man can: "Yes."

It should have terrified her, sent her screaming into the rainy night outside, but it was different now. Lisa wanted to be with him at any cost, and now that she could touch him, she didn't want him to have to work at all. If there was going to be more pleasure—and there *was* going to be more pleasure, crippling, intense, agonizing, brilliant pleasure—she wanted to be the one to give it this time. "Fine," she said, then kissed him hard. "Take me with you, take me back, I don't want to be here without you."

They embraced at first, and his tongue went into her mouth with all the force he had, and her hands caressed his cheeks and her tongue darted into his ear and her fingertips began pinching his nipples until she jerked her head back and down and bit them, bit them hard enough to draw blood if he'd been from among the living, and from the way he cried out and shuddered she knew he'd felt that bite all the way down to his groin; then her fingertips moved down his body, down toward his erection where they stopped and began to caress his testicles, then moved slowly up and down the inside of his thighs.

Around the bed, the audience of the dead leaned down closer, all of them whispering love and strength and *Join us, Join us* as Lisa took control of both their bodies, giggling and sighing and groaning, her hand working back to his shaft.

He closed his eyes and went with the sensation, hardening again, plumping bigger than he had yet been, and she knew it was going to hurt when he entered her this time but she didn't care, she wanted it to hurt so much because then something good would come out of all this pain, and there'd been so much pain for so long, it seemed it was all she'd known, but now the pain would be good, would lead to something even better, so she used her fingertips to help him swell even more and a moment later her lips replaced her fingertips, her tongue moving along the underside of his shaft and she knew he wouldn't be able to hold back for much longer, but she wanted to prolong it for him, the same slow, delicious way he'd prolonged it for her, so she lifted her head, moved up again until her breasts were by his face and she moved so slowly, playfully slapping his face with her breasts as she jiggled back and forth, letting her extended nipples move across and around his mouth before letting him have them.

He tongued them, moving his mouth from one to the other, slowly at first, then faster and faster, sucking them, biting them, back and forth. Her nipples were so firm, they were like pebbles, and then Lisa pulled them away for a moment and held his head between her hands and said, *"Now* who's impatient?" and he went at them more slowly and tenderly after that, but just as hungrily. While he worked at her nipples, she took one of his hands and guided it down to her clitoris, guided him into a gentle up-and-down motion and then, when he was doing it the way she showed him, she took her hand away and began to stroke him.

The dead surrounding them began to gasp in sweet, cold, grave pleasure.

When he was hard again, Lisa began, slowly moving down, straddling his body, taking his unbelievably swollen erection and slipping it inside of her, and it hurt even more than she'd thought it would, but that was okay, that was great, that was fine, because it was the most exquisite pain—a flash of searing anguish from without before it soaked through the flesh and lit the fire within, and she cried out, gasped, almost choking, but then he was inside and it was fabulous, she sighed and licked her lips, letting him thrust as deeply inside of her as he wanted. He was breathing fast now, all of the dead were breathing fast now, fast and now faster still, and she surprised everyone by lifting her body away, letting him subside again, but only a little, only for a moment, bringing her breasts back to his mouth so he could suck at the nipples.

He was heaving now—all of the dead were heaving—as he took his mouth away from her nipples and searched out her lips, brought his arms around her and held her, just held her, as if making sure she was still there and hadn't changed her mind. She pulled away after a few moments and kissed his nipples again while her fingers got him hard for the...*God, how many times had it been since they began?*...She couldn't remember and didn't care, all that mattered was that it was almost Over now, they were almost Finished, and she would be going With Him, and now he was hard for the last time on this side of life, and she bent down and lowered her head and went slowly. All. The. Way. Down. His. Shaft.

Taking it all in, then slowly moving up until her tongue circled his tip, and then her tongue went down the underside and he was losing control and she knew this was it, this was *The End*, so she let it happen, put her mouth around him again, moving quickly up and down his erection, licking, slurping, drinking him down, and a moment later he was biting his own forearm to keep from shrieking out loud as he thrust up, as he rammed upward, cramming the whole length of himself deep into her mouth, gagging her as the dead surrounding the bed reached down and, laying one hand atop another, held the back of her head down as she choked on bliss while he came and came and came in her sweet, warm, soft and— after a few more thrusts and clogging spurts—soon lifeless mouth.

Somewhere in this night, the dead *whispered* of love and sang a song of lovers reunited forever.

And Lisa, when they would found her a few days later, would be lying in her bed, quite alone, and very naked, and undeniably dead.

Suicide, some of them would say.

But if she were in such despair, others would wonder...why was there such unbridled *joy* frozen in her dead eyes?

And how, they would later wonder among themselves in the most quiet, private hours, if she and David had never slept together, *how* could the medical examiner determine that she was three to four weeks pregnant with David's child at the time of her death?

Only the dead knew for certain.

And to the living they offered not a whisper.

◆━◉◉━◆

Though difficult to imagine, you can find out more about David & Lisa in the forthcoming novel This Flesh Unknown, *available in 2001.*

FOGGY WINDOWS BOOKS

Anthology

INTERESTED IN A LITTLE MORE HEAT?

Starting in Spring, 2001 — HEAT, Volumes 1–5!

HEAT, Vol. 1—March, 2001

Incredibly hot short fiction from James Reasoner, Billie Sue Mosiman, Kristin Kathryn Rusch, Peter Crowther, Christine Matthews, Dean Wesely Smith, and many more!

HEAT, Vol. 2—April, 2001

The series continues! Twelve tales of erotic fiction from Stephen Mertz, Wendi Lee, David Bischoff, and Daniel Ransom, and other literary adventurers!

And look for these HEAT volumes soon!

HEAT, Vol. 3—May, 2001
HEAT, Vol. 4—June, 2001
HEAT, Vol. 5—July, 2001

Ready to sign up for more HEAT?

Visit us on the web at **www.foggywindows.com**
Or call us, toll-free, to RESERVE YOUR COPY TODAY:
888-797-4466

COMING FEBRUARY 14TH, 2001
OUR FIRST SIX NOVELS!

FOGGY WINDOWS BOOKS

FRONTLINES:
NICE GIRLS DO, BY LESLIE JOYCE

Set in Nice, France, during World War II, this novel features a young couple involved with the Resistance. Can they help the movement, stay safe and keep their love alive during this dangerous mission?

OVERDRIVE:
HOT WATERS, BY ERICA LYON

A couple forced to work together in their small commercial fishing business runs into a Russian drug-smuggling operation. It's high-seas adventure as they try to survive!

FLINTLOCK:
BLACKMAIL & LACE, BY DANIEL RANSOM

Best-selling author Daniel Ransom turns his hand to a Western novel of intrigue as a young lawyer searches for the truth about a very explicit diary and a bank robbery with the help of his beautiful wife!

UNDERCOVER:
DYING FOR IT, BY TIM WAGGONER

A husband and wife private investigator team looks into a murder and discovers a web of voyeur videos!

AFTERBURNER:
THE DIPLOMATIC TOUCH, BY DAVID BISCHOFF

It's outer space hilarity, mayhem, and temptation as a husband and wife duo of intergalactic diplomats try to recruit a new planet into their interplanetary federation. Unfortunately, the inhabitants of Nocturne III have a lot more on their minds than just talking.

CHIMERAS:
THIS FLESH UNKNOWN, BY GARY BRAUNBECK

Nominated for both the Horror Writers Association Bram Stoker Award and the International Horror Guild Award, Braunbeck's novel is the bone-chilling story of a couple whose erotic passions go too far and take on a unique life of their own!

THIS VALENTINE'S DAY IS GOING TO BE HOT!

Visit us on the web at **www.foggywindows.com**
Or call us, toll-free, to RESERVE YOUR COPY TODAY:
888-797-4466